BY LAUREN WEISBERGER

The Devil Wears Prada

Everyone Worth Knowing

Chasing Harry Winston

Last Night at Chateau Marmont

Revenge Wears Prada

The Singles Game

When Life Gives You Lululemons

Where the Grass Is Green and the Girls Are Pretty

Where the Grass Is Green
and the Girls Are Pretty

Where the Grass Is Green and the Girls Are Pretty

A NOVEL

Lauren Weisberger

RANDOM HOUSE | NEW YORK

Published in the United States by Random House, an imprint and division of Penguin Random House LLC, New York.

RANDOM HOUSE and the HOUSE colophon are registered trademarks of Penguin Random House LLC.

Hardback ISBN 978-1-9848-5556-5
International edition ISBN 978-0-593-24326-8
Ebook ISBN 978-1-9848-5557-2

Printed in the United States of America on acid-free paper

randomhousebooks.com

2 4 6 8 9 7 5 3 1

First Edition

Book design by Susan Turner

To Dana Zuskin, my sister. My shrink. My other life partner. The one who will never fail to laugh at the inappropriate, the unfortunate, and the unsuitable with me. I love you.

In memory of Susan Kamil. Our time together was far too short, but I'll be forever grateful for your guidance, support, and belief in this book—and me.

Where the Grass Is Green
and the Girls Are Pretty

1

Spinning for Boys

I think the reservation is under Marcus," Skye told the statuesque, Nordic-looking blonde who grudgingly acknowledged her at the door of Le Bilboquet. Presumably the hostess at this A-list restaurant didn't see a lot of people come in wearing maxi skirts and Birkenstocks.

"Mmm," the girl said, gazing at the screen in front of her, the kind that couldn't be read unless someone was standing at exactly the right angle. "Is that so?"

Skye flushed. An hour earlier she'd been happily sharing coffee with her old teacher friends in Harlem, but here she was nothing but an aging hippie. "It would be under Peyton Marcus, from ANN?" She hated the way she sounded as she said it.

The hostess's head shot up. "Oh! I'm sorry, did you say *Peyton* Marcus? All News Network?"

Skye forced a smile. "She's my sister."

"Of course!" The girl beamed. "We normally don't seat anyone until the full party has arrived. And naturally, we don't hold reservations for more than seven minutes, but please, follow me."

She led Skye past a cluster of tightly packed tables to a two-top positioned perfectly between the dining room and the sidewalk. With unobstructed people-watching on Madison Avenue, it was the type of table Skye would never, ever have been shown to on her own.

The hostess placed two menus on the table. "How funny," she said, smiling at Skye. "There isn't even a hint of a family resemblance."

"Yes, I hear that a lot," Skye replied.

"I mean, Ms. Marcus is just so fair! Her hair, her skin, her eyes . . ."

"Mmm, isn't that true."

"Well, anyway! I'll send her over as soon as she arrives," the young woman said before finally leaving.

Skye maneuvered herself into the seat with the inferior view and dropped her bag on the ground next to her. Instantly a uniformed waiter produced a tiny wooden stool and proudly placed the worn suede bag on it. Then, in either a bad fake French accent or a completely charming authentic one—Skye could never tell—he dramatically revealed a champagne flute and filled it with a bubbling, golden liquid. "With our compliments," he crooned, before sashaying away.

Skye tasted the champagne: dry and unbelievably delicious. The fizz went to the back of her nose, the warmth hit her stomach, and she sat back to enjoy the all-too-rare feeling. She wondered why she didn't drink more. Every now and then she'd pour herself a glass of wine on a random Tuesday night and feel rebellious and crazy, but then she'd inevitably fall asleep or get a migraine or both, and her freewheeling drinking would end for another couple weeks.

Skye felt a tap on her back and jumped. At the adjacent table, a blond woman with bass lips smiled. "Pardon me," the woman said. "But is your bag Saint Laurent?"

It took Skye a moment to understand. "Oh, this?" Skye pulled her imitation suede bag from its throne. "No, it's actually from Urban Outfitters."

The woman raised her eyebrows and forced a chuckle. "Oh! My. Well, *irregardless*, it's lovely." She turned back to her dining companion, a man half her age who had used the fifteen-second interaction to check his phone.

It's "regardless," Skye thought, feeling the blush cover her neck. *And you should get a full refund for those lips.*

Finally, her sister hurried in. "Hello, darling!" she said, smiling and leaning across the table to kiss Skye's cheek. Twice.

"Seriously?" Skye asked.

"What? We're French, at least for the afternoon!" Peyton pulled out her AirPods. "How long has it been since you've heard 'Don't Know What You Got'? Twenty years?"

"Is that Cinderella?" Skye laughed. "Way more than twenty. I made out with Harry Feldman in the temple coat closet at Samantha Weinstein's bat mitzvah to that song."

"Life was so much easier in the time of power ballads."

Skye laughed. "There was no emotion Whitesnake couldn't quantify."

"Exactly." Peyton sipped her champagne. "Now everything's gone to shit. My life is a hot mess."

Her sister looked more put together on a casual Saturday morning than Skye did ever. Peyton's coral-colored jacket, likely Chanel, topped a white silk T-shirt, skinny crop jeans, and peep-toe Louboutins in a gorgeous nude patent. Her blond hair looked freshly cut, colored, and blown straight so that the slightly turned-out ends grazed her chin and disguised her oversized ears, the one fault that Peyton hadn't yet corrected. She pulled off her Tom Ford sunglasses and tossed them into her bag, which was, of course, the authentic white leather Saint Laurent version of Skye's cheap imitation.

"Yes, I can see that. Remind me how, exactly?"

"The usual," Peyton said breezily. "The higher our ratings go, the more everyone freaks out trying to protect them. Jim, my very favorite sexual-harassing co-host, is being even more of a dick than usual. I've been working on keeping a list of really excellent on-air experts— I don't always love the ones the producers book—and that's been challenging to navigate. And there's so much to do to get Max ready for school. I mean, who would have thought my own daughter can't so much as book herself a hair appointment?"

"There's a difference between 'can't' and 'doesn't care.'"

The waiter swept in to refill Skye's champagne glass and swoon over Peyton, who asked for a bottle of pinot grigio.

"A bottle? It's eleven-thirty," Skye said.

"Thanks for the time check, Mom." Peyton turned to the waiter. "I'll have the Niçoise, please. Dressing on the side."

"Of course, Ms. Marcus."

He turned to Skye.

"I'll have the same, please. And also an order of fries."

The waiter nodded and disappeared. Peyton wrinkled her nose. "Fries?"

"You don't have to eat them."

Another waiter materialized, this one a young woman who was trying very hard not to stare at Peyton while she struggled to open the bottle of wine. Her fingers slipped. "Ohmigod, I'm sorry. I'm new, and . . ."

Peyton made a motion for the girl to give her the bottle and opener. "Here, let me." She expertly inserted the corkscrew, twisted it, and pulled it straight out with a refreshing pop. "I used to wait tables, when I was first starting out." She handed the bottle back.

"Thank you," the girl said. "That's so nice of you."

While she was pouring, a heaping plate of fries landed on their table. Crispy and hot, they were topped with sea salt, and Skye immediately popped two into her mouth. "Apparently, only brunettes with shit-brown eyes would ever order fries around here," she said through bites. "The hostess was very taken with our lack of physical resemblance."

"You may have gotten the shit-brown eyes, but I'd trade my baby blues in a heartbeat for the genetic aberration that allows you to eat like you're eighteen every day of your life. Do you even realize how rare that is after forty? I will gain a pound today by simply sharing a table with those fries," Peyton said, watching Skye chew.

Skye laughed. "I turned forty less than a year ago. You only have nine months to go. May as well enjoy them while you can."

"Dreading it. My metabolism is shot, just like my vagina," Peyton said, taking a long drink of the wine. "Have I mentioned that?"

"Only a thousand times."

"One lousy, completely uncomplicated childbirth all those years ago and still, it's never recovered."

Skye held up her hand. "Do not. The last time you likened it to the hanging slabs of deli meat at Gold's, I couldn't eat for two days."

"I won't, I won't," Peyton said, waving her hand. "I found a new physical therapist, who gave me a set of weights. Did I tell you this? You're supposed to start with the smallest one and work your way through the whole set. Apparently, by the time you can hold in the heaviest one, you're not peeing when you sneeze anymore."

Skye smiled. "And?"

"And I couldn't keep in the starter weight!" Peyton leaned forward. "Literally, the lightest one. For, like, *beginners*. You're supposed to wear it ten minutes a day and walk around, do your normal stuff, but it kept slipping out! My therapist said she'd never heard of anyone who couldn't keep in the lightest one."

"That's reassuring. She sounds really great."

"Right? Like, 'Wow! You have the widest, most gaping vagina of anyone I've ever worked with, and I'm a pelvic floor specialist, so that's really saying something.'"

Skye wiped tears from her eyes. She often thought how unfortunate it was that the viewing public never got to see this wickedly funny, outrageous side of her sister.

"It doesn't make any sense," Peyton continued. "One average-sized baby a hundred years ago. Thank god I didn't breastfeed." She cupped her breasts. "These are still passable."

"You'd be hung today if anyone else heard you say that."

"Please. Mothers today have it so easy. You get your hair blown out, your nails done, and you take a comfy Uber XL to the hospital at a mutually convenient time. It's all so civilized."

"It's supposed to be one of the most meaningful and beautiful experiences in a woman's life."

Peyton took another long drink of her wine. "Meaningful? Maybe. But the kind of women who think it's *beautiful* are the ones having babies in bathtubs in their living rooms. Hard pass."

Skye laughed. "Esther said her bathtub birth was really special."

Peyton rolled her eyes. "You know I love Esther, but please stop reminding me about her living room deliveries? It makes me judge her." She speared her salad. "How is she, by the way?"

"She's good, I think. Still not dating anyone, but trying." Skye pulled an iPad from her overstuffed bag, trying not to spill anything. "She's been advising me on the legal issues for the girls' residence, which has been extremely helpful. Want to see my mood board?"

"Yes, just don't call it that," Peyton said. She took the tablet and started to swipe and zoom through the different sections for carpeting, wall decor, furniture, and bedding Skye was considering for the five-bedroom home that was being converted into a residence for underprivileged girls, who would then attend Paradise's award-winning public high school.

"Wow, this looks *amazing*."

"It's really coming along."

"I'd say. What's your move-in date?"

"Labor Day weekend at the latest, if I want the girls to have an uninterrupted school year. If the funding comes in soon from Isaac's friend, we'll be fine."

"Henry can be a prick, but he'll come through with the money. It's the only thing he's good at."

"He's been nothing but wonderful so far," Skye said, forking the last of her salad into her mouth.

"He may only be funding this to meet some corporate responsibility requirement," Peyton said.

"That's fine with me. He can do it for whatever reason he wants, just so long as he does it."

Peyton grabbed the bottle of pinot grigio by its neck and hauled it out of the silver ice bucket. "I'm proud of you for getting this girls' residence idea out of your head and off the ground. And you're getting back to work after so many years off."

Skye stared at her.

"What?" Peyton asked. "I'm not *judging* you for your extremely extended maternity leave. I've just heard you drone endlessly how you're done with Girl Scouts and looking forward to something a little more . . . stimulating."

"How about you?" Skye said. "Max leaving for school? Your one and only baby girl, grown and flown?"

Peyton scrunched her nose. "More like irritable and entitled."

"You're too tough on her."

"On the child who's devastated to be heading to Princeton?"

Skye sighed. "Film school would have ruined her life? That's all I am saying."

"Can we not rehash this? My god, it's *Princeton*. Anyway, she's all yours this summer."

"I can't wait. Maybe you and Isaac could come up and stay, too?"

"Max definitely wouldn't want us there. And I'll be in the studio even more than usual this summer, making sure we can keep ratings firmed up going into fall." She pointed to Skye's phone. "You just got a text," she said, at the same time that her own phone vibrated to indicate a new email.

"How does Mom always know when we're together?" Skye muttered, glancing at the notification. "If she knew how to download the app—any app—I'd think she was tracking us."

Peyton swiped open her email and read, "Subject line: talcum powder."

"Oh, please don't," Skye said, placing two fingers and a thumb on the side of her forehead.

"'Dear girls,'" Peyton read in her best Marcia voice. "'There is some evidence, parentheses, not conclusive, end parentheses, that talcum powder increases the chance of quote ovarian cancer, end quote. I used it with both of you often. You may want to mention it at your next doctor's appointments. Love, Mom.'"

"What a useful email to get on a random afternoon in June! Thanks, Mom," Skye said.

Peyton snorted. "Why do you think she put 'ovarian cancer' in quotes? Like, it's not a real thing?"

"It still doesn't come close to her email about Aunt Hattie," Skye said.

"'Dear girls,'" Peyton started, reciting it from memory. "'I'm sorry to have to tell you that Aunt Hattie died last night. I'll email you as soon as I have the shiva information. In other news, I finally decided on colors for my new Camry. Silver cloud for the exterior, charcoal gray leather on the inside. Love, Mom.'"

Both women were in tears. Despite the fact that they'd recited this particular email to each other no fewer than a hundred times, it never got less funny.

"We should laugh while we can," Peyton said while dabbing her lips with a sheer gloss from a brand Skye had never heard of. "Because it's only a matter of time until we do this to our own daughters."

"Speak for yourself. I think it's well established that I'm the cool mom," Skye said.

"I would have made a good boy mom, I think." Peyton nodded thoughtfully.

"I'm pretty sure in Paradise they're spinning for boys. There is no way that many families are having all those boys naturally."

"Your town is so fucked up." Peyton tucked her blond hair behind an ear. "Why would anyone want *boys* that badly?"

"Sports, I think. The more boys you have, the more seasons you can cover and the more fields you can sit on and carpools you can drive and practices you can attend and teams you can coach. My working theory is that it's a way for unhappily married couples to avoid having to spend a second of time together on the weekends."

Peyton laughed. "I did warn you when you moved to the suburbs." She held her hands up. "I know, I know—outstanding schools, Gabe's job. But what did you expect? It's a tough crowd." She pushed back her chair. "Let's get out of here?"

They paid the check and wove through the restaurant, past the now friendly hostess, and out onto the sidewalk. A mother and daughter pair did a simultaneous double take when they spotted Peyton, who offered an enthusiastic wave and a bright smile.

"I don't know how you do it," Skye said, watching the exchange.

"What?"

"Constantly cater to your adoring public. Don't you ever want to go somewhere and not be recognized? Especially on a weekend."

"Nope."

Skye laughed. "You're a lunatic. I love you." She hoisted her scruffy bag onto her shoulder and held out her arms.

"Love you, too," Peyton said, walking into Skye's outstretched arms. "Send me ideas for Mom's present. And we have to get on a birthday plan for her soon."

"Copy that," Skye said. "By 'we,' I'm assuming you mean me?"

"Yes." Her sister made a mock-guilty face. "You're so much better at this stuff."

They hugged goodbye, blocking the flow of pedestrian traffic on Madison Avenue. Skye pulled back quickly, unwilling to inconvenience strangers. Peyton laughed at her.

"Love you," Peyton said, offering a little flat-palmed wave like Queen Elizabeth at the Trooping of the Guard.

"Love you, too." Skye stepped out of everyone's way and watched her sister stride down the street like it was a runway in Paris. Peyton could be self-absorbed and showy, sometimes downright impossible, but Skye couldn't deny that she loved that crazy bitch.

2

Good Things Come to Those Who Pay

B ack from commercial break in sixty seconds, stand by!"

Peyton sipped her coffee from her All News Network mug and turned her head sideways, toward the makeup artist who'd materialized to powder Peyton's forehead. The cameramen adjusted their positions for the upcoming segment while Sean, the EP, called over the studio's audio system. "Homestretch, everyone! Only six more minutes to the weekend."

Peyton could see a few people in the control room give a cheer. It had been a long week, and everyone was anxious to get home to their real lives that weren't counted in thirty-second increments or rated on a segment-by-segment basis. The living that took place out-side the brutal hours of five to eight in the morning, the blazing studio lights, and the relentless, unforgiving pressure of live national television.

Jim, her co-host, returned to their shared desk and lumbered to his anchor chair. Peyton wondered if Jim's frequent bathroom visits during commercial breaks were actually a cover for a quick set of bicep curls.

"TFGIF," he said, reinserting his earpiece. He smoothed his hair back, but not a strand moved under his industrial-strength lacquer spray. "A full bottle every three days," he'd often bragged.

It's not that Peyton didn't like Jim, it was just that . . . well, fine. She didn't like him. He was a damn good anchor, no arguing that, and their audience, which skewed female, absolutely loved his on-air personality—a kitchen-sink mixture of hyper-masculinity, unwavering positivity, and, when required, something that very closely resembled empathy. However, when the cameras were off, he reverted to his authentic self.

"Am I right?" he asked Peyton, looking at her.

"Huh?" Peyton asked. She'd just remembered that she needed to make a dentist appointment for that afternoon.

"Thirty seconds!" the loudspeakers announced. A PA appeared to refill both their water glasses.

"TFGIF," Jim repeated. "Get it? Thank fucking god it's Friday."

"Mmm." Peyton forced a smile as she pulled out the small Moleskine she kept in their anchor desk, in which she wrote down the constant to-dos she only remembered when least able to act.

Book dentist for 5 pm, she scribbled, before another thought occurred to her. Max had to schedule herself dentist, doctor, and gyn checkups before she left for college at the end of the summer.

"Twenty seconds!"

As she wrote, Jim took a loud, slurpy slug of whatever was in his ANN mug. Peyton wondered, for the thousandth time, if his coffee was laced with cocaine or crushed Adderall or at the very least some sort of black-market testosterone supplement. What else could make a seemingly normal man that *aggressive*?

"Ten seconds!"

Jim cleared his throat, pulled back his shoulders, and began making intimate eye contact with Camera 3, the one that would lead them back from commercial break.

"Peyton? You good?" Sean asked, this time through her earpiece.

She nodded. *Dammit!* She'd forgotten to check back with Skye about her mother's birthday. She circled the reminder, making it priority number one.

"And we have five, four . . ."

"Peyton, for chrissakes, move it!" Sean's tone was spiked with irritation.

". . . three, two . . ."

She closed her notebook.

The set went silent. Camera 3's red light blinked to indicate they were live. Peyton felt a surge of calmness. It was the opposite of an adrenaline rush, a sudden feeling of complete tranquility. Her brain, ping-ponging only seconds earlier, settled into that hyper-focused sweet spot, and Peyton morphed, without the least bit of effort, into her trademark warm composure.

"Welcome back," she said, smiling straight into Camera 3 as though it were a living room full of her favorite people. "To close out this Friday, we'd like to share with you one family's incredible story of fortitude and love," Peyton read from the teleprompter. They always tried to end the week with a fuzzy human-interest story to leave viewers feeling less suicidal about the state of the world.

"Logan Pierce is a nine-year-old boy who loves drawing, Legos, and cheering on the Astros from his family's home outside of Houston," Peyton read with just the right mix of gravitas and admiration, even though she was wondering which segment producer's pet border collie had written that moronic script. "So imagine the Pierce family's horror when Logan was diagnosed with pediatric lymphoma, a rare and life-threatening disease." But then, the mother's dignified sadness as she recounted Logan's diagnosis, treatment, and ultimate recovery captured Peyton's attention completely, an almost unheard-of phenomenon when she was on air and needed to juggle so many competing inputs. She was so absorbed by the woman's voice—and Logan's obvious sweetness as he cradled his infant sister—that she almost missed Sean's urgent breaking news announcement in her ear.

Her eyes darted to the control room, which had transformed from a calm, finely choreographed ballet to a chaotic rave. She glanced at the enormous digital clock above the cameras that counted the time to the second. *Shit.* They were still five full minutes away from eight o'clock, which meant that the breaking news would need to be announced on their watch.

"I'll take it," Jim murmured into his microphone. On the monitors in front of them, Logan's doctor described the effects of lymphoma on children.

"Negative," Sean's voice came back. "Too disruptive. Bad enough we have to cut short the kid. Go to commercial when this B-roll ends."

Both anchors nodded their understanding.

"They're writing up the intro now but it'll only be thirty seconds' worth of material," Sean continued. "The charges and a brief description. From there I'll talk you through it."

With this, Peyton felt a small jolt of anxiety. It wasn't panic, exactly, but something uncomfortable enough that it made her sit up straighter and breathe a little faster. Breaking news was always unpredictable.

The tape ended, and when the camera switched back to Peyton, she calmly told the viewers that they'd be back after a quick break. Almost immediately all hell broke loose.

"This better be worth it," Peyton said aloud to no one in particular.

"Seriously," Jim echoed. "We just bailed on a kid with cancer!"

One of the segment producers, Jenna, a prodigy in her mid-twenties who they'd recently poached from Fox News, announced, "FBI just confirmed simultaneous arrests for twenty-two individuals, some high profile, all charged with felony conspiracy and/or mail fraud."

"Who gives a fuck about mail fraud?" Jim boomed, reading Peyton's mind.

Jenna ignored him. "All twenty-two are affluent parents accused of buying their kids' way into elite universities," she told them through their earpieces.

"Thirty seconds!" came a voice over the loudspeaker.

Peyton felt a flush of adrenaline. "What do we know? Are we ready?"

Sean burst into the studio, a stack of papers in one hand and his signature large black glasses in the other. "Jenna, prompter?" he asked into the ether.

Jenna's disembodied voice confirmed that the teleprompter was set.

"I have enough information here to get us to the end of the show,"

Sean said, waving the printouts. "Read the prompter slowly, and we'll take it together from there."

"Ten seconds!"

Sean went back behind the control room's glass wall. Peyton watched as he pulled on his headset and jabbed his finger at the graphics guy.

"Buckle up, Buttercup," Jim said, once again arranging his face into an impressive facade of empathy.

". . . three, two, one . . ."

Camera 2 switched on, the one they primarily used for close-ups, and Peyton's eyes found the teleprompter.

"We are interrupting the emotional story of Logan Pierce to bring you breaking news," Peyton read, wondering if the slight waver she heard in her own voice was real or imagined. "ANN has confirmed that the FBI has arrested twenty-two parents of college applicants across four states and accused them of *purchasing* their children's admissions to certain elite universities. While we don't yet have many of the specifics, sources have confirmed that at least three of these parents are high-profile individuals."

The teleprompter stopped scrolling. She knew it had merely run out of words—those were the only sentences that Jenna had time to type—but Peyton stopped breathing. It was only Sean's voice in her ear that kept her from total panic. No anchor liked ad-libbing blind to millions of viewers.

"Breathe!" he barked. "I got you."

And as she inhaled, Sean relayed nugget-sized bits of noninformation to Peyton, which she synthesized and regurgitated back to the cameras: "No comment yet from the College Board"; "Waiting to hear from the Manhattan district attorney"; "The largest conspiracy ever involving college admissions."

Then Sean barked, "Jim, ask Peyton when we'll know more!"

Jim, without missing a beat, turned his upper body toward Peyton, furrowed his brow, and said, "When can we expect more information on this developing story?"

Sean said, "Peyton, end it," seconds before Peyton returned Jim's look and smoothly—she hoped—replied, "Our time this morning is just about up, but Suzanna and Alejandro will be closely following this story all throughout the nine o'clock hour." She turned back to Camera 1 on her left diagonal and said, "Stay right here for all the details on this emerging scandal. We are Peyton Marcus and Jim Atwood, and we'll see you bright and early Monday morning."

There was a three-second pause where no one moved, and then Sean announced, "We're clear!"

The studio broke into applause.

Sean materialized in front of the anchor desk. "Loved that you called it a scandal," he said, a slight sheen of sweat on his forehead. "Juicy!"

"Thanks for carrying me," Peyton said, her heart thumping hard in her chest. She pulled out her earpiece and collapsed back into her chair.

"Good show," Jim said, removing his earpiece. He stood up, towering over Peyton and Sean. He had the body of a former college football player and an uncanny knack for working the phrases "when I played football at Clemson" and "during my QB days" and "there's no training for life like D1 football" into regular conversation, to the point where Peyton felt like she should do a shot of Jäger every time he used one of them.

"Anyway, I'm out, girls," he announced, grinning at Sean to show how totally cool he was with Sean's gayness. "Have great weekends. Don't do anything I wouldn't do. . . ." He offered a meaty hand in a wave and barreled toward his dressing room.

"Is he wearing Drakkar?" Sean asked, scrunching his nose. He turned back toward his office. "Walk with me."

Peyton unclipped her microphone and jumped down off her seat. "Do we know anything else?" she asked.

"About?"

"About the college thing! I mean, we have covered this before,

have we not? Is this really still a thing?" Peyton hurried along the cor-
ridor behind him.

He pushed his office door open and flopped into his desk chair.
"It's always a thing. I'd bet half my class at Stanford got in by rowing
or playing volleyball. Or tennis. *So much tennis*. These idiot parents
certainly take it up a notch, but it never gets old hearing what the
wealthy will do to get their kids into Ivy League schools."

Peyton accepted the bottle of water he passed her. She hadn't
realized how thirsty she was. Her breathing returned to normal.
"Yeah, you're right," Peyton said, nodding. "This goes on all the time,
I'm sure. But these parents are probably different, at least if they
were like the last ones: literally faking photos of their kids and paying
strangers to take tests for them. I mean, who does that?"

"Exactly." Sean's desktop phone rang. "Yeah? On my way." He
stood up again. "Gotta run. If I don't see you before you leave, have a
great weekend." He kissed her on the cheek and pulled the door shut
behind him. It was a small courtesy but a fortunate one, since Peyton
felt a wave of nausea wash over her. Probably just lingering adrenaline,
she thought. The parents getting rounded up were nothing like her or
any of the thousands of other parents who killed themselves giving
their kids every possible advantage. Still, it was unsettling. A second
round of this, after they'd all just put the first one to bed? Peyton took
one last sip before she dropped to her knees and swiftly vomited up the
entire contents of her stomach into Sean's elegant wooden wastebasket.

It only took thirteen minutes in an Uber—a record—to get to her
private gym at Seventy-fourth and Madison, a second-floor loft space
so gorgeous that it could easily be mistaken for a movie set. Tucked
into one of the spacious, private changing pods, each featuring a
steam shower and vanity stocked with Malin+Goetz products, plus a
lounge area with a loveseat and gas fireplace, Peyton stripped off her
sapphire-blue sheath dress. She yanked on a pair of cropped leggings
and a tank with a built-in bra. It took four premoistened makeup
remover wipes to clean off the extra-thick layer of TV foundation and

a half dozen swipes with a boar bristle brush to break up the industrial-strength hairspray, and although every inch of her body screamed to sit down on the plush sofa—just for a minute!—she willed herself to keep moving.

"Hey, gorgeous," Kendric said to her, swatting her with a towel when she entered the cardio area. "Great show today. Now get on there and move that ass."

Peyton saluted and headed to the nearest treadmill. Sometimes she missed the frenetic energy of Equinox, but not the fact that everyone recognized her and would either stare at her, sneak pictures, or, worst of all, approach her for a chat. But here, at the hidden oasis that called itself a gym but charged like it was a fractional jet service, there were only two men in their sixties on adjacent treadmills and one woman in her twenties working distressingly hard on a stair-climber. Otherwise the place was empty. Abandoned! It was beautiful.

Peyton claimed the treadmill in pole position and plugged in her earbuds.

While she waited for the screen to load ANN, she set the pace to a brisk 6.0 with a 4 incline to get warmed up but was distracted by her own appearance in the fully mirrored wall. Lord. Not good. Everyone *looooved* to talk about how the wheels came off at forty, and Peyton always smiled and nodded and was not the least bit worried that it would affect her whatsoever. She'd spent her teens, twenties, and the first nine years of her thirties doing whatever she damn well pleased, and it never mattered. She'd smoked for a decade. Drank way too much. Ate like a teenage boy. Barely worked out. Never got more than five hours of sleep a night. And still, despite the fact that she was only five-five, which was at least four inches shorter than she would have liked, she'd always been trim, tight, and toned. But now? Still nine months shy of forty? It was a horror show. The barely noticeable lines around her eyes had become trenches. Her skin was sallow and gray, no matter how much she spent on exfoliators or eye creams or face oils. There was hair everywhere, except where it should be. And her body? It was like a switch had been activated that made her stomach paunch out, her boobs sag, and her ass start to spread in all the wrong directions.

When she'd shown up, nearly hysterical, at her OB's office, her doctor nodded knowingly. "Perimenopause," she said. "Normal."

"Normal!" Peyton screeched. "Look at me!"

Certainly accustomed to such outbreaks in her private Upper East Side practice, Dr. Kate smiled. "Cut down on carbs. Start working out, maybe get a trainer? I can recommend a great cosmetic derm."

In the last six months, Peyton had wholly committed herself—and what felt like half her sizable salary—to self-improvement. What choice did she have? Her career was based on her appearance. She made standing appointments at the derm and subjected her face and décolletage and, yes, even the tops of her hands to every imaginable laser and chemical peel legally available. One did red spots. One did brown spots. A third did fine lines and wrinkles. Another attacked errant hair. A fifth did general sallowness. A sixth worked on collagen production. For a short period of time she'd be pleased with the smoothed, lightened, hairless result. And then before she could so much as buy a new foundation, it would all come surging back, a veritable tsunami of wrinkles and spots and stubble.

Peyton wasn't a quitter. She upped her thrice-yearly Botox to every other month. That helped. So did the fillers in her cheeks and lips, and the vile-smelling oil she rubbed into her scalp to stimulate hair growth. Encouraged a bit, she turned to her body and began training sessions with Kendric, who charged more per hour than a shrink with a PhD. Despite having the most brutal schedule of anyone she knew—up at 3 A.M., in the makeup chair by 4:15 A.M., live on air from 5 to 8 A.M., and often hours more of meetings and researching, Monday through Friday—Peyton would drag herself out of the office and come straight here, where Kendric would put her through a savage circuit of bicep curls and dead lifts and cardio. She scored an appointment with a nutritionist who had traveled the world with Gisele Bündchen and Tom Brady and committed to eating exactly what the woman demanded. She forced down eighty ounces of water every day even though it made her pee every twelve minutes; she dipped her salad greens in the dressing instead of pouring it on top; she eschewed bread, pasta, cheese, and every other morsel of food that carried even the faintest suggestion of possible enjoyment.

None of it changed a thing, not one fucking bit. The second she focused on building muscle, her skin went to hell. Whenever she returned to her punishing regimen of lasers and peels, her gut returned. She was barely eating enough to sustain her workouts or her trips to the dermatologist, and yet all of that starving was doing nothing. Zero. The scale didn't move a single pound. The jeans she'd worn comfortably since college still didn't zip. No amount of injected poison or burpees or cold, hard cash could put so much as a dent into the damage wreaked by turning forty. Never mind she hadn't even turned forty yet! Her sister, on the other hand, was still skinny as hell, unwrinkled and fresh, without a modicum of effort.

The treadmill sped up automatically and Peyton switched from ANN to MSNBC, where Joe and Mika were discussing the new wave of college admissions arrests, including a doctor father from Beverly Hills who had explicitly offered a free gastric bypass to the squash coach at one of the UC schools if she would "recruit" his daughter. *Insane,* Peyton thought, as she increased the speed.

Peyton claimed she never watched the news when she wasn't in the studio, but that was a lie. She knew every anchor on every station. Got alerts from a half dozen news websites. Studied up on hirings, firings, and internal scandals. This was one competitive industry, and if you didn't keep up, you were left behind. She hadn't gotten to the morning show anchor chair by being lazy or uninformed. *Oh, hell no.* She'd done stints in Arkansas. South Dakota. Even one summer in Alaska. No one knew better than Peyton how important it was not to get too complacent. She was finally national, and not in the middle of the night. Next up was prime time. So long as she stayed strong and focused.

Ten minutes into her run, Peyton tired of *Morning Joe* and switched over to CNN. Poppy Harlow was an acquaintance, and she liked checking in with her show in the mornings. That day Poppy was on location in London, and Don Lemon was at Poppy's desk in the studio. Peyton was so preoccupied with adjusting the incline and trying not to hyperventilate that she almost didn't notice Don pressing a finger to his ear before he said, "Poppy? Just one moment here, we seem to have some breaking news." Almost immediately, an angry red graphic swirled on the screen, accompanied by a dramatic drumbeat: BREAKING NEWS. Peyton rolled her eyes. Was this going to be a new development or an entirely new story? They were all guilty of overusing that pronouncement. Yes, it got everyone's attention, but polls showed the viewership growing immune to it. A fire in the Pentagon where officials knew one hundred percent that it wasn't a suicide bomber *and* no one died? Save it. Record-setting market close in China? Please. Oil spill off the coast of Indonesia? Next. Anything short of an assassination attempt on the president or a dirty bomb on the subway didn't warrant the graphic.

But then Don was back, and he looked riled up. "We're going to take you live to uptown Manhattan, where my colleague Jamie is on the scene. Jamie, what can you tell us?"

A young man with a bow tie and a serious expression stared down the camera. "Well, Don, as you know, this story is still developing. What I can tell you is that the FBI is here today in a rather large show of force, something they don't do unless it's warranted."

Wow, thank you for that brilliant analysis! Peyton thought.

Wait. Peyton punched the emergency stop button on the treadmill and squinted at the screen. Was that *her* building in the background? The camera zoomed in on bow-tied Jamie, who could barely contain his excitement, and just behind him Peyton saw her very own doorman, Peter, standing rigidly on the sidewalk.

"What the . . . ," she murmured, more fascinated than worried. Someone in her building was about to be *arrested*? She felt a pang of panic but then remembered that cretin of a plastic surgeon who lived in the penthouse and constantly posted "before" and "after" pics of women's breast enlargements on his Instagram page under the handle @kingofboobs. He would cover their nipples with little pink heart stickers and then photograph himself cupping their breasts from every angle. He called his patients "gems," as in "Bringing you another work of art: We took this Dr. J Gem from saggy to superhero with 330 ccs." He would include a headless picture of a woman's body that looked perfectly lovely in the "before" picture and like a porn star in the "after." Every time Peyton saw him in the elevator or the lobby, he reminded her of his gratis boob job offer—after all, she was famous—and every time, she forced a smile and tried not to throw up in her mouth. It had to be him! Sexual harassment, or even all-out assault.

Was ANN getting scooped? She flipped through the channels, shocked to see Jim, back in *their* studio, leaning conspiratorially toward the camera.

"Now, bear with us, everyone," he said in his faux-folksy way that made her want to reach straight through the television and plunge her thumbs into his eyes. "As you can imagine, this is a very sensitive subject for all of us here at ANN, one that hits close to home."

Jim's left hand went to his left ear as he glanced skyward. An imperceptible nod. And then it occurred to her: the producers were updating him. Her producers! Ohmigod, was it Sean in Jim's ear? Why was she on a treadmill when Jim was still on air? Peyton was so transfixed that she almost missed the action unfolding on the screen as they flipped back to the external shot. The building's doors—her building's doors—swung open. Two men in dark suits emerged and looked around. Following them were two uniformed police officers, one male and one female, and between them was . . . her husband.

A small but loud group of reporters began shouting questions. Jim was narrating, but Peyton couldn't understand what he was saying. She leaned closer to the treadmill screen. Isaac looked, well, like Isaac. He was wearing a plaid flannel button-down, a pair of ratty khakis, and those wool running shoes every man, woman, and child in the top income bracket seemed to own. His hair was sticking straight up and his jaws were clenched so tightly that his neck muscles bulged. Peyton pressed her hand to her heart when she saw it: he was in handcuffs.

"As I said before, this one hits close to home. But here at ANN we put you, our valued audience, first, and have decided to cover the arrest of Isaac Marcus, husband of our own Peyton Marcus, for what it is: a newsworthy story," Jim said in a serious voice. "The FBI has been intimating that a second round of arrests in the college admissions scandal would be forthcoming, and it looks like today they are making good on their word."

"Oh my god," Peyton said aloud, or screamed, or whispered or merely thought—she had no idea.

Once again Jim pressed his ear. "Yes, I can now confirm that Isaac Marcus, husband of ANN's own Peyton Marcus, is being arrested in conjunction with the college admissions scandal. While we do not yet have the specific charge or charges, they will likely be similar to those we've seen both in previous years and earlier this morning—"

Peyton's phone buzzed from its perch on the treadmill's magazine holder. She grabbed it and started running for the exit.

It was Sean.

"Can't you shut Jim up?" she hissed into the phone. "Pull the plug already!"

"I'm sorry, P, I really am. He was just about to leave the studio, and then we got the second breaking news notice. . . . He just pounced."

"You can't possibly think that Isaac . . ." Peyton's voice trailed off as she ran past the check-in desk and out onto the sidewalk.

"No! But I can't stop Jim from covering this, whatever it is. And I certainly don't have to remind you that, executive producer or not, he doesn't listen to me."

Peyton's throat clenched. "I have to go. I have to figure out what's happening. I just don't understand. . . ."

"Let me know if I—"

Peyton ran the rest of the way to her building, where the scene from television was playing out in real time. She wasn't sure whether it was instinct or shock or just plain luck that kept her from screaming out his name, but Isaac spotted her before any of the cameras. He leaned in to say something to one of the detectives, who nodded and indicated to a uniformed NYPD officer to allow Peyton to approach.

"Oh my god, are you okay?" she asked, cursing her own inane question while wanting to reach out and touch his arm, his face, anything. The same detective who'd given her permission now sent her a warning look to keep her distance.

Cameras flashed from every direction. She could feel the buzz all around her. *Was that Peyton Marcus? Could they possibly be lucky enough to catch this husband and wife drama unfold live? Even better, was she really wearing leggings and a sports bra with no makeup?*

Then, somehow, Isaac's mouth was pressed against her ear, and she could feel his hot breath as he said, "Do not say anything to anyone. Not. One. Word. Do you understand?"

Peyton nodded, or she tried to, but the next thing she knew, the detectives prodded him into the backseat of an SUV and the door slammed shut. The glass was tinted so dark she couldn't see inside.

"What can you tell us about the charges against your husband?"

"Did this come as a surprise or did you know this arrest was coming?"

"Do you feel there's a conflict of interest in your reporting of the story that now involves your spouse?"

"Any word on next steps, either for Isaac or for you, professionally speaking?"

The questions came rapid-fire from every direction as Peyton stood, frozen. Then, out of nowhere, a hand on her elbow, which she swatted away until a familiar voice said, "Mrs. Marcus, this way," and Peter, her doorman, led her through the crowd and into the blessedly empty lobby.

She looked at him, uncertain what to do next, how to thank this kind man who had just saved her from certain hell.

He pressed the button to summon the elevator and held the door open for her when it arrived. "May I suggest you don't answer the landline for anyone?" he asked. "I will ensure no one comes up without your express permission."

"Thank you," Peyton whispered, just before the elevators closed. And then she remembered: Max.

"Max?" she yelled as she threw open the unlocked front door.

"Are you here?" Silence. There was no response, and Peyton was almost relieved to find her daughter's room empty. But where was Max and how could she reach her? She sent a first text: *Call me asap, it's important,* and then followed it with a second: *911!!!!* She pressed redial again but still got her daughter's voicemail.

What was she supposed to do in this situation? Call her mother? A friend? A lawyer? Yes, a lawyer. Her college roommate, Nisha, who'd gone on to Yale Law School and had left the U.S. district attorney's office to start her own crisis management firm. She was brilliant and a ballbuster, and she would know exactly what to do. *Stay calm. Call Nisha.* But when Peyton opened her phone, panic rose in her throat.

There was only one person to call.

Skye picked up on the first ring.

"Are you watching this right now?" Peyton asked.

At first, her sister said nothing. When she finally spoke, her voice was quiet and serious. "You are so totally and completely fucked."

3

The Guy Magnet

G rande vanilla latte, extra hot, no foam, for Max!" a barista called out from behind the counter. Max jumped up from her overstuffed wing chair and headed to the pickup station.

"Thanks," she said, noticing right away how cute he was with his shaggy, shoulder-length hair.

"Oh, hey, you're a girl," he said with a smile, revealing dimples.

Max looked herself up and down, as though she, too, needed confirmation. She blushed.

"Sorry," he said, noticing her embarrassment.

"No, no, it's fine," she mumbled, and practically ran back to her seat. What was wrong with her? Why couldn't she have a three-sentence exchange with a cute boy that she'd never see again? Humiliated, she took a giant gulp of her coffee, which burned her tongue and the back of her throat. She tried to choke down the burning hot liquid but had to spit it out.

Just call me the guy magnet.

She mopped her coffee-stained T-shirt and sneaked a glance at the counter. The cute barista wasn't even looking at her. Obviously. The coffee shop was teeming with attractive, professional-looking office workers grabbing breakfast, ones who could manage to respond to a bit of friendly chat.

Max swiped the touchpad on her laptop, where she was editing the footage she'd filmed of her boxing lesson the day before. For the last few months she'd been meeting her mother's trainer, Kendric, in her building's gym, and finally she felt like she was making enough progress, skill-wise, to film a session. She had secured her new camera to the lat pulldown machine with a Gumby-like wall mount, and now, as she watched the footage, she was impressed with what she saw. Twenty or thirty seconds of her best boxing moves would make a good opening to the day's vlog, and if she set it to good music and ended with both audio and closed-caption of Kendric saying "Way to crush it," she could easily segue into her thoughts on the recent Supreme Court ruling. The new graffiti font she'd been playing with would be perfect in both segments.

She scanned, cut, and pasted. Cut some more. All around her, people buzzed in and out, slurping their frappes and chatting into their phones, happy it was Friday morning, excited for the upcoming weekend. Not that she had any real plans. With Brynn gone and the rest of her graduating class off doing whatever fabulous things fabulous people did in the summer before college, Max didn't have much going on at all. Maybe some fishing with her dad. Certainly an argument with her mom.

Max took a sip of water from her new steel water bottle, which had been a gift from her mother. "I read it's the coolest one—everyone has them," Peyton had said. Which was so typical: If everyone had it, she should, too. Didn't matter if you liked it, or needed it, or if it was a genuinely good or useful product, so long as everyone thought you were cool for having it. It was so ironic. Everyone always accused teenagers of caring too much what their friends thought—had they ever met a Manhattan mother?

Like the boxing lessons, for instance. Her mother had managed to weasel her way into the one semi-sporty thing that Max loved and make it all about something else. Losing weight, namely, although of course she would never, *ever* say that. Instead, Peyton had always carefully couched it in socially acceptable phrases, likely all approved by some teen specialist shrink she consulted. Since Max was thirteen, her mother had been saying things like "Exercise makes everything more manageable" and "Good sweat sessions help so much with sleep" and "Workouts are chicken soup for the soul," which Max had obviously understood was code for "Don't get fat." Or really, "Don't get fatter." It was the same veiled way Peyton used to talk enthusiastically about food. "I love starting every meal with a big salad—it's a great way to fill up on the good stuff." "Clean eating is so important to good health." And Max's personal favorite: "The whole family is going to focus on eating better—we could all stand to pay attention more." Which was flat-out fucking ridiculous: her dad was naturally, genetically skinny and her mother basically dedicated her own existence to staying that way. It was so obvious that those comments were meant for Max and Max alone.

It was maddening. Had she put on some pounds the last few years? Obviously. It was called puberty. Had her mother heard of it? These little snippets had been poisonous when Max was a younger teenager, racked with body shame and angst, both made worse by her mother's focus on her own appearance; Peyton would deny she herself was obsessed, but Max had seen her go from being a pretty and professional news journalist to the stereotypical high-maintenance, smooth-faced, and ageless creature that a national audience demanded. But now, at seventeen, Max had finally realized that just because her mother still desperately clung to the hollow-cheeked look didn't mean Max had to. She was allowed to love her D-cup boobs and the roundness of her hips and to think her ass looked damn good in a pair of high-waisted jeans. So what if her thighs didn't have that ridiculous triangle gap that all the models flaunted on Instagram? Max wasn't a moron: she'd read about the unrealistic pressure on girls to be skinny. And the evils of Photoshop. And eating disorders. It was so irritating that, despite being proud of her own body, Max still had to hear the usual horseshit about diet from her own borderline-anorexic *mother*. Which of course Peyton would deny if accused. *Skinny? Who, her? No, no, of course not.* It was all about "health" and "taking care of yourself."

She finished editing the vlog entry and watched it through twice more to make sure she hadn't missed anything. Satisfied, Max hit Publish and held her breath as it loaded over her ever-slowing hotspot. When it gave confirmation, she exhaled and clicked off the site. A commotion of laughter by the front door caught her attention. Looking up, she saw three Milford classmates and immediately regretted not choosing a midtown or even Hell's Kitchen Starbucks. Max sank lower in her seat and turned her body toward the wall. When, three days earlier, she'd donned the required white dress and accepted her diploma, Max imagined that the whole of Milford Academy—the city block it occupied between Park and Madison and its entire student body, clad in its matching tartan plaid uniforms—would vanish. Poof! Gone from her life forever. And yet, here they were.

"Hurry, guys, we're going to be late!" the tallest one, Lucy, a gazelle-like girl with long, graceful limbs, called out. She was a nationally ranked fencer. Very sweet. Not the brightest, but clearly Carnegie Mellon's competitive fencing team didn't care. With her were Josephine (Stanford), whose father was a billionaire, and Anne-Marie (Cornell), who had both a hyphenated first name and an exotic accent, despite having been born and raised on the Upper East Side.

"Oh my, look at these!" said Anne-Marie, holding up a package of chocolate-covered graham crackers like they were rare, delicate butterflies. "Must. Have."

Max glanced over at the counter and noticed the cute barista was watching Anne-Marie, too. Shocker.

"Wait—is that Max?" Josephine asked, pointing in Max's direction. "Ohmigod, it is! Hey, Max!"

Lucy led the charge toward Max's chair. Was she wearing a crown braid? Was it professionally done? And how did she pull it off so well? Max touched her own wild curls and wondered when the last time was she'd gotten so much as a trim, never mind a Coachella-inspired updo.

"Hey," Max said.

"So crazy! What are the chances of seeing you here?" Lucy asked.

Oh, I don't know. Like close to a hundred percent, since I was

*stupid enough to pick a Starbucks equidistant between my apartment
and our school?*

But instead Max said, "Right?" drawing out the "i" in an effort to
sound friendlier.

Anne-Marie leaned closer. "What are you reading? I think my
mom is reading that book."

Max held her hardcover nonfiction on Alexander Hamilton aloft.
"Oh, this? It's pretty good. I'm actually meeting some friends here.
We're heading to the beach today, but I needed some caffeine first."
The moment the words left her mouth, Max felt a tsunami of shame.
Why did she care so much what they thought of her?

"Totally." Lucy nodded. "We're heading out east, too. Looks like
the weather is going to be great."

"Mmm," Max murmured. And then, remembering her effort to
be friendlier, she said, "Hope the traffic isn't too bad."

"Okay, well, it was nice seeing you," Anne-Marie said, yanking on
Lucy's arm. "We have to run. Bye, Max!"

"Have fun today," Lucy called over her shoulder.

Max watched the girls as they grabbed their drinks from the
counter, adjusted their milks and sugars, and walked out, laughing.
Only then did she notice their outfits: short skirts, cut-off denim,
bikini straps peeking out of cute linen cover-ups. They were *actually*
heading to the beach.

Fuck it, she thought, returning her attention to her book. But
Max couldn't get the thought out of her head. Who graduated high
school with virtually no friends? Had anyone cared when Max insisted
that Milford Academy was the wrong school for her? That its relentless focus on grades and STEM curriculum and the Ivy League *at all
costs* created an environment of Stepford preppy robots who would
kill one another for a leg up? Of course not. Did anyone listen when
she had asked—no, begged—for years to transfer to LaGuardia or
St. Ann's or Friends, all incredible schools with more creative offerings? Not even a little. Well, that wasn't fair exactly. Her dad *had* listened, but her mother always overrode him with what she called "the

irrefutable facts": Milford was *the* most prestigious school in the city and Max would have to be certifiably insane to voluntarily give up her spot, which, incidentally, had been secured for her in kindergarten. It was that emphasis on "the" that needled Max the most. *The* most prestigious. *The* hardest to get into. *The* one and only. As though all of life was a linear path, and each direction or decision or opportunity had a clear and undeniable value ranking—so long as you were the one in charge of deciding the values.

Whatever, Max thought as she returned her eyes to her book. All that high school bullshit was finally behind her. She'd move in with Aunt Skye for the summer, something she looked forward to all year long, and right after that she would head to college and start her new life.

Max pulled out her phone and WhatsApped Brynn:

i'm a loser. just ran into lucy, josephine, and anne-marie. At STARBUCKS.

She waited a minute and then remembered the crazy time difference with Hong Kong. Max tried to return to her book but couldn't concentrate, so she packed up her stuff and headed out. The cute barista called, "Have a good day!" and she gave him a shy wave.

It was warm for early June, and people were bustling up and down Lex, getting ready for the summer Friday. If she went home now, would her mother still be at the gym? She just couldn't handle a long Peyton chat at that exact moment—her mother was always extra worked-up after finishing a show. Debating this as she walked, Max almost didn't notice her phone beep.

ugh you can't do better than starbucks? Brynn had written.

there you are, Max pecked in reply.

what up?

just realizing I have exactly zero friends since you moved

friends are overrated, Brynn wrote.

Max smiled. *Totally.*

She checked the time. Her mom didn't usually get back from the gym until ten-thirty, so she could probably get into her room without risking a run-in. Her dad might still be there, either on the Peloton or making calls, but he didn't get on her nerves the same way. Max meandered a couple of blocks toward her building and stopped to sit at a bench outside a nearby florist. The sun was warm and the florist, an elderly woman with a cool punk haircut, gave her a thumbs-up. Swiping open her phone, Max logged into Instagram before she could stop herself.

First up in her feed was a photo of Lucy and Anne-Marie clutching each other in the backseat of a likely chauffeured SUV, pretending to kiss. Caption: *happy graduation to my other half, love you more everyday thanks for doing life with me* 🖤 🔌

Josephine, Lucy, and Anne-Marie together at a highway rest stop, each holding a bright blue Icee and cheering. Caption: *FRIENDS FOR LIFE.*

Another of the three of them, this time on top of the SUV in the parking lot, each hysterically laughing and flipping off the camera. Caption: *Going to miss these girls so much cuuuuuuuuuties!!!!!!!*

Fuck it, she thought, and angrily clicked off the site and over to the admin page of her YouTube channel, where Max was surprised to see dozens of new comments.

Loved this one!!!

Can you tell me what camera you're using?

Hi from the West Coast! You don't know me, but I'm a fangirl!

Max replied to each and every one of the people who DM'd her. She'd been proud of the entry, had a sense that it was one of her best yet, but she hadn't expected this level of enthusiastic feedback. Everyone was so supportive, so encouraging! Max knew she was talented. She instinctively understood how to capture emotion with a camera, and when there was none to capture, she could create it. Imagine what she could do with the right resources! She felt a brief pang that she wouldn't be starting at the Film Institute in L.A. this fall. Not that Princeton wasn't incredible—it was. As her parents reminded her on a second-by-second basis, just about every living, breathing rising college freshman on planet Earth would sacrifice a body part to matriculate there. She felt supremely bratty thinking of the reasons why it wasn't her first choice—too preppy, too conservative, too close to home—especially when she'd been the one who'd finally caved to her parents' relentless pressure to apply early decision last year.

"See what happens," her dad had urged. "I had the best four years of my life there."

"Go to a dedicated film school for *graduate* school," her mother had crooned. "But don't miss out on a world-class education first."

"The Film Institute is most definitely world-class," Max had argued, but in a rare showing of parental agreement, both Peyton and Isaac had held firm.

"Just apply," they said. The acceptance email had pinged into Max's inbox on a cold, blustery Tuesday last December, and Max knew there would be no further discussion of additional applications, film school or otherwise.

"You don't throw away a chance at a degree from the Ivy League." Her mother had declared this as an inarguable, scientific truism, akin to "Vaccines save lives," or "The earth revolves around the sun."

And, despite all his support of Max over the years, all his encouragement of her creative pursuits and his insistence on thinking independently, her father had agreed.

Max's phone rang. *Mom,* she immediately thought. *Calling to tell me that she's on her way home and ask where I am.* Max was about to silence the ringing when she saw that it was Brynn calling.

"What time is it there?" Max asked. "Wait, it's not even ten at night. I'm not sure why I thought you were already—"

"Max." Brynn's voice was tight, urgent.

"I'm here. Can you hear me?"

"Where are you? Turn on the TV right now."

"I can't, or I risk running into my mother and having to listen to how great she feels after—"

"Max, you need to get on CNN right this second. I'm sorry, I don't want to . . ."

"Okay, okay, give me a minute." Max put the call on speaker, opened her CNN app, and clicked on the "Watch Live TV" icon. It loaded almost instantly, but it took Max a couple seconds to understand what she was seeing.

"Oh my god," she murmured, leaning in close to the screen, just as her mother had done minutes before on the treadmill.

"Is that your dad?" Brynn asked.

"Oh my god. What's going on? Wait—that's our building. Oh my god. It says it's live! But I'm only a few blocks away. I don't understand."

"Where's your dad?"

"I—I don't know. Home? He was there when I left two hours ago, I think? I can't remember. Oh my god. Brynn! He's in handcuffs!"

"This must be a mistake," Brynn said. "Your dad would never get arrested for anything. He's such a . . . *dad*. Wait—is that your mom?"

Max watched in horror as her mother, wearing one of those ridiculous and much-too-young-for-her sports-bra-and-legging combos, ran up to the gaggle of people who surrounded her father. The cameras were too far away to pick up the sound, but she saw her father lean close to her mother's ear.

"I gotta go," Max said, jumping off the bench so fast she nearly knocked it over. She ran the remaining blocks to her building, and by the time she arrived, the crowd was beginning to disperse. There was no sign of either parent. She raced into the lobby.

"Peter!" she shouted. "What's happening?" She could see some of the people on the sidewalk turn to watch her.

The elderly doorman she'd known for years looked pained. "Maybe ask Mrs. Marcus," he said, glancing down at his feet. "I just put her in the elevator myself. She should be on her way up."

Max couldn't move. It wasn't until the elevator doors closed around her that she realized she'd stepped inside, and she held her breath as the floors fell under her, one by one, as she rose to an unknown future.

4

Overworked and Underpaid

'm dying," Skye moaned, kneading her right thigh through her
drenched leggings. "I don't think I can stand up."

Esther laughed. The women sat on wooden benches outside
the studio. "Remind me never to drag you to the regular Bikram," she
said.

Skye wiped away a stream of forehead sweat. "Didn't we just do
regular?"

"No, that was restorative. We barely moved."

"Skye!" exclaimed a petite and extremely fit woman in high-
waisted leggings and a crop top. "I've never seen you here before!"

"First time," Skye croaked.

The woman nodded and kept walking.

"Who's that?" Esther asked.

"Belinda Daniels. She has one in fifth, one in third, and one in K,
I think? She oversees the parent volunteers for the school library."

Two more women emerged from the studio. They were chatting
like they'd merely strolled down the block and not just contorted
their bodies in suffocating heat. Again, each wore coordinated
designer athleisure. The one in neon pink said, "Oh, Skye, I'm glad I
ran into you. Did you get a chance to go over the food for the Writers'

Tea? I know the email suggested scones, but these kids get so much junk! Maybe we should do something carb-free? I was thinking that fruit skewers with some healthy dips could be cute? And maybe batch up some smoothies—with paper straws, of course."

"Sounds great, Mal," Skye said with a thumbs-up. "I love it."

"And her?" Esther asked under her breath, as the woman and her friend headed toward the boutique.

"Mallory Salinger. She has twin girls in third and a special needs kid in first who's in Aurora's class this year, and we're both room parents. I've never officially met the woman she was with, but I see her at everything. Jane Benedict. I'm pretty sure her youngest is in fifth and then she has older ones, maybe one each in middle and high school? I hear she's planning to run for the board of finance."

Esther mopped herself with a hand towel. "I've been coming to this class every Saturday for nearly a year, and I don't know a single person."

As if on cue, a man in a black tank and black shorts noticed Skye. He sat down next to her, wrapping his sweaty, muscular arm around her shoulders. "What are you doing here?"

Skye tried not to think about their commingling sweat. "Hey, Kenny. This is my friend Esther. It's her fault I'm here."

The two exchanged pleasantries before Kenny said, "I have to run, but I'll text you later so we can get a date on the calendar for the next Museum Morning, okay? Mrs. Harney is all over me for the schedule."

"Definitely. We do need to get on that." Skye waved as he trotted off.

Esther raised her eyebrows.

"Kenny Goldberg. Goldman? Goldstein? Something Jewish," Skye said. "Stay-at-home dad. His husband travels constantly for work—like three out of every four weeks. It's got to be brutal."

Skye realized her slip the moment the words left her mouth. "Sorry," she said. "I didn't mean it like that."

Esther waved her off. "I wouldn't trade Trish for all the husbands in the world. She cooks, cleans, parents my children, and I don't have to sleep with her. She's the best."

Skye laughed. "Hey, you want to grab a coffee? Iced, obviously."

"Shouldn't we get back? I did dump both my kids on your husband."

"Please. I'm sure he plugged them all into a movie the second we left," Skye said, finally cool enough to pull on a lightweight sweatshirt as they crossed the street.

"Still, it was really nice of him to watch mine, too," Esther said. "Everything comes completely unhinged when Trish goes back to Trinidad."

"I don't know how you do it," Skye said. "I'm overwhelmed with one kid and no job. Which I know is ridiculous, but I can't understand how you manage two kids and a full-time job, all with no partner."

Esther shrugged. Her body was a straight line—no curves, nothing rounded—but her face was the exact opposite: heart-shaped with soft, indistinct features, like they'd been blurred by Photoshop. Naturally pink lips. Apple cheeks. Even her dark hair was thick and shiny, thanks to her beautiful Filipino mother. "You just do it. I mean, it's not like any of it was a surprise, you know? By the time you're shopping for sperm online, you usually have a pretty good idea what you're getting into."

"Still, you don't give yourself enough credit. Having one baby on your own is incredible. But *two*, while working fifty hours a week? That's superhuman."

They collected their coffees from the end of the counter and tucked themselves into a corner table.

"Whatever. You're the most involved parent I've ever met! Aurora is lucky to have you," Esther said, like a good working mom friend who had memorized the script.

"*Me?*" Skye rolled her eyes. "I'm basically a professional volunteer. I serve at recess duty, help kindergartners learn composting, break up squabbles in the cafeteria, alphabetize books in the school library, act as president of the PTA and treasurer of the newcomers' club, run the water slide station at Field Day, oversee the class scheduling at the Scholastic book fair, act as troop leader for Girl Scouts, and peddle school logo wear at the Election Day bake sale. The flip-sequined shirts are our bestseller, in case you're wondering."

Esther laughed. "You're the reason our public school is one of the best in the state. We need moms like you!"

"I'm not done!" Skye said. "I haven't told you about all the workshops I've attended. *So many workshops*. I'm not exactly sure what I'm supposed to do with my wealth of knowledge, but on top of the ones we did back when we adopted Aurora, I'm now an authority on stress, anxiety, social-emotional intelligence, overuse injuries from sports, ADHD, vaping, power parenting, gifted kids, and bullying. I've listened to experts tell me I should be Aurora's biggest advocate, and I've heard from other experts that I should back the fuck off if I want her to stand any chance of becoming a functional adult."

"Stop!" Esther laughed.

"I've also raised money. You name it—dogs, softball, literacy—and I've fundraised for it. I've sold everything from brownie pans to car decals, all so Abington Elementary could bring in famous children's authors and cultural dance troupes from Brazil and renowned jazz quartets for the second-grade assembly."

"Didn't we just host the Bush sisters? With their new children's book?"

Skye nodded. "I'm tired. And burnt out. And I know I shouldn't say it because I'm hashtag grateful and humbled and lucky, and I realize that, I really do, but . . ." She leaned in closer to Esther and lowered her voice to a whisper. "I'm also severely bored. I don't think I realized how bored until Aurora went to first grade full-time this past year. It's time for me to go back to work."

"Are you considering it?"

"For years, but it always seemed silly to hand over my salary to a nanny. But now that she's in school all day . . ." Skye's voice trailed off. "I'm just not thrilled with the idea of teaching around here."

"No?" Esther said, laughing. "I can't imagine why not."

"I'm going to get the girls' residence set and running, and then the plan is to look into getting a teaching job in the city again. Queens or the Bronx, maybe—it's not such a terrible commute."

"What does Gabe think?"

Skye shrugged. "He's supportive. I mean, if it were up to him, we'd bag the whole thing and move to Australia. He talks a lot about the higher quality of life we would have there."

"Yes, but no jobs. Or serious people. Although you probably wouldn't have all these lunatic parents, either." Esther stopped. "You're not moving to Australia, are you?"

"No! Absolutely not. Gabe's not serious about it. He loves Paradise, always says what a perfect suburb it is, straight out of the movies. But I do really miss the city. Maybe not living there so much, but teaching there. Connecting with all different kinds of kids, from so many varied backgrounds and perspectives. It was incredible to see how their cultures and traditions informed how they looked at learning and creativity: I loved watching them make that connection after days—sometimes weeks—of trying. I'm not explaining it well, but it was . . . different from here. Better."

"I can totally understand that," Esther murmured.

"I've put together an informal group of . . . what should I call them? Consultants, I suppose, for lack of a better word. Four total, all women of color, two educators and two mental health professionals, who will advise on the best way to smooth the transition for the girls. Aside from being tremendously helpful, speaking to them regularly has me inspired to get back to my educational roots."

Skye glanced at her phone when it shimmied on the table. "I hate to do this, but Gabe texted that his meeting got bumped a half hour earlier and he needs to get to the office."

Esther hit the table. "Let's go save him. Can Aurora come to us for the rest of the morning? It's easier to have her there—at least then my monsters have something to do."

"Skye! Is that you?" a voice rang out from somewhere near the coffee counter.

"No!" Esther whispered as she watched Skye wave back.

"They've already seen me!" Skye said back through a gritted smile.

Three women, nearly identical to the ones they'd seen at yoga, crowded around the table.

"Do you all know each other?" Skye asked. "This is my friend Esther. Esther, this is Becky, Denise, and Ana, all moms of . . ." Skye pretended to think for a second. ". . . third-grade boys, am I right?"

Esther brushed her bangs out of her eyes. "Oh, really? And you're all at Abington? My son is in third grade there, too."

Silence. All three mothers turned to look at Esther for the first time. She was suddenly interesting. Relevant. "Who's yours?" asked Denise, Skye's Girl Scouts co-leader.

"Crew. In Mrs. Goodwin's class."

"Oooooooh, you got Mrs. Goodwin this year? How's *that* going?" Ana asked, leaning forward.

Esther shrugged. "Fine, I think? Crew hasn't complained."

"She's supposed to be brutal!" Denise said, bouncing her waves. "Like, so old-school. Very strict. I mean, it's great that your son doesn't seem to mind, but maybe he's too scared to admit not liking her? In my letter to the principal last year, I *insisted* that we not get Mrs. Goodwin for third."

The others nodded. "A teacher like that can have lasting repercussions," Becky announced gravely. She tried to look concerned, but her Botoxed forehead was uncooperative, creating the impression that she was staring, either dispassionately or drugged, into space.

"Oh my, it's almost nine," Denise said. "I'm going to be late getting Bryson to his baseball game if I can't get to his lax scrimmage in Larchmont in fifteen minutes. I mean, who does the scheduling around here?"

Ana and Becky also stood and announced, in case anyone cared, that they had two swim meets, three softball games, and a six-hour soccer tournament between them. "Jake better not think for a single second that he's going to sit around and watch baseball all day," Ana said, slinging her enormous Chloé bag over her shoulder—its heavy, hanging metal lock narrowly missing Skye's cheekbone.

"That's why you have to sign them up to coach *everything*," Denise said authoritatively. "Having a husband around without a team to coach is like having another child." She turned to Skye. "I'll see you next week for our last Girl Scouts of the year. Will you check the schedule and confirm with the Snack and Stay mom?"

"On it," Skye sang brightly.

The three women left.

"Wow. They're . . . a lot," Esther said.

"You have no idea," Skye said.

"No, I'm starting to. You have to deal with that *every day*?"

Skye thought back to the parents of her fourth graders in Harlem, people who could have moonlighted as diversity models. There had been a radio DJ, a midwife, a social worker, and two dentists. A smattering of parents who worked for the city, mostly the MTA, and a few in-home health aides. There was one father with reputed ties to the Russian mob, although Skye had always found him extremely attentive and involved. A few of the parents she'd never even met, as they'd been unable or unwilling to attend Curriculum Night or the Christmas concert or the Valentine's Day party, and they never returned an email or phone call. Every year she would count the languages spoken by her students; one time there was a record-setting sixteen, not including English or Spanish.

"No," Skye said, gathering up their trash. "Definitely not in Harlem. A little more so when we first moved out here and I was still teaching in White Plains, but nothing is like Paradise. You know Denise?"

"The one just now with the Kardashian-sized ring?"

Skye nodded. "Last fall her husband got into a fight with another dad at their son's flag football game."

"A fight? Like, a disagreement?"

"A fistfight! A physical altercation! Two grown men rolling around on the field and shouting about the best way to get the team to the Super Bowl. The *Paradise* Super Bowl. For *children*. Thank god Gabe was there. He and another dad broke it up, but not before every single six-year-old on the team saw the whole thing. I mean, seriously:

I challenge you to come up with a single scenario with lower stakes than a first-grade flag football playoff game."

"I can't."

"Of course not. Because it doesn't exist."

Together they got into Esther's car and drove the short distance home. After saying goodbye to Gabe and watching out the kitchen window as Aurora made her way to Esther's backyard, Skye climbed into the shower and stood under the pounding water for a full ten minutes. When she came out with one towel wrapped around her chest and another knotted atop her head, she flipped on the television in search of a music station, but a blaring BREAKING NEWS graphic caught her attention.

"What now?" she murmured to herself, squinting at the screen.

The camera zoomed in on the face of the man being nudged into the backseat of an official-looking car. Skye frowned and leaned closer.

"Oh my god," Skye breathed. "Is that—?"

Skye glanced around their room, trying to remember where she'd left her glasses. What was going on? There must be some mistake. Where was Peyton, and what did she know?

The reporters on the screen started scrambling and shouting. "Can you comment on the charges against your husband?" one called out, louder than the others.

Despite her semi-blindness, Skye would know her sister anywhere. It was like recognizing one's own baby in a nursery of identically swaddled newborns. She stood so close to the television that water droplets from her hair peppered the screen. *Oh my god.* It was absolutely, one hundred percent Peyton. Skye had long gotten over the odd sensation of seeing her sister on the air, but this was different. Why was her sister wearing spandex and a sports bra? Why the crazy hair and red face and terrified expression? Skye realized she'd been so mesmerized by Peyton's appearance and Isaac in handcuffs that she'd missed the accusation. She sank to the floor, her body understanding that something terrible was happening, but her mind unable to process it. For that moment all she could think was: *Max.*

A phone rang from somewhere. She scrambled up and found it on the bathroom sink.

Neither she nor Peyton said a word. They waited, breathing together, both too terrified to speak. Then, finally, Peyton asked, "Are you watching this right now?"

Skye took a deep breath and said, "You are so totally and completely fucked."

5

We Have a Problem

For the twenty-second time in the past hour, Peyton's phone rang. She snatched it from its charging stand on the kitchen island.

"Kenneth, I don't have anything more to report than I did seven minutes ago," she said, trying to keep her voice even.

"Well, I have plenty to say," her agent of nearly ten years said with his standard gruffness. Bald and overweight, Kenneth was a throwback to the two-martini-lunch era. Old enough to be Peyton's father—maybe, in some circles, her grandfather—he was the best in the business, and he didn't take any bullshit from anyone, especially Peyton. Which she usually appreciated, but today she could have done without.

"I told you before, this is all a misunderstanding."

"That very well may be, and I hope for your sake it is, but it doesn't change the fact that ANN is—how shall I put this?—*displeased* at the fact that their favorite female morning co-anchor is making headlines of her own. I need some clarity, Peyton, if you want me to handle this for you. What the fuck is going on?"

Peyton touched two fingers to her temple. There was no way she could tell him the truth-truth.

"We've known each other a long time, Kenneth. You're just going to have to trust me that we don't have a problem here."

"Don't have a problem? Who doesn't have a problem? *I* don't have a problem, but it appears that *you* very much have a problem. Joseph is agitated, to say the least, and your boss is not taking kindly to me reassuring him that it's all a big misunderstanding."

Her phone beeped. This time it was Joseph calling her himself. Her stomach lurched. "I've got to take this," she told Kenneth, and hit Swap before he had the chance to respond.

"Peyton," Joseph drawled. "Care to tell me what in God's name is going on?" His Southern accent was slow, syrupy, but she knew him well enough to know that he liked to lure people in before crushing them.

"Joseph," Peyton murmured, trying to summon her most soothing and professional tone. "I know this looks bad, I do understand that, but I want to assure you that—"

"Looks bad?" he interrupted. "America's sweetheart's husband just got arrested on national TV! Now, tell me. Do you think the housewives in Oklahoma who tune in every morning for stories on hero firefighters really want to picture your husband in prison for bribery? For writing a check that's more than their family's annual salary to get your kid into an Ivy League school?"

"Isaac didn't *bribe* anyone," Peyton said, trying not to sound defensive. The official charge was mail fraud, which she didn't completely understand yet.

"Did you know about this?" Joseph asked, catching her off guard. "You must have. I know Isaac. He's a hell of a guy, and there's no way he would have done this without you."

"I don't—"

"I'm asking you point-blank. Were you involved in this? I need to know how much more in the shit we are before I can make a decision on how we're all moving forward." Peyton felt sweat prickle under her arms. "What role did you play in this?"

Peyton froze. Joseph loved her. He had wooed her from MSNBC with a series of lunches and dinners and turned to all-out stalking when she'd broken the story about illegal fracking in an Alaskan nature preserve. For the last five years, he'd mentored her and promoted her. He personally had sent her a magnum of Dom Péri-gnon with a gushing note when she'd won an Emmy for television news programming. Was it possible that he wouldn't even give her the benefit of the doubt?

"Can you hear me?" His drawl had somehow vanished.

"Joseph, I've already hired the best attorney, and you'll see that this has all been—"

"Clean. It. Up. Do we understand each other?"

Peyton opened her mouth to reassure him again, but her voice was blocked by another incoming call. Joseph hung up, and her screen showed that it was Nisha.

"Hi," Peyton said, finally exhaling.

"I spoke to Claire. She's using every connection she has—and trust me, she knows everyone—to get Isaac out before the weekend. She's there now. She's not making any promises, but she's hopeful."

"Oh my god, Nisha, he can't spend the night in a holding cell."

"If anyone can get him out, it's Claire. She's the very best."

"Thank you," Peyton whispered. She felt a flood of gratitude toward Nisha for getting Claire to agree to take the case. Back at Penn State, Nisha had been the ultimate party girl. Spontaneous road trip to the nearby Indian reservation casino? Three A.M. calzone run? Tequila shots for brunch? Skip the game to keep on tailgating? Spend the night? Nisha was always down. Not even Peyton knew that Nisha also studied as hard as she played until she'd gotten accepted to Yale Law School their senior year, the only one in their entire undergradu-ate class to do so.

"Remember, no matter what, you stay put. He can take an Uber home. The absolute worst thing right now would be a photo of you standing outside some police precinct flashing over every television in America. I cannot reiterate this enough."

"I know," Peyton said, and she did.

"Do not answer any calls you don't recognize. Assume your work email is being read, because it is. Hell, I'd assume your private email also is being read. Your entire focus right now should be on keeping quiet. That includes Max. I don't care if you have to confiscate all her electronics and lock her in her room—she cannot do anything stupid on social media or she'll jeopardize your entire family."

"I understand. I explained all of this to her already."

"Explain it again. And then once more."

"Copy that," Peyton said.

"This is not a drill," Nisha said tightly. It was jarring coming from someone who was usually telling an outrageous story about another misbehaving celebrity or billionaire. When Nisha had left her position at the U.S. Attorney's Office to open her own crisis management firm with two other women, Peyton had been delighted: her best friend had become a constant source of great material. But now? How had Peyton ended up as one of her clients?

"No," Peyton said.

"Listen, P? This isn't going to be easy. I want you to know that. But I'll be here to help you however I possibly can, okay?"

"Really, Nish, I appreciate that, you know I do. But this whole . . . situation is overblown. It's ridiculous, really, and it's not going to be a thing."

The beat of silence made Peyton check to see that their call was still connected.

"I'll call you when I know more," Nisha said quietly and hung up.

Peyton stared at her phone for a moment, her hands shaking. Nisha never sounded worried. Never. Clearly she didn't know the whole story, though, and once she did, she'd understand that everyone was overreacting. Peyton walked down the hallway and knocked on Max's door, but there was no response.

"Honey? It's me. Can I come in, please?"

"No!"

Peyton cracked open her daughter's bedroom door.

"Max? I just spoke to Nisha. She recommended the best lawyer in New York, a classmate of hers from Yale, named Claire."

Max said nothing. She was sitting atop her covers, staring at the open laptop on her outstretched legs, oversized headphones covering her ears.

"Can you hear me?" Peyton asked. "Max? Max! Can you please take those off?"

Max ripped them off angrily and threw them across her bed. "What do you want?"

"I was telling you that I spoke—"

"Yeah, Nisha and her lawyer friend. I heard you. Is there anything else?"

"She reiterated the need for all of us to keep a tight lid on things, but I know you understand that. I'm hoping Daddy will be home in the next few hours, and we can sit down and have a proper conversation about all of this." Peyton reached out to place her hand on Max's leg, but her daughter jerked it away. Her tight lips and gritted teeth had been the same since toddlerhood, an expression that only a mother would know: Max was trying not to cry.

"A 'proper conversation'? About my father ruining my life? Yeah, thanks but no thanks. I'm good." She leaned across the bed and yanked her headphones back on.

Peyton was lost for words. There were a thousand things she knew she should say, but not a single one was clear in her mind. Instead, she quietly closed the door.

Her phone buzzed immediately.

What's happening? Skye texted.

Lawyer hired. Hopefully Isaac home soon. Peyton pecked this out and hit send but then wondered: Was someone reading her texts? Did Nisha really mean no contact with anyone?

She walked into the family room, adjacent to the kitchen. It was small but comfortable, with lots of white and gray and subtle animal-skin prints. The whole apartment was like that: the three-bed, three-bath in a doorman building was certainly a luxury but far from extravagant, and what mattered most to Peyton was that it was cozy and chic. They'd only moved in a year earlier, when Peyton's promotion to morning anchor and ensuing salary bump kicked in, and she loved the place.

Although she knew she shouldn't, Peyton switched on the TV,

automatically set to ANN. Renee's face filled the screen, and Peyton felt a wave of nausea as she realized her friend and colleague was not only reporting on Isaac, but hadn't bothered to send so much as a text beforehand.

"We are hearing that charges have been filed against Isaac Marcus, husband of ANN's own Peyton Marcus, by the district attorney's office. Reports are saying that Marcus, a part-time real estate investor, has been accused of conspiracy and mail fraud. It is alleged that he paid a 'fixer' to secure his daughter's admission to Princeton University, where he himself is an alumnus."

Peyton exhaled. Frustration and impotence rose in her. She grabbed her phone.

Seriously? You couldn't even call me first? she wrote, her fingers banging the buttons.

She regretted it as soon as she pressed send. Of course, there was no response, even as Renee handed it off to Dean, the host who took over at 5 P.M. Come to think of it, not a single one of her friends among her TV Moms group had called or texted, despite the fact that they typically messaged at all hours, nearly every day. They'd all met as young reporters in their twenties and become allies in a hypercompetitive and cutthroat industry. They'd changed from TV Chicks to TV Moms—and fifteen years later, only Peyton and Renee were still in the business—but these were her work friends. The ones who had her back. The women who had sneaked in sushi and champagne to the hospital after she'd delivered Max, and brainstormed brilliant ways to get revenge on sexual-harassing co-workers at the networks where they worked, and planned dates and dinners when any of them were single, depressed, divorced, or alone on birthdays. And yet her entire world was blowing up, and Peyton hadn't heard a word from any of them? She checked her phone again. Her mother had messaged another three times, Skye twice, Kenneth had left a voicemail, but there was still nothing from the lawyer or Isaac.

She started to pace the apartment, taking long strides up and down the center hallway, starting in the foyer, passing Max's room, the bedroom that served as a shared office for Peyton and Isaac and a guest room with a pull-out couch, and finally, their airy bedroom with a western-facing view of the treetops in Central Park. The kitchen and family room, which flowed together, took up the space opposite the bedrooms, and although the layout was straightforward—some might say unimaginative—Peyton loved how contained it kept their little family. Ducking into their office, Peyton glanced at the picture she'd only just framed and placed on her desk: her and Isaac at this year's ANN holiday party, looking happy and handsome in their formal wear. At forty-two, Isaac had hair as thick and dark as the day they'd met. Sometimes he would pull it tight with both palms and show her his supposedly receding hairline, and she would roll her eyes and tell him he was losing his vision, not his hair. And also, he should fuck off, because it wasn't remotely fair that Isaac got more handsome with every passing year. The creases around his mouth made him seem perpetually happy, and the bit of salt and pepper in the two-day stubble he typically sported somehow looked extra masculine. His eyes, an unnatural shade of bright blue, hadn't dimmed or dulled a bit. Staring at the photo, she felt an unfamiliar panic rising. How had things gone so badly wrong?

The front door opened and she jumped. What the hell? Was that Max going out? No, she wouldn't. The doorman wouldn't let anyone up without her permission, unless . . . could it be Isaac? She'd only hung up with Nisha an hour earlier; there was no way he could already be home. There was no way he wouldn't have called her.

"Isaac? Honey? Is that you?" She pulled nervously on her fitted cotton sweater, the blue one, his favorite, as she strode down the hall.

Her husband was kicking off his shoes and looked up when she walked into the foyer, but he didn't say a word. Even now, after they'd spent eighteen years together, his lopsided grin was enough to quicken Peyton's breath. Not that he was grinning.

"Oh, thank god," she said, wrapping her arms around his chest. She brushed a lock of hair out of his eyes and stood on her tiptoes to kiss him, but he pulled away.

"Where's Max?" Isaac refused to meet her eyes. His voice was cold and hard.

"She's in her room. I told her we'd give her a little time, but that we'd all sit down and have a talk over dinner tonight." Peyton tried to make her voice reassuring, the way she'd often done with Max as a toddler and then again as a teenager.

Isaac didn't say a word but made his way down the hallway to Max's room.

"Mackenzie?" He knocked three times, then three more. "Open the door, please."

Peyton couldn't hear what her daughter said in response, but she knew there was zero chance of Max opening that door to the father she felt had betrayed her. Isaac returned a moment later.

"How could you?" he asked, his anger palpable. "After our whole conversation! After I explicitly told you not to get involved. After you promised you wouldn't! What in god's name have you done?

Peyton walked over and gingerly took his hand, which he shook free. "Come sit down, okay? I'll pour us a little wine, and we can have a—"

"You *covered* this fucking story, Peyton. Two years ago! You spoke about it so often, you couldn't stand to report on it for another second. You saw what those idiots did. How they broke the law. *How they went to jail.* And then you go and do it yourself?" His voice was low, a growl.

Peyton filled two glasses with pinot grigio and looked at him. "Those parents were consciously and deliberately breaking the law. They paid people to take the SATs *in place of* their kids. Made their kids pose for pictures like they were getting recruited for sports they *never even played.* I mean, that's completely insane—and entirely different from what you and I talked about."

"You don't think writing a check qualifies as breaking the law?" Isaac asked.

Peyton shook her head. "Not unless building a science lab or a stadium at a school also qualifies. People do that all the time—have done it for generations—and no one throws *them* in jail. Of course I wouldn't cheat like those people did."

"Oh my god, Peyton. Please tell me you don't believe what you're saying. Tell me you understand there's a difference—in real life, but also in the eyes of the law—between writing a check to a bullshit charity to get your kid into college and making a donation to the school where the entire community stands to benefit. Please."

Peyton shook her head stubbornly. "It's not like that."

"Like what?" Isaac asked.

"She never would've gotten in without a little push. You know it, and I know it, too."

Isaac stared at her, his eyes wide.

Peyton took a deep breath. "Did you think that because she had great grades and decent test scores she was going to get into Princeton? Because that's just plain crazy. And don't deny that you wanted her to go there every bit as much as I did."

"Of course I want her to go there," he hissed, a mottled red spreading across his neck. "I want her to go there because I loved it. Because the professors and programs are amazing and the campus is gorgeous and I think she'd find her people there in a way that she never managed to in that suffocating, soul-crushing Milford Academy that we forced her to attend because that's where all the 'right' families went."

Peyton recoiled even though they'd had the conversation about Milford a hundred times before. "We sent her to Milford because it's the finest preparatory school in the city, and they get the most kids into the best schools every year. You know that. We agreed."

"Well, who are the idiots now? We could've sent her *anywhere* if you were just going to buy her way into college."

"Isaac, honey," Peyton said quietly. "Princeton is the perfect school for Max. I did what needed to be done. What hundreds, if not thousands, of parents all over America do to give their kids every advantage."

Isaac took an angry gulp of his wine. "She had a 4.0 and 1480 SATs. Max is a rock star of a student. She would've gotten in on her own."

With this, Peyton's eyes widened. "No one loves Max more than I do, and we both know that she's an extraordinary human being. But as an applicant to an Ivy League school? She's a dime a dozen."

"That's a lovely way to talk about our daughter."

Peyton held up her left hand and opened her fingers one by one. "She's a white Jewish girl from Manhattan: strikes one, two, and three. Never played first violin in the New York Philharmonic, strike four, never started her own globally successful internet company, strike five, never identified a new species, strike six. No substantive yet fascinating physical or psychological traumas, strike seven. She hasn't overcome poverty, racism, or any kind of discrimination to get where she is now, strike eight. Her parents are straight, and as far as we know, so is she—strike nine. Must I continue?"

"By all means, make it an even ten," Isaac said, his voice tight.

"Despite all of these incredible advantages—or maybe because of them—she got a 4.0 and a 1480, which are probably on the lower end of scores to these schools—strike ten. Do you see what I'm saying?"

"I can't," he said, standing up.

"Please don't go," she said pleadingly. She couldn't remember ever seeing him like this. Her palms were uncharacteristically damp, her heart beating in her chest.

"We talked about this, Peyton. I made my thoughts on it super clear. You *promised*." He sounded genuinely hurt, and that, more than the cold anger, made Peyton feel queasy.

"Isaac, I only did what—"

He strode across the family room and turned. "One last thing. Tell me why you wrote the check from my account."

Peyton's eyes flew up. "Your what?"

"You wrote the check from my business account, not your individual checking account. Or our joint one."

Until that moment, Peyton hadn't thought for a single second which account she had used. "I couldn't find any other checkbooks. I used whatever one was sitting on your desk. Obviously, I didn't try to, like, hide the paper trail or whatever. It was just a donation. I never thought for a second . . ."

He nodded. "You never thought for a second that you were going to blow up your daughter's life." He stared at her with an anger she couldn't ever remember seeing from him and then strode out. A moment later she heard the door to their shared office click shut.

Peyton took an enormous glug of wine, although it was hard to swallow with the knot in her throat. It was true, they had talked about it last summer when Max was starting her applications, and she had promised him that she would drop it. She *did* drop it. But when the insanity of applying to schools intensified at the beginning of Max's senior year, and both her daughter and her husband were wrecks about the entire process, Peyton thought of the guest she'd had on her show. And still—*still*—she hadn't called him. She'd promised Isaac she wouldn't. But when the man had *called her*, as though he somehow had a camera in their living room and knew how stressed they all were, she answered. And listened.

She swallowed again and thought back to that very first night she'd brought it up to Isaac, a Friday in late August, when they'd met at their neighborhood Italian joint for dinner.

"I had an interesting guest on the show today," she had mentioned, casually she hoped, after they had sat down at their usual table.

Isaac had scrunched his nose then, too. "Was today that actor, the one who blew the whistle on Johnny Depp? I'm blanking on her name. . . ."

"Yes, but after her, I interviewed this revered college counselor. You should hear the way people talk about him—like he can wave a magic wand and get your kid into Harvard."

"I don't want our kid to go to Harvard. She'll become one of those Harvard people who finds a way to work 'Harvard' into every conversation."

"We should be so lucky," Peyton said.

"Max is *not* going to Harvard."

"It's really a moot point, because she is never going to get *into* Harvard. But anyway, this guy came on to promote his new book,

Cracking the Code, where he explains the best strategies for identifying your target school's priorities and then figuring out how to align with them."

"Let me guess," Isaac said, grinning. "For the bargain price of twenty-two ninety-nine, he'll divulge all his secrets in a hardcover."

"The book is not the point," Peyton said, waving her hand. "The point is that I was speaking to him afterward in the greenroom, just, you know, telling him that Max was a senior and did he have any advice for her."

"And?"

"He asked where we were applying, and whether or not we had any personal connections to the schools. When I told him that you had graduated from Princeton, he said he has a very close friend on the Board of Trustees there, and that he'd be happy to talk to him on Max's behalf."

Isaac had stopped eating. He looked at her. "Why would he do that? He doesn't know Max—or us."

"It's one of the services his company offers. So long as we make a donation to his educational charity, he'll work his personal connections and advocate on her behalf. Of course, he can't make any guarantees, but he has a ninety-five percent success rate—higher when the student has credentials in the right range, like Max."

"An educational charity? What charity?" Isaac looked confused.

It had taken all of Peyton's effort not to show her annoyance. He was focusing on all the wrong things!

"I don't know. He tells you which one," she said, struggling to keep her voice even. "The suggested donation is fifty thousand, which, don't get me wrong, is not nothing. But when you look at what the college counselors around here charge for a handful of appointments and some essay editing, it's actually a fair deal."

"I don't care if he'll do it for ten bucks."

"Oh, come on, Isaac! What you're not acknowledging is that we've *already* paid to get Max into the best possible school. Her tuition has been over fifty thousand dollars a year, starting in kindergarten. We hired a private field hockey coach in third grade. Remember the professor from Columbia with a PhD in applied mathematics to tutor her in algebra? Or the nearly twenty grand we paid last summer so she could 'volunteer' to build homes for needy families in Costa Rica? We've done all these things with the express intention of giving our child every conceivable advantage so eventually she could get into the best possible college. How is this different?"

Isaac examined his plate. "When you lay it all out like that, I'm not proud of some of the decisions we made. But this isn't a good idea."

Peyton smacked the table then—she cringed now merely thinking about it. "You're missing the point! What about the checks you already write to Princeton each year? Was it a coincidence you started the year Max was born? Can you honestly say you'll continue donating after she goes to college? Have you been giving money to support the school and show your appreciation or to increase the chance that she gets admitted? Be honest."

"Both," he said. When Peyton tried to interject, he held up his hand. "Our ten or fifteen grand each year isn't affecting Max's admission. It takes millions to do that."

Peyton leaned toward him. "But what if it didn't?"

They ate the rest of the meal in silence until Isaac said, "I'm not interested, P. And you shouldn't be either."

"Then what have we been doing for the last seventeen years?" Peyton asked.

Isaac cleared his throat. "Look at me," he said, his voice comforting, peacemaking. "I don't want to fight. I know you only have Max's best interests at heart. But I need you to promise me that you're not going to talk to this *Cracking the Code* guy again. Okay?"

"But I think that if—"

"Peyton James Marcus. Promise me. We'll support Max in every way, and I know—and you know too—that she's going to get in somewhere great. And that she'll love wherever she ends up going. Promise me you won't do anything further with this guy."

Peyton again opened her mouth to say something, but again, Isaac cut her off. "Promise me."

She sighed. "I promise."

"No calling him back. No following up. No checks written, to him or some charity, or anyone. Promise?"

"I said it already! I promise."

She'd sulked the rest of the meal, but he had either not noticed or pretended not to notice, and they'd never talked about it again.

Now, staring at the ceiling, unable to remember a time when her even-tempered husband had been angry enough to storm out of the room, Peyton took a deep breath and acknowledged that she had broken her promise. In all their years together, she couldn't think of a time he'd been really and truly angry with her. Life with Isaac was an adventure; he was her constant, and had been from the very beginning, starting when they were only still dating, and it was her first weekend off in months from the local Queens network where she'd been working the graveyard shift. Peyton had desperately wanted to go to a hotel, maybe order room service, and lounge near a beach or a pool for a few days. Sleep, make love, drink fruity cocktails. But Isaac had been so convincing! He was different from all the meatheads she typically dated. He was good-looking, but not gorgeous. Didn't really care much about sports, either watching or playing them. He'd majored in philosophy at Princeton and minored in English literature. He was kind, thoughtful, and affectionate, and man, could he be adamant when he thought something was a good idea. Almost nothing could have gotten Peyton off that chaise longue and onto a filthy, smelly charter fishing boat except Isaac's patient and persistent pleading. And even though she'd vomited for five straight hours, more than two dozen times, and was so dehydrated she'd needed to go to the emergency room for IV fluids, she still couldn't keep from smiling at him that night as they sat on their hotel room bed, eating takeout pizza straight from the box and recounting the fish they'd caught. Peyton hadn't planned it or thought about it, but the moment she'd blurted out the words "Will you marry me?" she knew with a thousand percent certainty that it was exactly what she wanted. For a split second Isaac looked shocked enough to fall off the bed, but then he'd scooped her up into a bear hug, sending the pizza flying onto the floor, and kissed her face. Her hair was still flecked with puke and his clothes still stank of bait and fish, but they'd agreed right then and there to do forever together.

Forever meant forever. Through all the twists and turns that life brought. Peyton knew it, she thought, as she finished her wine and went to find her family. Isaac knew it, too. They would find a way through this. He would forgive her, wouldn't he? The alternative was too awful to fathom.

6

Florals for Summer

Max heard the low voices, the doors closing on two separate rooms. She slammed her computer shut. She had to stop obsessively refreshing the headlines across multiple sites. If it wasn't enough that her father had gotten arrested that morning on national TV in front of the entire world and she would be forever known as the girl whose father bribed her way into college—and really, it was enough—it seemed like the only picture circulating in the media of Max was her freaking *senior portrait.* No matter that she had a very edgily artistic picture on the "Meet Max" section of her channel, or a whole host of carefully edited photos on her Instagram page. She closed her eyes and the photo appeared behind her closed lids: the ridiculous Milford blazer, the bouncy blowout her mother had insisted on despite Max's protestations, the lipstick that looked far pinker in the photo than in real life. Christ, who *was* that person? It bore almost no resemblance to the real her, with her wild curls and bushy eyebrows and the additional three piercings she'd since gotten in her left ear. That photo was plastered all over social media, where every troll with an internet connection had something to say about it, and none of it was nice. Plus, now she had to feel like a shallow, self-obsessed snob for worrying about a photo when her entire life was falling apart in real time, but my god, she was only human and no seventeen-year-old should have to endure this level of public humiliation. Without warning, the tightness in her throat gave way, once again, to hot tears, and Max wondered how she could possibly deal with the rage she felt toward her own father.

Her phone pinged. It was a picture of Brynn's Cavalier King Charles puppy that her parents had bought her as a combination consolation/bribe when they'd relocated her to Hong Kong for her senior year. At the time Max had wondered how it was possible Brynn's parents were even capable of making decisions that horrible, but if the last twenty-four hours proved anything, it was: don't challenge parents, because they *always* rise to the occasion.

Soooooooooo cute. He's gotten so big, Max wrote.

He's still peeing on my parents bed. I love him, Brynn wrote back.

Max leaned over and looked under her bed. Cookie growled back at her ferociously. *Whats it like to have a dog that doesn't bite?*

Whats it like to understand what everyone's saying? I've taken three years of Mandarin and still can barely speak a word.

Whats it like to take a gap year and travel the world?

Whats it like to live in a minuscule apartment with both your parents, two little brothers, and no friends/guys/life of which to speak about in this weird, weird city? I feel my situation is worse right now.

In case you forgot, my father spent the day in JAIL because of a BRIBE FOR ME!!!!

There was a pause, and then the three dots appeared. *Yeah, you're right. You win.*

Max grinned and Snapped back a picture of Cookie baring his teeth.

When does he get out? Is it the same as on TV? You pay bail and he comes home? Brynn wrote.

Max pecked back three question marks, followed by *I guess so? He just got home. They're fighting.*

Family dinner, I hope?

Obv

Sounds like a blast. Miss your mom's boiled proteins and steamed vegetables.

I'd be so out of here if only I could leave. Paps everywhere downstairs.

Look on the bright side: you're famous!

Max snorted. *I'm the most hated spoiled monster in all the land. Who's going to believe I had nothing to do with this?*

She heard a knock on her door, and her heart did an extra little beat. Her mom opened the door without waiting for a response, and even amid the biggest family crisis ever, she looked like she stepped out of a fucking catalogue.

"Hi, honey. Daddy's showered. He's pretty hungry, so we're going to eat." Her mother glanced at Max in her sweaty boxing clothes. "Do you want to shower before dinner?"

Max had been planning to shower, but now, having been prodded like a toddler, there was no way she was going anywhere near the bathroom.

"Nope, let's eat now. What'd you order? Please say it's a salad."

"Oh, Max. Give it a rest," she said, eyes downcast.

"I was joking!" Max said.

Her mother sighed and pulled the door closed. Max climbed out of bed but couldn't bring herself to walk into the kitchen and actually see her father. What was she going to say? What was *he* going to say? She'd spent the entire day playing different scenarios in her head, trying to explain how this could all be one big mistake. Intellectually, she knew she should be a rational human and accept the obvious truth. After all, it wasn't like the FBI was known for lying. But he was her *father*. The one who insisted on meeting all her friends before she could go to their apartments. Who cooked every breakfast for her and who always helped with her homework and who had muddled his way through a humiliating but endearing lecture on periods and another on only having sex when you're in love. He was the one who admitted that he, too, had experimented with drinking and weed in high school, and while he wasn't encouraging it, he was much more open-minded about an occasional beer or joint so long as Max understood: no pills. None. Of any kind. Ever. Pills were unknown, dangerous, terrifying, and he'd made her swear on her life multiple times that she'd never, ever take a pill from an unknown source.

There was no way on earth her father—who constantly harped about helping others and being kind and all that dad stuff—would have gone and done something knowingly *illegal*. And not only illegal, but something that had the potential to ruin *her* future and *their* relationship. It wasn't possible. All these years it had been her mother who was so freaking hung up on college, constantly advising Max on which APs to take and charities to volunteer for and ideas for assuming "leadership positions." Max got it. It didn't require a PhD to see that her mother's obsession with the Ivy League stemmed from her own feelings of insecurity in high school, when Peyton's own parents paid more attention to Skye, who'd gone to Amherst, and treated Peyton like the sweet but slightly dumb party girl. But her dad had always talked her mom down from the ledge: *Max is an excellent student; she has a wide variety of authentic interests, which means much more than mere résumé-building fillers; there are literally hundreds of incredible schools she could go to for a top-notch education and an all-around amazing experience; the Ivy League, while prestigious, is hardly the be-all, end-all.* He'd said a million times that he could envision her happily ensconced in a small liberal arts college in the Northeast, or an exciting city university in Chicago or Boston, or a dedicated film school in Los Angeles. Had he been lying that entire time? Did he truly believe, like her mom, that there were only eight colleges worth attending, eleven if you added Duke, MIT, and Stanford? Did he believe it enough to pay one of those schools—his very own alma mater—to have her admitted?

"Max, come before everything gets cold!" her mother called from the kitchen.

She took a deep breath and walked into the eat-in kitchen. "I'm right here!" she said, taking her usual seat at the built-in banquette.

Her father was freshly showered, but he couldn't hide his exhaustion—it made him look haggard. And sad. "Hey, sweetie," he said, placing his hand over hers.

She pulled her hand away and grabbed for the salad bowl, trying not to notice his hurt expression. In addition to salad, there was a bowl of steamed broccoli, a small platter of asparagus spears and lemon slices, and three pieces of plain grilled chicken, none bigger than a deck of cards.

"My god, I bet you got better food in the clink," Max said.

"Mackenzie!" her mother said sharply, but her father gave a little laugh.

"Let's just say they didn't use whole wheat noodles," he said with a smile, referencing their old inside joke. Whenever her dad would come tell her dinner was ready, Max would ask what they were eating. One totally ordinary night a few months earlier, when Max had been muddling through a brutal chem assignment, her dad appeared in her room and closed the door behind him. "Yes, there's a salad, because your mother would divorce me if there wasn't. And the so-called chicken parm is grilled and missing the cheese, and the marinara sauce is sugar-free. However, it is served over linguini and"—he lowered his voice to a whisper—"I did not use whole wheat noodles. Repeat: did not use whole wheat noodles. Can I trust you with this information?"

Max suppressed a sigh. My god, didn't he get that he'd betrayed her? Should she ask him point-blank why he did it? Put him on the spot and make him explain how he could have been so insanely, madly stupid? She was just about to open her mouth when her mother said, the strain evident in her bright tone, "I can't even explain how spectacular it was to see peonies in this quantity. I mean, they must have been flown in from Hawaii that morning. Do you think that's possible?"

It was Peyton's superpower, this ability to change the subject to something benign, inane, or both. It was literally what she got paid to do, and my god, she was good at it.

"Neither of us have any idea what you're talking about," Max said flatly, without looking up.

"Remember the luncheon I was asked to speak at last week? For children's literacy?" Peyton asked. When no one responded, she continued. "The expense of it all! For a charity event. That's what always has me wondering. I understand the theory that without the fabulous, over-the-top party you can't lure in the big donors, but still! It must have been hundreds of thousands of dollars in flowers, and I can't stop thinking how far that money would go toward helping kids learn to read instead of *decorating for the event* that's meant to help kids learn to read."

Max and her father sat in silence. Max chewed her tasteless chicken.

"So, I'm sitting at my luncheon table, listening to Salman Rushdie read, for heaven's sake—like that's something you get to hear every day, right? And I can't even concentrate on what he's saying because these insane peonies are blooming right in front of me."

"Florals for summer? Groundbreaking!" Max said, and looked up, but her mother said nothing.

Her father winked at her, but she pretended not to see. It was exactly like the wink he'd given her last week, when she'd emerged from the subway in the Financial District and handed him one of the two Yoo-hoos she'd brought.

"Vile stuff," he said, opening it and taking a long swig.

"Disgusting. All chemicals." Max drained her bottle in a few swallows.

"Cancer in a bottle," Isaac said, finishing his and winking at her. "Don't ever tell your mother."

"Some men have affairs. Others engage in nutritional betrayals. I get it," Max said, nodding.

They swiped their MetroCards and ran to make the number 1 train, which had just pulled into the station.

"How was your meeting?" Max asked, after they'd found a seat together.

"Fine, just fine. Here, look." He pulled out a folded sheet of paper, smoothed it on his leg, and said, "Here's my plan. Tell me what you think."

He'd researched three potential fishing spots, each of which they planned to scope out, but he was most hopeful about their first stop, the Belt Parkway Promenade.

"We have a lot to get in this summer, kiddo," he said, his voice cracking the tiniest bit.

Max poked him gently in the arm. "You know I'm not leaving home forever, right? It's just college. I'll be back. You can't get rid of me that easily."

He smiled, but it seemed tinged with sadness. "I know. But this is the beginning of your real life. Your adult life. Of course, you'll be back to visit, but it won't ever be like this."

Max peered at him as the train hurtled into darkness, the interior lights flashing on and off. "Are you crying? Dad, I'll only be an hour away! You can come visit whenever you want!"

"I'm just . . . so proud of you. Of who you are and what you stand for. And you're going to love college so much. I know you weren't completely sure about it, but Princeton is going to be in-credible. Literally anything you can dream of studying is available to you."

"Yeah, I think so, too. I've been emailing with a sophomore who's currently enrolled in an Intro to Digital Arts and Culture class, and she says it's amazing. She's working on analyzing femininity in the digital age by studying Instagram accounts. I mean, how cool is that?"

"It sounds incredible. I can see you loving it so much there. All that high school crap about who's invited to what party or whatever? It's just gone. Over. Done. You're going to meet so many kinds of people with different backgrounds and upbringings and ideas. . . ." He sighed. "I would do it all over again."

"Oh, come on! The homework, the finals, the all-nighters? You would not!"

"In a heartbeat."

"Is being old really that bad?"

Her father laughed. "Yes. From a learning perspective, at least in my world, I think it's garbage. Sure, it's great not having parents or professors tell you what to do. You can go anywhere or do anything that circumstances allow. But in the twenty-five years I've been out of college, I haven't learned as much as I did in the first semester of my freshman year. You read, and you grow professionally, but . . . It's hard to explain. The emphasis on learning for learning's sake—for the pure pleasure of knowledge—never happened again for me." He shrugged. "Maybe it's just not a priority anymore, not with kids and jobs and mortgages and all that."

Max considered this. She thought of both her parents as smart, fairly engaged humans. Did they totally understand any of the social changes that were taking place in her generation? Of course not. They still expressed incredulousness when Max told them that this boy came out as gay or that girl came out as transgender, and that it wasn't a thing. That these were un-newsworthy announcements. They struggled with the idea that people had pronoun preferences. They could not grasp the concept that a whole lot of her friends, and maybe even Max, thought of sexuality as fluid, and something that happened on a continuum, not a fixed point on a straight line. Hell, they'd probably freak out if she wanted to marry someone who wasn't Jewish one day, despite being the least religious people she'd ever met. And they were the liberal ones! The New Yorkers! But still, when it came to politics, current events, obviously the news—her parents always put on a very impressive show. Multiple newspapers arrived every day; her father read loads of novels; her mother could name every senator from every state, and most representatives. But Max understood that wasn't the kind of learning her father was talking about. That kind of pure, academic focus had long given way to headline scanning and endless sessions of staring at their phones. Both of them always seemed so insurmountably *exhausted*. Was that all parents? Or just hers?

A notification had popped up on her phone. She swiped it open and her administrator's page told her she'd gotten 130 new subscribers in the hour since she'd posted her last video.

"Hey, Dad? Check this out." She handed him her phone and pointed to the number. "That's how many people are currently subscribed to *To the Max*. How crazy is that?"

"Eight thousand people? And you don't know them all?"

Max laughed. "I barely know any of them! I mean, I feel like I do—we message each other—but aside from a few city friends, you guys, some random other friends—no, it's all strangers."

"That really is incredible, Max. You've got such a talent. I can't wait to see what you're going to do with it."

"I was thinking reality TV. Maybe, like, a trashy dating show? I've also heard there's big money in porn. . . ."

Her father clutched his chest, and she laughed.

"Even hearing my sweet baby girl say that word nauseates me," he said.

Max snaked her hand up under his forearm and linked their arms together. She rested her head on his shoulder, something she couldn't remember doing in ages. "I love you, Dad. I promise I won't go into porn."

He kissed the top of her head and squeezed her arm. "I know you won't, sweetheart, but let's take one moment here and acknowledge a truth: I won't hesitate to have you murdered if you do."

The train pulled up to their stop and the doors opened. "This is us," she said, jumping up and holding her hand out for her dad. "Come on, old man. Let's go scout some spots."

"Max? Honey?" Her father's voice pulled her back to the present, and Max found herself sitting across the table from him.

Max squinted. "Was everything you said last week complete bullshit? It had to be. How could you drone on and on about my 'promising future,' knowing it was only happening because you bribed someone?"

Everyone was silent for a few seconds before her mom put down her fork and said, "Sweetheart, we understand this, this . . . situation . . . is stressful. But it's only temporary."

"Oh yeah? It's not really feeling so temporary." Max gazed directly at her father. "I can't believe you'd do something like this. You, of all people." She could see the words register on his face.

"There's been a big misunderstanding," her mother said. "And we need you to trust us when we tell you that we're going to get everything straightened out. No one has broken the law."

"A *misunderstanding*?" Max looked between her parents. "So, you're telling me, on the record, that Dad *didn't* try to buy my way into Princeton? That the *FBI* got it wrong?"

Her parents exchanged a look. No one said anything.

"Okay then," Max said. "So, he did completely ruin my life—all our lives—by paying to get me into a school that, irony of ironies, I didn't even want to go to in the first place! Amazing, Dad. Great call."

"Princeton is an incredible school," Peyton said quietly, setting her fork down.

"That's not the fucking point!" Max screamed.

"Let's all just calm down for a second, okay?" her father said. "We're all under a lot of stress. Max, sweetheart, please don't scream at your mother. And, Peyton, can we lay off the 'incredible school' stuff?" He turned back to Max. "Max, I know this is . . . horrible for you. Beyond horrible. But please understand: This may *seem* like the end of the world today—trust me, I spent the afternoon in a jail cell, I get it. But it's not. I swear to you that this will get better."

Max laughed bitterly. "Get better? How? When Princeton kicks me out and I can actually go somewhere I want?" she said, having not even considered that as a possibility until she uttered the words.

Her parents looked stricken. "Honey, you are brilliant and talented, and your future is so bright," her father said slowly. "We're going to get through this, I promise you that."

Her mother nodded.

Max stared at her plate. "I'll take it over from here, Dad. As much as your whole 'we're going to get through this' bullshit sounds good, I think you've done more than enough."

She couldn't sit there anymore; it was all too much. "I'm done," she said, standing up. And without waiting for a response, she fled to her bedroom.

7

Business as Usual

The underwear itself didn't reveal much. They were soft cotton in a perfectly nice shade of turquoise with lace trim. They looked like the dozen or so other pairs in various colors that had been in her top dresser drawer for the last however many years, ever since the day when, in a fit of wedgie-induced frustration, Skye had purged every last miserable pair of thongs and skimpy-cheeked bikinis from her life and replaced them with full-coverage hipsters. Maybe they weren't the sexiest underwear, but they were hardly *hideous*. Skye was glancing at the laundry room folding table when it hit her: the perfect-condition turquoise ones must have been left behind by Carol, her mother-in-law, when she'd visited from Australia earlier that month.

"Oh my god," she gasped. "This isn't happening."

"What's not happening, Mommy?" Aurora chirped from her post on the hallway floor, where she was stretched out on her belly, chin in her hands, waiting patiently for Skye to escort her back to the kitchen.

"Nothing, chickpea. Why don't you go pour yourself some cereal? I'll be there in a minute."

Skye pulled her phone from her back jeans pocket: 7:37 A.M. Everyone would be long awake, she knew, and maybe it would be normalizing to text about something ridiculous like underwear instead of the fact that her sister's husband had been arrested on national TV the day before.

Skye began typing into the group message that included her mother and sister.

Just discovered I wear the same underwear as Carol!!! she pecked.

So? Peyton replied.

So??? That's all you have to say when I tell you that I wear same UNDERWEAR as my MIL??

She's very attractive, the girls' mother, Marcia, responded.

Yes, she is very attractive. She's also 68! How can I own the same lingerie as her??

I've seen your bras and panties. None of them qualify as "lingerie," Peyton wrote.

Agree, Marcia typed.

Thank you both for your support.

I think its a way more interesting reflection on Gabe, Peyton wrote.

"It's," Skye typed. *You need an apostrophe.*

As usual, her sister ignored this correction. *I mean, don't you think its FASCINATING that your husband doesn't mind that you and his mother wear the same underwear???*

Why the f would he know what kind of underwear his mother wears? Skye pecked like a crazy person.

I've been telling you this forever. Your too old for multiple ear piercings and too young to be wearing granny panties, Peyton wrote.

It's "you're," Skye wrote.

Marcia wrote: *And that tattoo of yours. NOT GOOD.*

You know about that???

Of course. A mother knows all.

From Peyton: *I told her like 4 years ago. She knows all about the starfish that looks like its swimming out of you're ass.*

It's is with an apostrophe! And Y-O-U-R ass!!!

I don't have a starfish swimming out of MY ass! Peyton fired back.

Skye smiled.

Gotta run, Peyton wrote. *Max is up. And she's still not speaking to either of us.*

Rightfully so! her mother typed.

And for the record, the starfish looks like it's swimming IN to my ass, not out of it . . . , Skye typed. She waited thirty seconds for a response, but when it became obvious her mother and sister had moved on, she sighed and stuck her phone back in her pocket. She folded her mother-in-law's underwear into a neat little square and wondered if she should mail them.

"Come on, chickpea," she said, reaching down to help her daughter up. "You need to get dressed for art class."

It took a bit of wrangling and slightly more yelling than she would have liked, but Skye managed to get Aurora dressed and fed by eight-fifteen. Although Aurora was supposed to do her "three things" each morning—brush her teeth, make her bed, and put on her clothes by herself—the routine had started to unravel in January, and by the first of February it had completely fallen apart. The only saving grace had been a refresh of Aurora's braids the week before, which shaved at least fifteen minutes off the morning. They would last for two months, and Skye again sent silent gratitude to the two angel hairdressers at the salon specializing in Black hair who advised, oversaw, and executed her daughter's hairstyling when Skye—despite watching endless YouTube tutorials and even a few in-person lessons—could still not get the hang of it.

"Daddy!" Aurora yelled when Gabe appeared in the kitchen, ginger hair still wet from the shower. His outfit—lightweight blazer with suede elbow patches, fitted jeans, and sneakers—could have been equally at home on a college campus as it was at the boutique architecture firm where Gabe was a partner.

"How's my favorite girl this morning?" Gabe asked in the Australian accent that charmed everyone who heard it. He stole a strawberry from Aurora's plate and grabbed an apple from a carved acacia bowl that sat in the middle of the kitchen island.

"It's Saturday!" Aurora declared. "Why are you going to work?"

"You remember that I design houses for people?" he said as he sliced his apple. "Well, even though today is Saturday, it's the only day the people could meet. So I am going to my office to meet them."

"Can you drop her at art class on your way?" Skye asked. "I told my mother I would swing by, and I'm already late."

"Sorry, honey, I've got to go right now." His three-day scruff scratched her cheek when he kissed it.

"It's two minutes out of your way."

He looked up; his blue eyes squinted. "It's two minutes out of your way, too. Marcia can wait. My clients can't."

"It's just that I'm not dressed," Skye said. "And I won't have time to come home after I drop her."

"Stop fighting!" Aurora said, placing her hands over her ears.

"We're not fighting, sweetheart, we're discussing," Gabe said. He looked at Skye, eyebrows raised in question.

"It's fine, I'll drive her," Skye said. "I'm going to run up and get dressed. I'll be right down, okay? Aurora, get your shoes on, honey."

Gabe kissed her on the lips this time. "Keep me updated on the Peyton situation, okay? I'll call Isaac this afternoon."

Skye nodded and started to climb the stairs. She didn't have time to shower if she was going to get Aurora to the class on time, so she tucked her favorite RBG T-shirt into her jeans and slipped on her go-to floral Birks. She sprayed her roots with dry shampoo and exhaled in frustration when the white residue ended up all over her shirt. After swiping and brushing at her shoulders like a mental patient, she quickly twisted her wavy brown hair into a bun and yanked a few pieces loose around her face.

By the time she got back downstairs, Gabe had already left.

"Look, Mommy, it's Aunt Peyton!" Aurora said, pointing to the TV in the family room, just like she did every morning. "Her hair is so pretty. And so is her dress."

Skye glanced at the television, and sure enough, there was Peyton, sitting next to that admittedly attractive buffoon of a co-host, looking every bit the perfect news anchor: straightened blond hair bobbed to just above her shoulders; crisp, emerald-colored dress with a conservative boatneck; flawless makeup highlighting a gleaming white smile that had cost more than a car.

Skye clicked off the television before Aurora realized that Peyton wasn't actually on air that morning and the clip was actually a news story about her uncle's arrest.

"We're leaving in one minute. Snack bag and shoes, please! And don't forget to bring your painting."

The scene in the parking lot of Abington Elementary, even on a Saturday morning, never ceased to amaze her. During the week, a calm, orderly procession of Land Rovers and Tesla SUVs deposited well-scrubbed and fashionably clad children into the care of young, cheerful, and almost unnervingly attractive teachers—each of whom held an advanced degree from a prestigious university. The picture-perfectness continued inside, where the young pupils learned math on state-of-the-art Smart Boards and received individualized reading instruction from trained literacy specialists. Throughout the day they would browse the school's expansive library, dine on locally sourced organic food in the sun-dappled cafeteria, and play on the beautifully manicured playground, which was designed by experts in children's development and funded entirely by the PTA. Physical education, art, music, coding, foreign language, chorus, student government—was there anything these five- to ten-year-olds couldn't do? And this was *public school*. Skye thought of the crumbling elementary school she and Peyton had attended in Lancaster, Pennsylvania, with its mismatched desks and cranky, past-their-prime teachers who wouldn't hesitate to turn off the classroom lights, throw in a VHS tape, and literally disappear for the duration of class. For nearly six full years, starting in kindergarten, Skye's school lunch had consisted of salted tortilla chips topped with liquid Velveeta, a plastic cup of mandarin oranges in syrup, and a juice box of Hawaiian Punch. No one noticed. No one talked about it. No one *cared*. And now here she was, thirty years later, sending her daughter to a school where the mothers had started a petition—oh, who was she kidding, it was a *movement*—to replace the cafeteria's Yoplait with Siggi's, which had two grams less sugar per serving, even though it cost five times as much.

Aurora climbed out of the Subaru's backseat and waved to Skye.

"I love you, chickpea! Have fun at art. I'll be back to pick you up for lunch," Skye said. She watched her daughter happily skip to the front entrance. Paradise wasn't her first choice of communities—it was too white and too wealthy—but for Skye and Gabe, when a job opportunity arose there, like so many other families looking to escape the city, they ultimately made their decision based on one thing: the schools. And no one could claim that they didn't deliver.

To get to her mother's apartment in White Plains, Skye drove through downtown Paradise, a couple of intersecting streets the locals called The Village. At first glance, The Village looked like the quintessential New England town, with its narrow streets and old-fashioned storefronts. Trees and benches dotted the charmingly uneven cobblestone sidewalks. Chalkboard easels announced store hours or menu offerings; Parisian-style bistro tables were topped with potted flowers; nearly every shop provided a water bowl for all the chocolate Labs and golden retrievers who accompanied their owners. But just past the sweet facade, there existed an entirely different world, one where the lady who worked the register at the stationery store wore a fifty-thousand-dollar diamond ring, and the cobbler's worktable was stacked with Gucci luggage and Louboutin pumps. Sixteen-year-old kids tried to guide Range Rovers, unsuccessfully, into parallel spots while blasting Ariana Grande on their state-of-the-art sound systems. For every bakery and children's clothing store, there were ten designer shops: Tiffany, Vince, Theory, Joie, Alice + Olivia, Rag & Bone. Even a sweet little Saks Fifth Avenue outpost and, on the very edge of town, a brand-new Tesla dealership. Every time Skye went to The Village, whether to run an errand or meet a friend for coffee, she couldn't help but wonder how she'd ended up living there.

As she neared her mother's place, Skye's phone rang. She almost screened it, but the 917 area code persuaded her it was an old Brooklyn friend or co-worker.

"Hello?" she called loudly into the empty car. Gabe was always making fun of her for shouting on Bluetooth.

The voice on the line was anything but friendly. "Am I speaking with Skye Alter?" a man asked.

"Who's calling, please?" Skye asked back, already nervous.

"This is Leonard from Pacific Financial Services. Is this Skye Alter?"

She considered lying, but really, what was the point? They would find her one way or another. "This is she."

"Ms. Alter, I'm calling to inform you that you are currently three months and three days overdue on your Discover card. As of this morning at nine A.M., your balance is thirty-two thousand, six hundred seventy-seven and thirty-two cents. Would you like to make a payment now over the phone?"

Skye inhaled. Last time she'd checked, it had been closer to twenty-eight thousand. It wasn't so different, but crossing the thirty-thousand mark felt significant.

"Ma'am?"

"Yes, I heard you," Skye said. "I'm actually in the middle of a meeting right now, it's not a good time."

"Is there a better time when I should call you?" the man asked. He was polite but insistent.

"Later, please," Skye said, and disconnected the call. Her heart was beating faster. She'd never even intended to open the damn card—who used Discover anymore?—but they'd offered so many perks: free miles and zero interest and a credit to use in her favorite restaurant in the city. All her other credit cards were linked to her and Gabe's joint accounts, but for some reason she'd kept this Discover card a secret and had started charging all the housewares for the new residence on it. She had assured herself that as soon as the financing came through, she would reimburse herself for everything from kitchen utensils to bath towels. Gabe wouldn't get anxious from all the little notifications popping up on his phone, because they only popped up on hers. But everything had added up so quickly, and she'd never managed to tell Gabe that they were actually thousands in debt. She'd never had any interest in shopping before—not for clothes, or household items, or anything other than complete necessities—

but a compulsive desire to make the residence perfect had struck something inside her, and now it sometimes felt like she couldn't stop.

Her forefinger automatically went to Peyton's name on her dashboard screen, but Skye left it hovering. How could she ask her sister to ease her own anxiety when Peyton's life was literally falling apart? They'd talked on and off throughout the day before, but she hadn't heard from Peyton again since Isaac had gotten home. What was happening with them? Were they fighting? Meeting with lawyers? How was Max? She'd texted her niece but hadn't gotten a reply from her either. Was it business as usual in the Marcus household, despite the fact that the entire United States was publicly discussing their family? As insane as it sounded, it was possible that Peyton was still convinced it was all a huge mistake, her combination of relentless positivity, motivating anxiety, and complete delusion colliding together to create the Peyton they all knew and mostly loved.

She'd been like that as long as Skye could remember. Which was why it was nearly impossible to keep from calling her: Peyton always had the right answer. It didn't matter if she knew nothing about the problem, or the people involved, or any extenuating circumstances— she had a strong opinion about how to fix it, or at least how to proceed. Skye tried to conjure her sister's confident advice as she drove. What would Peyton advise? March over to Gabe's office and announce that she had fucked up? Downplay the issue by saying she'd gotten a tad carried away with her Amazon ordering but tell him not to worry? Continue blatantly lying by omission and tell him nothing until the whole thing was resolved? She could imagine her sister saying each of them, and it was torturous not to call her.

Marcia walked out from her two-bedroom condo on the ground floor the moment Skye pulled into the parking lot. She shaded her eyes with her hand and watched as Skye hauled a giant Bed Bath & Beyond bag out of the trunk.

"Thank you, dear," she said as she held the door open for Skye. "I do appreciate the effort, but I'm perfectly happy with my old one."

The smell of pumpkin spice hit her the moment she stepped inside. "Mom, it's June. Isn't it a little early for pumpkin spice?"

"It's never too early. Besides, the extra-large candles were on sale at HomeGoods last week. I bought six. Do you want one?"

Skye swept her arm across Marcia's counter to clear some space and hauled the box out of the bag. "I'm all set, thanks."

Marcia tugged on her cotton tunic, which, paired with mom jeans and flats, made up her daily warm-weather uniform, and leaned in to examine the box. "Dear, this looks very expensive. Not to mention much more high-tech than I need. I don't need all those buttons! Certainly not a digital screen. Coffee is not such a complicated thing, and I told you: my old one works just fine."

Skye stopped unpacking the new machine and pointed to Marcia's coffee maker in the corner. "The cord is being held together by duct tape and the carafe is cracked. You drink coffee all day long. Can you please just not argue about this one thing?"

"Fine," Marcia sighed. "But you're going to have to write all the steps down on a piece of paper and leave it on the fridge for me."

"I know," Skye said.

After making a test pot and then a real one, Skye took her coffee mug and sat opposite Marcia in the small, cluttered living room. Pictures of Marcia's travels in mismatched frames—some the wrong size—covered the walls, and every surface was filled with tchotchkes.

"How's your sister?" Marcia asked. "She won't answer my calls. Who doesn't speak to their own mother at a time like this?"

Skye grimaced. "I haven't actually spoken to her since yesterday. Isaac was just back home. It's still all over the news. I had to physically intercept Aurora from watching."

Marcia took a sip, her thin lips pursing around the mug.

"Isaac is not a stupid man," Marcia said. "He's smarter than she is. I can't understand why he'd do something like this."

"We all know what kind of man Isaac is. Maybe we should give him the benefit of the doubt."

"Yes, I agree, but the facts seem increasingly harder to deny.

Besides, didn't someone do this already and get caught for it? That silly actress from that nineties sitcom? I mean, why are we doing this again?"

"None of it makes sense," Skye said. "Not to mention that Max was perfectly capable of getting into college on her own. She's the brightest one in the whole damn family."

Marcia clucked. "What I wouldn't give to be a fly on their wall right now."

"Mom!"

"Don't take everything so seriously," Marcia said, waving her free hand and splashing a little coffee on her tunic. "Your sister is right, this is all going to blow right over. With everything that's going on in the country, in the world, no one cares about something like this."

Skye stared at her. Marcia was usually right about most things. A retired nurse, she had worked double shifts after the girls' father left them for his dental hygienist when they were ten and eleven, respectively. He went on to have an entirely new family—two boys this time—a scenario he seemed to prefer since they rarely ever heard from him outside of birthdays and Hanukkah. But Marcia? The woman could hold her own. She *knew* things, and not just medical ones: who was going to win the upcoming election; when all the good sales started each season; how to make bouillabaisse; drive a stick; and get stains out of anything. She was an expert-level deal hunter, traveling exclusively with elder-hostel-type groups at the very last second when they posted their bargain-basement prices, and she was a badass about where she'd go, which was pretty much anywhere that wasn't actively engaged in all-out war. She was also certifiably crazy, certain that it was perfectly acceptable to return cooked meat to its marinade for "extra flavor," that all those "food safety" rules—she always used air quotes with that phrase—were a hoax and a conspiracy. She simply didn't believe the appliance repairman who told her that her twenty-two-year-old dishwasher was so clogged with cemented-on food that it'd be healthier to let the dog lick the plates clean. The woman had never met a doctor she trusted or a restaurant meal that was right the first time. She was tough, hardworking, and enough of a wackadoo to keep Skye and Peyton constantly on their toes. But on this one, Skye was certain her mother had it wrong.

"I don't think so," Skye said, shaking her head. "Having a household face and name associated with something as juicy and high profile as an FBI investigation? And cheating the system when you already have every advantage? People don't merely overlook that."

"Everyone will forget about it by Monday."

"No. This has the potential to upend her entire career." Skye glanced at her phone again, looking for a message from her sister. "Peyton must be panicked."

"Men do far worse things every day than try to help their own children. This is dead in the water. Just give it time."

Skye stood up and took Marcia's mug for a refill. "Do you think she knew? I mean, how could she not, right?"

Marcia shrugged. "I always say it's impossible to know what goes on in someone else's marriage. Even your own daughter's. I think we have to wait and see how it all develops. So in the meantime, tell me what's going on with you."

Skye handed her mother the steaming mug. "Isn't it nice to have hot, fresh coffee? Aren't you so grateful to your older daughter for bringing you this luxury?"

Marcia's eyes narrowed. "You look like you're going to cry."

Although she didn't feel on the edge of tears whatsoever, the mere suggestion of them by her own mother coaxed them forth. In a flash Marcia was beside her on the couch, rubbing her shoulder and murmuring, "There, there."

"Don't let all this stuff with your sister upset you so much," Marcia said. "She's a tough cookie, that one. She'll handle it."

"You're right."

"How's Gabe? And Aurora?"

"They're fine. All good."

What would her mother, who'd taught both her daughters to use cash and balance their checkbooks and use credit cards only for security reasons, think of the fact that Skye owed a debt the equivalent of a year's teaching salary? Or that the project she'd been working on for two years—literally, the thing that justified her existence beyond merely being a hyper-involved parent of one lovely and easy six-year-old—was still not finalized? Skye wished that just one time her mother would speak of her in the same glowing terms she talked of Peyton: as someone who was tough and determined, just like her. And although Marcia had never said it—hadn't even really implied it—Skye knew her mother was disappointed that her older daughter's fancy education and years of public service had slowly unraveled into . . . nothing.

"Why the tears, sweetheart? Go on, you can tell your mother."

Just as Skye was opening her mouth, the doorbell rang and her mother bustled up.

"Dianne!" she heard her call from the front door. "What a lovely surprise! Come in, come in. I have the most fabulous new coffee machine; you must have a cup."

Her mother appeared in the living room with a woman wearing a nearly identical tunic, leggings, and Tevas. "Skye, you remember Dianne, don't you? Her son-in-law is the chief resident at Columbia Presbyterian, isn't that right?"

"Actually, it's HSS," Dianne said. "And it's my daughter-in-law."

"Isn't that wonderful?" Marcia crooned, not hearing a word. "Skye, love, will you make Dianne a cup of your special coffee?"

Skye smiled wanly and headed to the kitchen. She could hear the two women discuss their shared dissatisfaction over their book club's most recent selection. When she returned with a cup for Dianne, her mother said, "Sit, dear. Visit with us."

"I have to pick up Aurora," she lied.

"Okay, but please remember to write me out the instructions for the coffee!"

"Mom, it's automatic. There are no instructions. You put the pod in the holder, close the lid, and press the button with a cup on it."

Marcia covered both eyes as though Skye were offering a detailed description of how to dismantle a complicated HVAC system. "You know all I'm hearing is blah-blah-blah. Please. Write it down."

"Dianne, it was nice to see you. Mom, I'll talk to you later." In the kitchen Skye grabbed a notepad that Marcia had clearly lifted from a local restaurant and wrote:

OPEN LID
INSERT POD
CLOSE LID
PRESS BUTTON

Skye stuck the memo on the fridge with an Iceland magnet and walked back to her car. She managed to get her seatbelt buckled and ignition on before the tears returned. But this time she was all alone.

8

All Talk, No Ambien

"C ome on in," Nisha said, sweeping open the door to her spacious Gramercy apartment. "The boys are finishing up breakfast, and then I'll kick them out."

Despite the early hour, Nisha looked chic in skinny jeans, a silk button-down, and a pair of fur slide slippers. Her thick black hair was pulled into a casual chignon, and although she wore no makeup, she still managed to look bright and rested.

"I'm so sorry to interrupt your Saturday morning," Peyton said as she and Isaac followed Nisha into the mammoth kitchen.

"We know this is family time," Isaac said. "We really appreciate you letting us crash in like this."

"Stop it!" Nisha shook her head. "You *are* family. Besides, we couldn't exactly meet at the office in light of the paparazzi outside your building. This is much better optics. Old friends having brunch. Speaking of which . . . Boys! Where are your manners?"

Sitting at the kitchen island, an expanse of gray and white marble so vast it looked like a playing field, was a row of four mop-headed boys. In front of them an enormous lazy Susan featured a bonanza of waffle toppings, all in coordinating black dishes: blueberries, chocolate chips, strawberries, rainbow sprinkles, slivered almonds, Nutella, homemade whipped cream, and a bowl of maple syrup with a coordi-

nating honeycomb-shaped serving stick. Each child was intently concentrating on either procuring, decorating, or chewing a waffle.

"My god, this is quite the spread," Peyton murmured.

"It's all Lydia. I didn't even know we had a waffle maker until she
pulled it out this morning," Nisha said. And then she thundered,
"BOYS!" Her face softened to a smile the moment they froze and
looked up. "I'm not sure if you noticed, but we have guests. What do
we do when guests are here?"

Immediately, as though she'd nudged them with an electric cattle
prod, all four boys leapt from their counter stools and arranged themselves in a single-file line.

"Nice to see you, Mr. and Mrs. Marcus. I'm Finn. I turned six last
week."

"Hello. My name is Lucas and I'm five years old."

"Hi, I'm William. I am three and three-quarters!"

"I'm Chammy. I'm two."

"His real name is Sammy," Lucas announced. "But he can't say
his S's yet."

Peyton and Isaac exchanged a look. Quietly to Nisha, Peyton said,
"I see them, what? Twice a month? I've known them all since birth.
Do we really require introductions?"

Nisha shrugged. "Lydia has started making them do it. She says
it's good practice. Who am I to question her?"

"Peyton, Isaac, good to see you!" Nisha's husband, Ajit, walked
into the kitchen. His hair was still wet from the shower and Peyton
could see a tiny spot of shaving cream under his left earlobe.

He and Isaac embraced, clapping each other's backs. "Good to
see you, man," Isaac said. "Sorry to crash in like this." He waved his
hand at the children, who had resumed their feasting.

"Don't be ridiculous. It's a nice change of pace." Ajit stuck a mug
under a built-in espresso machine and pressed a button. "Latte? Cap-
puccino? Drip?"

Soon Lydia, the nanny, was summoned to take the boys to the
park, and after much wrangling with shoes and socks and strollers
and scooters and balls and snacks, Nisha motioned for everyone to

move to the living room. It was typical New York mid-century modern, with low-slung couches, an uncomfortable backless chaise, and two Eames accent chairs. Under the wall of windows that looked out onto Gramercy Park sat five sherpa-covered beanbag chairs, each personalized with a boy's name and stocked with books in an attached side pocket.

"Looks good, right? They never sit in them," Ajit said.

"They never sit, period," Nisha added.

"I don't know how you do it," Peyton said, shaking her head. "Five!"

As if on cue, an overweight woman in scrubs appeared. One meaty hand held a swaddled newborn in the space between her shelf-like bosom and shoulder, and the other clutched a Boppy pillow and burp cloth.

"Oh my god. Didn't he just eat? Like ten minutes ago?" Nisha asked.

The woman shook her head. "Just feels that way, Mama. It's been two and a half hours, and Teddy's rootin' for sure."

Nisha sighed and accepted the swaddled baby.

"Give a call when you're done," the baby nurse said, and vanished.

Peyton watched Isaac avert his eyes as Nisha unbuttoned her shirt and whipped out her left breast, which she expertly positioned over the baby's mouth so he immediately latched on.

"Oh, come on, Isaac," Nisha laughed, noticing his gaze was fixed on the floor. "Get over it. It's just a boob."

Ajit laughed. "I can now see breasts—like, nice ones, on models or TV or wherever, and all I can think about is, 'I wonder how her production is?'"

Peyton had once asked Nisha if they were good with two or if they'd roll the dice and try for a girl, and Nisha had laughed. "I didn't start until I was thirty-five. I figure I have, what? Five, maybe seven years total? If I'm lucky? We're going to cram as many in as humanly possible, and I couldn't care less what they are, so long as none of them look like Ajit's mother."

Peyton sipped her coffee and rested her hand on Isaac's knee, but immediately he moved his leg away. The fourteen hours he'd been home had been horrible. The second Max had fled to her room during dinner the night before, Isaac disappeared into their office. She'd waited up most of the night, but he never came into their bedroom; in the kitchen that morning, he couldn't look at her.

"I, um, I just wanted to thank you guys for doing this . . . whole thing," Peyton said, waving her arm.

Everyone nodded. The room was silent except for Teddy's little sucking sounds.

"So?" Nisha said, swinging the baby onto her shoulder, where she expertly whacked his back. "Who's going to start?" She looked between Peyton and Isaac, who each stared at their hands. "Okay, good. I will. This is a real shit show you've gotten yourselves into."

"I would just like to say—" Peyton held up her pointer finger, but Nisha glared at her.

"Nope. That invitation to speak just now? That wasn't sincere. I actually don't want either of you to say one word."

"But let me just—"

"Zip it!" Nisha said at the same time that Teddy let out a loud burp. "What I'm not sure either of you understand here is that I am not your lawyer, and therefore you are not currently enjoying attorney-client privilege. So I am the only one who's going to talk. Got it?"

They both nodded.

"As this whole dog and pony show that we are putting on for the press hopefully demonstrates, this is a breakfast among friends, nothing more. The fact that I'm a crisis manager obviously complicates things, but we stick to the story, which also happens to be true: we are old friends from college, and this is a social visit. Now . . . you were happy with Claire?"

"Absolutely," Isaac said. "Thank you for the recommendation. She seems great."

"She is. Best criminal attorney in the city, if not the entire East Coast. Listen to her," Nisha said.

Isaac nodded and Peyton noticed that he was clenching his hands together, twisting each finger around the other. Peyton felt a stab of panic, so sharp it felt like she couldn't fill her lungs. It was bad enough that the entire country thought Isaac had done this horrible thing. How could she let their oldest friends think the same?

"There's something you need to know," Peyton said, rushing to tell them before Nisha cut her off. "It was actually—"

"Nope!" Nisha's voice was raised to nearly a shout. "I do not need to know whatever it was you were about to tell me. Ajit doesn't need to know. Not to put too fine a point on it, but we *refuse* to know."

Peyton exhaled.

"Let me just point out a few facts," Nisha said, latching Teddy onto her other breast. "Whichever one of you—and I am forbidding you from telling me—did the actual communicating with the college fixer is somewhat immaterial. The public will assume that as a married couple you acted together, or at the very least knew of each other's actions."

"But that's—" Isaac started to speak, but the intensity of Nisha's glare stopped him mid-sentence.

"I'll just point out a few obvious things here. The amount of money alleged is somewhat small in relation to some of the other admissions arrests—that's the bit of good news. Also good is that it was a one-time check, which is a lot easier for a judge to swallow than an ongoing program of lying or cheating, as we saw a couple years ago with those accused who falsified photos, hired test stand-ins, et cetera. Obviously, no one can predict the future, but if I had to guess, I would say you—Isaac—will be looking at one of the more lenient sentences. A few weeks, perhaps a couple months at most if the judge has a hard-on for this sort of thing. Certainly, hundreds of hours of community service and a fine, but I'm sure you know that."

Peyton felt her eyes widen. Perhaps it hadn't been *ethical*, that much she could admit. But she truly didn't believe it was illegal, considering it seemed like something people did, in one form or another, all the damn time.

"You look surprised?" Nisha asked.

"I just . . . you really think there's a . . . I mean, *jail*?" Peyton prided herself on being succinct and articulate, but it felt like her brain had narrowed to a single, dark tunnel.

"I can't tell you what to do, but I can point out this: regardless of whose idea this was—and again, I do *not* want to know—I can tell you that Isaac has significantly less to lose, professionally speaking. Peyton, were you to be officially implicated, never mind convicted, I think it's not an overstatement to say you would never work again."

"This just all seems like . . . such an overreaction," Peyton said, but no one else acknowledged it.

"So, what are you saying?" Isaac asked, his voice breaking slightly. "Just give it to us straight."

Peyton's mouth was suddenly so dry she could barely swallow.

Ajit had taken up an interest in a loose thread on his jeans pocket.

Nisha peered at them both. "Isaac, you acted one hundred percent alone. It would also help, significantly I think . . ." Nisha paused here, as though she knew the next part would be the hardest to hear. ". . . if the two of you were to separate—for the sake of appearances only, of course—until this is resolved."

No one spoke.

Ajit tore at the thread.

Peyton tried to wet her lips, but her tongue felt like sandpaper.

Even Teddy had stopped nursing and had fallen into a deep, silent sleep.

"I think you both need to keep in mind that there are two battles we're facing here: the legal one, of course, but also the one on social media. Think whatever you will about cancel culture, but it's real and it's vicious. This case will be tried by the media, by the bloggers, by the influencers and the randoms who sit anonymously behind their keyboards. And they are typically not so forgiving. Peyton, regardless of what you did or didn't do—and I repeat, I don't want to know— you will want to be very, very careful."

"Exactly how?" Peyton asked quietly.

"Separate, first and foremost. Do not be seen in public together, no matter what. Then we should probably get you involved in some high-profile charity work, preferably education-related. You'll also want to have your social media manager call me and we can go over some messaging."

Peyton swallowed hard, and only then noticed that her fingernails were digging into her palms. She knew what Nisha was saying was true, but worse than that was that none of them were even talking about Isaac—his life, his career, his reputation, all blown up because of something Peyton did.

Finally, Isaac cleared his throat and stood. "Nisha, Ajit, thank you so much for your advice and your hospitality. I think we've taken up enough of your—please, don't stand. We'll see ourselves out."

Peyton felt a rush of relief that at least he'd said "we." She kissed Nisha's cheek and rubbed baby Teddy's head.

"Thank you," Peyton whispered. She had so many more questions.

"Stay strong, P. And remember, everyone makes mistakes. This is a particularly stupid one, I'm not going to lie. But this too shall pass."

"Did you really just say that?" Peyton asked, her eyes wide.

Nisha, not ever one for physical affection, looked at Peyton and then pulled her into her arms. "You're so strong, P, one of the toughest, most badass women I know. I'm not going to tell you that this will be easy, but it won't be forever. Just promise me you'll remember that, okay?"

Nothing was working that night—nothing. Not the chamomile tea or the CBD gummy bears or those ridiculous homeopathic relaxation drops she bought by the carton at the Union Square farmers market. Not the hot bath or the steam shower or the forty-five minutes of mind-numbing pedaling Peyton had logged on the Peloton. She'd put back two glasses of pinot grigio and only had a headache to show for it. Ditto for the four squares of dark chocolate she'd ferreted out of her secret stash in the pantry freezer. If there was ever a night to smoke weed, this was surely it. But even the thought of taking a few hits from the pen a friend had given her sent her into paroxysms of paranoia. Why was she the only woman on the Upper East Side—hell, possibly the only woman in all of Manhattan—without a reliable source of Xanax? It was ridiculous. No one should have to face the last twenty-four hours without the very best.

The night table clock screamed 1:06 A.M. She flipped onto her side, careful not to jostle Isaac, before realizing that he was still sleeping on the pull-out in his office. Peyton leaned over and rooted through her nightstand. Her hands closed around a blister two-pack of green NyQuil gel tabs, long expired. *No matter,* she thought, tearing it open, raccoon-like, with her teeth. She washed it down with the remnants of her wine and prayed to some unknown higher power, asking for sleep but pretty please not unintended death, à la Heath Ledger, who had made some unfortunate mixing choices but surely never meant to kill himself. Dear god, how would it look if she died in her own bed, the very next night after her husband was arrested? No one would ever believe it was unintentional. Max would think her own mother didn't love her enough to stick around and see her through the rough times. Nisha would blame herself for coming down too hard. Skye would be devastated for the rest of her life that she hadn't recognized the signs. And Isaac? Not only would he be carted off to jail for a crime he didn't commit, but they'd surely throw in a murder investigation, because, well . . . dead wife.

She collapsed against the pillow and closed her eyes. Per all of the "good sleep hygiene" articles she'd collected, her bedroom thermostat was set to 62 degrees, her custom-made blackout shades were securely closed, and two industrial-sized white-noise machines whirred from separate corners. Peyton pulled up her covers, which were the finest feather down, and tried to breathe slowly. Three counts inhale, five counts exhale, just as all the apps advised. The fucking breathing was making her even more anxious. Was she doing it right? Why couldn't she stay committed long enough to anything to make it an actual habit? All the time downloading these apps, everything from macro tracking to sleep hygiene to step counting. But did she stick to any of it? Show it the kind of ruthless commitment she showed her work? Absolutely not. It was always just another half-assed attempt at what she secretly hoped would be a quick fix. Obviously, something was wrong with her brain. Or her personality. What was the definition of insanity? Lying in place, hour after hour, staring, and waiting for sleep, when all you wanted to do was leave that prison of a bed.

Prison. She thought of Isaac sleeping on the pullout, undoubtedly unconscious. No matter the current hell that had recently defined his every waking hour. No drugs needed, no breathing exercises, no complicated accoutrements. He only needed to rest his head, close his eyes, and embrace the deep, beautiful sleep that effortlessly followed. Peyton had been wildly jealous of his sleeping gift since the very beginning of their relationship, when she still pretended to be normal. Back then she would snuggle next to him and quietly wait for him to fall asleep before climbing out of bed to pace the apartment. Now she went straight to pacing.

Why wasn't that damn NyQuil working? she wondered.

A wave of nausea washed over her. They were going to treat him like a felon! Her husband. Never mind he hadn't actually done anything wrong—that was bad enough. But didn't anyone understand that Isaac cried while watching *Parenthood,* for god's sake? How could you put a man like that in *jail*? The one who never rolled through stop signs or skipped a Sunday night call to his ninety-eight-year-old grandmother. How many times had Peyton tried to go through the E-ZPass lane without an E-ZPass while driving a rental car? Or made it out to the parking lot before noticing the case of water underneath her shopping cart that she hadn't paid for—and hadn't gone back inside? Or—she flushed even thinking about this one—pretended not to notice an elderly person on the packed subway car so *she* wouldn't have to be the one to volunteer her seat? If anything, she was a deficient human being with a lack of integrity. But Isaac? He was the type who paid his taxes not out of fear of reprisal, but because it was his duty as an income-earning citizen. He overtipped and under-complained. He showed up! At every funeral, at every bris, at every school play and field hockey game and insignificant classroom celebration. He was her moral compass, and she was sending him to jail.

Enough. She couldn't take another second of the mental looping. She suddenly remembered the banana muffins Nisha had insisted she take home. Peyton sat up and felt a stab of pain near her ankle.

"Dammit!" she scream-whispered. She thrust her leg straight, half expecting the Land Shark to be swinging by his teeth from her flesh, but he hadn't even left a mark. The dog was a fucking expert-level abuser. Her phone buzzed from the pocket of her robe as she padded down the hallway to the kitchen.

You up? From Skye.

Obv, Peyton replied, sticking one of the muffins into the microwave.

You okay?

The thought of typing suddenly seemed overwhelming, so Peyton dialed her sister.

"Why are you awake?" she asked Skye, her voice low, although she knew there probably wasn't a reason. They'd both been insomniacs from childhood, a genetic gift from their mother.

"The usual. You?"

The microwave beeped. Peyton pulled out the muffin and started to slather it with peanut butter. "Mmm, same," she said, through a huge bite. "Is that Mr. Big I hear?"

Skye snorted. "Who else? I will forever contend that 'To Be With You' is one of the best songs ever written."

With this, Peyton couldn't keep herself from laughing. "It's one-thirty in the damn morning and you're listening to Mr. Big and what? Feeling understood?"

"Do you remember the first time Mom let us go to a concert alone together? We told her it was James Taylor, even played her 'You've Got a Friend' so she wouldn't worry, and then we went to see Guns N' Roses?"

"*Remember*? It was one of the best days of my life. When they played 'Welcome to the Jungle' and Axl swung his hair around and Slash lit his guitar on fire . . . it was the sexiest thing I think I'd ever seen."

"Bieber and Swift really can't compete," Skye said. "So . . . any update on sick people?"

Peyton pressed her fingertips to her forehead. "I recognize that you're trying to distract me from thinking about Isaac, and I appreciate it. Let's see, Brad's wife published an update on CaringBridge today since I think he was still too groggy from the surgery."

"Which one's Brad again?"

"The high school boyfriend of my best camp friend's best friend. Do you remember Erin from Camp Everest? Well, her best friend used to date Brad."

Who else would understand why she carefully tracked the medical progress of complete strangers? For years she'd figured she was alone in carefully reading about, tracking, and researching the horrible diseases and misfortunes that afflicted people she'd never met. But Skye understood, because she did it, too.

"And what's the prognosis? They were waiting for pathology results, right?"

"It's not good. Glioblastoma. Stage four."

Skye whistled. "That's *extremely* not good."

"Yeah, his wife says that they're going to fly to Germany for some experimental treatment, but the life expectancy after diagnosis is like nine to twelve months." Peyton stuck another muffin in the microwave.

"I followed a young woman who was diagnosed the first week of her senior year of college and she was gone before graduation," Skye said quietly.

"Yes," Peyton said, allowing herself to feel the pain and unfairness of dying so young, even if she'd never met either Brad or Skye's young woman. After all, if she subjected herself to their pain—even a fraction of it, by proxy—then wouldn't it somehow inoculate her family against getting the same disease? If she dove deep into someone's profile who was fighting, or dying from, ovarian cancer or ALS or a brain tumor—really tried to understand and empathize with their suffering—didn't it guarantee her own safety? At least from that particular horror. Which is why she read broadly and indiscriminately, following links on Facebook and Instagram to GoFundMe and CaringBridge. Her cameraman's mother's pastor who'd dropped dead three weeks after finding out he had pancreatic cancer. Her dry cleaner's nephew whose undiagnosed melanoma had spread to his lungs and liver. The first cousin of one of her sorority sisters who'd become a paraplegic after diving into a shallow lake. And by far the worst ones of all, the ones she could barely read through her own choking tears: the children with bald heads and cartoon hospital sheets and sad smiles. It was twisted that she and Skye did this, wasn't it? But there was some strange comfort in knowing she wasn't alone.

The microwave beeped, and this time Peyton dunked the muffin directly into the peanut butter jar.

"How's Isaac doing?" Skye asked.

Peyton swallowed. She *had* to confide in Skye and tell her that it was she, not Isaac, who had gotten them into this horror show. They may not be able to tell anyone else, but Skye would understand. Would she be judgy and patronizing? Undoubtedly. But this wasn't the kind of secret she could keep from her sister. She would tell her, Peyton promised herself, before they hung up.

"He's okay, all things considered," Peyton said, trying to clear the peanut butter from the roof of her mouth.

She heard a splashing sound. "Are you peeing?"

"Sorry," Skye said. "And how's Max? We texted and she claims she's fine, but my god—this is a national news story and it centers around *her*."

Peyton took another bite and slowly chewed. "I wouldn't say she's great. I'm sure she's obsessively reading all the coverage. We both keep trying to talk to her, but she flat out refuses."

"Thank god she's already graduated. I can't imagine how much harder this would all be if she were still at Milford, hemmed in by all that uniformity. It would be a nightmare."

Peyton rolled her eyes. Typical Skye, couldn't ever resist a dig about Milford. "You live in *Paradise*. You can hardly take the moral high ground here. But seriously, it might have been better if this had all happened while she was still there. That place specializes in parental scandal."

"Milford?"

"I've seen noncustodial abductions, a dad who underwrote his kid's cocaine-selling business, and not one but two fathers busted for patronizing high-class prostitutes."

"You're joking."

"Those weren't even the interesting ones! I must have told you about the time they arrested the chauffeur of a fifth grader for traveling to Syria to attend a jihadi training camp? Oh! And there was a senior girl who apparently went on an extended European 'spa retreat,' and whose parents—at nearly fifty years old—coincidentally adopted a newborn at the same time because they 'simply couldn't resist.' You know how it is—just a plethora of white, European babies waiting to be adopted, you know? And of course, all the run-of-the-mill financial crimes: fraud, money laundering, tax evasion. Even an insurance-related arson charge. Mail fraud is practically quaint."

"Sounds like a lovely community."

Peyton snorted. "Yeah, but at least it's nothing that these kids haven't seen a hundred times before." Suddenly she felt dizzy and exhausted. "I think the booze and NyQuil are finally kicking in. I'm going to go."

"Booze and NyQuil? Should I be worried? Can't you find something a little higher quality than that?"

"Obviously not, or I wouldn't be sitting in my kitchen at one A.M., huffing whole milk and peanut butter and talking to you."

Skye laughed. "Sleep well. I'll keep my phone on in case you want to call back."

"Mmm," Peyton whispered, as she padded down the hallway. "Sorry I didn't ask about your life at all."

"No worries. A husband out on bail earns you one entirely selfish call."

"About that. There's something I need to tell you, and I don't want you to—"

Isaac appeared in the office door, his robe hanging open over a pair of pineapple boxers. His expression was serious.

"Skye? Never mind, I'll call you in the morning, okay?" she said quickly, and hung up. She moved to wrap her arms around him, but he slid past her.

"I think Nisha's right," he whispered, no doubt to keep from waking Max.

"Right about what?"

"About us needing some time apart. From each other," he said to the hallway carpet.

Peyton could feel her eyes widen. "She was only suggesting that for appearance's sake."

He didn't respond.

"Isaac. Look at me!" She whispered too, but her voice was urgent.

He ran his hands through his thick dark hair. Finally, he lifted his gaze to meet hers. "I need some time to think about everything—you, us, Max, how all of this happened. It's not forever. And I don't care what you tell people."

"But, Isaac, we just need—"

Abruptly he turned around and said, "Don't tell me what *we* need! You gave up that right the second you broke your promise. Have you considered for one minute how all of this is going to play out for Max? Or me? *We* certainly doesn't seem to be your default these days. I'm going back to sleep in my own bed; you take the office." He slammed their bedroom door.

Peyton stood there, shocked, staring at the back of the door. She could hear the toilet flush, the covers rustle, and then nothing. He hadn't locked it—nothing was preventing her from climbing into bed next to him. But the pitchfork had returned to her temples, and her stomach had started to cramp. *What have I done?* Her body on autopilot, she sank to the floor of the hallway and curled herself into a ball. Max's room was only a few feet away, and Peyton didn't want her daughter to find her like that, but she couldn't move. She wasn't sure how long she lay there, shivering, before she finally fell into a dark, drugged sleep.

9

Matchy-Matchy

Skye stared at her laptop screen, wondering how to address the email. *Dear Parents* wouldn't do, since one of the girls was being raised by her grandparents, and another was in foster care. *Dear Guardians* sounded so cold. Chewing on the pen propped between her teeth, she finally decided on *Dear Parents and Guardians*.

Dear Parents and Guardians,

I'm excited to be writing with an update! As you already know, we have purchased the home that will be used for our girls' residence while they attend Paradise High School. A local architect—my husband—has drawn plans to transform the space to fit our needs, and I've already begun sourcing the furniture and soft goods that will make it feel like home. We are expecting the last of our financing any day now from a generous local investor, and we will immediately begin the renovations needed to make the space our own. I'm thrilled to write that we are on track for a late-summer move-in, and the girls will hopefully be ready to start the school year with the rest of the Paradise students.

Please don't hesitate to get in touch with any questions or concerns. I look forward to greeting each of your girls soon!

All the best,

Skye Alter
Executive Director, Serenity Home for Girls

She read it, spell-checked it, and, feeling satisfied, hit send. The clock on the kitchen counter read 2:46 P.M. Less than a half hour until she needed to meet Aurora's bus. She should really go for a walk— she hadn't left the house all day. Feeling a burst of motivation, Skye went to close her laptop, but the little icon of the Amazon cart caught her eye, and she clicked on it. It was already full from earlier that morning. Eight desk lamps with dimmers. An assortment of drawer organizers. An enormous rice maker. Wall-mountable shampoo dispensers. Click, click, click. One product took her to the next and the next, every minute a new screen popping up, showing her something she hadn't realized the residence needed until it blared its own benefits like a bragging Real Housewife: *Enriched! Redesigned! Back in stock! 2,041 five-star reviews!* Click, click, click, her fingers went, adding things to the cart almost faster than her brain could process them.

It took twenty minutes to edit and purchase the cart, which meant another exercise opportunity squandered. Taking the stairs two at a time, Skye grabbed the first sweatshirt she saw, pulling it on as she headed back downstairs and out the front door. It wasn't until the driveway that she realized she'd pulled her old Amherst zip-up that was two sizes too big and so gloriously mushy and over-washed that it felt like silk against her bare skin. She and Peyton had bought them together at the campus store on a random weekend when Peyton had come to visit during Skye's junior year.

"I'm never going to take this off," Peyton had announced, as she spun in front of the store's floor-length mirror. "I'm going to go back to Penn State wearing this so everyone will know that my sister is smart enough to go to one of the best schools in the country."

Skye could remember searching Peyton's face, hyperalert to any hint of jealousy or mockery, but there was none. "Come on, I'll buy it for you," Skye said, pulling the sweatshirt from Peyton's hands.

"You mean Mom and Dad will buy it for me," Peyton said, laughing. "But you have to get one, too. Let's be matchy-matchy."

Skye already owned a half dozen Amherst sweatshirts, but it was easier to buy another than stand in the way of Peyton when she had her mind set on something. They'd worn their matching sweatshirts all across campus to Skye's apartment, arms linked, and Skye could still remember the feeling of walking with her sister, laughing and singing, a few rare rays of the Massachusetts sun warming their faces. When they'd arrived back at Skye's off-campus apartment, Peyton had poured them vodka cranberries from a bottle of Absolut she'd brought with her, and they sipped and gossiped while they got dressed.

Skye could remember that night, twenty years earlier, like it had happened the previous week.

"You're wearing *that*?" Peyton had scrunched up her nose at Skye, who'd emerged from her bedroom in a shapeless burgundy maxi dress.

"Yes."

"But it's just so . . . awful."

Skye sighed. "It's a dress. I don't really care."

"Well, that much is obvious." Peyton disappeared into Skye's small bedroom. "Can you come in here for a minute? I think we can do better."

Resisting Peyton was like standing on tiptoe in front of a rogue wave. Skye rolled her eyes but followed her sister. "What?" she asked, hand on her hip. Peyton's perfect denimed ass stuck out from Skye's closet.

"Here, look! These are bordering on cute. I bet they'd be flattering, too." She tossed a pair of wide-legged trousers to Skye, who caught them. "Then . . . let's see here," she said, flipping through hangers. "Pair it with . . . this!"

Skye accepted a sleeveless white silk shirt that her mother had bought her for an internship interview last summer, and she shrugged it on over her head.

Peyton tucked Skye's shirt into the jeans, added a belt she ferreted out from god knows where, and said, "Wait, I'll be right back." She returned with her own overnight bag, from which she removed a handful of necklaces and a pair of red patent leather pumps that had at least three-inch heels.

"No freaking way," Skye said, eyeing the shoes.

"It's a cocktail party!"

"At my professor's house! And one I'm hoping to ask to be my advisor."

"So? Since when aren't you allowed to look good? Are you worried he won't think you're smart if you wear heels?"

Skye rolled her eyes, but the answer was simple: yes. That's exactly what she was worried about. "It's 'she.'"

"Whatever. Just try them," Peyton urged, and once again, Skye submitted. She slipped her feet into the shoes and glanced in the mirror and nearly fell over staring at the reflection that peered back. The wide-cut pants made her waist look even smaller than normal and her legs like they were a mile long. The silk shirt skimmed her small breasts and highlighted her narrow shoulders, and although she wasn't sure what was doing it—the heels, or just her own awareness— she seemed to stand taller and look more confident.

"You see?" Peyton said.

Skye couldn't stop staring at herself.

"It's the best I can do with this." Peyton waved her arm toward the closet. "It still kills me that the sister without a shred of fashion sense got the better body and face. That feels really unfair. Come here, I'll do your makeup and they'll think you're a complete shallow fucking idiot by the time I'm done with you."

Peyton went to work, and ten minutes later Skye examined herself in the mirror. She was glowing. It was almost unnerving how pretty she looked and felt. How had she never known how gifted her sister was with a random assortment of drugstore makeup and some old brushes? She watched as Peyton zipped herself into a black sheath dress, curled her eyelashes and then her hair, and literally painted on a perfectly proportioned face in fewer than fifteen minutes. "Let's show this professor biatch that she cannot, should not, mess with the Alter sisters," Peyton announced, jutting her hip out in front of the mirror and blowing herself a kiss.

Skye felt a flash of irritation. Or was it something else? "Look, I'm all for having fun, but can you please remember that these professors are . . . serious people? They're scholars, not partyers."

Peyton's eyes widened. "Of course," she said, nodding gravely. "*Scholars*. Noted. Got it. You know, because I've never met a real, live *professor* before."

"P, that's not what—"

"Come on," Peyton laughed as she walked out the door. "I'm just teasing you."

Peyton yammered on about her sorority as the girls walked across the Main Quad at dusk. "I had no intention of running—zero—but they basically begged me to. I mean, social chair determines the entire social schedule of the whole sorority for the year. It's, like, why we joined a sorority in the first place," Peyton said, waving her arms. She stopped and looked around at the ivy-covered buildings, the massive expanses of green grass, and the fiery color of the changing leaves. "My god, it's gorgeous here."

Instead of agreeing, which she did—even after three years on campus, she could barely believe how beautiful it was—Skye said, "I can't imagine going to a school where the Greek system has such an enormous influence."

Peyton peered at her. "Oh, yeah?"

"I mean, nothing against fraternities and sororities," Skye continued, "but thank god that's not the scene at Amherst."

Skye felt awful the moment she said it. Peyton had driven five hours to visit her for the weekend, and she'd been nothing but great the entire time she'd been there: she'd whipped up cheddar cheese popcorn and milkshakes last night when they stayed in and watched a movie; she'd made a thousand comments about Amherst being spectacularly beautiful; she'd been super friendly to Skye's roommates and friends. There was the styling and makeover, and the fact that Peyton had cheerfully agreed to accompany Skye to a cocktail party at her history professor's house, a task even Skye was dreading.

"Are you trying to be a raging, snotty bitch?" Peyton asked. "Because if so, you're doing a really good job."

"Sorry," Skye said. "I didn't mean it like that."

"Just like you didn't mean it when you also reminded me that Amherst doesn't even *have* a journalism major? I'm guessing because you're all supposed to major in English literature instead? That's much more elite. But guess what? I've wanted to major in broadcast journalism since I was fifteen, and I'm happy to be at a school where I can do that. When I transfer to main campus next year, I'll be in one of the best programs in the country."

Skye thought about Peyton's life at Penn State, where despite being on a small branch campus in the middle of nowhere, it seemed her sister had carved out a pretty great niche for herself. She thrived as the social chair of her sorority, adored her lacrosse player boyfriend, and spent her weekends going to football games and her weekday mornings at the campus television station. Peyton seemed to embrace college, actually, in a way that Skye couldn't really imagine. Of course, she loved the intellectual rigor of her classes, and the access to world-class professors, and she had been lucky enough to meet a handful of really great friends from all over the world. But she certainly wouldn't describe her three years so far as *fun*.

"I'm insufferable," Skye said. "I'm sorry."

"Wait, please, dear sister, can you use a word that a state schooler at a *branch campus* might understand? Please?"

Skye jabbed Peyton in the arm. "This is it," she said, relieved at the change of scenery. "But we're still early. Let's wait here for a little."

"Let's just get this over with," Peyton said. She climbed the porch stairs and rang the doorbell before Skye could stop her.

"I'm not ready!" Skye scream-whispered, suddenly desperate to turn around and leave. One-on-one with some real conversation and no small talk? Fine. But Skye hated big groups and parties and knew she was awful at faking it.

"What are you so stressed about? It's cocktails! It's your professor! We'll have two glasses of bad wine, smile, and leave." Peyton fluffed her hair. "Seriously, I don't know where you get your social anxiety from. It's so strange to me."

Skye didn't have a chance to respond, because the door swung open and Professor McCann and another woman smiled at them.

"Skye, you are the first to arrive!" Professor McCann said, stepping back so the girls could enter.

"Professor McCann, I hope you don't mind that I brought my sister?" Skye asked. She hated hearing her voice shake.

"Come in, come in," the professor said, ushering them to the surprisingly traditional living room, where a few platters of cheese and crackers were stacked on top of coffee table art books. "This is my wife, Brenda. Brenda, this is Skye Alter, a junior history major, and her sister . . ."

"Peyton," Peyton announced with a huge smile and a proffered hand. "I know Skye has been looking forward to tonight for weeks, and I'm so glad I'm able to join her. Thank you for having us."

Skye inhaled. It was too much. Peyton was always too much. She needed to tone it down a little, not be so casual and enthusiastic. Show proper respect. But to her surprise, Professor McCann smiled warmly and said, "Please, both of you, call me Amanda. Come, sit down."

Brenda, who was surprisingly attractive and looked at least ten years younger than middle-aged Amanda, poured each of them a glass of white wine.

"Oh my goodness, look at that sweetness!" Peyton crowed, and again Skye cringed. Couldn't she keep it down? But it was too late—Peyton had already leapt up and headed toward a mammoth, furry dog. "Oh, good boy! Aren't you just the most gorgeous thing! Who is this?"

Professor McCann's face lit up in a way Skye had never seen in class, or anywhere else. "That's Martin. He's very pleased with the attention."

"Oh, of course he is," Peyton crooned, sticking her face in Martin's. "He's an Alaskan malamute, isn't he? I've always wanted one, they're just the most beautiful creatures ever! Does he shed?"

"A ton!" Brenda answered, sipping her wine. "But he's worth it."

"Yes, he is! Can I ask you both—does he hate the summertime? Growing up, a friend of mine had a malamute, and I remember it used to beg to go outside all winter long and then it would just plop right down in the snow."

Skye nearly bit her tongue at Peyton's insipid line of questioning, but then she realized that both Professor McCann (she just couldn't call her Amanda) and Brenda appeared to be enraptured by this conversation. She was the one who was sitting there stupidly, saying nothing.

When Peyton had exhausted every possible line of inquiry about the dog, she began to ask about Brenda's career, their historic home, even their summer plans. She chatted so easily, so effortlessly, that Skye soon lost any self-consciousness about Peyton's behavior. She began to feel grateful. What would Skye have done if she'd arrived alone, before any other guests? She couldn't think of a single damn thing to say or ask! Maybe she'd have inquired about something Professor McCann had assigned in class, but it was rude to talk about work at a party, wasn't it? Or was it? She took a long swig of her wine and savored the feeling of the first sips hitting her empty stomach. Thank god for her sister.

By the time more students arrived, Peyton had made Professor McCann belly-laugh with an off-color but funny joke about hand jobs, and Brenda had sat beside Peyton, captivated by Peyton's charming retelling of some travel mishap. She'd always known her sister was more socially adept, but Skye had almost forgotten to what extent. The new sorority, college-loving Peyton was even more socially gifted than Homecoming Queen Peyton, and that was saying a lot. When, a couple of hours later, they thanked their hosts and left, Skye was almost hyperventilating with appreciation.

"Thank you," Skye breathed.

"You're welcome," Peyton said as they pulled the door behind them.

"You totally saved me."

"What was the big deal? I know they're supposedly hotshot, fancy professors at this super prestigious school, but they're just people, you know?"

"I think I forget that sometimes."

Peyton grinned. "Everyone loves dogs and hand-job jokes, remember that."

Skye laughed. "Noted."

"Can we go to a real party now? A bar? *Something*?" Peyton asked.

Skye looped her arm through her sister's. "Yes," she said, squeezing it. "I owe you that at least."

Now, hugging herself and the fantastically comfortable sweatshirt, Skye frowned as she walked to the bus stop. Her sister was batshit crazy in so many ways, there was no denying it. But she loved her. And now, with everything that was happening to Isaac? The fallout for Peyton was going to be extensive, likely in ways they couldn't yet fathom. After too many years and so much sacrifice, she would lose so much. Skye vowed to step up and be the decent, supportive sister Peyton had always been to her. She fired off a text to Peyton: *Call you soon,* and then knelt down to greet Aurora, who stepped off the bus and ran straight, blissfully, into her arms.

10

Brilliant Harvard Clichés

The irritating birdsong alarm drove her crazy. Peyton usually needed the rage to motivate her out of bed at three-thirty in the morning, but today she was already awake, unsure whether to be glad or horrified that it was Monday. Instinctively she rolled over to Isaac's side and reached for him, but again, his side was empty. Hauling herself into the shower, Peyton allowed the scalding water to pound her shoulders as she gave herself a pep talk. Sunday had been . . . horrible. In a misguided attempt to smooth things over, Peyton had bustled around the apartment, desperately trying to please her family—pancakes for Max, lattes for Isaac—but both refused to speak to her. At one point Max tried to leave to go filming around the city, but a particularly determined paparazzo had sent her fleeing back home. Isaac had locked himself in their shared office for most of the day; Peyton could hear bits of his conversations with his best friend from childhood, who lived in Norway, and his elderly father, whose Alzheimer's blessedly made the current situation—at least for him—a non-event. It seemed the only one who wanted to hear from her was Kenneth, who had called no fewer than four times to blurt out unhelpful and unsolicited advice along the lines of "Keep your head down and plan to be on air first thing Monday morning." Peyton had barely slept. But today was a new day, and she was more determined than ever to make it a good one. No one knew better than she how quickly stories like this cycled in and out of the news. She would show up at work today and crush it, like she always did. What they were saying about Isaac—she still couldn't quite bring herself to admit *what she'd done*—just didn't stack up against the main news stories or even the previous admissions scandal. After a day with some space from one another, they could all have a good long family talk when she got home that afternoon.

Newly energized, Peyton pulled on jeans and a T-shirt and tip-toed to the kitchen, where the microwave read 3:45 A.M. She triple-checked her phone to make sure she'd read Sean's text correctly, and was reassured by his firm, confident wording: *You are confirmed for this morning. Business as usual.* The coffee machine hissed out its last drop, exactly on schedule, and she poured herself a heaping mug with almond milk and a shake of cinnamon. A text popped up from the studio's car service announcing that her ride had arrived. Moving quickly, Peyton printed out the briefing papers that one of the PAs emailed each night and stuffed them into her Goyard tote. She picked up her gym bag, grabbed a Greek yogurt and a plastic spoon, and peeked into Max's darkened bedroom. Struck with an overwhelming urge to press her lips to Max's warm cheek, she tip-toed in. Terrified of waking her, Peyton stood on the fuzzy area rug and watched her daughter sleep peacefully. How many times had she held vigils like this when Max was little? A hundred? A thousand? All the fevers and nightmares and recess dramas and home-work anxieties. All the "I'm scared of the dark"s and the "there's a monster under my bed"s blended right into each other, knitting together the fabric of Max's childhood. And now Peyton sat and gazed at her beautiful, sleeping daughter and wondered—like every mother on the planet—where all the time had gone. Her thoughts flickered to the situation with Max and Isaac, but she pushed them away again.

"Mom? What are you *doing*?" Max groaned, rolling over, sound-ing slightly irritated but not excessively so. "You know it's weird to just stand there and watch someone sleep."

"You're not *someone*," Peyton said, wanting desperately to reach out and stroke Max's hair the way she had when she was younger.

"Is everything okay?" Max pushed her mane of wild, wavy curls from her face. "What's wrong?"

"Nothing, honey! I'm leaving now. I was only . . . looking at you."

Max opened her other eye. "What's going on?"

"Oh, honey," Peyton said, sitting at the very edge of Max's bed. "Everything's fine! It's a new day! I mean, it's not fine as in resolved. But we will *be* fine."

"Right," Max said. "Everything's great."

"Go to sleep, sweetie, I didn't mean to wake you. I have to go to work. I love you."

Max pulled the covers over her head in response, and Peyton quietly pulled the door closed behind her. She made her way downstairs and into the waiting Town Car.

"Have a good show, Mrs. Marcus," Peter, her doorman, said as he closed the car's back door.

It wasn't one of her usual drivers, but thankfully someone had told him that Peyton didn't like to chat in the morning. As they flew down a mostly empty Park Avenue, Peyton propped her briefing papers on her lap and tried to concentrate. With any luck it would be a normal day: no breaking news, no emergencies, no office conflicts. The junior-level staff would glance away from her, feeling awkward and uncertain about what to say, but the more senior producers and execs would be their best blunt selves. She imagined them murmuring no-nonsense things like "Shit happens" and "We're here for you," before handing her a stack of updated papers and the outline for the morning's show. Everyone would keep it tight and professional, exactly as it needed to be, regardless of what might or might not be happening in anyone's personal life. There would be hair and makeup. A countdown from Sean, after which Peyton would say, "Good morning and thanks for joining us today," with exactly the right amount of gravitas and enthusiasm before skillfully leading them into the day's top stories. And there would be that feeling, the same one every day, that incredible high whenever the studio lights blazed hot on her face and the camera blinked green to indicate that she was being broadcast, live, into millions of American homes. The hours were barbaric and the workload crushing and the stress level sadistic, but she fucking *loved* it.

When the driver pulled into ANN's gated drop-off carport, a PA opened the car door. "Good morning, Peyton," chirped Sahara, a petite brunette with pockmarked skin but a winning smile. "This is for you." She handed Peyton a piping hot latte and led the way through the cavernous basement hallways to the elevator that would whisk them to the ninth floor. Peyton sensed nothing amiss in the girl's reaction to her.

"Thank you," Peyton said, taking a sip. "Did you have a good weekend?"

"I did, thank you. Did you?" Sahara blushed.

"Yes, it was very nice," Peyton lied.

Sahara stared at her feet. Suddenly, although they'd been having this same exchange for over a year now, the awkwardness between them was palpable. When the elevator doors opened, it felt like Sahara wanted to bolt.

"I'm just going to grab the latest briefings," she said, again without meeting Peyton's eyes. "I'll bring them to hair and makeup?"

"My desk is fine," Peyton said, and frowned as the girl speed-walked down the hall. Peyton dropped her bags in her corner office and walked into the adjoining closet, flipping on the lights as she did. Strange that no one had done that yet, she thought, as she approached the racks of jewel-toned dresses and suits. Although she was perfectly capable of choosing an outfit on her own, typically Bev or Roger liked to wander by and weigh in. From a rack toward the back, she pulled an emerald-green sheath dress in a heavy viscose with the slightest of sweetheart necklines and grabbed a pair of coordinating green pumps from the wall of shoeboxes. She changed quickly in her office and, grabbing the papers Sahara had left on her desk, walked to hair and makeup.

People waved and said good morning, as usual, as she walked past their desks, but there was a certain tension she couldn't ignore. One producer, an overconfident twenty-something man fresh from their rival network, also asked how her weekend was. Was he being friendly, or was that passive-aggressive? They were all polite and professional, but Peyton couldn't escape the feeling that everyone from the interns to the senior producers was watching her, like she might crack at any moment. They'd always watched her—she was the talent, who typically got coddled and accommodated on set—but this was a different kind of watching, a careful, nervous one, and she could feel her back and chest grow damp with sweat.

When she got to hair and makeup, she paused at the door, surprised to hear Isaac's name coming from inside.

"There's no way they're going to keep letting her on the air," a woman said. "Talk about conflict of interest." Peyton could tell from the voice that it was Bev, who'd been styling hair at ANN for a hundred years and had opinions on absolutely everything.

Roger, her assistant stylist, agreed. "I mean, Peyton covered the story the last go-round! And now Isaac . . ."

"It looks terrible," chimed in a third voice, Karen, the senior makeup artist and Peyton's favorite. "I feel so badly for her."

"Oh, come on! You think she didn't know?" Roger asked. "Does *your* spouse go around breaking the law without your knowing?"

Karen laughed. "If I could keep a spouse, he could do whatever he damn well pleased."

Peyton glanced down at her dress, which suddenly looked garish in the bright hallway lights. She took a deep breath, plastered on her bright TV smile, and swept into the room.

"Good morning, everyone!" she sang in her cheeriest voice.

"Peyton!" Karen said with surprise, as though Peyton didn't materialize at this exact time every morning.

"Happy Monday, everyone." She looked around conspiratorially and, lowering her voice, said, "Anyone been sexually harassed by my co-host yet today? No? Well, the day's still young."

The three of them laughed politely.

Peyton shivered. "Roger, how's your mother feeling? Happy to be out of the hospital?"

Roger nodded. "Much better. Thanks for asking."

There was a beat of silence, long enough for the unusual formality to register.

"Come, sit!" Roger said, his voice higher than normal. "I know you have a headlines meeting today, so let's get you in and out."

Lowering herself into her usual chair, Peyton held her breath as Roger pumped the foot pedal and raised her up.

"How was everyone's weekend?" Peyton asked, her eyes closed so Karen could start on her lids, as she usually did. "Give me all the dirt!"

No one responded. When Peyton opened her eyes, she saw Bev carefully examining her makeup brushes while Karen organized the already neat product bottles. The only sound was from one of the television monitors mounted on the ceiling, a commercial for Downy dryer sheets.

"Gorgeous Sunday, wasn't it?" Roger said. "I mean, when is it ever that warm in June?"

Peyton swiveled her head around. "The weather? We're really playing it like this?"

Roger giggled but wouldn't look at her. "I just—"

"Look, you all obviously heard about Isaac. I mean, there is probably no one left in the country who didn't hear about Isaac," Peyton said, finally exhaling. "Let's stop acting so weirdly. It's fine! I assure you, the entire thing was a giant misunderstanding, and it will all be cleared up momentarily. You don't have to feel awkward around me!"

Roger began to spray her hair with dry shampoo as Bev dabbed a contouring brush into a tray of deep plum eye shadow.

"You're all good, girl!" Bev said, tapping Peyton's brows with the back of her knuckle to indicate that Peyton should close her eyes. "We don't judge here!"

"Of course you do!" Peyton said, sounding more screechy than she intended. "That's why I love you all!"

"Fine," Roger said, switching on his blow-dryer. "We do judge. But not you! Or Isaac! He's a total sweetheart. There is no possible way that man would ever—"

Roger stopped talking mid-sentence, and the room went quiet enough that Peyton's eyes flew open.

"Sean!" she called from the chair. "Why are you creeping around there? Come in!"

"Morning, P," he said, looking pale.

"Sorry I texted you so late last night. I couldn't sleep, surprise, surprise. Listen, I couldn't stop thinking about Naomi. Did she . . ." Peyton stopped. Why was he looking at her like that?

"Come to my office for a quick minute?" Sean said.

"Can it wait until we're done here?" Peyton asked. "I was already a tad behind, and if they don't get a chance to really spackle it on today, I'm going to scare the viewers."

"Sorry, P, it, uh, can't wait."

Before Peyton could react, Bev, Roger, and Karen all started rushing to the door.

"I'm going to grab some coffee. You two want?" Bev asked.

Roger and Karen each murmured something indistinguishable about either a bathroom visit or another urgent errand, and in a flash, all three had vanished.

Peyton peered at Sean. His red hair was nearly the same shade as Gabe's, but Sean wore his close-cropped and neat, trimmed every three weeks to the day. Typically, he was an immaculate dresser, but today his button-down was already wrinkled and slightly untucked, and she noticed he had day-old stubble, something she had never seen before.

"Are you okay?" she asked. "Is it Naomi?" Judging from his grave expression, Peyton worried his daughter might be sick.

He shook his head.

"My god, you look like shit. Talk to me."

"They're pulling you."

"Pulling me? *When?* You can't be serious. Sean, are you serious?"

"Today. I just got the call, I'm so sorry, P, you know this isn't my—"

"Wait—like, after today's broadcast, right?" She checked her watch. "I'm on in nineteen minutes."

Sean looked down.

"Joseph, that bastard," she said through gritted teeth. "He did this on purpose. Had me come all the way in. . . . I'm dressed! Sitting for hair and makeup and *now* he decides to pull the plug? Is that even *legal*?"

"I really don't know anything beyond what they told me, which was: she doesn't go on today." He held his hands up in surrender. "I think they were still in a meeting about it until minutes ago."

"A meeting? A goddamn *meeting*? At four-fucking-thirty in the morning?" Peyton started to pace. "What am I supposed to do now?"

Sean looked even more pained. "I guess go home? I'm sure you'll be hearing from him soon."

"Go *home*?"

"I'm sorry, P. I really am. I know Isaac and—"

She covered her eyes with one hand, held the other outstretched. "Please."

"Don't shoot the messenger—you know what our friendship means to me, which is why I'm giving it to you straight, why I always have: This may not be fair, or even legal—I'm not an expert on that end of it—but this"—he waved his hands—"shouldn't be surprising. You are at the center of a national . . . story. You're going to have to let it play itself out for a bit."

"And what does that mean exactly?"

"Peyton, you're upset, and I get it. This show is nothing without you, and everyone knows *you're* the reason ANN moved into the top slot. The rapport you and Jim have on the air—which I recognize is horseshit in real life—is impossible to replicate. I've got to get back to the control room now, but I'll tell Sahara to get you a car. Call me the second the show is over, okay? Or forget it, I'll call you. Answer your phone!" He squeezed her shoulder, and before she could say another word, Sean was gone.

Dizzy, almost drunk, Peyton stumbled out of makeup and nearly ran into Karen, who was rounding the corner.

"Everything okay?" Karen asked.

Peyton answered only with a maniacal laugh and wobbled toward her office on the nearly five-inch heels. The digital banner clock above her desk blared the time, 4:47 A.M., and both her office and cell phone were ringing insistently.

Leave, leave, leave, she urged herself, as she cast about her office, which typically felt like a sanctuary from the mayhem but in the last thirty seconds had started to feel like a coffin. *Move, move, move.* She grabbed her Goyard tote, spilling the small amount of coffee still left in her cup onto the floor. No matter. Someone else could deal with that. Into the tote she threw her phone, a bottle of kombucha from her mini fridge, and the framed photo of Max and Isaac that she'd kept on her desk through every job since Max was born: in it, Max was a week old and naked, and Isaac was holding her entire body in the palms of his two hands.

She careened into the hallway, where Sahara, looking terrified, waited.

"I've, um, called down for a car. It's waiting on the Fifty-first Street side, and, uh—"

Peyton ignored her and practically dove into the open elevator, where she stood facing the back wall for what felt like an endless hour until the doors blessedly shut. In the last few minutes her phone had only stopped ringing long enough for whoever was calling to redial. Digging it out of her bag, she saw that it was Kenneth.

"What the fuck is going on here?" she asked, in lieu of hello.

"Peyton, I've been trying to reach you for—"

"They didn't tell me until I was in makeup! Practically in front of the entire staff! Did you know about this?"

His voice was garbled, filled with static.

"Can you hear me? Ken?" She released a long, low guttural sound—an actual growl.

The elevator opened and she hobbled out, but there was never good reception on the windowless ground floor. "GRRRRRRRRR!"

Finally, she stepped outside into the still-dark morning and heard Ken's voice clearly. ". . . a process. I can't say that I'm shocked, to be perfectly honest, and I'm not trying to say 'I told you so,' but—"

A driver leapt out of the front seat of an idling Town Car when he saw Peyton and opened the back door, but she mouthed, "No, thank you," and kept walking despite the fact that she had no plan, no destination, and nothing was open.

Kenneth was still blathering on. ". . . get it all ironed out in the next couple days. Until then, keep a low profile and don't say anything to anyone."

"This is insane! Are they not aware I have a *contract*? That they can't just cancel me?"

"Peyton? It's Joseph on the other line, I'll call you back. . . ."

The call disconnected. Peyton rounded the corner to Rockefeller Center, which was deserted except for a few early commuters.

She sat on the edge of a fountain and texted her TV Moms group.

Guys! I just got basically thrown out of the studio! Can you even believe that!

Despite the early hour, the replies popped up immediately, but they were lukewarm at best.

Bummer

Sorry to hear that.

hope all is okay!

Hope all is okay? Peyton nearly threw her phone. All was clearly *not* okay, and where were her damn friends when she needed them? These were the women who had one another's backs when things went down at work, when bosses got lecherous or co-workers snippy or hard-won raises didn't materialize. But now, her entire world had seemed to spin off its axis the last forty-eight hours and not one of them actually *called*. Images flashed in her mind: Max looking devastated; her typically placid husband staring at her in anger; even Nisha, her unflappable friend, who could barely bring herself to look Peyton in the eye. Her throat tightened and she willed herself not to cry.

She hailed a cab and went back to the apartment. Isaac and Max were still asleep. A quick text to Nisha went unanswered, but as Peyton was pouring a cup of coffee, her phone rang.

"I'm sorry, did my text wake you?" she asked Nisha.

"Wake me? It's quarter to six. What kind of life of leisure do you think I lead?"

"Nisha, they pulled me off the air today! Can you believe that? I wasn't the one who was arrested!"

"What did they say, exactly?"

"There wasn't a lot of detail. I was already in hair and makeup, and the EP came in and said that corporate didn't want me to go on today. That I should go home and they'll be in touch 'in a few days.'"

Nisha was silent.

"Are you there?" Peyton asked.

"I can't say I'm surprised."

"You're not surprised? That they yanked me from the air twenty minutes before I was going live? Seriously?"

"Listen, this has to run its course—this is how all these things work. I stand by what I said on Saturday: Time to lie low. Distance yourself from Isaac. Can you go anywhere for a week or two? Hamptons? The Vineyard? You must know someone with a house on Nantucket?"

Peyton groaned and shook her head. This was really happening, then. She was off-air. Her mind ran through her friends and the singular lack of offers of help and support since Friday. She glanced toward Max's closed bedroom door. "Max is leaving this week to spend the summer at my sister's house in Paradise. . . ."

"Great! Go with her! That's perfect, actually. Close enough that you can hop back when needed, but out of the city and out of the spotlight."

"She won't be thrilled if I tag along. And I'm not sure my sister would—"

A high-pitched scream came through the phone. "Samuel! How many times do I have to tell you not to bite your brother? Peyton? Listen. I don't know how else to put this, but you don't seem to understand that this whole thing isn't just going to disappear. You may not have been the one on the news, but in the court of public opinion—the one that really matters, I'd argue—you and Isaac are interchangeable."

Peyton opened her mouth to respond, but Nisha cut her off.

"P, I'm sorry, I've got to run. It's like *Lord of the Flies* in my kitchen right now."

"Of course, I'm sorry, thanks so much for—"

Nisha had already hung up. Before she could think too much about it, Peyton called Skye.

"Shouldn't you be on air right now?" Skye asked when she answered, instead of saying hello.

"Yes, that's exactly where I should be. Listen, quick question: What do you think about me coming to Paradise for a few weeks? Maybe even the summer?" she asked, half hoping that Skye would veto the whole thing, or tell her it was a crazy idea.

"Well, it's an easy commute, especially when you've got a car service. And of course it would be nice to spend some time together without one of us having to drive forty minutes home afterward. Mom would love it." Skye paused. "Would Isaac come too?"

Peyton pretended like she hadn't heard the question. "Should I try to rent something? I can't very well crash in on you guys the whole summer. That way Max could stay with me, too, which I'm sure would thrill her to no end."

"One of Gabe's partners has a cottage he rents out."

While Peyton considered that, Skye added, "His wife emailed a big group. Their tenants fell through or something; I'm sure they'd be very flexible. Max could stay with us, or you guys, or go back and forth. Think how lovely it would be for the girls."

"It would be nice to have everyone together," Peyton said automatically, although she couldn't believe she was having a serious conversation about moving to *the suburbs* for the summer. Peyton poured herself more coffee. "Send me the info?"

"Will do. It's nothing fancy, so you know."

"'Nothing fancy' as in 'You're probably not going to love the countertops' or 'nothing fancy' as in 'It's decorated with mallards and plaid and you might even find a cat or two'?"

Skye laughed. "Probably the latter."

"Terrific. Well, considering it's already late June, my network has canceled me, and my family is barely speaking to me, it will have to do."

"Peyton Marcus does not get canceled!" Skye said.

"Tell that to ANN. Apparently I went from beloved morning host to persona non grata in zero point two seconds."

"Come here this summer. We'll get you back into fighting shape, okay? Check your email, I'm sending it right now."

They hung up. Realizing she was starving, Peyton settled on a whole pineapple that she'd purchased despite not knowing how to cut the damn thing. As she hacked at it, she thought of Isaac, his wanting to separate. She thought about Max, whose entire life had been turned upside down, and about Skye, who still didn't know the whole truth. She thought about Nisha, who had reminded her as she was leaving that this, too, shall pass. *This too shall pass,* Peyton murmured to herself, carving the pineapple into pieces, growing angrier and angrier as she repeated it. *This too shall pass.* What the fuck did that even mean? Of course this too would pass, Peyton thought. But would any of them survive it? *This too shall pass.* What was this going to do to her family, to the rest of their lives? To Isaac's real estate career? Max's reputation, her very future? *Huh, Nisha? Where are all your brilliant clichés for* that? The knife sliced into Peyton's thumb, near the knuckle. Peyton knew she should clean it, or at least try to stem the bleeding, but she could only stand still and cry as the blood and tears blurred, a long quivering flow of sadness.

11

Chicken Dance

Max heard the knock on the front door from her room, and she knew it was Peter, the doorman, with a luggage cart. "Mrs. Marcus," she heard him say. "Whenever you're ready."

"Max! We're ready!" her mother yelled, despite the fact that Max was neither far away nor deaf. How had this happened? On top of all the other shit, how had her perfect summer gotten hijacked?

"Coming," she muttered, tossing a few last-minute things into her oversized canvas tote bag: her travel case of watercolors and brushes; a massive pouch of chargers and backup batteries for her cameras and laptop; the bunny and the kangaroo she'd slept with since she was a child. She could hear her mom and the doorman loading up the cart.

"Mackenzie Marcus!" Peyton yelled.

"I'm on my freaking way!" she screamed, much louder and slightly more maniacally than she'd intended. She was briefly embarrassed to sound like a lunatic in front of Peter, but she figured her yelling voice was probably not a secret to her doorman.

Max walked into the foyer and watched with a small level of satisfaction as her mother took in her outfit. Ripped boyfriend jeans (not a Peyton fave), old Grateful Dead T-shirt of her dad's (even less of a Peyton fave), and the biggest offenders of all, her trusty old Doc

Martens. She was too old for this behavior and she knew it. Max didn't even like the boots anymore, and no doubt would've left them in New York for the summer if they didn't piss off her mother so effectively.

"Honey, are you ready?" her mom asked.

"I'm standing here, aren't I?"

Her father appeared in the hallway. He'd been wearing the same sweatpants and shuffling around the apartment in the week since the arrest. Max had barely said a dozen words to him, which she knew he found excruciatingly painful, but she didn't know where to start.

"I'm going to miss you, kiddo," he said, looking at her with sad eyes.

Max said nothing.

"I thought you'd be happy escaping here—and me."

"She's annoyed I'm going too," her mother announced.

Max wanted to object or at least half-heartedly deny, but she couldn't. There was a moment of awkward silence before her mom said, "But that's okay! Because we're going to have a great time. I can't believe it's the summer before college. The last time I can order you around and watch you sleep and be a hovering, annoying mom."

"Yep. Last one," Max murmured. She sneaked a look at her father, who was staring at her with a look in his eyes she couldn't quite identify.

"Max?" he said quietly. "I love you, sweetheart. I know you're angry."

She let him kiss her cheek, and it took all her willpower not to throw her arms around his neck. It was so confusing, loving him so much and being so angry with him, too.

"I'm going to wait in the lobby," Max announced. She took the elevator downstairs and wondered what the goodbye between her parents looked like. She hadn't heard any outright screaming the last week, but tense voices had emerged at times from behind their closed bedroom door. Not in a million years had she ever considered her parents would get divorced—they were almost nauseatingly affectionate with each other—but that was before. Now, who knew? They were separating for the summer, no matter what she called it.

Her mother appeared, eyes unmistakably puffy, and motioned for Max to get in the car. Peter tried to hand Peyton a bundle of mail, but Peyton was oblivious, so Max grabbed the pile and popped it in her backpack. She climbed into the front seat and watched as her mother painstakingly adjusted the seat and the mirror.

"You have a license, right?" Max asked. She'd wanted to lighten the mood, but her joke came out sounding more obnoxious than she'd intended.

"Of course I do!" Peyton snapped.

"I only meant that Dad always drives."

"Well, that's just because he likes to drive, not because I don't know how." Her mom steered their Audi onto Park Avenue and narrowly avoided clipping a yellow taxi's bumper.

"Jesus, Mom!" Max said, instantly feeling badly.

But her mother had set her jaw in that determined way, the one that announced to the world that she had zero fucks to give.

"Aw, this kitchen is so sweet," Aunt Skye said as she ran her hand over the butcher block countertop.

"It's very . . . antique," Peyton said, rooting around, looking for a bread knife.

"I love that it's rustic," Max said, admiring the painted green cabinets with their elaborate arched carvings. "It feels homey."

"That's one word for it," her mother said.

Skye pointed up. "Look at that cross-beamed ceiling. I've never seen anything like it."

Her mother began to slice the bagels they'd brought from the city. Peyton brought them, despite the fact that she judged bagels to be as calorically destructive as Big Macs and probably hadn't eaten one in twenty years. If ever.

"I love this house," Max said. "It has charm. I love that it doesn't look exactly like every other house, the way our apartment does. It's not fifty shades of gray."

"Do you like the cobwebs, too?" her mother asked.

"Peyton!" Skye admonished. "It's a summer cottage, it's meant to feel like the country!"

"Well, it succeeds."

"How long until the fireworks?" Aurora asked from her perch on one of the wicker barstools.

Skye walked over and stroked her daughter's cheek with the back of her hand. "Not until it's dark out tonight, chickpea. You're excited, aren't you?"

"Yes, I can't wait!" Aurora squealed. "It's my first real ones."

"Just a minute," Max said with exaggerated seriousness, scooting in next to her cousin. She looked at Skye but pointed at Aurora. "*She's* coming with us tonight to the fireworks? After dark? Is she even old enough?"

Skye nodded solemnly. "She is."

"I am! I really am! And by the time we get home, it's going to be two hours after my bedtime!"

"Maybe even three," Max whispered, smiling as the little girl's eyes widened.

Aurora climbed onto Max's lap and rested her head against her shoulder, and in a second Max was transported back seven summers, after her failed sleep-away-camp experiment, when Aurora was only a baby and Max would hold her for hours, trying to soothe her colicky cries. A few times she had given up and cried right along with her, which had been oddly cathartic. Often they would fall asleep together, curled on the couch or the shaggy carpet in Aurora's room, and Max would feel warmer and safer than she could ever remember.

Max's first time at sleep-away camp had been an epic fail. Nobody had forced her to go that first summer—in fact, her dad actively tried to talk her out of it—but she was ten, and living in the city, and had two parents with demanding full-time jobs. All of her day-camp friends were going. All of her school friends who didn't have summer houses on Nantucket or Montauk were going. The videos online sure made it look awesome, what with the zip lines and the horseback riding and the waterskiing and the s'mores. Smiling girls who made friendship bracelets and braided one another's hair filled the catalogues that arrived like magic at her apartment. They spoke of "forever friends" and "my summer home" and "live ten for two," and Max would study them and think how wonderful it all looked. And, as she soon found out, it wasn't false advertising: everything really *was* wonderful. There were more activities to try than she'd ever imagined, her bunkmates were almost all sweet and funny, and the food was even better than it looked in the pictures. No one sat across the table from you and commented on what you ate, or how much, or whether or not it was healthy. No one cared what you wore or how your hair looked. But none of that prevented or stopped Max's crushing homesickness. It had hit her on the third or fourth day and increased over the next two weeks. By the middle of the third week—a time when the last holdouts had gotten over missing home—Max was more miserable than when she started. Soon even the camp director agreed it was time to go home, that it might be best to wait and try again the following summer, and Max was ecstatic until the woman returned to her bunk and told her, grim faced, that her parents had just taken off for their long-planned two-week vacation in Greece.

She'd cried nearly the entire night, so much so that when Uncle Gabe had shown up in the camp's office the following morning, Max thought she was hallucinating. He spent the six-hour car ride from Maine to Paradise telling her all about the little girl that he and Skye had adopted, how they'd gotten the call out of the blue a few weeks earlier and could still barely believe it themselves. When Max walked into their house and saw Aunt Skye feeding a fussy six-week-old Aurora a bottle, she started crying all over again. She'd always wanted a little brother or sister. And now, a cousin! For the next two weeks Gabe and Skye took care of Max like she was their own daughter, feeding her home-cooked meals and snuggling with her in front of the TV, and Max learned how to take care of Aurora, helping with bottles and diaper changes and bath time. When her parents returned from Greece, Max refused to leave Paradise, which was just as well because Max's nanny had gone home to visit her own family for the summer and both Peyton and Isaac needed to get back to work. Max never again went back to camp, but she returned to Paradise every summer after that.

"Max?" She felt a tug on her hair and looked down at Aurora. "Are fireworks scary?"

"Scary? No, sweet girl, they're beautiful! Sometimes they make a loud boom, but that's part of the fun. I think you're going to love them."

Max plucked a plain bagel for Aurora and a salt bagel for herself. She was spreading the cream cheese when she heard a strangled bark come from outside.

"Where's Cookie?" she asked, jumping up in panic, her bagel falling face-down to the floor. The entire property was gated, so they'd let Cookie out to run free, but suddenly Max was filled with visions of rabid raccoons, coyotes, and foxes, all determined to find and eat her snack-sized pup.

Cookie's growl, which was surprisingly threatening for a four-pound dog, grew louder as Max ran, but almost immediately Max could see that Cookie was the hunter, not the hunted. A dozen or so chickens toddled around, in and out of bushes, clucking and pecking and occasionally flapping, except for the one large hen Cookie had backed up against a tree with a snarl and her bared, miniature teeth.

"Cookie!" Max scolded, reaching down to scoop him up. "No hurting the chickens!"

Aurora was right behind her. "You have chickens?"

Max frowned. "I don't think these are ours?"

Peyton ran outside. "I see you've met our new summer residents. Aurora, Max, meet the Ladies."

"I'm sorry, the what?" Max asked.

"The Ladies! I'll leave it to you two to name them, but they're all ours through August."

Skye stepped from the porch into the grass and shielded her eyes from the sun. "What did you say?"

"She's crazy, right?" Max said, as though her mother wasn't standing right there.

"What? I heard you all talking about getting chickens this summer. Well, I went ahead and made it happen," Peyton said, with a sweep of her arm.

Only then did Max notice the coop, which looked like a small-scale Frank Gehry house built around the base of a massive European beech tree. It was whitewashed like a real home and had two floors, a lofted area with a balcony, and wide swaths of screened areas for the chickens to enjoy the fresh outdoors. There were window boxes filled with impatiens and a pair of small French doors in front. The hens themselves came in assorted colors and shapes, each impeccably groomed and capped with lipstick-red combs atop their constantly pecking heads. Lined up side by side, they looked like the Victoria's Secret Angels of chickens.

"I love them!" Aurora squealed, and started to chase a beautiful jet-black hen that ran with surprising agility.

Aunt Skye laughed so hard that she was nearly doubled over.

Max's mother shrugged, clearly delighted. "Pretty nice setup, huh? It's all wired, with heaters or air conditioners or whatever. And of course there's a Nest Cam so we can all watch them from our phones. The farmer recommended a nice lady in town who will make them organic food, so that's all squared away."

Max couldn't help it. Despite herself, she started to laugh. And soon, like Aunt Skye, she had tears streaming down her cheeks. "Mom, tell me this is a joke. You *rented* the chickens? You cannot be serious."

Her mother smiled. "We are in a suburb where three-year-olds have their own chess coaches. You think it was hard to find a few rental chickens?"

Later that night, as Max was tying a towel around her wet hair, she heard an errant cluck from below her window and started laughing all over again. Yes, of course she'd rather be staying at Skye's house as she'd been every summer, but her mother was trying, she had to give her that. Their cottage was sweet, and she loved that her room had a built-in window seat. The chickens were hysterical. And at least so far, her mom wasn't being as controlling as humanly possible. The fireworks, which Max would have skipped if it weren't for Aurora, turned out to be great. Not the actual show—that had to be pretty much the same in every town across America—but the experience of packing a picnic and taking it to the local high school field and eating under the stars. It all felt so wholesome, so all-American, such a welcome departure from city life. As usual, a few people had recognized her mom, but they'd been chill about it—no selfie requests, and no reference whatsoever to her dad's recent legal trouble. Max was accustomed to being the plus-one to her famous mom, but she had dreaded the day someone recognized her as the girl who needed her father to pay her way into college.

She pulled on an oversized T-shirt and climbed into the metal-framed twin bed with her laptop. As Max scrolled through her daily footage, trying to figure out which parts to edit together, she decided to stick to the chickens. Everyone would be doing Fourth-related posts, and was there anything less interesting than watching someone else's fireworks show? Maybe someone else's concert experience, but it was a close call. She'd located a hysterically funny meme of Trump doing the chicken dance in his boxers when her FaceTime rang.

"Hi!" she said to Brynn when her friend's face appeared on her screen. "Wait—it's daytime there. Are you behind or ahead of us? I can't ever remember."

Brynn laughed, which made it look like the freckles on her face were blending together to create a single cohesive tan. "Ahead. It's the next day already here. So, guess what? You've gone global!"

Max felt an awful sensation in her stomach, similar to when she rode that horrid swinging pirate ship ride at amusement parks. "Global?"

Brynn held up a newspaper. It was covered in indecipherable Chinese characters, but the picture was unmistakable: it was her senior portrait, and it was placed directly next to her mother's publicity headshot.

"Oh, fuck me," Max said.

"What? Don't they say all publicity is good publicity?"

"My mother keeps repeating the same trite thing about how the news cycle will forget all about this soon, blah, blah, blah. But my fucking god, it's been over a week, and they're now writing about it in *Asia*? This really sucks."

"Sorry," Brynn said. "I hate to even ask, but have you considered what you're going to tell people when you actually get to campus?"

Max yanked her backpack into bed, ferreting through it for her headphones. "What do you mean?"

"I mean, *I* know you had the grades and the scores to get into Princeton on your own, but no one *there* is going to think so."

Max exhaled. "What can I do? Am I supposed to walk around with a giant poster of my GPA and my SATs? Have them tattooed on my forehead? I mean, people will think whatever they're going to think." She wondered if Brynn was buying her bravado.

"Totally," Brynn said. "Although for the record, I think you should bail on the whole thing and come with me."

"I tried that already," Max said, "and my parents flipped the F out. Said you were entitled to a gap year because your parents moved you to a foreign country for your senior year. But I, apparently, am not."

The jumble of mail that the doorman had given her when they were leaving tumbled out from her backpack when she removed her headphones, and Max began to sort it into piles for her parents.

"Does everyone get this many catalogues?" she murmured as she thumbed through the Sharper Image one. "Did you know they sell vibrators on, like, every page? They don't even try to pretend they're something else."

Brynn laughed. "There's a girl here who wears that Goop necklace one? And just in case anyone isn't sure what it is, she tells them. It's like, okay, we got it, you're super into self-pleasure. Good for you."

As Max sorted through the letters, an envelope with a bright orange return address stood out. Princeton. It was probably another announcement of some Orientation Week activity, or an invitation to meet incoming students from her area at another picnic or BBQ. Every few weeks since she'd been accepted, Max had received some type of communication from the school, and each time she felt her initial apprehension disappear a tiny bit more. There were just *so many* incredible opportunities, classes, professors, programs. Despite her initial misgivings that Princeton would be a mere extension of Milford, the students in the photos looked like a glorious mix of sizes and shapes and colors. Although she'd never admit it to her parents, Max now had a very good feeling about the place they'd pressured her so intensely to attend.

But what if it wasn't a picnic save-the-date or an invite to coffee with the Fine Arts department heads? Her breath quickened. What if this was the notification she'd been secretly terrified of receiving?

She tore open the envelope and started to scan.

Dear Ms. Marcus,

This past December we were pleased to offer you admission to the entering freshman class. This offer was extended on the basis of your superior academic record and your standout application. However, as new information regarding your admissions process has come to light, I'm afraid I have no choice but to rescind your admission to Princeton University.

"Oh my god," Max breathed. Her stomach roiled.

"What are you reading?" Brynn squinted into her own screen. "Who's it from?"

"I'm going to throw up."

Brynn continued to plead for information, but Max kept reading.

Be assured that we will also be addressing the accused party on the Princeton Board of Trustees, as new information continues to emerge. Princeton prides itself on being an institution of higher learning that is based on honesty, fairness, and, above all else, integrity.

Please accept our best wishes for your future academic endeavors.

Sincerely,
Patricia Palmer, PhD,
Dean of Admissions for Princeton University

Max read it once, then twice and, to be absolutely certain, a third time. She didn't remember hanging up on Brynn, but the screen had gone dark. *Ohmigod, ohmigod, ohmigod.* The word reverberated in her head as the nausea intensified. *This isn't happening, it can't be happening.* But of course, it was. She read the letter one more time, but none of the words changed. Stumbling out of bed and toward the bathroom, she made it with only a second or two to spare before the contents of her stomach came hurling up. When finally the vomiting subsided, she slumped to the floor next to the toilet, back against the wall, and waited for the numbness to follow.

12

My Friends Don't Woo-Hoo

The sweat poured down her face and chest and collected in a tiny pool between her breasts. Finally, blessedly, her Apple Watch flashed the indication that she had completed her exercise ring for the day.

"Thank god," Peyton murmured, as she slowed to a walk. She was only a quarter mile from Skye's house, but she'd be damned if she was going to run another foot. By the time she rang her sister's doorbell, it felt like the blazing mid-morning sun was crisping her skin.

"Skye? You here?" Peyton asked, pushing open the front door when no one answered. "Aurora?"

A cartoon was playing in the family room, and breakfast dishes were still out on the kitchen table, but there was no sign of her niece or sister. Peyton climbed the stairs.

"Anyone home?" she called.

"My room!" Skye yelled back.

Peyton walked to the end of the hallway and into Skye and Gabe's room, which had a chic, boho vibe, just like her sister. The mismatched, layered vintage rugs and hanging rope chair somehow looked high-concept, and the beautiful carved-wood headboard reached toward the ceiling and served as the perfect backdrop to an assortment of woven, embroidered, and fringed throw pillows in varying shades of brown, rose, and plum. In one corner a lone prickly pear cactus jutted from an enormous terra-cotta pot.

"Whoa!" Peyton said when she saw Skye, who was applying lipstick at a whitewashed, shabby-chic vanity. "What's going on here?"

"I'm meeting a bunch of local moms today to talk about the girls' residence."

"Oooooh, let me come!"

Skye turned around, frowning. "Why would you want to? These things are pretty awful. I have to hit them up for money without seeming like I'm hitting them up for money."

Peyton flung herself on the bed. "That's one of my superpowers! Plus, I have nothing better to do."

"Was it weird not going to work today? I can't remember the last time you missed a broadcast." Skye rubbed something on her cheeks; Peyton wanted to tell her it was too shimmery for morning time.

"Pouty Vivian with her bass lips and blinding veneers was in my seat this morning." Peyton picked up a paperback from Skye's night table and put it back again. "Whatever. It's only temporary. A few days, at most. I'm sure I'll be back on the air by the end of next week."

Skye was silent in that quietly judgy way of hers that always made Peyton want to scream.

"Take me," Peyton said. "I'll help you."

"No."

"Come on! I want to meet your friends! Will Esther be there? I haven't seen her in ages."

Skye snorted. "No, she's at *work*. Plus, this isn't her crowd. It's not my crowd, either. My friends don't woo-hoo."

"Huh?" Peyton asked.

"You'll see what I mean."

Peyton jumped off the bed. "I'm coming!"

"I'm leaving in two minutes, and you're not even dressed."

"You're telling me these Paradise women won't welcome someone in workout clothes? It's their *uniform*. It actually makes me very accessible, I think."

Skye walked out of the bedroom and Peyton followed her.

"Where's Aurora?"

"Playdate. I have to pick her up at twelve." Skye grabbed her car keys from the table in the mudroom and turned to Peyton. "Are you serious? You actually want to come? Even with everything that's going on? What happened to lying low?"

Peyton shoved past her sister to the garage, where she climbed into the passenger seat of the Subaru and called, "What are we waiting for?"

Shaking her head, Skye climbed in beside her. "They'll be so impressed. A real, live celebrity in their midst."

"See? That's the spirit!"

Skye backed out and started to navigate through the leafy streets. "My god, I'm dreading this so much."

"Don't stress! These things are easy. Remember, keep it light. Be appreciative. Don't pressure. Float the creation of a possible board—these women love boards!"

"That's a really good idea."

"If you approach it as primarily an update and not a solicitation, they'll feel respected and respond better. But if they do seem amenable—and trust me, they also *looooove* giving away money for public credit—keep the focus on tangible items they can buy rather than the poverty of the recipient children. Shopping: fun. Poverty: depressing."

Skye laughed. They pulled into the sweeping circular driveway and past a half dozen Land Rovers and Tesla SUVs—the same ones from the school, or maybe different ones entirely. "I can do this," she said.

"You can do this! You've already purchased the house—all from raised funds! That's so impressive. Now you show them how they can *decorate* it!"

"I still need the real cash from Henry to do all the construction. I mean, this is a small, run-down family home and it needs to be converted to a residence where eight girls and two housemothers can sleep, study, and eat. There's a lot of work to be done from a conversion standpoint and—"

"*Boring!* You are boring me! That all might be true, but I want to hear about fluffy towels and cute duvet covers, not plywood and particleboard. Next!"

"Okay, I hear you. Can I tell them that their donations will also go toward hiring the necessary staff and helping with weekend transportation for—"

Peyton pressed both hands against her ears and started humming loudly.

"Gotcha. Stick to back-to-school clothes and throw pillows."

"Ding, ding, ding!"

After she parked in front of a Suburban covered in stickers from Nantucket, Martha's Vineyard, and Cape Cod—with an I ♥ MY SWEET LAXER and a HOCKEY MOM thrown in—Skye shot Peyton a warning look and rang the doorbell.

"What's that look for?" Peyton asked innocently.

"Behave yourself," Skye said.

"Hiiiii!" sang Vanessa, the homeowner, as she swung open the door, a madly yipping Maltese under her arm. Her hair was white-blond down to her pink scalp, the kind of blond you just knew was natural, and her body was long and muscular. And of course, she wore high-waisted bike shorts, a too-cropped-for-her-age tank, and a pair of $200 sneakers in an aggressive shade of hot pink.

Peyton discreetly poked her sister in the side.

"Hi!" Skye sang back, too loudly. "I hope you don't mind, but my sister wanted to tag along."

"Oh my, that's *right*! I totally forgot your sister was Peyton Marcus," she lied, as though this wasn't the primary biographical fact most women in Paradise filed away for Skye—or that Peyton wasn't standing right there.

"Can I just say, I *love* your tank? I could never pull it off, what with my crazy short torso," Peyton said, reaching out to tap Vanessa's shirt. "But it looks *so* good on you. My god, woman, what's your secret?"

Vanessa's white scalp flamed red, and she couldn't mask her delight. "Stop it! You are so amazing on TV," she breathed, not even bothering to hide her awe. "I mean, on mornings when I'm not at the gym, I, like, never miss your show. Oh, look at me, I'm so rude. Come in, come in!"

Vanessa led them into an expansive open space, where the Paradise Kitchen (white marble countertops, double Miele dishwashers, Viking stove with cherry-red knobs) gave way to a Paradise Family Room (gas-burning fireplace, Restoration Hardware Cloud sectional in gray linen, wall-mounted TV the size of a mattress). Vanessa had also clearly abided by the Paradise Rules of Home Decor and proudly displayed Diptyque candles, fur throws, a gorgeously styled bookcase that contained no actual books, and a family photo collage featuring towheaded children frolicking in autumn leaves, on New England beaches, and on puzzlingly uncrowded ski slopes. All four kids were so universally gorgeous—so unnervingly without flaws—that one couldn't be faulted for wondering if Vanessa had simply failed to remove the frames' stock photos before hanging them.

Skye had told Peyton in the car that the six women in attendance were all generous donors and zealous fundraisers. Together they'd helped Skye raise enough money to purchase the residence—no small feat even considering the home was a bit run-down and located close to the border of New Rochelle, a less desirable town. These women were ballbusters, accustomed to getting exactly what they demanded, whether that was a particular teacher for their fourth grader, a seven o'clock reservation on a completely booked Saturday, or a check toward the "really important cause" of their choice. Among them they had an MD, two JDs, a PhD, twenty children, and god knew how many millions. They had dated celebrities and married the most eligible men. They regularly traveled to exotic countries, could speak intelligently on current events, could recommend "the very best" person to do anything: landscape the yard, book first-class tickets on miles, eliminate that irritating pocket of fat between bra strap and underarm. They instinctively knew what to wear to every event, whether it was a fundraiser gala, a moms' night out, or a Sunday afternoon bar mitzvah. Their skin was smooth and plump thanks to Botox every ninety days, Juvéderm every six months, and five-hundred-dollar creams as often as needed. They could throw an elegant dinner party for twelve with two hours' notice. "Sold out," "booked," or "unavailable" simply didn't apply to them. Neither did waiting in lines of any kind. They expended stupendous amounts of time, money, and effort ensuring that their children had the very best of everything, including but not limited to an endless stream of therapists and services for young children with no discernible diagnoses; Invisalign for every tween daughter who complained about the social suicide of metal braces; new luxury SUVs—chosen for their "safety features"—for every freshly minted teenage driver; and the usual array of expensive electronics, designer clothes, and mind-blowing vacations. And while Skye was put off and intimidated by these women, she admired their ruthless determination.

"Hi, everyone," Skye said, a little timidly.

The women turned and cheered. "Woo-hoo! Welcome!" they called, as if Skye had just walked in with a giant platter of margaritas and diamond jewelry.

"Look who we have here!" Vanessa called like a charity auctioneer. "The one, the only, Peyton Marcus!"

Mimosa glasses froze in midair; conversations stopped midsentence. Every woman turned and beamed like Oprah had just gifted them a new car.

"Hi, y'all!" Peyton drawled, despite the fact that she'd never lived one minute of her thirty-nine years south of Pennsylvania. "Thanks for letting me crash your party today. My sister here tells me that you are literally *the* most organized and influential group of women in town, so I forced her to let me tag along!"

A round of applause quickly turned into hoots and cheers. "Woo-hoo!" they called.

"We love you, Peyton!" a woman who was wearing bandages from a recent rhinoplasty called.

"I can tell, I already love y'all right back!" Peyton plopped herself on a couch right in the middle of two women, whose faces contorted with delight. "I'm here for the summer to enjoy the fresh country air, so I hope we can all get together again—maybe drinks at my place next time?"

Skye pressed her fingertips to her forehead.

"Woo-hoo!" one called.

"Totally in!" cried another.

"Done!" Peyton said. "Let's hear about the incredible things my sister is planning for the residence you all kindly made possible, and then we'll pick a date."

Skye accepted a mug of coffee from Vanessa and, after looking around for a place to sit, perched awkwardly on an ottoman. "Thanks so much for coming this morning. I know everyone's so busy and . . . well, I just really appreciate it."

"We're happy to help," said Laura, who'd made managing partner at Deutsche Bank before having a breakdown and quitting for good.

"I'm . . . so excited! Here, look at these updated plans," Skye said, flipping open her laptop and positioning it so everyone could see. Peyton willed her to focus on the fun stuff.

"This is the family room. It'll have a fireplace and a piano, so the girls can learn to play. Over here, we're going to knock down a wall to double the size of the existing kitchen. Upstairs, there will be four bedrooms, each with two beds and two desks, plus a fifth room for the housemothers. And it's not definite yet, but I'd love to finish the basement and fill it with beanbag chairs and loads of books—a place where they can entertain friends and just hang out."

Vanessa whistled. "It's looking incredible." She pointed first to a picture of the dilapidated house as it currently stood and then to Gabe's 3D rendering. "I can't believe you're going to go from that to this!"

"We are. Because of you!" Skye said. "Major construction costs plus staff salaries and insurance will be covered by an investor, and I'm hoping we can raise a bit more on top of that, maybe here today even for, um, the fun stuff like all the duvet covers and furry rugs and throw pillows, that kind of thing."

Skye sneaked a glance at Peyton, who was nodding encouragingly.

Rosemary, a mom of two who was pregnant with twins, asked, "Who's the investor?"

"It's a hedge fund owner who's based out of Rye," Skye said. "Apparently, he hired a firm to oversee his 'corporate responsibility'"—Skye air-quoted these two words—"and they advised that the fund make a public donation to a local charity, for goodwill. Presumably so they can't be accused of not caring while they rake in millions or billions?" She said this last part with a laugh, but no one laughed with her.

"Perfect." Laura nodded, sipping her mimosa. "Friend of Gabe's?"

Skye shook her head. "Actually, a friend of my brother-in-law's. They went to college together. Regardless, I'm so thrilled that—"

"So, a friend of your husband's?" Nicole asked, leaning toward Peyton.

The room fell silent; the air felt electric.

Peyton broke into her very brightest and warmest and most authentic fake TV smile. "Yes, Henry is a dear friend of Isaac's. They've known each other since their Princeton days." She paused. "You've all heard about the ridiculous accusations against my husband, yes?"

Peyton waited, nodding her head encouragingly, until all the women were nodding with her. She waved her hand like she was brushing away a pesky mosquito. "Obviously all a huge misunderstanding. You know how carried away the media can get, am I right?"

The women laughed, so delighted with Peyton's self-deprecation that they seemed entirely willing to overlook certain details, like the involvement of the FBI.

"Anyway," Peyton continued. "Henry's terrific. His company has made boatloads over the years, and I, for one, don't think he could have possibly chosen a more deserving project to support."

"Totally," Vanessa said, nodding. The others murmured their agreement.

The moment passed, and Peyton was relieved that no one followed up with more pressing questions about her personal life that she would have to artfully dodge. Instead, Skye scrolled through her

Pinterest boards and Houzz folders, showing the women her ideas for everything from bedspreads to backsplashes. They oohed and aahed, all experts at affirming one another's shopping acquisitions, while Skye showed them everything she'd already bought, and all the things left that she still needed to buy: great big piles of sheets and towels and backpacks and sneakers and desk supplies and kitchen appliances and toiletries and books and even small, individual faux fur rugs for next to each girl's bed.

"Skye?" Peyton asked in her cheeriest voice. "What do you think of having a vegetable garden installed in the backyard?"

"Oooooh, I love that idea!" Nicole said. "I have a guy who could install it. He's the best."

Peyton knew that Skye could picture it perfectly. Organic cucumbers and squash, more snap peas than anyone could eat. A healthy outdoor activity that the whole house could be involved in.

"I love it," Skye said, clapping her hands together. "Not only would a garden help with the grocery bill, but it would also be a great source of comfort and distraction to the girls, who will probably be homesick, at least in the beginning."

Vanessa added, "I'd be happy to talk to my contractor, see if we can't put in a little gazebo for shade, maybe a swinging bench? Thoughts?"

Before Peyton knew what was happening, she saw her sister's eyes well up. "I only cry for good things, I swear," Skye said, wiping away tears. "Stick me at a funeral, and I can't cry to save my life."

The women laughed politely and soon someone changed the topic to travel soccer. Peyton excused herself, and from the privacy of Vanessa's Paradise Powder Room—potted orchid, monogrammed guest towels, Molton Brown hand soap—she looked at her reflection in the mirror and smiled. It felt so good to help Skye in this small way.

Skye was waiting for her outside the bathroom. She threw her arms around her sister. "Thank you," she said. "You were amazing."

Raucous laughter came from the living room.

Skye started to walk back toward the group, but Peyton grabbed her arm. "I don't do travel soccer. I don't do preschool playground politics. I'd be very happy to do who's sleeping with whom, but that's not what they're discussing right now. Get me out of here."

Skye laughed. "Copy that. Extraction in ten."

"Make it five."

"Meet me in the car; I'll do the goodbyes."

The ride home felt like old times: Peyton loved the two of them laughing together, recounting the absurdity of the morning, how *perfect* these suburban women appeared, at least on the outside.

"Thanks again," Skye said, pulling into Peyton's driveway. "You were brilliant in there."

Peyton climbed out and bowed. "It's just knowing your audience. Talk later?"

Peyton called out Max's name as she walked in the front door, and again as she climbed the stairs to take a shower.

"Honey? You home?" She peered into Max's room, but it was empty. Her bed was a rumpled, unmade mess, and there were papers strewn all over the desk, which was extremely out of character for her typically meticulous daughter.

"Max?" Peyton walked into the room and picked up the first thing she saw, an opened but empty envelope from Princeton. With a rising sense of dread, she cast around the room until her eyes found a crumpled piece of paper on Max's desk chair. It only took a few seconds to read the first couple of sentences, which told her everything she needed to know.

"Max! Mackenzie!" she screamed, flying back down the stairs. When had Max gotten the letter? How could she not have told her? Peyton checked the kitchen again and the sunroom, but both were empty. She thought of Isaac: Did he know? Had Max called him? Had Max gone back to the city without telling her? Pulling her phone out of her pocket, Peyton was just about to text Isaac when she heard a ruckus from outside.

"Max, honey, are you out here?" she called as she stepped into the backyard. The Ladies were going crazy, flapping and squawking, feathers flying all over, as Cookie the Land Shark chased them in circles. In the furthermost corner of the yard, flopped on the ground with her legs crossed, sat Max.

Before Peyton could say a word, Max peered at her and called, "Looks like you saw the letter. Pretty sweet, huh?"

Peyton's stomach cramped.

"I mean, it's not like any of us should be surprised, right? What else did we really think was going to happen?" Max stared hard at her right thumbnail, picking the cuticle.

"Oh, honey," Peyton said, her voice cracking. "I'm so sorry."

Max's head snapped up. "No! You don't get to get all weepy here. This isn't about *you*. It's about me. And Dad." Max gave her nail another hard dig and it began to bleed. She stuck it in her mouth and sucked.

Peyton lowered herself to the grass and tried to put her arms around her daughter, but Max leaned away. "Don't," she whispered, and wiped a tear from her cheek.

All around them the chickens kept clucking as Cookie continued his streak around the yard.

"Max, I know this is the very last thing we all wanted," she began, taking a deep breath. "I know I speak for both of us when I say that your dad and I—"

"You speak for Dad? Is that so? Let's see about that." Max swiped her phone a couple times until there was the familiar sound of Face-Time ringing.

Isaac picked up on the first ring. "Max? Honey, I'm so glad you called! I, um, wait, hold on one second, let me fix the light here so I can see you better."

Peyton glimpsed the screen and saw Isaac in a hoodie and joggers, his hair still bed-tousled as he leaned against the kitchen counter. His face was awash with joy that his own daughter had called him, and it hurt her heart thinking of what would come next.

"Really, Dad, you don't need better lighting to hear the news that I have been officially excused from Princeton."

There was some rustling and Isaac said, "Sorry, honey. You must have cut out. What was that?"

"Princeton. Told. Me. To. Fuck. Off."

The rustling stopped, and with it Peyton's breathing.

"I mean, this should not be a surprise, right?" Max said, her voice rising. "Probably not the craziest revelation that one of the finest institutions in the country—your words—isn't super enthusiastic to welcome someone who had to lie and cheat her way in."

"Max, you didn't lie *or* cheat, I hope—"

"No, but *you* did! I suffer the consequences."

From behind them, Firetruck let out a long, mournful cluck.

"Oh, honey. I don't know what to say. I can't . . ." Although she could no longer see the screen, Peyton could hear Isaac's voice breaking.

"What's there to say?" Max spat toward her phone, her anger barely concealing the fact that she was trying desperately not to cry.

"Max?" Peyton said softly.

Her daughter turned to her with surprise, as though she had forgotten Peyton was sitting there all along.

"Daddy and I can't even imagine what you're feeling right now, but we both want you to know that—"

Max stood up abruptly and stared at Peyton with such fury and sadness that Peyton was stunned into silence. "Just save it, Mom. Save it for when I'm living at home forever and even the colleges I could've gotten into all by my pathetic self won't have me. Because I really don't want to hear your sanctimonious bullshit right now. Or his." Max turned her attention back to the screen. "Thanks for literally ruining my life and erasing my future. I hope you're happy."

She jabbed End Call with her thumb and, without another word, ran back into the house. Peyton grabbed her own phone, desperate to speak with Isaac privately, to figure out how they were going to fix this. Surely they could appeal to the dean? Write letters explaining that Max had nothing to do with any of this, beg them not to punish her for the sins of her parents? She was already composing the email in her mind as she dialed Isaac: when they put their heads together—certainly as far as Max was concerned—there was nothing they couldn't fix.

The phone rang and rang. When his voicemail answered, Peyton hung up and called again. This time when it went to voicemail, she tried FaceTime. Finally, desperate, she activated the Find My iPhone alert on Isaac's phone, which would make it beep incessantly. They only used it in emergencies, when one couldn't reach the other, but there was no doubt this qualified as a crisis. She beeped it once, twice, three times before a notification came through that Isaac had removed permission for Peyton to view the location of his phone.

Peyton stared at her phone. He was gone. Max was gone. And she had nowhere to go.

13

Bounty of Goodness

They'll be here any minute," Peyton mumbled while she stood in Max's room, arguing with her daughter over a drab green jumpsuit. She knew she shouldn't say one damn word about Max's clothes—probably true at all times, certainly true in light of the last twenty-four hours—but she couldn't help herself. It was normalizing. Even if Max got annoyed with Peyton, at least she was *speaking* to her. "I don't know, honey, it would just be nice to see you in something a little more . . ."

"Feminine? Isn't that what you mean to say?"

"No. I was going to say 'dinner appropriate.'"

"It's family!" Max said with irritation. "Why do you care what I wear?"

Peyton was quiet. Max was right—why was she always nagging at her over her clothes and hair when she knew it was every bit as pointless as when her own mother had done it to her? Pointless, yes, but also patently ridiculous in light of the actual issues in their lives at the moment. She just wished Max would take a little bit more care of herself; it would help so much with mood and confidence. Who didn't feel better when they looked their best? Max had some lovely features. Why did she always knot her beautiful, wavy hair into a ball on the top of her head? Or never wear makeup? Or cover her curvy, youthful body in ugly, shapeless clothes?

"It's your grandmother's birthday," Peyton said, picking clothes up off the floor. "I think she'd like to see her granddaughter dress for the occasion."

"Oh, spare me. Grandma doesn't give a shit what I look like, or anyone else for that matter. This is *your* thing." Her daughter's tone was more hostile than ever.

"I know you're upset," Peyton said, trying to make her voice as soothing as possible. "You have every right to be."

"You sound exactly like Dad. Did you coordinate your messaging?"

Peyton watched Max swipe open her phone.

"'Dearest Max,'" she started to read. "'I know you're upset with me right now, and you have every right to be.'" Max looked up at Peyton. "He's written me some variation of that every day since this all went down."

Peyton felt her throat tighten. The damage this was doing to Max and Isaac's relationship was the most tragic part of the entire hellish, horrible nightmare. She wanted to reach through Max's phone and reassure her husband that their daughter still loved him, that she was lashing out now, but the wounds would eventually heal and everything would soon go back to normal. The way it used to be before she made the worst decision of all their lives.

"He's trying the best he can," Peyton said. "He loves you so much. So do I."

"Uh-huh," Max said. "Sure feels like it."

The doorbell rang. There was more to say, but Max made it clear she was finished with the conversation. Peyton headed downstairs and was momentarily stunned by Skye and her family. They were so gorgeous, so natural, so effortlessly fabulous, that it could take her breath away. Gabe with his oddly attractive reddish hair and soulful eyes and sexy beard, all very reminiscent of Prince Harry; Aurora's flawless skin and shoulder-length braids and hand-knit fisherman sweater; and of course Skye, with her long skirt and wild eyebrows and freaking perfect complexion despite the fact that she didn't own any makeup and had never—ever!—had a facial.

But now Peyton felt foolish thinking how much time she'd spent (hours? days? weeks? *years*?) on her family's appearance. Scouring stores for all the right things: Brunello Cucinelli for Isaac's cashmere sweaters and Vineyard Vines for his casual wear; Carbon 38 and Bandier for the workout gear Peyton bought in excitement when Max had started her boxing training sessions; and Bergdorf's for her own extensive and well-curated work, evening, and casual wardrobes. It was Oscar Blandi for hair and Neve, no last name needed, for nutritional advice and Dr. Bittman for skin care and celebrity trainers for fitness. Still, their lives had imploded in the most spectacular sense; how little any of that had actually mattered.

"Hi, guys!" She stepped aside so they could enter. She plastered on a smile.

"Aunt P!" Aurora called out in delight, throwing her arms around Peyton's midsection. "Where's Max?"

"Upstairs. Still choosing her outfit," Peyton said.

"Hello, dear!" Marcia trilled from the porch.

"Hi, Mom," Peyton said. "Happy birthday!" She kissed her mother's cheek and felt her damp skin beneath her lips.

"Where's my other granddaughter?" Marcia asked. "I brought back the most marvelous Buddha from Bhutan and I want to show her."

"She'll be down soon. Come, let's sit."

They all followed Peyton to the cottage's cozy screened-in porch, which had white wicker furniture with overstuffed floral cushions. Peyton poured glasses of pinot grigio for her mom and her sister and handed Gabe a bottle of beer. Aurora left to find Max.

"So, Mom, tell us about the Himalayas. I can't believe you only just got back last night," Skye said, and Peyton sent her a look of gratitude.

"Please! This is my sixty-seventh country. I certainly know by now that no one is interested in my travels."

"That's not true," Peyton protested with little conviction. "We love the slideshows."

Marcia barked out a laugh. "I leave next week for Budapest. A quickie. Seven days, seven hundred bucks, all in. I just got an email that they have an opening this morning. Anyone want to join? Maybe Max?"

Max walked into the room, Aurora trailing behind her. "Hi, Grandma," she said, kissing her grandmother's cheek. "Where are you off to?"

"Budapest. Fabulous culture and food. Why don't you join me?"

Max shot Peyton a slightly panicked look.

"Max is working this summer," Peyton said, trying for enthusiasm.

"Yeah, I'm helping take care of this one," Max said, playfully twisting one of Aurora's braids around her finger, "and I also got a job at an ice cream shop in town." She cracked open a can of Coke and sat down next to Peyton, who heard her daughter murmur under her breath, "Now that I'm never going to college, it might be my forever job, too."

"So!" Marcia said. "Where's Isaac?"

Everyone froze.

Marcia looked around. "What, are we pretending this is not happening?"

"Mom!" Skye and Peyton exclaimed simultaneously.

"What?" she crowed. "We're *family*."

Peyton sighed. She noticed that Skye took a monster swig of wine. Gabe studied his phone intently.

"Lighten up, everyone, it's my birthday! And you know no one loves their sons-in-law more than I. Isaac can do no wrong in my eyes. Everyone knows those FBI men are just a bunch of anti-Semites."

"What are you saying about Uncle Isaac?" The small voice that came from the doorway was quiet. Aurora glanced from her own mother to Marcia to Peyton, like she was watching a tennis match.

Skye opened her arms and murmured, "Come here, sweetie," but it was Max who walked over and took the little girl's hand. "We were just saying how much we all love your Uncle Isaac. That's all."

Peyton marveled, gratefully, at how every ounce of the impatience and sarcasm Max directed toward her these days simply evaporated whenever Max was around Aurora.

"Heath in first grade said Uncle Isaac is going to jail!" Aurora said, and then dove into Max's arms.

"Jail?" Max said with exaggerated incredulity. "Well, that's just the craziest thing I've ever heard. And what kind of name is Heath? It's like Keith, only they forgot the 'k' sound! You can't believe anything that someone named *Heath* says."

Aurora appeared to consider this. "He was the best reader in our class. He's a Level N. *And* he has a Fitbit."

Max kissed the top of her head. "A Fitbit? No way!"

Aurora nodded. "He does."

Max looked at Peyton and raised her eyes. *See? All forgotten.* Peyton sent her a grateful look in response. "On second thought, why don't we leave these grown-ups here to talk about their boring grown-up things, and you and I go check the coop for eggs?"

When the girls left, Marcia looked at Peyton. "She's a good girl, that Max. Grades in the top of her class. Confident. Nice to her grandmother. Would be even prettier if she wore something besides combat boots, but that's just a phase. She would've made the loveliest bat mitzvah of everyone's grandchildren in my entire book club if her parents had just encouraged her to respect her faith."

Peyton pressed her fingers to her forehead. "Can we please not right now?"

Marcia clucked. She turned her attention to Skye, who visibly flinched under her gaze. "Skye, sweetheart, how's everything going with the residence?"

Skye cleared her throat. "Good, I hope. Fingers crossed, the final funding should come through any minute, and hopefully we'll be ready for the girls to start in September."

"I think it's wonderful what you're doing!" Marcia said.

Skye smiled. "Thanks, Mom. That means a lot."

"Finally putting that top-notch education of yours to use! I'd hate to see an Amherst degree go to waste on carpools and soccer games."

Gabe cleared his throat.

Peyton jumped to her feet. "Did I just hear the doorbell?" She had not heard the doorbell, or any sound whatsoever, but at that exact moment, it rang. "Yep, there it is. Dinner's here! Let's relocate to the kitchen."

Peyton signed for the delivery while Marcia went to fetch the girls.

"Why does she get to me so much?" Skye asked, helping her unpack the food.

"Because she's your mother," Peyton said.

"Yes, but she's yours too, and you seem much better equipped to deal with her!"

"Better equipped? She called me from Bhutan with some local SIM card she'd purchased, and after the nineteenth question about how I thought Isaac would survive in prison, I pretended I couldn't hear her and hung up."

Skye shook her head. "I don't have the strength for this today."

"Sure you do. I'll pour you another drink and you'll get through this family dinner the same way people have from time immemorial: with a seething, low-grade rage and a serious buzz."

Later, after the cake was devoured, and Gabe drove Marcia and Aurora home, and Max disappeared to her room, Peyton headed to the porch for another glass of wine with her sister.

"Do you have something stronger?" Skye said.

"Tequila? I have a bottle of the good stuff here somewhere." Peyton rummaged through a box from the New York apartment.

"Yes. Double, please."

Peyton filled two rocks glasses with ice, poured in an excessive amount of alcohol, and added a squirt of agave and lime juice.

Skye tasted hers immediately. "Heaven," she said. "One thousand percent worth tonight's migraine."

The cottage's backyard was small but completely private, enclosed on three sides by evergreens, and the simple pool—little more than a rectangular hole in the ground—was dark.

Peyton tossed Skye a towel and laid one out for herself. When they'd settled into side-by-side chaises, Skye said, "I don't know why family dinners are so . . . exhausting."

Peyton sipped. "I think that's pretty much the textbook definition of 'family dinner.'"

"What's wrong with us?" Skye said. "We should be grateful we even *have* a family, that everyone's alive and healthy."

"We should be," Peyton agreed. "But we're damaged."

"Oh, please. We're fine."

"Fine? We both built good careers, married nice men, and have healthy daughters. Neither one of us, or our husbands or children—knock wood, spit three times—has any horrible disease, we're financially comfortable, and we have generally peaceful, productive lives filled with family and friends. Current legal drama notwithstanding."

"Okaaaay . . ."

"And yet, we're miserable!" Peyton slapped the mesh underneath her. "I think I'm only realizing it now because I finally have twenty seconds of free time to string together, but seriously: what the fuck is wrong with us that we, of all people, can't be happy with the absolute bounty of goodness that we have?"

"I don't know what you're talking about. I have a gratitude practice."

Peyton laughed. "This amorphous anxiety we both have is toxic."

"I'm not anxious," Skye said, draping her hand over her eyes.

"Okay, but you're bored out of your mind. How's that stay-at-home-mom thing working out for you? Are we not allowed to acknowledge here that a large part of that dissatisfaction is driving your single-mindedness with regard to the girls' residence?"

Skye sighed. "Did I tell you about Aurora's friend's mom? She asked me the other day if Aurora wanted to join the 'private squash group' she was putting together. Apparently, squash is the new fencing, and all the Ivies are looking for it."

"I have heard that," Peyton murmured. "I think it's a good idea."

"No! These kids are six years old. We were finger-painting at that age! Literally playing in dirt. And our kids? They've already begun college prep."

Peyton was silent. She knew Skye had deliberately told the story so she could segue into a conversation about Max and Isaac. She waited.

"Soooooo . . . ," Skye said, trying to look casual while she sipped her tequila. "Now that we finally have a quiet second alone . . ."

"Please don't. Not right now."

Skye sat up straighter. "Can you just explain to me what Isaac was thinking? Because I can't wrap my head around his thought process. This whole thing is so *not Isaac*. I will never forget how he advised me to report that principal I suspected of stealing and selling the school supplies. You must remember that? I mean, Isaac was insistent that it was my *moral and ethical obligation* to report the guy, even if his actions didn't hurt anyone directly, and even if it threatened my own job. This doesn't track!"

"It's not so simple."

"Really? Then explain it to me."

"It's just that . . . things are complicated." Peyton clenched her eyes shut so she wouldn't have to see Skye's expression, but she could feel her sister's outrage.

"Well, that's why I'm asking! *What's* more complicated? For the first time in as long as I can remember, you're pushing me away. Did you know what he was doing? Were you involved? And what on earth is Max going to do now that Princeton rescinded her admission?"

Peyton opened her eyes.

"Yes, she told me. Jesus Christ, Peyton. How are you of all people being so freaking chill about all of this?"

"I'm far from *chill*," Peyton said. "I'm going to fight that decision with every tool available to me. I've already written to the dean of admissions, the president of the university, the entire board of trustees. I've explained ad nauseam that Max had nothing to do with this, that she had no knowledge of anything. That all the mistakes made were mi— Isaac's. I'll do whatever I have to, to make sure they understand that Max is exactly who she presented herself to be!"

She so desperately wanted to confess to Skye, to tell her everything. But something had stopped her the last few times she'd had the opportunity, and it was happening again. What if Skye didn't understand? What if she couldn't find a way to forgive Peyton for screwing up Max's life? What if it was like the time when Peyton was fifteen and had ended up in Skye's bedroom at one in the morning, crying, after she'd lost her virginity to a boy she didn't even like? Peyton had wanted her big sister to hug her close, tell her that all would be fine, but sixteen-year-old Skye hadn't even tried to hide her horror.

"You did *what*?" she'd asked, flicking on the overhead light. "With *him*?"

Peyton could remember how cold she'd felt standing there in her skimpy, off-the-shoulder dress, how desperately she wanted Skye to hold up her covers and invite Peyton to climb in next to her. But her sister had stared at her, mouth agape, eyebrows furrowed.

Much the same way she was staring at Peyton now.

"What's your plan?" Skye pressed. "I'm not Mom, P. This whole little story you're telling everyone that he's staying in the city to 'deal with things' while you live somewhere else for the summer is ridiculous. Are you separating?"

"No, absolutely not!"

"Because you wouldn't be unjustified. There are plenty of women who wouldn't stand idly by while their husband broke the law and ruined their kid's life."

I don't understand why you slept with him. *You don't even like* him. *Why are you the least bit surprised that he wouldn't even drive you home?*

"Can you tone it down?" Peyton asked, stung by the honesty. "Or better yet, can you cut me a little slack? Maybe just try to *act* understanding, even if you don't actually understand?"

"I'm sorry," Skye said. "You can't just wave your magic wand and fix this."

Peyton finished her tequila and noticed, for the first time since they'd been out by the pool, that she was properly drunk. She felt a hand close around hers, and her eyes flew open.

"Let's just hang here for a few more minutes? I'm not ready to go home yet," Skye said.

Despite the slightly sick feeling that was starting to set in, and the fact that she still wanted to call Isaac, Peyton nodded. Her sister's hand on hers felt warm, safe. As long as she sat there, she wouldn't need to think about anything or anyone else.

"Yes," she whispered. "I'd like that."

14

Small Cone with a Side of Anorexia

Max climbed the stairs out of the freezing cold water, loving the cottage's pool, even if it was unheated. She was the only one who would swim in it. One good thing in the shit show of her life. "I'm going to change for work," Max said, wrapping a towel around her waist.

Her mother and Aunt Skye looked up from their coffee. Aurora was sitting at the porch table with them, gluing plastic gemstones to neon Popsicle sticks.

"You're starting today?" her mom asked, obviously surprised. "I didn't even know."

"It's an actual real, live job, Mother," Max said. "I don't get to choose my own hours. Can I take the car? Or can someone drop me off?"

She was proud of herself for getting a job in addition to babysitting Aurora. Back in March she'd taken the train from the city to Paradise and walked the whole town, hitting every store and restaurant she could find, asking if they would be hiring summer help. Every place in town rejected her, citing her inexperience in retail or restaurant service, but her very last stop, an ice cream shop unimaginatively called the Ice Cream Shoppe, offered her a job.

"I can drive you," Aunt Skye said. "We're supposed to meet friends at the playground, so we're heading out anyway."

"Great, thanks," Max said. She bounded up the stairs to the room she'd claimed—the one at the far end of the hallway with the little window seat—and peeled off her suit. After a quick shower, she laid her uniform on the bed: a light pink polo shirt with *The Ice Cream Shoppe* embroidered on the chest and the kind of knee-length khaki shorts worn only by elderly female golfers in Boca Raton. Max sighed as she buckled the pink grosgrain belt with navy ice cream cones and pulled on her white ankle socks and Keds. Keds! It was brutal. Savage. She looked like a cross between a *Friday Night Lights*–type cheerleader and a WASPy chick who'd grown up sailing at her family's Chappaquiddick compound.

Max jutted out her hip and, pointing to her ridiculous belt, snapped a selfie. Brynn was going to die. She sent it to her and felt a sharp pang of longing for her friend. How much better would this summer be if Brynn was taking the train out to visit every weekend, like they'd planned? As Max walked downstairs in her hideous outfit, she made a silent bet on whether her mother or Aunt Skye was going to laugh harder, but it was Aurora who trolled her first.

"Look at Max!" the little girl trilled, pointing. "She is wearing fancy clothes for the first time!"

"Okay, okay, get it all out now," Max said, pretending to be upset.

"Aww, sweet," her mother crooned. "It reminds me of how I used to dress you when you were little. If I could just give you pigtails . . ."

"Styling," Aunt Skye said, with a wink.

"I'm glad you all like it, because now that Princeton is off the table, I may be scooping ice cream for the rest of my life," Max said coolly.

Max watched her mother and Skye exchange glances.

Aurora clapped. "I will come visit you every day. Will I get free ice cream?"

"You bet. Now come on, I have to get going." Max waved goodbye to her mother and climbed into Skye's Subaru. Brynn Snapped her back with a picture of herself laughing and a caption that read, *Baaaahhahahahahahha LOSER!!!!!!*

When they pulled up to the store five minutes later, Aunt Skye said, "Good luck, sweetie. Do you want us to come by later for a cone?"

"Maybe not my very first day?" Max said. "Definitely next time, though."

"Understood. Need a ride home?"

"Nah, I'll walk," Max said, slamming the door behind her. "Bye, Aurora. Have fun with your friends!"

She watched as the car pulled away and felt a wave of anxiety. What did she, a spoiled private school kid with exactly zero real-world experience, know about working? There was obviously going to be a cash register and a soft-serve machine to operate, and considering Paradise's proximity to New York, probably a fair number of demanding customers. The woman who'd hired her, Darlene, hadn't really told her much. Was she the manager or the owner? Max still didn't know.

She pushed open the door, which set off a chorus of tinkling bells.

"Hello?" Max called out tentatively.

A door to the back area opened, and a boy appeared. He was basketball-player tall, long and lanky, so skinny that he looked more like a giraffe than an athlete. What was that word? Loping. He loped when he walked and hung his head like he was trying to make himself shorter. His own pink polo looked shrunken on his impossibly long torso, and his shorts were laughably short.

"Hey," he said, raising his chin in her direction.

"Hi. I'm Max Marcus?" Why did she always have to phrase everything like it was a question the second she met anyone male? She should try to project confidence. At the very least she could state her own damn name!

But he didn't seem to notice. "Cool," he said, wiping down the counter in front of him with a damp rag. "What can I get for you, Max Marcus?"

Finally, he looked at her. He was pretty much a mess—zits on his chin, bad haircut, dorky wire-rimmed glasses, but when he smiled at her Max immediately smiled back. Not in a flirty way whatsoever. But still. *Nice.*

"I'm not here for ice cream? Today is my first day? Of work?"

The boy frowned and walked over to a hanging wall calendar. "'Mackenzie to start,'" he read. "You're Mackenzie?"

Max laughed. "Yes, sorry. I go by Max. But my real name is Mackenzie. Unfortunately."

"Why unfortunately?"

"Have you ever met someone you actually think is cool named Mackenzie?"

The boy raised his eyebrows and made a point of checking out her outfit.

"This is not by choice!" Max said. "Obviously. And I wouldn't say you're exactly rocking it, either."

This time he burst out laughing, and Max noticed he had perfect teeth.

"Touché," he said, holding his hand out. "I'm Ogden."

"Ogden?"

"Ogden Worthington the Third. At your service."

"Wow," Max said. She never would've guessed that one. Ever.

"Just kidding," he said with another flash of the good teeth. "My real name is Oliver. Oliver Stroker. Which, as you can imagine, has me wishing for Worthington the Third."

"Your last name is *Stroker?*"

Oliver nodded. "Would anyone make that up?"

"I'm so, so sorry," Max said. "I promise never to complain about Mackenzie again."

"It's okay. I'm used to it. After years of masturbation jokes, I can take just about anything."

Max laughed.

"So, here, come on back," Oliver said, lifting a partition in the counter to let Max walk through. "Darlene is at, like, her third workout of the day or something, so I'm supposed to get you started."

Max followed him into the back room. Oliver had to duck to go through the door.

"Put on one of these," he said, handing her a pink apron to tie around her waist. "And wash your hands over there."

The bells out front tinkled, and they looked at each other. "Your first customer," Oliver said, pushing open the swinging door. "Hello, ma'am," he said to the blond woman in workout clothes. "Welcome to the Ice Cream Shoppe."

The woman was staring intently at the gallons in the freezer and didn't glance up. "I'll have a kiddie cone of mint chip, please," she said, never taking her eyes off the ice cream.

"Yes, ma'am," Oliver said. He turned to Max and raised his eyebrows, which, now that she was noticing, were very close to a unibrow. "You're up."

"What do I do?" she whispered, frantically looking around.

Oliver plucked a metal scooper from a pot of water and handed it to her. "Surely you can take it from here," he said.

Max took the scooper from him and asked the woman which type of cone she would like.

"Um, which has the fewest calories?"

Max looked to Oliver, who just shrugged.

"I'm not sure, actually. Definitely not the waffle cone. But between the wafer and the sugar cone, I'd have to say it's a toss-up."

The woman glared at her. "You really don't know? You *work* here."

Max blushed. "Sorry, it's my first day."

Big sigh. The woman conceded to a wafer cone, and the moment Max managed to get the smallest chunk of ice cream into her scooper, the woman almost screamed, "That's enough!"

"It's not even a full scoop," Max said reasonably. "A kiddie cone is one full scoop."

"That's plenty, thank you," the woman said. She pulled a credit card out of the waistband of her yoga pants and thrust it across the counter.

Oliver showed Max how to ring through the sale while the woman tapped her foot impatiently. Thirty seconds later Max handed the woman the cone and watched as she took two bites and promptly threw the rest out, cone and all. She left without another word.

"Is that normal?" Max asked.

"Totally," Oliver said, nodding.

"What sort of alternate universe is this?"

"What, the shop or the town? Or both? Welcome to Paradise! Every single woman in a ten-mile radius has a pathological fear of sugar. Like, more than home invaders. Or cancer. It really is the biggest anxiety around."

"I mean, I live in New York City. It's not like I've never been up close and personal with disordered eating. But what the fuck?"

"I worked a kid's birthday party last weekend. The piñata had pencils in it."

Max burst out laughing. "Stop it."

"Just wait until the post-dinner crowd comes in. All the kids and dads ordering cones and shakes and sundaes. All the moms ordering kiddie cups so they don't accidentally give their daughters eating disorders by starving in front of them, and then they either throw them out or throw them up. It's really a highlight."

Max considered this. "I've never thought about it before, but my mother always orders a kiddie cup when we get ice cream."

"Sounds like you'll fit right in."

Max punched him on the upper arm, and Oliver pretended to wince in pain. "Come on, I'll show you how to work the soda fountain machine. If you can't make an ice cream float using Diet Coke and fat-free frozen yogurt, you're going nowhere."

Max followed Oliver into the back room, trying to suppress a smile.

"So, Princeton, huh? Pretty good school. You must be smart. Or very well connected," he said, yanking open a drawer full of metal utensils.

Her stomach did an immediate free fall. She hadn't mentioned a word about college. He must have been lying to her before, when he pretended he didn't know her name. Obviously, he already knew a lot more than that. "Please, don't hold back," she said sarcastically. "Is this where you tell me what a shit my father is?"

Oliver stared at her. "Your *father*?"

"Clearly you heard all about me on the news. So why deny it? Especially if you're going to be a dick about it."

"The *news*? I have, like, *no idea* what you're talking about."

"How else would you know about Princeton?"

He pointed to her backpack, which she'd tossed on a stool in the corner. Hanging from the front zipper was a woven keychain featuring a large orange *P*. "I mean, unless that's for Pitt or something. That's cool, too. Despite my parents' very best efforts, I'm no school snob."

Her relief was so intense she laughed. "Oh my god, I'm such a mess."

"Want to tell me what that was all about?"

"My dad's one of the people who paid to get their children into college," Max said matter-of-factly. "Twenty-two arrested this go-round. Is this ringing any bells?"

Oliver made a valiant effort to keep his expression neutral. "Yeah, I heard about that. I didn't realize you were that chick."

"Lucky me! I'm not going there anymore." Max strode over to her bag, unhooked the keychain, and tossed it in the wide-mouth garbage can.

"Shit, I'm sorry."

Max said nothing. She was so sick and tired of her mother and Aunt Skye's platitudes about how everything would be fine, it would all work out in the end, sometimes things happened for a reason. And her father! He'd been emailing her every day, but it didn't seem entirely possible that he could love her and wreck her life at the same time.

"What's going to happen with your dad?" Oliver asked.

Max shrugged. "My parents don't give me straight answers about anything, but I'm guessing he'll probably have to do at least some jail time. Just judging from the whole Lori Loughlin situation. My mom's out here with me for the summer and my dad stayed in New York. So take from that what you will."

Oliver nodded.

"But I don't really know. Supposedly he wrote a check to some college advisor, who passed it on to a trustee, who advocated for my admission. It's not like they had me posing in swimming pools wearing goggles and onesies, pretending I was a polo player."

"I get that," Oliver agreed. He appeared to consider something. "My parents would one thousand percent do the exact same thing. For all I know, they have. I'm going to be a senior this year, and it's literally all they talk about."

"Ugh, it's endless! Mine forced me to go to this super elite private school my entire life even though it couldn't have been less *me,* and then they turned into absolute psychos when it came time to apply for college. I wanted to go to film school. And on top of it all, I actually thought my dad was a good guy. I'm such an asshole."

Oliver folded his arms across his chest and leaned against the kitchen counter. "I'm sure he still is a good guy. They just go crazy over this school stuff. I can't wait to get out of the house. My parents probably can't wait for me to leave, either. They'll finally be able to get divorced and not feel like they're fucking me up forever."

"You think they will?"

"Definitely. They *hate* each other. I'm the youngest—my two sisters are gone already—and trust me, they're counting the seconds. It's like, dude, I know exactly what's going on here, neither of you are fooling anyone. Just end it already, it'd be better for everyone."

"They fight all the time?" Max said.

"Not at all. They do horribly vindictive things to fuck each other over. My dad loves wine. He's a real connoisseur dick, reading about it and collecting it and whatever. He had a whole cellar designed for it; you know the type. So anyway, he's away on business a couple weeks ago and a giant delivery arrives at our house from one of his favorite vineyards—some vintage or grape that he's been waiting to get for, like, his whole life—and my mother left it all out on the front porch. Totally on purpose."

"Why?"

"Why not? Because she knew he wanted it? She was annoyed she had to deal with it? I have no idea. All I know is that it sat in the sun for four days and was completely ruined. Nearly ten grand flushed down the toilet so my mother could stick it to my father."

"Ten thousand dollars in *wine*? I'm sorry to ask, but why are you working here for minimum wage?" Max asked.

"Why are you, Ms. Manhattan Private School with the parents who throw enough cash around to interest the FBI?" He grinned.

She rolled her eyes but was delighted. "Touché."

"I've been working here every summer of high school. My parents wanted me to get an internship at an investment bank, but the college counselor they hired when I was thirteen—for thirty thousand a year, by the way—convinced them colleges care more about 'character' and nothing builds character like an old-school, grunt-work job. Apparently, it makes admissions officers nostalgic for their own youth, or something like that. It all sounds like bullshit to me, but I'm not complaining. I actually like working here, crazy anorexic moms and all."

"Speaking of which, you said you'd teach me how to make a milkshake. I want to learn how to make it just right for all the starving mothers who will throw it out—or up."

Oliver bowed, his arm outstretched toward the commercial-sized blender. "Your wish is my command."

15

Cartel Tequila

Okay, girls, can I have your attention, please?" Denise used the same peeved tone she likely spoke to her flag-football-brawling husband with every night. "Let's make sure we remember our manners and say thank you to Mrs. Teller, who has kindly volunteered to be our Snack and Stay mom this week!"

"Thank you, Mrs. Teller," ten girls dutifully sang.

A harried-looking Tracy Teller frantically passed around wax paper bags of apple slices and Honest juice boxes. "I hope these are okay?" she asked Skye and Denise, indicating the juice. "I know we're supposed to bring water, but the store was all out of the little bottles. At least these are organic!"

"They're perfect," Skye said at the exact time Denise said, "We really need to stick to water," and began collecting the boxes. "Calories and allergies!"

Skye had once suggested to Denise that they didn't really need a Snack and Stay mom, since the two of them already attended every meeting and the girls were generally well behaved. "Why inconvenience everyone else when we're here anyway?" she'd asked, and Denise had looked at Skye like she'd proposed they scrub all the school's toilets.

"We underwent twenty-five hours of training to be Girl Scout troop leaders," Denise had answered in a huff. "We got certified in CPR and first aid. We learned how to use EpiPens! We filled out hundreds of pages of paperwork. We attended seminars and underwent background checks. All for *their* daughters! Don't you think the least *they* can do is bring in some Goldfish each meeting?"

Skye had refrained from pointing out that neither of them had done *any* of those things for anyone else's kids; they had done them so they could both spend more time with their own daughters, to see how they interacted in a group, to gather intelligence on which girls were sweet and which were already bitchy, even as first graders.

Now Skye focused on guiding the group through snack time, the Pledge of Allegiance, and the Girl Scout Promise, which each girl recited holding her hand over her heart: "On my honor, I will try: to serve God and my country, to help people at all times, and to live by the Girl Scout Law." Finally, it was time to gather everyone into a circle and discuss how the troop would spend the money that they'd earned selling cookies that year.

Skye pointed to Esme, a gentle giant of a child, both painfully shy and exceedingly tall for her age. "Esme, sweetheart? Can you think of something you'd like to do with the money our troop earned this year?" she asked with an encouraging smile.

Esme stared at the floor but whispered, "Use it to buy toys for kids who don't have any?"

"That's a wonderful idea, Esme," Skye said. Tracy Teller nodded enthusiastically. Denise gave a constipated smile.

"And how about you, Bella? What do you vote we do with our cookie money?" Skye asked.

Bella pressed a glitter-painted forefinger to her lips and appeared deep in thought. "I know!" she said. "Let's give it to old people! Like my grandpa who lives in a great big house with all other old people. We could give it to them to cheer them up!"

The next three girls, including Aurora, also had community-service-minded ideas: use the money to build a playground; hire clowns for sick kids in the hospital; donate it to the town library. And then it was Denise's daughter's turn.

"I think we should use the money to get a limo and go to Serendipity!" Lia said. "They have the best frozen hot chocolate *ever!*"

"Yeah!" shouted the Burberry-clad McNally twins. Chloe, the louder one, said, "Limos are awesome! We went in one for my uncle's wedding and it had all these lights and bowls of candy and we could drink all the Pepsi we wanted."

"And the grown-ups had wine," her sister said authoritatively.

Aurora leaned in close to Skye. "Mommy, what's a limo?" she asked, and as Skye was debating how best to avoid answering her question, Denise stood up.

"Well, girls," she said, raising an arm for silence. "It sounds like we have a lot of great ideas here. How about we put it to a vote?"

Skye's head snapped up. She tried to catch Denise's eye to convey that this was a terrible idea, but she could feel the woman's steadfast refusal to glance in her direction.

"All in favor of buying toys for needy children?" Denise asked, and two of the ten girls raised their hands.

"And how about the library? Who would like to see more books there?" Another two hands timidly went up.

"And who votes to use our hard-earned money to go to Serendipity in New York City?" she asked, her voice raised in excitement. She clapped her hands together and leaned forward. "For the world's *best* frozen hot chocolate?"

All ten girls immediately shot their hands into the air. Seeing that it was unanimous, the girls jumped up and danced and shimmied around, hugging one another and cheering like they'd just won the lottery. Even Aurora, who moments before had so sensitively suggested that they hire clowns for sick children, was pumping her fists and screaming, "Limo!"

It took nearly ten minutes to calm everyone down enough to get started on the meeting's craft project, and as soon as they finished, their moms appeared for pickup. By the time Skye and Denise had offered a detailed report on each child, it was late. Aurora and Lia were waiting for their mothers by the cafeteria entrance, but it was obvious their patience was waning.

"Denise? I, uh, wanted to talk to you about the decision today. On how to best use the money?" Skye hated the timidity in her voice, but there was something so damn daunting about dealing with that woman.

"Oh, the Serendipity thing? The girls decided that for themselves."

"Well, no, not really. I mean, when you put something to a vote for a group of young children, it's not exactly fair to—"

Denise pulled a mirror from her heavily logo'd Gucci bag and touched up her lipstick. "I don't mean any disrespect by this, Skye, I really don't, but I have a BA in government from Duke and a JD/MBA from Harvard. I think I can handle the allocation of seventeen hundred dollars in *cookie money*." She plucked her phone from the bag's outside pocket and tucked it between her ear and her shoulder. "I'm on my way, sweetie. Just sit tight." She nodded gravely. "I hear you. Be strong. I'll be there in ten minutes."

"Is everything okay?" Skye asked.

"Fine," she said, cinching her shearling coat. "My god, with the level of drama, you'd think she was stuck in an abandoned elevator shaft somewhere and not at her best friend's house." Denise headed toward the cafeteria's exit but got distracted by the garment rack that acted as the school's lost and found. She eyed a purple Moncler puffer in a ridiculously adorable small size and plucked it off a hanger. "Do you believe how irresponsible these kids are?" she asked Skye. And then: "Lia! Your coat is here! Did you even know it was missing?"

Skye watched Denise jam the $650 children's coat into her bag as her phone rang again. "Dammit, Beatrix, I told you, I'm on my way!" Just when Skye thought she'd left, Denise popped her head back into the cafeteria. "Skye? Don't worry, honey. I get where you're coming from. And it's very sweet. You have my word that if there's any money left over after our group outing, we'll buy some toys for tots. Okay?"

Skye reflexively smiled. "Sounds good," she said automatically, even though nothing was good.

A moment later Aurora appeared in the doorway. Her white tights were a bit torn and dirtied at the knee, and her brown eyes were big and wide, the way they got when she was trying hard to hold them open. "Mommy?" she asked. "Can we go home now?"

Although her daughter had recently grown too tall and heavy for Skye to comfortably carry, Skye scooped her into her arms and pulled her tight. Aurora wrapped her legs around her mother's waist and rested her face on Skye's shoulder. "Come, chickpea," Skye murmured into her daughter's warm neck, which smelled faintly of orange-vanilla body wash. "Let's go home together."

"I still can't believe we live in a place with homes like this," Skye said as Gabe pulled their Subaru around the circular driveway.

"Agree," Gabe said, handing a uniformed valet the key. "This looks like the house from *Wedding Crashers*."

They walked slowly toward the house, not ready to commit to entering. "I can't stop thinking about that Girl Scout meeting earlier today," Skye said. "I know it's ridiculous—it's Girl Scouts—but how did I come to co-lead a group whose sole purpose is community service and we end up discussing limos the whole time?"

The front doors swung open to reveal an imposing foyer with the type of ostentatious double sweeping staircases that rich people the world over loved. Why be limited to one staircase when you could have two? Skye almost made a comment to Gabe—double staircases being one of their ongoing jokes, something that he, as an architect, especially loathed—but the view in front of them immediately silenced her.

"Wow, look at that," Gabe breathed, and Skye followed his gaze straight through to the backyard, if you could call it that, where an expansive green lawn accented the unobstructed views of the water. The evening was so clear it was possible to see across the Sound to Long Island, where the water reflected the day's last light. A sailboat bobbed in the distance, its grand mast waving, and a couple of small speedboats zipped by.

"It is so spectacular," Skye said. When a waiter came over to offer them berry mojitos made with freshly picked blueberries, black-berries, and mint, Skye and Gabe each took one and clinked their glasses.

"How do they source an all-blond staff?" Gabe asked, glancing around. "I mean, you can't exactly advertise for that."

Skye laughed. "Like, not only *must* you be white, but also you must *not* be brunette."

"Oh my god, Skye, is that you?" a woman shrieked from behind her. Skye saw Gabe's eyebrows rise as she slowly, anxiously turned around.

The woman, a mom with a daughter in Aurora's class, launched herself at Skye, throwing her arms around her neck and kissing her cheek with such force that Skye had to suppress the urge to push her away.

"Ohmigod, I am so happy you're here," the woman said, sounding like a teenager. "Love your outfit. Very casual."

Was that an insult? Or a compliment? Skye glanced down at her wide-legged cotton and linen jumpsuit.

"Hey, Patricia," Skye said. They had both been class moms for the girls' kindergarten class the year before, and Skye was still scarred from the experience. "Have you ever met my husband, Gabe? Gabe, this is—"

"Oh my god, of course! That's the connection! You're partners with Alan, am I right?"

Gabe smiled politely, trying not to appear unnerved that this stranger knew all about him.

Patricia placed a hand on each of their arms and pulled them into a huddle. They were close enough that Skye could admire the complete perfection—no, the *artistry*—of her veneers. "It's all *her* family money, am I right?" she whispered loudly enough for anyone standing within six feet to hear. "I mean, don't get me wrong, I know architects do *very* well"—with this, she fluttered her lashes at Gabe—"but not waterfront-estate-with-servants well."

Skye gritted her teeth.

Patricia leaned in again and loudly whispered, "I also heard that they hired a surrogate for the twins, and not for any actual medical reason. Remember when they took the older kids to Brazil for 'sabbatical' a couple years ago? Apparently, they also took the surrogate, an obstetrician, and a baby nurse with them, and while the twins were delivered and dealt with by the team, Kelly had a full Mommy Job at a super elite private clinic in São Paulo. The same place they did Jennifer Aniston's boobs, so obviously *very* discreet."

Skye could see Gabe's eyebrows shoot sky high, and she had to exert maximum effort not to laugh. It wasn't all that often he got a solidly strong dose of Crazy Paradise Lady.

"Anyway!" Patricia grabbed her nonexistent midsection. "I could use a nice trip to Brazil, too. Oh! There's Richard. Honey! Come over and say hello!"

Richard looked crestfallen that he was summoned. He was short and bald but powerfully built, his shoulders and biceps barely contained by his expensive button-down shirt.

"Hey, man," he said flatly, offering his hand to Gabe. "Great to meet you."

"Richard, be a dear and take Gabe to meet everyone. They're out by the bonfire." And before he could protest, Patricia clamped both hands around Skye's upper arm and dragged her toward the pool.

"Don't worry, Gabe will be fine," Patricia said, perhaps noticing Skye's trepidation. "Richard knows everyone. We have this group of friends that we, like, do everything with—holidays, vacation, all the kid stuff—and they're very outgoing and *loooooove* to party. Gabe will be well taken care of, if you know what I mean. . . ."

Skye searched Patricia's unlined, mostly frozen face. She *didn't* know what she meant. Offered a cocktail? Cocaine? Friendly chat? Hookers?

A crowd of women closed in around her.

"Ohmigod, I love that straw satchel! So chic!"

"You have a daughter at Abington, right? How was it last year with Mrs. Kalman? Kind of a cold bitch, don't you think?"

"Are you the Skye who's sisters with Peyton Marcus? Christ, I can't even imagine what she's going through right now! It's horrible."

Another one chimed in: "Oh, please. The whole thing is so ridiculous! I can name five people off the top of my head who have made sizable donations to get their kids into schools. I don't understand what everyone's freaking out about."

There was a moment of silence before the group all started to nod their heads. "It's just bad luck," one woman said.

Skye did her best to remain neutral. It was true: these women, more than anyone, could understand and sympathize with her sister. Most of them would likely do—or had done—whatever was conceivably within their means to help their kids get into the best schools. Still, Skye was relieved when the conversation turned to someone else—or rather something else: whether it was better to buy the Williams-Sonoma brand Vitamix or the original—and it was only then Skye realized she'd broken into a full sweat. All the party guests had moved to the backyard, but it was like an invisible bouncer had stood at the French doors and directed all women to the pool and men to the bonfire. Incredibly, there wasn't a single exception: the entire party, probably close to sixty people, had been divided by gender.

The same hot blond waiter from earlier, or perhaps a different one, offered Skye another mojito from his tray. "Where's the restroom?" she asked.

"I'd recommend using the one in the game room—no one's in there right now. Straight through the living room and to your left."

She thanked him and walked briskly, like she would if she were alone on a dark street and needed to project confidence, praying her body language said, "Don't speak to me." Skye exhaled a sigh of relief as she closed the bathroom door.

She pulled out her phone to text Gabe, thinking he could meet her in the deserted game room and they could plan their escape, but on her screen was a text from Esther.

What are you up to?

Why, have you heard anything from Henry?

Esther had received an email from Henry's associate the day before. It had been vague, but it hinted at some sort of delay with the financing. When she'd called to tell Skye about it, Esther had sounded unconcerned, but it had sent Skye into a panic.

Nothing. Stop worrying! It's going to be fine. A slight delay is hardly a reason for concern.

Skye snorted. Easy for Esther to say: she wasn't the one who'd already started spending the money. She considered her reply but then, frustrated with typing, tapped her friend's number.

Esther picked up on the first ring. "Tell me I'm way, way too old for Tinder," she said as a greeting.

"You're *waaaaayyyy* too old."

"Seriously? I downloaded the app, and it's actually pretty fun to swipe."

"Are there even single men around here?" Skye peeked out and, seeing that the coast was clear, stepped out of the bathroom. Directly in front of her was a massive black leather couch, an expensive and finely crafted version of something you might find in a fraternity basement.

"You'd be surprised. I have no idea why you'd live in a suburb if you were single—like, without kids—but people do."

"Isn't there an old-people version of Tinder? What's it called? I can't remember."

"I'm offended."

"Esther! Tinder is for twenty-two-year-olds looking for random sex."

"I may not be twenty-two, but what makes you think my intentions are pure? And that app that you're thinking of? It's called My Time, or something like that, and the ads show people in their seventies."

Skye laughed. "Dating is overrated. So is marriage sometimes. Gabe told me we were having a surprise night out. I was hoping for pasta. Guess where we are?"

"Not an Italian restaurant?"

"Alan and Kelly's house. For a *party*."

"Ugh! Probably not a great time to tell you that I'm wearing joggers and no bra. I gave both kids melatonin tonight, and I'm settling in to binge old seasons of *The Crown*."

"I hate you."

"How bad is it?"

Skye glanced toward the entrance of the game room to make sure no one was nearby. Lowering her voice, she said, "Bad. As usual, men on one side and women on the other. It's like an Orthodox wedding. Or the *Titanic* cigar room."

Esther laughed. "Let me guess. They're serving freshly muddled, organic watermelon margaritas with Himalayan pink salt."

"Very close. Freshly muddled, organic blueberry mojitos with farm-sourced mint leaves."

Skye twirled a lock of hair around her finger, feeling grateful not only that Esther was her friend, but also that she'd agreed to use her finance background to help coordinate the various funding. "He thought this would distract me from the whole situation with Henry, but I can't stop thinking about it. What do you think is happening?"

Esther sighed. "I don't know, honey. It could be anything. Maybe someone in his family got sick? Or he had to take an emergency trip overseas and doesn't want to deal right this moment?"

"Or he doesn't want his name associated with a close relative of Isaac Marcus, indicted criminal?"

There was a beat of silence before Esther conceded, "Or that."

"It makes me sick even to think about it."

"So don't! Go try to have fun. At least find out more details on that couple who swapped spouses? Weren't all of them best friends for like a decade now and then the one wife and other husband started sleeping together and then the other two started, and basically they all decided to switch?"

Skye smiled. "Someone said the kids don't even really care because they were such close family friends already that nothing much has changed."

"See! There is valuable information there. Find out more and call me later."

"You won't answer," Skye said, laughing.

"Nope. I'll be enjoying every free second of my children's medicated unconsciousness. But I'll call you tomorrow. Love you!"

"I love you, too," Skye said, hanging up. She had to will herself to leave the room, where she almost smashed directly into Gabe.

"Oh, thank god it's you," she said, kissing him lightly on the lips.

"Where have you been?" he asked, placing both his hands on her shoulders. "I got stuck talking to a group of guys about tequila. A very serious, intense conversation about their favorite private distillers. Something about small batches? It was . . . ridiculous."

A wave of relief washed over Skye. Here he was—her husband. And even though he'd dragged her to this place, he hated it, too.

Gabe continued, "One of them kept bragging about flying his tequila back from some Mexican town on a private jet? Needing to avoid customs because it was harvested or baked or brewed by an infamous cartel? This, apparently, is an enormous source of street cred for a Paradise banker."

"Enormous," Skye agreed. "I must have spoken to his wife at some point, because she had extremely impassioned opinions on how the various Vitamix models blend the margaritas she makes with the tequila her husband imports from drug lords."

"Let's get out of here?" Gabe stood and extended his hand.

She grabbed it and squeezed. "Immediately."

They drove to their favorite vegan restaurant in town and ordered açai bowls topped with almond butter and chocolate chips for dessert.

"Mmm," Skye said, licking her spoon. "Even better than those craft cocktails."

"That woman—Patricia? My god, honey. I hear you talk about the moms around here, but I don't think I realized . . ."

"I mean, she was particularly bad. There are some nice, normal people around here . . . just not enough. I don't know, I . . ."

Gabe peered at her. "What?"

"Nothing," she said, swallowing another spoonful.

"What were you going to say?"

"I miss Harlem sometimes. I know the schools are incredible here, but I just can't help but feel that . . . I can't put my finger on it, exactly. That this crazy wealthy town with all these hyperintense, type-A people, isn't really our scene. And of course the lack of diversity. What's that going to look like for Aurora as she gets older?"

"We've talked about this, honey," Gabe said reasonably. "We agreed that it was a good compromise: the chance for Aurora to go to public school instead of some fancy private or charter school, close enough to the city that we can pop in anytime, and no crazy long commute every day for me."

"I know, you're right. About all those things." She tilted her head. "I think the stress from the financing is bleeding into everything else. Not only are the girls and their families depending on this for the school year, but I'm depending on it to save my sanity in this town. Is that awful to say?"

"It's not awful at all. It's honest, and I get it."

"I'm just not sure how we ended up here."

Gabe was quiet for a moment. "Maybe it's time for you to go back to teaching? It didn't make sense when Aurora was younger, but now that she's in school for full days, and we're done with the baby stage . . ."

She felt like she'd been punched. "We're not a hundred percent done, are we? I mean, it's not completely out of the realm of possibility that we would have another baby."

"We're not?" Gabe put his spoon down.

"I don't know. We weren't planning on another. But it's *possible*."

"Anything's *possible*," Gabe said, his easy, affable laugh returning. "But that doesn't mean it's probable."

"Who knows? It could just be as easy as me going off the pill. We've never actually tried to get pregnant. Maybe it wouldn't be a problem at all."

"Honey." Gabe's voice was low, soothing. Like he was talking down an agitated toddler. "We've always agreed that neither of us felt the need for biological children, what with how many kids are already out there who need families. Has something changed for you?"

Skye considered this. Her commitment to adoption as the right answer for their family hadn't changed—they both felt so strongly about adopting a child in need rather than having their own—but she couldn't help feeling the baby pangs. Maybe it was hormones? The dwindling fertility that came with turning forty? Or the sadness of realizing that an entire phase of parenthood was behind them, never to return again. Gabe was an only child, so it had always seemed natural to him, but Skye often wondered if they were doing her a disservice by not giving her a sibling. Whenever she brought it up, Gabe assured her that their love and attention was all Aurora needed, that their family was perfect the way it was, and for the most part Skye agreed.

"Nothing's changed," she said, although she wasn't sure. "I . . . I can't believe our baby is almost seven. It doesn't feel real."

Later that night, after they'd made love and Gabe's breathing had softened to a steady, quiet snore, Skye thought back on the night. Was her recent baby fever nothing more than anxiety over Aurora growing up? Or was it her body telling her that yes, maybe they should try, that they weren't actually finished yet, that their family wasn't complete? To fill the void that she couldn't possibly fill with the PTA and the Girl Scouts? Despite her policy never to surf in the middle of the night, she pulled out her phone. A text notification from Esther on her lock screen read: *Ugh, just read the email. I'm so, so sorry. Mourn tonight, back to work tomorrow!*

Instantly a dull thudding started in her chest. Skye shivered as she opened her email and held her breath as she clicked open the email from Henry, her investor. Her eyes scanned so quickly that she missed whole sentences, but it didn't take long to get the gist. *Due to the current legal situation with Skye's family . . . no longer moving forward . . . the appearance of impropriety . . . unfortunate circumstances . . . too risky at the present time.*

Her hands were shaking and hot tears fell from her face. She read and reread the email, hoping that she'd missed something the first time, but it was all right there, in writing. Over. All her hard work, for nothing. And worst of all, eight families whose dreams she would now have to shatter.

16

Character Clause

The row of Town Cars outside of Hudson Yards stretched more than a block long, waiting to deposit their well-dressed couples at the red carpet. Peyton examined them all as her own car inched forward. There were Mika and Joe, in coordinating black suits, and Rachel Maddow in a dapper tuxedo, and that blowhard from Fox whose name she could never remember with his WASPy-looking wife, and Anderson Cooper with Andy Cohen as his date for the evening. There were at least a dozen other anchors, and Peyton had to remind herself that after forty years in the business, Joseph, the network head of ANN, knew everyone. She was still reeling from Skye's call earlier that morning, telling her that Henry had yanked the funding; her sister was devastated, and Peyton was nauseated by it. She *had* to figure out a way to help—she would straight-up hand her sister the money if she had it—but she felt horribly responsible for this unexpected ripple effect of misery. When it was finally her turn to climb out of the car, Peyton's anxiety spiked even more: she desperately wished Isaac were with her. But she took a deep breath and talked herself down: She went to work events alone all the time. She could make conversation with a piece of furniture. And most importantly, she looked freaking amazing in her borrowed McQueen dress, which had a black corset covered with a hundred tiny red rosettes and a full, floor-length skirt that was adorned with small, silver . . . what? Brackets? Studs? Some sort of hardware that sounded awful in description but in reality made the dress look like the perfect juxtaposition of European princess and Hollywood glam.

Three young women she knew from ANN's PR department were waiting outside the door with clipboards and earpieces, and each turned to watch Peyton walk the carpet. There were no paparazzi—this was still a media party, after all—but Peyton, with the designer dress and the splurge-worthy Louboutins and the random passersby all turning to stare, felt like she was headed into the Met Ball. She would show all of them! It had been one week off-air, and it was enough already. The paps had long left their New York apartment, the news cycle had moved on to cover the latest Supreme Court drama, and even Kenneth, when pressed by Peyton, conceded there was a chance—however slight—that Joseph would confirm her return to the show at the party that evening. Why else would her invitation remain both extended and encouraged? she'd asked. She was still part of the team, an indispensable part. It would be proven tonight, she hoped, when her exhausting daily calls with Kenneth, Nisha, and Isaac's attorney would all be worth it. She'd return to her rightful seat at the anchor desk, and she could focus one hundred percent of her efforts on continuing to needle, beg, and persuade Princeton to change their mind. Thrusting her shoulders back, Peyton reminded herself to smile, to laugh, to radiate confidence. To *show no weakness*. She strolled the carpet like she was head of network and waved to the PR girls.

"Have a wonderful night, Peyton," one of them said as she held the elevator door open.

"Thank you," she said, smiling.

The momentary respite of the quiet elevator was shattered the instant the doors opened on the fifth floor.

"Well, look who it is!" Jim boomed, taking a giant slug of his cranberry-colored cocktail. "Gentlemen, please excuse me."

Don't worry, they're thrilled to get rid of you, Peyton thought.

"Well, don't you look gorgeous," he drawled, putting both his hands directly on her hips, something Peyton—and all women—hated. "Very fashionable."

"Thanks, Jim. You look nice yourself."

"I'm glad you showed up, P. It's a real classy move, I have to say."

"*Showed up?* To our boss's sixtieth birthday party? That we've known about for five months?"

"Well, you know, with everything . . ."

They faced each other silently. Finally, Jim grinned, leaned in close enough that Peyton could smell the booze on his breath, and said, "Tell Isaac we're all supporting him. I mean, we certainly can't say so on air, but I challenge you to find me one person in this room who wouldn't do anything to help their kid. Am I right?"

Peyton furrowed her brow. Was Jim being supportive? Or a dick? It was so hard to tell. "Thanks, Jim."

"That said, you better be really careful. Not everyone here is as understanding of your . . . *predicament* as I am."

Dick. She should have known.

"Time for a cocktail, Jim. I'll see you soon," she said, and bolted.

Thankfully, Sean and his husband, Booker, were chatting at the bar. Sean whistled when he saw her. "Gorge. Like seriously, A-list, top-of-the-line, cliché-worthy hot," he announced.

"Agreed," Booker said. "That dress! McQueen?"

Peyton kissed each of their cheeks. A waiter walked by with a tray of champagne flutes, and she took one.

"Thank you both. Jim just made some veiled threat. Or maybe it was a warning? I, for one, think viewers are sophisticated enough to understand my husband and I are actually two separate beings. Apparently Jim does not." She drained her champagne.

Sean gave her a weird look.

"What? Why are you looking at me like that?"

Sean and Booker exchanged a glance, and Booker said, "I'll catch up with you both in a bit," before practically running away.

"What was *that* all about?" Peyton asked.

Sean coughed. He looked uncomfortable.

"What? Tell me!"

He exhaled. "Look, P, I don't want you to think that this has been some sort of discussion at work, or something formal, or anything like that. It's just me, as your friend, looking out for you. As a *friend*."

"Okaaaay." Peyton's throat constricted just the smallest bit: Sean wasn't just a friend, he was her work husband. If something was going on behind the scenes, he needed to provide all the details.

"Look, this is totally off the record, but I think you should know that there's been talk. . . ."

"What kind of talk?"

Sean glanced around. "The kind that says the network may not cycle through this . . . hiatus as quickly as we'd hoped. And . . ."

"Please continue."

"And they may want you to take a little time."

"A little time? I took a little time."

"More than a week."

"They can't do that. I have a contract!"

Sean gave her a pointed look.

"Well, don't I? My ratings for the last six months are higher than ever, they can hardly claim it's performance based. . . ."

Sean cleared his throat. "Look, I'm only the EP and certainly not privy to the conversations taking place on the twenty-second floor. As far as I know, nothing's been decided. But I thought you'd want to know what I'd heard."

Peyton nodded. "Thank you. I appreciate it."

Sean held out his hand. "Come on, let's put in some face time so we can get out of here as fast as possible."

Peyton took it and squeezed. "Thanks for telling me. A lot of people wouldn't have had the nerve."

Sean led her straight to the host's table, where Joseph was holding court. An inappropriately young model hung on his arm.

"There she is!" Joseph called out. His tuxedo somehow shimmered. His smile was somewhere between benevolent and leering, and as usual, Peyton couldn't decide if he was a brilliant, supportive mentor or a closeted sexual predator with a predilection for teenage girls. "My favorite morning person! Darling, do you need another drink?" He turned toward a bow-tied waiter and made a motion with his hand.

"Happy birthday," Peyton said, leaning in to kiss Joseph on his itchy gray beard. "What a spectacular party! I love this space. Hudson Yards got so much flak in the beginning, but I really think it's come into its own. Don't you?" Peyton knew she was rambling, but it's what she did in awkward social situations, and mostly, people were appreciative. Joseph, however, merely gave her a grin that could have meant "I adore you for making such an effort at my party" or "I'm a pervert at heart who can't be rehabilitated."

Joseph shook off the gorgeous young thing who was clinging to his arm like a barnacle.

"Peyton, let's take a walk," Joseph said, ignoring Sean. He navigated his way around the table without spilling a drop of his martini, and Peyton marveled: he was sober. Totally sober, completely in control, and, judging from his completely inscrutable expression, either going to fire her, promote her, or molest her.

"Everything okay?" Peyton forced herself to ask. It was better to get this over with; the not knowing was torture.

"Fine, fine, darling. It's just that—how do I say this?" Joseph stopped walking, not seeming to notice that the crowd had parted and collectively moved backward, creating a ring of space around them both. No one could hear what he was saying over the music, but she prayed there weren't any lip-readers in the room.

"You're scaring me," Peyton laughed, and it sounded hollow, and terrified, to her own ears.

"I'm going to be direct here. Your husband is fucking up our optics." He raised his eyebrows.

"I'm sorry, my husband is . . ."

"It's a cluster fuck, Peyton. Look, any remotely intelligent human being understands that these things happen. He didn't kill anyone, I get that. But the rest of America is not pleased that their morning sunshine is married to a felon."

Peyton felt like she'd been sucker punched. No one had dared use that word yet. Isaac wasn't a felon—he was the guy who had an endless supply of cringe-worthy dad jokes. Who didn't ever remember to match his belt to his shoes. Who wrote her sappy, singing cards on her birthday.

"I'm sorry you feel that way. But certainly you know that I'm still the same person, Joseph. And I think our viewers understand that, too."

"Oh, cut the horseshit, Peyton. That mom in Kansas who tunes in every morning to see the smart and sassy Peyton Marcus now sees a woman who talks to a convict in an orange jumpsuit through a plexiglass wall."

"Joseph, nobody is in jail. I don't think that—"

He cut her off. "Look, you know how I feel about you. How *everyone* feels about you. You're primed for prime time, love. You're on the short list. I'm not telling you anything you don't already know. I want our audience talking about how you nailed the coverage on the school admissions scandal, not about how your hubby bought your kid's way into school. You understand?"

Peyton stared, too shocked to speak. She could feel the mounting sense of dread wash like a cold wave across her neck and arms.

"The summer, that's it. Take the rest of the summer, go to the Hamptons, rest and relax. You'll be back, better than ever, in the fall, and this will have all blown over by then."

"The entire *summer*?" Peyton knew she'd been reduced to a bumbling idiot, but even with Sean's warning, she felt blindsided. Joseph couldn't have known—or cared—that she was already commuting from Paradise, and this wasn't really about location: she could barely process that he planned to bench her for the next *six weeks*.

"Exactly," Joseph said, smiling. "A little break will be good for everyone."

Suddenly the shifting landscape started to solidify. A "break" was the first step toward something more permanent. Morning anchors with massive ratings didn't take sabbaticals. Hell, they rarely even took sick days. Come to think of it, happily married couples also didn't take "breaks" either, regardless of how their crisis managers—or husbands—framed them. The sinking feeling in her stomach was starting to intensify, like she was on the downward curve of a too-steep coaster. This was horrible, all of it. She forced a deep breath and stepped closer to Joseph.

"Joseph, I appreciate your looking out for my mental health and well-being, I really do. But let me be the first to assure you. I'm fine. I've got this. You've known me long enough now to know that the last thing I need or want is a summer off. I have some great ideas for the type of human-interest segments we discussed in our last meeting, and I'm in the process of compiling a comprehensive list of experts with good on-air personalities who can take us through each one of them."

He stroked his beard dreamily, and Peyton wondered if he was listening. But then Joseph leaned in close enough that she could smell his cologne and said, "Peyton, sweetheart. Let me be a touch more transparent: your *needs and wants* are not, at this moment, my primary concern. This leave of absence is not optional. Now go, enjoy the party. Did you try the mini lobster rolls? Flown in fresh from Maine this morning!" He offered her a little salute as he floated away, and Peyton didn't know which felt worse, her cold, clammy dread or her seething hatred for the man who controlled her future.

"To Paradise, please," she told her driver as she scrambled into the backseat, yanking her studded skirt with her.

"Then, into her phone: "Nisha? It's me."

"Peyton. Wait—hold on one second." A baby wailed in the background.

"I'm sorry. You must be right in the middle of bedtime. We can talk later if—"

"It's perfect timing! I'm in my office. My nanny brought the baby here to nurse because I couldn't get home in time. What's up?"

Peyton breathlessly explained what had transpired at the party. "That can't be allowed, can it?"

Nisha sighed. "Obviously I haven't seen your contract, and I'm not an entertainment lawyer, but I would imagine that the network left a few loopholes for *situations* that arise. They can claim just about anything—likely they'd invoke the character clause if you tried to fight it—but of course you won't fight this if you want to keep your job."

"*Character* clause? Are they allowed to do that? Invoke that for something, um, Isaac did?"

"I know this is terrible, P, I really do." She paused for a moment. "We've known each other a really long time, and whatever happened—however this all went down—I'm sure neither you nor Isaac ever expected it would look like this. You're both good people. Everyone makes mistakes. It's especially hard that yours—and that's the collective 'you' I'm using—has to get played out in the court of public opinion."

Even harder than being strong was hearing the concern in Nisha's voice. It was an odd but welcome relief. Nisha wasn't exonerating her, not at all, but this was the very first time anyone close to her had shown even the smallest hint of understanding. What Peyton had done was morally and ethically inexcusable, possibly even unforgivable for what it was doing to the people she loved most. Given the chance for a do-over now, she never, *ever* would have made the same stupid decision. But she couldn't go back, so now more than ever she needed to start working on a plan to make it right.

The baby started to scream again. Peyton thanked Nisha profusely and told her she would call her back the following day. She immediately dialed Kenneth, but her call went straight to voicemail. She tried Isaac, but he didn't answer either.

The driver was about to turn onto the FDR so he could take the Midtown Tunnel, when Peyton said, "You know what? On second thought, I'm going to go to Seventy-sixth and Park. Thanks."

The car pulled up to her building, and Peter opened the car door. His eyes widened in surprise. "Mrs. Marcus," he stated.

"Thank you, Peter," Peyton said breezily, as though she weren't sneaking into her own building. She climbed out of the backseat, careful not to wrinkle or rip the Alexander McQueen dress, and headed directly for the elevator. She paused for a moment when the doors opened on her floor. Why hadn't Isaac answered her call? There was no way he was sleeping already—it wasn't even nine. Did he have friends over? A *woman*? Peyton shook the thought away, knowing it wasn't true, but she couldn't bring herself to type the code into the keypad. She knocked.

The footsteps she heard were Isaac's—she could tell he was wearing his old Adidas slides by the noise they made on the hardwood floor.

"Who is it?" he asked, but the door swung open before she could respond. *"Peyton?"*

She was relieved to see that he was wearing his usual summer pajamas—orange Princeton sweat shorts and a plain white undershirt—and holding the remote in his hand. "Hi. Can I, uh, come in?"

Immediately he stepped back and opened the door wide, motioning for her to enter, but Peyton was certain she could see something else in his expression.

"Why didn't you call?" he asked, embracing her briefly and kissing her on the cheek, like she was a friend's wife and not his own.

"I did," she said, trying to keep her voice light. "You screened me."

He didn't confirm or deny this. Peyton suddenly felt aware of the dampness under her arms.

"That's quite the dress." He sounded noncommittal, aloof. So different from her Isaac, the one she often thought of as golden retriever–like in his general enthusiasm for life.

"Tonight was Joseph's birthday party," she said, as though she hadn't told him a half-dozen times over the phone.

They walked into the kitchen. She could hear John Oliver's voice coming from the TV in the living room and felt a momentary wash of relief that at least this, Isaac's favorite show, had stayed the same.

He pulled a chilled bottle of water from the fridge, carbonated it in the countertop machine, and poured himself a glass over ice. "Want some?" he asked.

Peyton shook her head. He knew she hated seltzer. Had he already forgotten? Although she would have sworn a hundred times in a thousand ways that it was impossible at this point in their relationship to share an awkward silence, there it was.

She stared at the kitchen floor.

He studied the wall.

"Sorry to, um, just stop by like this, but I wanted to tell you in person that I'll be taking a leave from work the rest of the summer."

His eyes darted to hers. "Why would you do that?" he asked, sounding genuinely bewildered.

"It wasn't my decision."

"Christ." He combed his fingers through his hair. "Here I am, taking the fall for an absolutely asinine decision you made against my advice—all to save your career—and now you're taking a *leave of absence*?"

"I didn't *choose* this. Joseph told me in no uncertain terms that all the media attention surrounding your—our—situation isn't good for the show's 'optics.' He ordered me to lie low this summer and reassured me that I can come back as soon as it all blows over."

Finally, Isaac raised his gaze to meet hers. They'd only been apart a week, but he looked like he'd aged years. He took a deep breath. "I'm not sure if you're in denial or what, but we need to be straight about something: this is not going to just 'blow over.' I am likely going to serve a jail sentence. Our daughter has been kicked out of college before she even had a chance to matriculate. Now, despite both our efforts to save it, it looks like your career is in serious jeopardy, and with it, our financial stability."

"We have enough saved to get through the summer!" Peyton cried. Her determination to remain strong was slipping away.

"We do, yes. But after that? What if this isn't a temporary leave? What if you can't move to another network? You know how mortgaged we are now, how high our expenses are! Everything is dependent on your salary. I'm not saying this to make you feel worse, but we need to talk in real terms here."

The tears surprised her as much as they obviously shocked Isaac. Peyton almost never cried. But that night, standing in her own kitchen next to her husband who suddenly felt like a stranger, she couldn't stop the surge of emotion, the guilt and sorrow all rolled into a painful ball deep in her throat.

"I'm so sorry," she whispered. "So, so sorry."

"What were you thinking?" Isaac asked. "I don't understand— you're so much smarter than this."

Peyton shook her head. "I know now how wrong it was, on every level."

"Yes, but why didn't you know *then*? We talked about it! You covered this story when the first go-round happened two years ago. Why on earth wouldn't you think the same rules—and consequences— applied to us, too?"

"I wasn't thinking! Or I was thinking about it all wrong. Here was this man, someone the producers vetted to come onto the show to discuss his widely acclaimed book, and he was offering us an edge. That's all I saw it as—a little push. My god, there's a girl in Max's grade whose family hired an ex–professional water polo player from Russia and installed him in his own studio apartment in their building so he'd be available for on-call, twenty-four/seven training sessions. For four years! And all this reputable expert on college admissions wanted us to do was write a check to charity and he'd put in a good word with his friend, a trustee. You can't tell me that everything isn't done through personal connections: city private school admissions, internships, finance jobs. I convinced myself that this was the same thing."

"Well, obviously it's not. Legally, ethically, or otherwise. It's totally different."

"I know," Peyton whispered, and for the first time, she did. Her tears started again. "I know you must think this is all an extension of my Ivy obsession, but you have to believe me when I tell you that I was blinded by wanting to help Max."

"But Max didn't need—"

"I see that, too. But I couldn't then. She struggled in high school. Not academically, of course, but to find her place, to fit in. I know that was partially our fault too, by forcing her to go to Milford, but it's hard to turn down the finest private school in the city when they want your kid. And I . . . I just kept thinking back to how it felt when I realized all my friends were leaving for big, beautiful campuses, all over the country, ready to start their lives, and I'd be staying behind, in town, because I hadn't taken school seriously."

Isaac opened his mouth, but Peyton held up her hand. "I see now how unfair it is to put my childhood baggage on Max. She's a great kid, and she had the brightest future before I stepped in and screwed it all up for her. And you."

"She still does have a bright future. Not at Princeton, certainly, but that never really mattered to her in the first place. The only thing Max needs from you is unconditional love. That's it. For you, her mother, the most important person in her world, to see who she is and to love her for it. Where she gets her degree . . . in the grand scheme of life, as you and I both know, it's irrelevant. It's about family, about sticking together, about loving each other."

"But . . . it's not just about Max. I do think she's going to be okay, in spite of everything I've done to screw it up for her. But what about for you? I know we agreed that it's the quote-unquote 'smart move' for you to take the hit for this, but I can't stand it! And not just what the media is saying, but our friends, our family! It makes me literally sick to my stomach that any of them would think you were capable of something like this. Your job, too. All for what? Preserving my career? How is that fair?"

"It's not fair. But it's our only choice. It's the right choice for our family. One day, not long from now, when we both decide the timing is right, we're going to tell Max the truth about what happened. The one thing I can't live with is lying to our daughter."

Peyton nodded. "I agree a hundred percent." She was terrified of the idea—her relationship with Max was already fraught—but she wouldn't let Isaac take the fall with their daughter. The mere thought of Max's reaction to that development sent her into gasping sobs.

Isaac stood and walked to her, his arms outstretched, and she fell into him like he was the last safe place on earth. It wasn't until he wrapped himself around her that she realized it was the first physical contact they'd shared since before that hellish day of his arrest.

"Shhhhh," he murmured, the way he used to when Max skinned a knee. "We're going to have to figure out a way forward through this."

"You mean together, right? Please tell me you mean together. I know this separation was supposed to be in name only, strictly for appearances, but it's morphed into something real, and that scares me. It scares me so much. I don't want—" Her voice broke, and she didn't think she could finish, but she took a deep breath: "I don't want to lose you."

His silence frightened her, maybe more than she'd ever been frightened before, but she exhaled when he said, "We'll get through this. Together. Because we have no choice."

His arms around her felt warm and strong and safe. She stood on her tiptoes and pressed her lips to his, felt a dizzying joy when his familiar mouth yielded so easily into her own. Peyton was still crying as their mouths found each other, and it quickly grew more urgent, but then Isaac pulled away.

"No," he said.

A wave of panic washed over Peyton. Never, ever had he refused her. She pulled away and looked at him, trying to hide her own surprise.

"I'm not ready."

"Okay, of course, I understand," she said, and she did. She missed him desperately, wanted nothing more than to lie next him in their bed, to fall asleep beside him. But she understood.

Once again she stood on her tiptoes and tenderly pressed his upper lip between her own. "I'll wait for you as long as I have to."

This time it was Isaac who nodded, looking too emotional to respond.

"And not only that, but I'm going to fix this. I don't know how yet, but I'm going to make this better . . . for all of us."

Isaac looked at her, his face questioning, but he didn't say anything else before he walked out of the room.

Peyton watched him as he left, and prayed to the universe that she hadn't ruined the very best thing in her life.

17

Like a Psycho

Max stumbled into the cottage's kitchen at 6:45 A.M. and found her mother curled up in one of the old wicker chairs, sipping coffee in a silk robe, ANN playing on the television.

"Morning," Max mumbled. She headed straight for the Keurig.

"Hi, honey," her mother said mindlessly, her eyes fixed on the television, where some smoking-hot woman was sitting in her mother's usual anchor chair, and that repulsive co-anchor of hers was leering at her in the grossest possible way.

"Mom, it's been over a week. Why do you watch? Isn't it torture?"

"Sure is," her mother murmured. She sipped her coffee and turned back to Max. "What's your schedule today, sweetheart?"

"Can we please lay off the questions until I've had one cup of coffee?" Max said.

Her mom rinsed her cup in the sink. "I'm going to be meeting with a few local women who—" She stopped mid-sentence when the show returned from commercial break and Jim's voice sounded like it was being piped directly into their kitchen.

"We're lucky enough to have an incredibly accomplished and gorgeous—am I allowed to say 'gorgeous'?" he said. "Well, I hope so, because that's exactly what she is, gorgeous. An accomplished and *gorgeous* guest who will be joining us to shed light on the stress caused by cyberbullying."

Max filled her cereal bowl and sat down next to her mother at the floral banquette. "Does it bother you that he objectifies women like that?" she asked, chewing a huge spoonful of granola.

"Yes, it most certainly does. He's a chauvinist pig, the very worst kind of good-old-boy media type for whom Me Too simply doesn't apply. While I find him unpleasant to work with, at least he doesn't hold any real power or influence over me. I'm far enough along in my career that I feel confident enough to brush him off. But I often think of the younger women who work on the show—many not much older than you. I'm sure I don't even know half the ways he's vile and possibly predatory toward them, but what I do see enrages me."

Max considered this. It was interesting to hear her mother talk like this: the woman was usually so focused on flowers and fitness. "So what can be done? Don't you have to do something?"

Peyton smiled at her daughter. "Yes, of course, we all do. I'll continue to report any incidents I see to upper management. I'll continue to mentor the young women in our offices, give them guidance and support for how to deal with male superiors like Jim. But so much of this is going to be on you—your generation, coming of age in this new and exciting time when women can finally demand what they deserve. That's where *you* come in."

Max took a sip of her coffee. "I'm guessing you had to deal with a lot of Jims in your career," she said.

Her mom appeared to think about this. "Not so many, thankfully, but enough. You'll have to as well, regardless of what field you go into. But hopefully they'll be fewer and farther between, and the world will have continued to shift in the right direction." Her mom paused. "I know it doesn't feel this way, particularly now, in light of everything—but I'm so excited for your future. Whatever direction you choose to take it, I hope you'll let me stand by your side, cheering you on."

"Sure, Mom," Max said automatically, before getting up to refill her coffee. But as she stood at the machine, her mother's words reverberated. For the first time in as long as Max could remember, her mom had said something authentically supportive. She smiled to herself.

"I'm going to jump in the shower," her mom said. She leaned over and kissed Max on the cheek. "I love you, sweetheart."

"I love you, too."

The warmth from the chat didn't last long. All it took was Max flopping back down at the table and reflexively opening Instagram to send her into an anxious spiral. Her classmates' usual pictures had shifted into summer mode: all Hamptons, all the time. At the old-school Carvel on Route 27 upon arrival. Hitting up Drybar in Bridgehampton. SoulCycle in East. Intermix in South. The Hampton Coffee Company in Water Mill. Golf courses, tennis courts, riding stables. Polo. So much polo. Swim clubs. Wine tastings at Wölffer despite the fact that no one was legal. At the beach in string bikinis. At the beach in thong bikinis. At the beach in $450 lemlem cover-ups. At the beach for a bonfire party. Max only knew one person in her entire class, Brandon Simmons, who was working an actual paying job, if one could reasonably call giving sailing lessons at the Southampton Yacht Club an actual paying job. And come end of summer, each of them would be packing their bags and heading to dorms all across the country—but mostly in the Northeast—where they'd begin the best four-year adventure of their lives. And she would be scooping ice cream.

There was a knock at the front door.

"Anyone here?" she heard Skye call out. She let her aunt in.

"You look totally beautiful!" Max told her. Skye was wearing a pair of baggy linen pants that were cinched at the waist, a tight white ribbed tank, a tangle of super cool beaded necklaces, and a pair of beat-up Birkenstocks. Her tan skin literally glowed and her brown hair fell in the most amazing beachy waves down her back. And best of all, she wore no makeup. She was basically Max's hero.

"Ugh, I just can't," Skye said, running a hand through her waves as she followed Max into the kitchen. "Where's your mom?"

"She's upstairs, supposedly taking a shower," Max said. "But I suspect she's actually watching her show. Her ex-show. I don't think it's healthy."

"Oh?"

"She's a wreck. She doesn't get dressed anymore. Like, leggings-all-day-long type of situation. She's eating ice cream right from the container. Not drying her hair. Watching that damn show every single morning. It's like she's grieving. I feel badly for her, but I don't know what to do."

Skye furrowed her brow. "Moping is not very your mother."

"Since that party where they canned her, for the summer, she's barely left the house," Max said, holding up a mug in question toward Skye, who nodded.

Skye sat down at the kitchen table, a knotty, uneven farm table that Max loved.

"What's going on with you?" Max asked. "You're here early."

Her aunt didn't say anything at first, only twirled a piece of hair around her pointer finger. Max had learned, and not from her mother, that sometimes it was better to talk less, to wait.

"I lost the funding from my major investor," Skye said, staring at the table. "And without it I don't know how we can open the residence. Or pay for what we already committed to. I had to email the families and tell them. It was a pretty rough night."

"I'm sorry. I can't imagine."

"This single dad, Emilio, he's a widower with three daughters. Two of them were going to come here in September. He's devastated. The others are, too."

"So, what happened with the investor?" When Skye said nothing, Max said, "It's because of my dad, isn't it?"

Skye looked down. "Not directly."

"What does that mean?"

"It means, I don't want you blaming your dad for this," Skye said.

"Even though you are."

"It's complicated, honey. I understand Henry, my investor, not wanting to take what was supposed to be an enormous charitable contribution from his company and . . . I don't know . . . sully it with potentially negative media associations. It's the world we live in now. I just feel like I failed these families. Crushed their dreams, after building them up . . . it was one of the worst things I've ever had to do."

Max slapped her hand on the table. "You didn't fail at anything! My father did. It's because of *him* your investor bailed."

Skye shook her head. "I don't understand any of it. Your father wouldn't do something like this."

"Yeah, except he did. What is their obsession with the Ivy League? I mean, I'm asking seriously. I get that it's, like, extremely prestigious. That the professors and campuses are the best in the world, and that you're on some short-list path for success with a degree from one of them. But still! None of that can possibly explain why people lose their minds over getting into these schools. . . ."

Skye sipped her coffee. She smiled at Max. "You are wise beyond your years. Have I ever told you that?"

"Only, like, every time we see each other."

Skye glanced toward the door. "Are you sure your mother is upstairs?"

"Mom?" Max called out, louder than a regular speaking voice, but not loud enough to actually be heard if her mother was in fact holed up in her room, watching her replacement on ANN.

No response.

"You know part of the reason why your mother is so hung up on prestigious schools, yes? Regarding her own background?"

"She went to a state school," Max scoffed. "My god, the travesty!"

"It's not just—"

"I mean, come on! Penn State is a great school! You can't tell me that she—"

"She didn't start at Penn State," Skye said quietly.

Max set down her mug. "She didn't?"

"No. She spent her first year at a local community college near Lancaster. She didn't get into Penn State when she applied, or any-where else. Her grades were horrible."

"They *were*?" Max couldn't believe it—her mother had never mentioned anything about bad grades or community college. "But she's so smart! The entire country listens to what she has to say."

"She *is* smart! That hasn't changed. And I'm sure she'd kill me for telling you this, but I guess that's sort of what aunts are for, being the oral history of our siblings. . . . Anyway, the truth is that she basically blew off high school. She partied too much, skipped classes, all that kind of stuff. She got rejected from everywhere she applied."

Max whistled. "I didn't know that."

"When the reality of that set in, and all her friends left for college and she was at home with Grandma, well, I think it was a dark time for her. A lot of other people might not have recovered from that, just sort of figured that they weren't meant for college. But not your mom. She immediately enrolled in community college and worked her ass off for a year—literally, she worked two jobs and went to school full-time. Then, when she was finally able to transfer to Penn State her sophomore year, she just kept on working. It took her a fifth year to graduate, but only because your grandmother refused to pay for her college after what a disaster she'd been, so she had to keep up her paying jobs, too."

"How could she have never told me any of this?"

"If I had to guess, I'd probably say she was ashamed, even though she should have been so damn proud of herself for turning it around. But I'm sure she feels like she's been making up for that mistake and working to prove herself ever since. She's a fighter, your mom."

Max considered this. She'd often wondered why her mother worked as hard as she did, with the demanding schedule and work-load, and she'd always chalked it up to her blind ambition. A win-at-all-costs attitude that, suddenly, didn't seem quite so repellent as it had before.

"But I'm the furthest thing from a partyer," Max said. "I mean, I barely have friends. She couldn't have been worried about me flunk-ing out of school."

"I'm sure she wasn't worried about that, honey. But I imagine there's some part of her that sees all this opportunity in front of you—literally, the whole world, stretched out ahead of you, exactly as it should be—and it panics her to think that in some way it won't be perfect. And of course, it won't be perfect—no one's life is! But—and I'm speaking from experience here—moms are irrational when it comes to their daughters whom they love more than anything else on earth." Skye reached across the table and patted Max's hand.

"It does explain why she freaks the fuck out any time I even float the idea of not going to college. Or at least taking a gap year."

"Yes. Don't forget, the entire time this was happening with her, I was on a full academic scholarship to Amherst. Which, I don't need to tell you, Grandma never, *ever* shut up about. I knew it then, but I can see even more clearly now how that made everything even more difficult for your mom."

"Yeah, that would suck. At least I don't have any über-brilliant older siblings to overshadow me."

Skye hugged herself. "It wasn't easy. For either of us. I still think about the time when your mom won Homecoming Queen—she was the first junior to do it in the history of the school—and we all missed it because Grandma and even Pop both came to watch my orchestra rehearsal instead. Nothing special, just a rehearsal. But they made it pretty clear to all involved what they prioritized that night."

"That's brutal," Max said. "I didn't know about that either."

"I'm only telling you all of this so maybe you can understand where your parents are coming from a bit more, you know?"

"Yeah. I do. But that doesn't solve your problem. What are you going to do now? It can't just all be over."

Skye appeared to consider this. "There's a conference every year in DC. I haven't gone in ages—I never had time once we adopted Aurora—but it's a great networking opportunity, especially for information on grants. Lots of connected people in the NGO and non-profit world. It's been an easy path for me to lean on your parents for their connections, but I should be taking responsibility myself for finding new people. The conference is coming up, so I think I'll go this year."

They both heard footsteps on the stairs and then Peyton appeared in the kitchen, wearing sweats, wet hair half up. She stopped and looked at Skye. "Hi! I had no idea you were here."

"Just chatting with your lovely daughter," Skye said, smiling at Max.

"Max, sweetie," her mom said, "Skye and I are going to catch up a little on the screened-in porch. Do you have something to do?"

Max looked sideways at her mother, giving her a look of disbelief. "Mother. I am seventeen years old. I'm perfectly capable of amusing myself."

She watched as her mom gave Skye a look by raising her eyebrows and said, "See what I deal with?"

"You're being a bit smothering, P. I have to be honest."

Max high-fived her aunt. "Thank you. It's nice that someone understands."

"And you," Skye said, pointing at Max, "should not be so bitchy to the person who gave you life. Who apparently ruined her vagina in the process, as she never misses an opportunity to tell me."

"Okaaaaaaay," Max said, holding up her hand. "I'm out." She scrolled through her emails while Aunt Skye and her mother went to the screened-in porch. She counted to twenty and then crept quietly to the door, where she could clearly hear what they were saying.

"Has she talked to Isaac yet?" her aunt asked.

"Define 'talked.'"

"Peyton. He's her father. They're so close."

"I'm not sure if you've noticed that Max does whatever she wants, whenever she wants to, and I have very little input these days. But yes, we have talked about it. And I do think they've been in touch, although it's strained."

Max's phone vibrated, and she silenced it immediately, relieved that neither Skye nor her mom had heard it.

Her mother continued. "Did I tell you that after she got the notification from Princeton, she made a comment about not going to college at all? I don't think she was serious, but my *god*. What would we do if she's serious?"

I am serious, Max thought. *And you don't have to do a damn thing.*

"Max is a smart girl with excellent common sense. Maybe taking a little time to figure things out isn't the worst thing in the world," Skye said.

"What, so she can mope around and work on her *blog*? No, thank you," Peyton said.

Rage surged up Max's throat. All her mother's supposedly unconditional love and support from that morning hadn't meant a thing.

"Between that, my 'extended leave of absence,' and the latest call with the lawyer, it's been a banner week."

"What did the lawyer say?"

"Nothing's official yet, but she said the judge will probably give Isaac two to six weeks in jail, community service, and a large fine."

Skye whistled. "Two weeks for trying to game the system and wrecking your daughter's life in the process?"

Max had never before understood what people meant when they called silence "deafening" until that very moment. She was scared to shift, breathe, even blink. Even though she couldn't see either her mother or her aunt, she could physically feel their tension.

After what felt like hours, Skye very quietly said, "I'm sorry."

There was another silence. Max had the strange sensation that her mother wanted to say something else—maybe even was about to—when Skye's phone rang.

"It's Gabe." And then into the phone: "Hey. I thought your meeting wasn't until nine." More silence. "Got it, I'm leaving now."

"Gabe's first meeting got moved up, so I have to get home to Aurora," Skye said. "Let's finish this later? I hate to leave like this."

Max beelined to her bedroom just before she heard the front door open and then close. A moment later there was a knock at her door.

"Max? Sweetheart? I'm going to head to town to do some grocery shopping. Need anything?"

"All good!"

"All right. Keep in touch with me, okay? Let me know if you go anywhere?"

"Copy that," Max said. She waited until the footsteps disappeared and then headed back to the kitchen. Her thumb hovered over her phone, coming so close to pressing the "Dad" button in her Favorites list, but Max didn't do it. What would she say when he answered? *I miss you desperately, but I also hate you intensely. Not forever, just at this moment in time. And also, can we go fishing soon, because that's basically my favorite thing in the whole world?* Or, *I worry about you going to jail and Mom completely losing it?* She'd sound like a psycho. Instead, she poured herself another coffee and debated taking a run to clear her head.

What a strange freaking morning, Max thought, as she changed into one of her heavy-duty sports bras, a tank top, and a pair of sweat shorts. It wasn't until she was nearly a mile from the house, settled into her running rhythm, that Max felt a strange pang of loneliness and realized: she wished she'd asked her mom to join her.

18

He Was Married

K eep walking," Gabe urged.

Skye and Aurora diligently followed, the ground crunching beneath their hiking boots. Although the fresh night air felt wonderful, Skye still felt like she couldn't fully fill her lungs. Her mind was on a loop reel: residence, debt, uncertain future.

"Are we there yet, Daddy?" Aurora asked. They tromped a dozen steps farther and emerged from the cover of the forest. A clearing of some sort stretched out before them, surrounded on all sides by trees and lit only by hundreds of stars.

"Here," Gabe declared. "We call this area the Sanctuary, because it's the area of the park reserved just for the animals. What are some of the things we could see here tonight?"

The three of them huddled together and gazed upward into the spectacular night sky.

"Bats?" Aurora offered in her sweet, six-year-old squeak.

"Yes, definitely bats. Although it may still be a bit early for them. What else?"

"Snakes?" Skye could see that her daughter's eyes were wide.

"No, probably not snakes. But wait a minute." Gabe fumbled around in his backpack and pulled out his phone. "Close your eyes for a minute."

Aurora immediately clamped her eyes closed. A deep, realistic-sounding *whoo-whoo* hoot filled the air.

"That was my phone," Gabe whispered. "But wait."

They stood in silent anticipation, the only sound the rustles from their windbreakers. A moment later, deep from the mysterious darkness off to the left, came the faintest *whoo-whoo* in response.

"Daddy, an owl!" Aurora yelled in excitement.

"That's called a great horned owl. They are common around here, but they're very hard to spot. They like to stay hidden. But sometimes when we call to them, they call back," Gabe explained.

Aurora whispered loudly, "Do it again, Daddy."

The electronic owl hoot from the Bluetooth speaker Gabe clipped on his backpack once again filled the air. And again, as though on cue, the real owl called back to it in a quieter, more reserved *whoo!*

Skye breathed in the crisp night air and smiled as she watched Aurora race around the clearing in excitement, laughing.

"Well?" Gabe asked, wrapping his arms around Skye and burying his face in her neck. "Are you happy?"

Skye nodded. Camping a weekend in July had become a family tradition. After news of the funding, Skye hadn't wanted to go, but she was glad now that Gabe insisted.

"It's perfect," she said, kissing his cheek. "I needed this. Tonight reminds me of that first night, you know, with us? I remember walking over to your apartment, and there were so many stars in the sky. My god, it feels like a hundred years ago," Skye said.

"The first time we met? Or the second?" Gabe asked.

Skye swatted him.

Aurora had found a large puddle and was leaning over to examine it.

"What? It's a fair question!"

Skye forced a laugh. It was crazy it still bothered her, all these years later, something as unimportant as how they'd met. Who really cared? Couples met all the time online, or drunk in a bar, or while they were in relationships with other people. It only mattered what you did after that, what kind of partnership and life you built together, right? But sometimes Skye couldn't shake the feeling that their marriage—despite being one of the best things in her life—had somehow had a cursed beginning.

She'd spotted him for the first time in Religions of the World. He wore a flannel shirt over a Phish T-shirt. Reddish-blond hair pulled into a ponytail. Sneakers holding on for dear life. Not that Skye liked her guys preppy—far from it, that was Peyton's domain—but she didn't normally go for the patchouli-loving pot smokers, either. Yet from the moment she saw him, Gabe seemed different. He had an enormous, almost electric smile that he flashed unsparingly and the sort of easy, constant physical affection that made everyone around him, men and women, want to stay close—a very Australian trait, she soon learned. A backslap here, a hug there, a hand squeeze or a shoulder rub: Gabe was comfortable with physicality in a way so many American men were not.

They'd ended up at Gabe's off-campus apartment, the exact sort of male undergrad abomination one would expect, complete with wall-sized tapestries and lava lamps and a bong so tall it rivaled the height of the resident Bernese mountain dog, Larry. There were books on every surface and framed color photographs of various birds, mountains, and seascapes vying for attention with dramatic black-and-whites of stupas, prayer flags, and monks. Gabe gave Skye and their two other classmates a brief tour of his photographs, and then they all got down to the real business of the evening: getting high and discussing how to best incorporate Buddhism's end-of-life traditions into their group presentation.

She was stoned, yes, but she didn't blame the weed for what happened that night. At some point the others left and Gabe and Skye were alone. When she leaned over and kissed him, he seemed momentarily surprised. Yet when he kissed her back, and their tongues touched for the first time, it felt inevitable. They made out in the living room for three minutes or three hours, she honestly couldn't have said, and when he grabbed her hand and led her into his bedroom, Skye remembered feeling grateful. It was 2002 and back then no one breathed a word about consent, and surely what happened next would not have met present-day criteria. But twenty-two-year-old Skye knew exactly what was happening. They both did. She couldn't remember a lot of the details from that night, but she knew it was one of the best of her life.

Only afterward, he didn't call. Skye began to obsess. What on earth was she thinking, sleeping with a guy she'd only just met? Surprise! It actually felt pretty lousy to have a one-night stand, despite the fact that every so-called empowered friend and tattered waiting-room copy of *Cosmo* swore that no-strings-attached sex was nothing but fun, fun, fun. Graduation followed a couple weeks later, and except for awkward nods in their final few classes together—and a group presentation that could only be described as downright uncomfortable for everyone involved—they went their separate ways: she back to Pennsylvania, where she'd live with Marcia until she saved enough to move out on her own, and Gabe back to Melbourne, where he'd spend the summer before applying to graduate school.

"Mommy! Daddy! Help!" Aurora's panicked wail instantly broke Skye out of her memory. Gabe wrenched away from Skye and sprinted toward Aurora. Blood poured from her nose.

"Ohmigod, baby, are you okay?" Skye said, dropping to her knees beside her daughter.

"My boot kicked my nose!" Aurora sobbed.

"Here, love," Gabe crooned, using his own scarf to mop up the blood. "It's starting to slow already. You're going to be just fine."

Gabe took her by the hand and began to walk, trying to distract her with a ghost story.

Skye looked after them. Absolutely not one thing in her and Gabe's history would have predicted they would have ended up here, like this, together. She hadn't even planned to attend her ten-year reunion, but naturally, he was the very first person Skye spotted when she walked into the tent on the Main Quad, and in spite of herself, a strange sensation shot from her stomach to her throat. Gabe at thirty-two looked even better than Gabe at twenty-two. His reddish hair was still long but the ponytail was gone, replaced by a man bun. And so help her god, despite every critical word she'd uttered on the subjects of man buns and the kind of men who chose them, Gabe somehow made it look *hot*. He wore tight gray jeans and a white T-shirt; his rumpled blazer with rolled-up sleeves gave him that intellectual-hipster look that Skye found irresistible.

He saw her right away, and his face broke into a huge smile as he covered the distance between them in quick, confident steps. "Skye," he breathed, his cheek kiss coming precariously close to the corner of her mouth, his accent even more pronounced. "It's so good to see you."

She knew immediately she would sleep with him that night. Why wouldn't she? She was single and he was gorgeous and, really, what could be better than a one-night stand that didn't count as one? A freebie! He wouldn't add to her number of sexual partners, a statistic she knew was utterly meaningless in this age of liberated women, but one that, regardless, she carefully tracked.

They drank. They danced to nineties hits. She told him she'd gone for her master's at Columbia's Teachers College and had spent three years afterward working for an educational nonprofit in Uganda. She was currently teaching fourth grade at a charter school in Harlem, where she lived in a small but charming garden apartment and was trying to get back to Africa. He told her he'd surfed and waited tables for a few years back home in Australia before going back for his master's in architecture at NYU. He was also living in the city, in Brooklyn, although his own apartment featured neither charm nor a garden; he'd been grinding it out as a freelance architect for years, but his student debt and general life of genteel poverty was making him think about accepting a position with a firm.

He told her he was married.

Unhappily, of course. Basically estranged. All the details one might expect from a seemingly decent guy who was about to cheat: his wife was anxious, unhappy, dissatisfied. They had married too young, too soon after meeting, and they'd both changed so much. They didn't have sex anymore. They had an understanding. He suspected she wanted out of the marriage, too.

And Skye believed him.

When she asked, because she couldn't help herself, Gabe told her that the first year of his marriage was the hardest of his life. But then other details emerged, small asides that were even more telling. They had a beagle together named Walter. They'd ended up in Brooklyn because *she'd* gotten a job there. He called her Nicki even though everyone else called her Nicole. She'd graduated from MIT, and he said this with pride. Later, when she was back home in Harlem, Skye found a picture of the wife online. Nicole was leaning against a railing, in front of a cemetery or ruins of some kind, and looking directly at the camera. Her expression was inscrutable. The sunglasses perched on her head glinted in the light. Skye realized Gabe had likely taken the picture, that he and Nicole had been sightseeing somewhere, right before they'd gone back to their hotel and probably made love, just as she and Gabe had.

Remembering that time, a deep, involuntary shiver shook her, made her suddenly angry to be standing alone in the dark park. "Aurora! Gabe! Let's go!" she shouted as loudly as she could manage.

There was no response. She called Gabe on his phone. "Can you guys come back? It's really dark here."

"Sorry, sweetheart. Aurora found a nightcrawler and we got distracted. We're on our way."

They'd begun to email after the reunion, which had progressed to long, meandering phone conversations late into the night. Skye wondered where Nicole was when they spoke for two, three, sometimes four hours at a time, but she never asked. When, six months later, Gabe appeared, unannounced, at Skye's Harlem apartment, she thought her heart would burst with excitement. He'd found her! He wanted her! He felt it, too! She was floating, euphoric, more in love with him than she'd ever been with anyone. But the moment he announced that his divorce had just been finalized, Skye had felt a thunderous roar deep inside her head. *Wait—you left your wife? For me? But we barely know each other!* As the days turned into weeks, these worries were followed by other ones. Had Skye just ruined another woman's life? Did the fact that Gabe cheated *with* her make it more likely that he'd cheat *on* her? Could a relationship ever succeed if it began in such a dishonest way? Was she dooming herself to repeat her parents' relationship, where her father had left her mother with no warning at all?

But Gabe constantly reassured her. He was excited, filled with plans. He kept insisting they trust their instincts, that they were older now and knew their own minds, that they knew when things were right. They would settle down somewhere lovely; she could teach and he could find a steady position at a great firm. They would raise a family. His happiness was exhilarating, and it all happened so quickly. Within a few months they'd moved in together, and soon he'd proposed in front of her family, and any worries about how they'd met had gotten swept away in a flurry of planning.

Eight years ago. How was that possible? Things were calm now, familiar. Solidly good. Weren't they? All Skye had to do was look at the little girl holding his hand and those old feelings came rushing back—anticipation, excitement, and love all wrapped into one person. Her daughter. From the moment the phone rang and the adoption agency had announced, "You matched with a baby girl," all of Skye's doubts had vanished. Aurora was more perfect than Skye could have ever imagined, and parenthood had turned out to be the biggest surprise of her life, with its richness and complexity and, yes, fear and exhaustion, too. She wouldn't trade it for anything in the world, although just for a while—with the plans for the residence—she'd wondered if she could have professional fulfilment, too. The thought of it gave her a pang of intense anxiety.

Sensing something, Gabe took Skye's hand in his left and reached for Aurora's with his right. Together, the three of them trekked back to the tent hand in hand. They built a fire and made hot cocoa, topped Aurora's with marshmallows and theirs with Baileys they'd packed in a stainless steel water bottle.

"You know this is the anniversary of the week we got the call from the agency," Skye said, after Aurora fell asleep, sprawled between them.

"Is it really?"

"My god, that was the best call we've ever gotten."

"It certainly was," Gabe agreed, stroking Aurora's cheek.

Skye opened her mouth to ask if he really, truly didn't sometimes think about another child, but she stopped herself. The night had been perfect. She adored that despite both of them becoming actual adults with actual adult responsibilities, Gabe made sure that they took the time to honor what sometimes felt like their previous lives. When they both had endless time and loved the outdoors. When everything was simpler. Instead of bringing up a subject that might disrupt the mood, she snuggled next to her daughter and reached across to take Gabe's hand. "I love you," she said.

Gabe gave her one of his lopsided grins that she adored and pressed his head against Aurora's shoulder. "I love you, too."

19

Close Your Fucking Mouth

Where are you right now?" Nisha asked. "What's that noise?"
Peyton glanced to her right, to the overweight man
who'd crammed himself into the seat next to her and
whose headphones were blaring music. "I'm on the train to the city,"
she whispered. "There are a few things I need to take care of."

"So, I did some research," Nisha continued, as if Peyton hadn't
said anything. "A colleague of mine recommended a charity auction
in Paradise next week. I made a few calls and you're going to be the
guest of honor. How's your tennis?"

"My tennis?"

"It's at a local country club. Very posh. Whites required; I'll email
you all the information. But it will be high-profile people, local media,
and best of all, all the money raised will benefit underprivileged, first-
generation college students. It's exactly the right cause and message.
Peyton, are you there?"

"I'm here," she whispered, her hand over her mouth. "When we
agreed to rehabilitate my reputation, I thought you were going to
suggest . . . I don't know . . . an interview or something. I'd give a tour
of our New York apartment, a real at-home-with-Peyton-Marcus type
of—"

"It's next Friday evening. I'll send you the details. You are going to project quiet confidence and authenticity. Also, remind me to talk to you about your social media."

"What about it?"

"I want you to humanize your Instagram and Facebook. Keep Twitter to newsy stories like it is, but put a softer face on your other accounts."

"Softer face?"

"Right now it's all entirely professional: you at the anchor desk, in your office at work, interviewing people on location or traveling for a story. In normal times that's exactly what we'd want. But now I want you including some more personal bits—pictures with Max, with your family and friends, vacations, that sort of thing. Even Isaac. Don't focus on him but also don't shy away, either."

"Really?"

"Listen, I've got to run, but keep it in mind and we'll talk more about it soon."

Before Peyton could say another word, she heard a click.

Peyton stared out of the window as the suburbs rushed past. There was no claiming that a haircut or some Botox was going to fix her problems, but she needed to take some sort of *action*. She was planning to call Sean and see if he'd meet her for a quick coffee outside the office, and after that, she hoped to swing by Kenneth's office and check in with him in person. For the morning, she'd made the appointments. All the appointments. It was going to cost a fortune, something that added another line of stress to her forehead, and that she had rarely considered when her paychecks were regularly being deposited, but it had to be a priority. First she'd fix her face and then her life, and you couldn't put a price on that.

From Grand Central, she walked to the Oscar Blandi salon, where Marco, her colorist, made no effort to hide his horror.

"It looks like dishwater," he said, holding up a section of Peyton's hair and grimacing like he'd detected a bad smell.

"I know, it's been a—"

"No, I take it back. It actually looks like sewage." His two assistants nodded. "Have you been . . . *swimming*?"

Peyton looked at him through the mirror her chair faced. "Yes, a couple times. I know it's a little dry and the gray really needs—"

"Gray roots I can fix. This is the color of algae."

Peyton held her right hand across her heart. "No more pools, I promise," she vowed. Did these people not realize her entire life was falling apart? That her problems ran much deeper than hair?

Three hours later and looking like a new person, Peyton picked up a salad on the way to her nutritionist's office. After settling into the pale pink waiting-room couch, Peyton opened the takeout container, carefully poured only the faintest drizzle of balsamic onto her salad, replaced the lid, and shook it vigorously. When Neve materialized, the first thing Peyton noticed was the way the twenty-five-year-old's collarbones jutted through her silk shell like miniature unicorn horns.

"Peyton," she murmured, either too cool or too hungry to smile.

"Neve! It's been forever. Thanks for fitting me in today. I've really started to let everything go, and I hope to be back on air shortly, so . . ." Peyton followed Neve into her office and waited for her to settle on her yoga ball chair before taking the smallest, most delicate bite of her salad. A nibble, really. Perhaps not even more than a single piece of lettuce.

Neve scrunched her nose and stared like Peyton had just lowered her entire face into a banana cream pie. "What's *that*?"

Peyton swallowed and dabbed her lips with a paper napkin. "Sorry, I thought you said this was a working lunch?"

Neve shook her head. "No. I meant we'd be meeting *during* my lunch hour. Eating is probably not the most efficient use of our time, considering we're here to talk about your diet."

"Right. Of course." Peyton felt her face redden as she tried to fit the lid back on her bowl. A few pieces of dressed lettuce ended up on her linen dress.

"Oh my," Neve murmured again, not moving a single inch to offer assistance.

"Sorry about that! Here, let me tuck this back in the bag and . . . there. Where were we?" Peyton clasped her hands together and tried to appear repentant. The diameter of Neve's upper arms was just so *distracting*.

"Have you been journaling your food?" Neve touched a fingertip to her sunken cheek. "Let's go through this worksheet together on which foods to avoid." Peyton promptly tuned out. What could Neve possibly tell her that she didn't already know? Limit carbs. Increase vegetables. Protein at every meal. Fruit sparingly. Sweets not at all. It was ridiculous already. Everyone knew *what* to do—the problem was *doing* it. Or really, *not* doing it. Neve typically had one and only one piece of advice for her clients, which boiled down to *close your fucking mouth*, but since she couldn't say that, they were instead forced to negotiate endlessly the issue of whether corn and beans were considered proteins or carbs.

Back in the cab and now in a full, anxious sweat, Peyton texted Sean to ask if she could swing by the Starbucks in the ANN lobby. His response was immediate: *Would love to see you, but today is chaos. Next week?* She couldn't remember the last time her work husband had said no to a quick coffee, but then again, she also couldn't remember the last time she wasn't at work. Finishing her salad in the backseat, Peyton tried to mentally prepare herself for her next appointment. Even though Dr. Lydia Bittman was an actual MD—both Yale-trained and board-certified—her office looked and felt more like an Aman spa. The front desk, where Peyton was greeted by an Asian woman in an elegant print blouse and coordinating skirt, gave no clues to its purpose: no obvious computers, no phones, no papers. Nor did the waiting room give the slightest hint that it was a prelude to actual medical care. Tufted upholstered chaises, half a dozen in all, took the place of regular chairs, and each was separated by a gauzy linen curtain and lit warmly by a softly glowing Himalayan salt lamp—the real kind, not the cheap Chinese versions from Amazon. Hardcover art and photography books, mostly Rizzoli, replaced the usual tattered magazines. There was no automated coffee machine in sight, only a handblown glass tea set and an assortment of exotically named leaves in delicate pouches. Invisible speakers played soothing spa music. Beautiful, uniform flames blazed from a wall-mounted gas fireplace despite the outside temperature of 85 degrees. The only other patient, a pregnant woman in her thirties, lay in a chaise with closed eyes while an attendant in a starched white uniform massaged her feet.

Peyton could already feel the kneading pressure of the woman's strong hands on her own sore legs. A cup of iced tea sounded heavenly, too. She'd almost forgotten how tough the city could be on a late July day when the temperatures reached the high eighties and the cement was emanating heat. She would call Kenneth to check in, and then her assistant, to hear what was happening at ANN.

"I'm early," Peyton announced to the beautiful receptionist. "But I'm very happy to wait."

"Well, you're in luck. The doctor had a rare cancellation," the woman said with a curt smile, one that seemed to say *Don't even think of trying to give me an insurance card, because that's about as useful around here as a food stamp.* "She can see you right now."

Peyton was whisked back to an exam room, which looked like a luxury hotel suite, and within seconds Dr. Bittman swept in wearing a tailored pantsuit with a leather belt whose bright orange "H" buckle could be seen from a distance of three city blocks. The heels were Louboutin, their telltale red soles and S&M-inspired studs leaving no question as to their provenance. An oversized Rolex watch and a thick gold Cartier bangle completed her look. Peyton was strangely accustomed to the fact that her doctor now bore a striking resemblance to Michael Jackson. It used to worry her that Bittman's nose looked like it was melting into her face, and that her lips resembled small sausages, but Peyton—like every other patient in the practice—soon came to realize that none of this mattered. Bittman could look like a character from *Game of Thrones*, so long as she made *you* look good.

"Peyton," she said. "Wonderful to see you. How's Isaac managing?"

Peyton appreciated the directness. Most people had no idea what to say.

"He's taking it one day at a time," Peyton said, as though they were talking about cancer.

Dr. Bittman nodded. "And you? I haven't seen you on TV for a bit now. Everything okay there?"

Peyton clenched her jaws, no longer enjoying their little chitchat.

"Fine, thanks so much. Just taking a little breather. It was my choice. I've barely taken any time off, so . . ." *Stop talking!* Peyton silently urged herself. *Stop being so defensive!*

Dr. Bittman got the message. "Great. What brings you in today?"

"Oh, just a little touch-up on the Botox, please. I'm afraid I've let it go too long this time."

Dr. Bittman slid next to her on the couch and produced an intensely bright light from the pocket of her pantsuit. She shone it directly on Peyton's face.

"Mmm," the doctor said softly. "Yes."

"Let's maybe do the same as last time? The forehead, the eleven, and the crow's feet? I was happy with that."

Dr. Bittman was quiet. She squinted a bit more and said, "The Botox is a given. But I do think you're ready for something a bit more . . . potent."

"What's more potent than botulinum toxin?" Peyton asked.

Not a hint of a smile from Bittman. Instead, she outlined Peyton's jaw with her fingertips. "It's not uncommon in my forty-something patients to see their jawlines slackening and their skin developing that crepey look. You have some darker-than-normal discoloration under your eyes and some fine lines and sunspots."

"What do you recommend?" Peyton asked, desperately wanting to know and not wanting to know.

"A PRP facial."

"A what?"

"It stands for 'platelet-rich plasma' and it's the gold standard when it comes to increasing collagen production and skin elasticity. It will also reduce your fine lines and wrinkles and add volume where you need it. Colloquially called a vampire facial. I've been recommending them to all my patients over forty."

Peyton inhaled. "I'm not forty yet."

"It's a simple, in-office procedure. We've had terrific results."

"What kind of plasma is it?" Peyton asked.

Dr. Bittman frowned. "Your own. We draw blood from your arm and then use a centrifuge to separate out the platelet-rich plasma. Then we apply that to your face, and it works its magic. It's like liquid gold."

"I, uh, don't really like the sight of blood, especially my own. I'm not sure I could have it smeared all over my—"

"We don't *smear* anything. We use a micro-needling technique to get it under the skin, really allow it to soak in."

"Needles all over my face?"

"If you can handle Botox, you can handle this. We'll get you good and numbed. Monique will massage your feet during the procedure. It'll be over before you know it."

It was all starting to sound a lot like the last treatment that Dr. Bittman insisted was imperative, some sort of facial laser. The doctor had promised—and provided—numbing and massage with that procedure too, but Peyton could still recall the exact sensation of having her face blasted by something that felt like a hot glue gun. The so-called anesthetic cream had been as effective at numbing her pain as a layer of freshly applied peanut butter.

"And the downtime? What will that look like?"

"A touch of redness and swelling at the time of injection. Perhaps some dryness and peeling a week later. That's it. It's nothing."

Peyton snorted. "That's what you told me when I did the IPL."

"And?"

"And it looked like I had full-blown syphilis for three weeks."

Dr. Bittman didn't deny this. "Was it worth it?"

"Yes," Peyton said, with no hesitation. Every freckle, sunspot, red spot, brown spot—every tiny little skin imperfection or discoloration—had slowly grown darker and darker and darker. During that time, makeup artists at ANN would only use disposable application brushes. Isaac had wanted to book her an appointment with an infectious disease specialist. But then, slowly, the dark spots started flaking off, and within a week every single one was gone.

Vanished! Like a cosmetic fairy had descended from the heavens and waved a giant magic eraser across Peyton's face. She looked flawless. Eventually it all came back, and faster than she might have hoped, but for those glorious few months, Peyton knew what it felt like to attain the unattainable. She felt a wave of something like nostalgia: how long ago was it when she dealt with her so-called problems on air by looking better, tighter, younger? Now it all felt so empty, and not just empty, but hopeless and ridiculous, too. The despair came at her like a shovel: swift, surprising, almost physical. She inhaled sharply, all too aware of her new reality, and how absurdly she was behaving.

"Well?" Dr. Bittman asked.

"I'm in," Peyton said, sticking out her right arm. She took another breath, trying not to cry. "Take whatever you need."

Hi. Going to swing by apt to shower before meeting the TV Moms for dinner. Ok by you? Any chance we can have a drink afterward?

It felt strange to be texting Isaac like he was a new boyfriend instead of her long-married spouse, but it felt even stranger to show up unannounced and unexpected in her own home.

He didn't respond, which left Peyton sitting in her own lobby, wondering what to do. She'd give it five minutes, she decided, and then go up. When she hadn't heard back from him after fifteen, and the new night doorman eyed her suspiciously, Peyton stepped into the mirrored elevator. Her hair still looked great with its fresh color and blowout, but predictably, her face was starting to swell.

There was no response to her first doorbell ring or her second, and when she finally unlocked the door, she had the odd sensation of being both panicked and relieved to find the apartment darkened and empty. She'd been hopeful that that night in New York, after Joseph's party, would have changed something between Isaac and her. If not fixed, then at least softened. But as soon as she'd awakened the next morning, he'd encouraged her to return to Paradise for Max, and the strange, emotional distance they'd been keeping between them returned. How weird was it to stand in your own home and not have any clue where your husband was? Again she shivered, hugging her arms tight to her chest.

She was looking forward to seeing her TV Mom friends that night. Over the past few weeks they'd been quieter than usual, to the point where Peyton wondered if they hadn't set up a side group without her. Eventually, all had offered some version of a supportive message, but they'd felt a little forced, a bit half-hearted at best. Dinner with the girls was exactly what the doctor ordered: they would bitch and laugh and gossip, confess and cry, and start all over again. How long had it been since she'd seen them? More than a month, she figured, doing the math. Certainly before the whole situation, as she'd taken to thinking of it. She'd had to push hard to get everyone to commit to dinner that night, especially considering that these women would usually do just about anything to escape their husbands and children.

She made her way to the kitchen, and her phone pinged.

Sorry this is so last minute but Roger has to stay late at work tonight. Have fun without me!

Peyton felt a flash of irritation. Renee employed not only a full-time nanny whose sole responsibility was caring for one four-year-old child, but also a round-the-clock baby nurse to "tend to" their three-month-old. In what universe did it matter if her husband was going to stay at work or fly to Bangladesh?

Whatever. Renee's compulsive addiction to childcare staff wasn't going to ruin the night; the remaining four of them would still have fun.

She replied a *We'll miss you!* and pulled a Diet Coke from the fridge. Should she try Max? Check in and make sure she was okay? Was that caring or smothering? Helicoptering or appropriate? As she mentally debated this, the next cancellation text popped up.

Ugh, so sorry. Crisis at work. Must deal. Will meet up later if anyone still out. xx

Peyton stared at her phone on the bathroom sink. Kate was a jewelry designer with her own boutique on Madison Avenue. What kind of crisis, exactly? A broken clasp? But whatever, drinks for three was way more intimate, and the two women she liked the most were still in. Peyton headed to the master bath and began filling the tub.

Her phone pinged again.

Don't kill me but I'm out too. Four girls in Harper's camp group have LICE! Suddenly so itchy. I have the lice lady coming to check us all as soon as she can get here. Love you guys and sorry to miss.

Marianne and Peyton knew each other from their stints as pages at NBC and had kept in touch all these years. At some point post-kids Marianne had given up anchoring and pursued a career as a segment producer at *The View*. Not even lice, merely the *possibility* of lice? This had to be some kind of joke.

Dina, the last holdout, texted almost immediately, this time only to Peyton: *Hey! Looks like we are last ones standing. Rain check? #exhausted #stressed #neednetflix*

Peyton stared at her phone. *Exhausted?* Hadn't Dina just returned from a weeklong junket sans kids to the new luxury meditation spa in Northern California? What, exactly, was she so stressed about?

Of course! Loving the idea of a night in too. xx

Sighing, she trudged to the wine fridge, filled a massive water glass with rosé and some ice cubes, and headed back to the bathroom. Taking extreme care not to splash any water on her face, Peyton slowly submerged herself into the steaming water. Exhaling, she dried her hands on a washcloth and texted Max what she hoped was a casual *Hello, how are you, did you find the salmon I left for you in the fridge?*

Peyton took a giant slug of her wine. This cancellation wasn't a coincidence, it was coordination. She texted Skye:

City mom friends all just canceled on me super last minute. It's me, isn't it? They don't want to be seen with me now?

She waited for a response, but none came. She texted Isaac again, two question marks this time, but nothing. Polishing off her rosé, she debated what to do.

She added more hot water, scalding really, and groaned. Nothing, nothing, felt as good as the oversized soaking tub in her city apartment. She wore a terry-lined shower cap to protect her new blowout and kept the tub level lower than usual to reduce the chance that any moisture would dilute the potency of her freshly plasma'd face.

What had she done? The apartment was empty, her phone was silent, and everyone else was getting on with their lives. Even Max, the most innocent victim in all of this, was doing her best to forge forward amidst impossible circumstances. How had she misjudged so badly? Acted so recklessly?

She remembered, clear as day, the night after the discussion about the college fixer, after Isaac had told her—unequivocally—that it was a bad idea. That they'd gone home from the restaurant and made love, their conversation about the fixer all but forgotten. It stayed forgotten for weeks—months, even?—until Peyton got an email from Max's guidance counselor about college tours, and the whole thing sent her into a tailspin of panic and anxiety. Even back then Max had occasionally murmured questions about why college was absolutely necessary. She wanted to go to *film* school. Travel the world. Take a gap year, which any sane person could see would significantly reduce the chance that her daughter ever made it back to a college campus. Suddenly, with that one email, Peyton was thrown back to Max's entire childhood, and her own. The hoops they'd jumped through to get Max into the "right" preschool. The classes, courses, tutors, coaches, extracurriculars, volunteer opportunities, camps, trips, and lessons they'd endlessly researched and debated, trying to choose exactly the "right" things for their daughter. The memories of that fateful day, twenty-two years earlier, when seventeen-year-old Peyton had opened her seventh—and final—college rejection letter and understood, for the very first time, that she had no one to blame but herself. All of it had come rushing at her like a river of remorse and regret and fear . . . so much fear. She hadn't planned to call the guy, truly, she'd intended to honor her promise to Isaac, but when he called her to "check in," it didn't sound like a big deal. It was a three-minute conversation, if that. *Write this check, mail it here, you'll be helping a great cause and I, in turn, will help your kid.* Did she know as she jotted out the amount, first in numbers and then in letters, that something wasn't right? Of course. But then the ever-tightening lump in her throat started to loosen as she signed her name, and it relaxed even more as she sealed and addressed the envelope. The night he'd cashed the check and sent her a thumbs-up text emoji, Peyton slept seven consecutive hours for the first time in three weeks.

As she stared at her perfectly pedicured toes, in the silence of the empty apartment, her family estranged, Peyton could no longer hide from the truth. With the conviction that she knew best, with one moment in time where she couldn't stand another second of worrying, she'd gone and ruined all their lives. Before she could help herself an ugly sob escaped, and tears streaked down her cheeks. It was only when Peyton went to wipe her eyes with her wet hands that she realized she'd dragged water all over her preciously plasma'd face. She laughed a kind of seal-like bark. Slowly, she lowered herself deeper into the water until it covered her head completely, and then, knowing full well what she was doing, she scratched at her face with her fingernails until every last inch of flesh was clean.

20

Rainbow Blow Jobs

Max rolled the gigantic yellow broom-and-mop-combo contraption into the back room and shoved it against the wall. "Done," she said, wiping her forehead. "The front of the store is spotless."

Oliver was sitting at the owner's desk with a pile of cash and credit card slips next to him, reconciling the night's sales. "I'm just about . . ." Oliver leaned his freakishly long torso over his notebook and squinted at it. He scratched out a few things with his pencil. ". . . finished. Let's get out of here."

He placed the sorted envelopes in the store's safe and locked the door behind them. The best part of the Ice Cream Shoppe was that they closed early, at nine, on Monday nights.

"What are you doing now?" Oliver asked, as they walked to the four-spot parking lot adjacent to the store.

Max shrugged. She knew he was just being nice. Their weeks of working together had confirmed beyond any doubt for both of them that they were only friends. Not so much as a hint of romantic or sexual tension between them. And Oliver was exactly the friend she needed now: smart, sarcastic, irreverent, and self-deprecating. He read the newspaper every day. Had opinions on politics and current events and pop culture. But he wasn't only interesting, he was also *interested*. In other things and people besides himself and his appearance. Brynn had been like that, too. And then she'd left.

"I'm meeting some friends. Why don't you come?" Oliver asked, pulling open the driver's-side door of his beat-up Toyota Camry.

"My mom is waiting for me to watch tonight's *Below Deck*," she said.

"So? Watch it tomorrow. A bunch of us are meeting at the diner. It's a fun group."

Max considered this. She felt guilty bailing on her mother, who she had started to suspect was actually lonely out here in the suburbs, with no husband and no friends, but Oliver had a point. They could watch TV any night. It wasn't like either of them had anything resembling a life. "Let me text her," Max said and typed out: *Work friend invited me to hang out with him and his friends. Do you care? I'm fine to come home too.*

The three dots appeared instantly. *Go, honey! Have fun!!!!!* her mother replied. Max sighed. It was obvious that even her mom thought she was a loser.

K. Thanks.

Another instantaneous three dots. *No curfew, just enjoy and keep in touch, ok, lovie???* She added three red hearts and two kissing emojis at the end.

Her phone beeped with an incoming call. Her father. Again. Part of her loved that he called every day, and the other part found it infuriating. Her decision to answer or screen never had any rhyme or reason—it was entirely dependent on her mood at the moment—and their conversations so far hadn't been particularly productive.

Oliver looked over her shoulder. "Answer it!"

"It's not a good time right now," Max said.

"He's your father! Just answer."

Even though the timing was terrible, Max swiped to answer.

"Hey, Dad," she said quietly.

"Max! Oh my god, how *are* you?" His excitement was so tangible that it instantly made her feel guilty.

"I'm okay. Just finished up with work, and I'm about to meet a few friends."

"Wow, that sounds great. I don't, um . . . I wanted to say hi. To hear your voice."

Oliver poked her in the arm. "Talk to him for a minute," he urged. "I forgot something inside."

"Sure you did," Max murmured.

"What was that, honey?" her dad asked.

"No, nothing. Sorry. So . . . how are you?"

"I'm fine, fine. I'm much more interested in you. How's work going? Are you still watching Aurora? How did you meet your new friends?"

When Max didn't respond, he apologized. "Sorry, I don't mean to barrage you with questions. I'm just . . . surprised you answered. Happy surprised."

"Dad, we can't just pretend like everything's normal and I tell you all about scooping ice cream and that Aurora learned the backstroke. It doesn't work like that."

"No, of course not. I just . . . I miss you."

Why was it so hard to say it back when she felt the same in every cell of her body? She wanted to scream through the phone, tell him that she hated him but also loved him, and by the way, what the fuck was he thinking? But when she opened her mouth, she couldn't make herself say the words.

"What do you think about me coming out there?" he asked. "So we can talk?"

"Can I think about it?" Her voice shook a little.

"Yes, absolutely. I'll call you tomorrow and maybe we can set something up?"

Oliver walked back outside, smiling at something on his phone.

"Sure, Dad. Listen, I've got to run."

"Okay, honey. I love you so much. Please don't ever forget that I—"

"Love you, too," she said gruffly, before the tears could start in earnest, and quickly hung up.

"You good?" Oliver asked, and in a very nice, gentlemanly way he walked around to the passenger side to open her door.

Max looked down at herself. She had a huge hot fudge stain near her right breast. "I'm wearing my uniform."

"I am, too. Who cares?"

Max climbed into the passenger seat. Oliver slammed her door closed and got in the driver's side. When he turned the key, Eric Clapton began playing from the speakers.

"You like Eric Clapton?" Max said. "I thought only my parents did."

"I like all that old music. My dad made us listen to it when we were kids, and then I actually started to like it."

They made easy chitchat on the five-minute drive to the Trivet, and Oliver got a spot right in front of the large-paned windows. As they walked toward the entrance, a long-haired boy sitting inside gave them the finger.

"That's Aiden. He's cool but can be a dick."

Max walked through the door that he held open. "I know the type well."

They walked over to the table. In addition to Aiden, there were two girls and another guy, and even though her mom always said that remembering people's names was a learned superpower, Max immediately forgot all of them. Leni. One of the girls was named Leni, the one with the long blond hair that had at least three inches of Manic Panic blue on the ends.

The one who'd given them the finger scooted over in the booth and motioned for Max to take a seat. Oliver sat in the opposite bench and there was a beat of awkward silence.

"Well, I'd ask how you guys met, but it's pretty obvious," Leni said, laughing and shaking her blue-tinged hair.

"We're not dating," Oliver said, too quickly. Max knew he didn't mean anything more by how fast he blurted it out, and she tried not to let it sting.

"I'm here for the summer," Max said, to say anything. "I actually live in the city."

"Wooooowwww, the *city*!" the other girl breathed. This one had a nose ring and a choppy, uneven bob, almost like she'd cut it herself. "I've never been but I've heard great things!"

"Really?" Max said, and knew instantly she'd been played.

"No, not really," the girl laughed. "It's a thirty-minute train ride away. We probably go every weekend."

"Sorry," Max said, feeling herself blush.

"No, it's fine!" the girl said, with a wide smile. Max was relieved to see it was kind and not mocking. "Just giving you shit. It comes from a place of total insecurity, nothing else. I've lived in this stifling suburb my entire life, and truth be told, I'm totally jealous of anyone who hasn't."

One of the other boys—not Aiden or Oliver—asked Max where she went to school.

"Milford," she said quietly, praying they wouldn't hold it against her. "I graduated this year."

"Tough place," the boy said sympathetically.

"Brutal, actually," Max said, and everyone laughed.

The boy spoke again. "My family just moved out here from the city. My brother got kicked out of Dwight and nowhere else would take him, so . . . suburbs."

"Ah, Dwight," Max said.

"The one and only," the boy said. Then he and Max, at exactly the same time, recited, "Dumb White Idiots Getting High Together."

The entire table laughed, and a warmth spread over Max's chest.

The waitress came over and they ordered one of every fattening thing on the menu. Max tried to envision any of the Milford girls even thinking about eating the heaping plates of mozzarella sticks, cheese fries, and tater tots that soon appeared.

Leni gnawed on a chicken finger and looked at Max. "Why are you out *here* for the summer? I mean, like, why here and not the Hamptons or somewhere cool?"

"Oh, well, my aunt lives here, so we rented a house near hers,"

Max said, carefully wiping her mouth after dipping three fries in ketchup.

"Sucks for you," the other girl said. "It's so boring out here."

Max smiled. "It's not so great there either, trust me."

"Yeah, right!" the boy who had just moved to Paradise said. "You don't know hell until you've lived in the suburbs."

Max laughed. "But I thought you guys have crazy parties all the time. Like, every time someone's parents leave the house, you roll in the kegs and invite two hundred people!"

"Not often enough," Aiden said. "Everyone's parents have cameras now. Mostly, we do this." He gestured at the table.

"My father will be very relieved," Max said. "You should hear him go on about the drinking and driving. Like, he's positive that all kids do in the suburbs is get wasted and drive around. And offer innocent girls like me rides when they're wasted."

The other girl who wasn't Leni nodded. "That's not totally inaccurate. We should introduce our parents. A couple weeks ago I was going to a friend's birthday party in the city and both parents sat me down and asked if I'd ever been to a 'lollipop party' because they read about it on Facebook. But seriously—Oh. My. God."

"What's a lollipop party?" Leni asked, and Max was glad she did, because Max had no idea, either.

"Well, according to my mother—who, by the way, was a virgin until she got married at twenty-six—it's a super common party that's going on, like, basically every weekend in the city, where the girls all put on different color lipstick and then blow all the guys in the room. Then it makes a rainbow!"

"Awesome!" Oliver said.

The girl rolled her eyes. "Yep. My mom actually said 'perform oral sex' in front of my dad. They were both very, very concerned about the city's culture of constant blow jobs," she said.

And that was it. In seconds all of them were hysterical. Max was laughing so hard that she accidentally drooled some Coke down her chin.

"Lipstick rainbows!" Aiden howled.

"Like, how do I possibly have time for studying or swim practice with all the blow jobs I'm giving?" the girl said, and all four of them laughed until they cried.

"My moms are convinced that I'm going to be sexually assaulted every time I leave the house," Leni said. She turned to Max. "They're lesbos." Max nodded and Leni continued, "Their biggest regret in life is not sending me to an all-girls school, but they were too scared everyone would accuse them of hating men. But seriously, they *do* hate men. Or at least high school boys."

"I don't know, I feel like I can get over your moms thinking every boy is a rapist," Oliver said. "They haven't hung out with guys in, like, a hundred years. What bothers me is how my dad is convinced that I'm one step away from becoming a full-fledged heroin addict."

Aiden nodded furiously. "Mine too. They read something about how kids today all are stealing their parents' Vicodin and oxy and then once they can't find any more, they head straight to the needles. It's like, chill the fuck out. Nobody *does* that."

"My parents, too," Max and Leni said at the exact same time, causing everyone to laugh once again.

The girl whose name Max still didn't know said, "If I have to hear my parents use the words 'gateway drug' one more time, I'm going to kill myself."

"Like, I almost wish I had a life as exciting as they think I do!" Max said. "I've smoked weed, what? Ten times? And the first three I didn't even feel anything. Why do they all think we're such junkie sluts?"

"It's the Facebook, I'm telling you," Leni said, pushing a blue and blond wave off her shoulder. "My mom can't stop looking at it. Like, every second of every day. She belongs to all these moms' groups and all they do is talk about all the crazy things that could possibly endanger their children. It's insane."

"Yep, my mom, too," Max said. "She's on it constantly. Half the time they're telling each other where to get Botox and the other half they're talking about us. I think it's sad."

Everyone nodded.

She had no idea why—she hadn't planned on sharing it—but before her brain could process what she was doing, Max blurted out, "The real reason we're out here is because my dad got arrested for, um, trying to buy my way into college and my mother likes to run away from her problems. But now it's my problem too, because Princeton rescinded my admission."

There was a beat of silence and then the girl with the nose ring said, "Parents really suck."

Max felt a wave of something—relief, gratitude, the extremely rare sensation of feeling understood—and she shrugged. "If you knew my dad, you'd think it was impossible he did it. But the FBI doesn't lie. . . ."

"Have you seen him in jail?" The one boy whose name she couldn't remember—not Aiden or Oliver—peered at her with curiosity.

"Lucas!" Leni and the nose-ring girl said at the same time.

But Max appreciated his directness. Not one of her so-called friends or classmates or whatever they were in New York had had the nerve to ask her directly about it. Instead, she could picture them perfectly, madly texting one another behind her back, all certainly outraged and delighted by the juiciness of the whole scandal.

"It's fine," Max said. "He's not in jail now, although he might be soon. He stayed in the city. It's pretty fucked."

The waitress returned and brought them all Coke refills.

Aiden held his glass aloft and looked at Max. "To Max. Good to have you out here, even if it sucks for you."

Max smiled at him.

"And of course, to rainbow blow jobs and heroin!" Leni said, holding up her own glass. "May we all have even a fraction of the fun our parents think we're having!"

Max laughed. Everyone cheered and Oliver put his fingers

between his lips and made a perfect cab-hailing whistle. Max looked around the table. These were definitely *not* the popular kids at Paradise High School. They kind of defied characterization, actually. They were a wonderful, weird mix, Max thought. Actually a lot like her.

21

Troop Leader

Can you please pass the saag?" Isadora, the woman seated to Skye's left, asked.

Skye hoisted the platter of chicken saag to Isadora. "The food here is delicious," she murmured.

"Right?" Isadora asked. "I haven't had great Indian in the longest time. I never thought it would be good in DC of all places." Her posh English accent and meticulous table manners stood in stark contrast to her appearance, which included bobbed, platinum-streaked hair and a delicate silver septum ring.

"You were telling me what you've been doing since Uganda," Skye prompted gently, both out of genuine curiosity and a desire to fill the silence.

Isadora brushed some loose hair from her cheek and scooped chicken onto her plate. "Right. So, after I left Uganda, Massimo emailed me to say that they were putting a team together for hurricane relief in Haiti and I said yes. I'm still not sure why. To say it was a hardship posting is an understatement. But in the two years I was there, our team rebuilt, staffed, and reopened twenty-six schools."

"That's incredible," Skye said, sipping from her bottle of beer, trying not to feel envious.

"It was a very rewarding experience," Isadora said, taking a small bite.

Skye knew that she would hear plenty of stories like Isadora's at the conference. She was almost afraid to ask, but she forced the words out. "And now?"

Isadora set down her fork. "Now? I've been in Somaliland for the last thirteen months, trying to help write their new educational charter."

"Somaliland?"

Isadora squinted at her.

Skye wanted to disappear directly into the restaurant's shiplap walls. It wasn't that long ago she could name every country, territory, capital, and region on the entire African continent. She could speak articulately on the challenges facing each country; she had intelligent, informed ideas on how best to help. But now? The only topic on which she could speak with authority was which online retailers offered free shipping and returns.

The whole weekend had been like that. No one was openly rude, but it was quickly clear that Skye's life trajectory was very different from those of her former colleagues. Over a breakout-session lunch earlier in the day, Skye had listened to an old friend describe his work in Laos with Smile Train: the man traveled all over the insular, rural country looking for children whose cleft lips needed correction and then arranged for them to receive the free, life-changing surgery. Another colleague of Skye's—one with whom she had shared an apartment in Kampala—was now based in the mountains of Bhutan, helping to implement a revolutionary family-planning and birth control program. A third was back stateside and overseeing the entire Teach for America program. It was incredible! In a few short years these people—her friends, her colleagues, her *equals*—had gone on to do astonishing things. It was inspiring and demoralizing and depressing, all at the same time. She remembered so clearly her own time in Uganda, when she'd worked with a local organization to increase access to education for children from rural villages. By the end of her three-year stint, they'd ensured twelve hundred additional students had access to schools. It had been the most gratifying work of her life.

Skye turned to the woman sitting on her other side and forced her way into the conversation. Her name was Amelie and she'd grown up in Cologne, Germany, but had lived in twelve countries since childhood.

Amelie nodded. "And you? I remember from the introductions during cocktail hour that you used to work in Uganda? Where are you now?"

"Paradise," Skye said flatly. Then she laughed, loudly, like a crazy person.

Amelie peered at her, clearly confused. "I'm sorry, I'm not familiar with it?"

Skye leaned closer to Amelie, as though she were confiding something of great importance. "I'm a Girl Scout troop leader. Co-leader! Can't forget the 'co-'!" she said, before dissolving into a fit of giggles.

Amelie pulled away, looking at Skye like she was highly unstable. "Isn't that lovely," she murmured.

Skye couldn't tell whether she was actually laughing or veering dangerously close to crying. "Excuse me," she managed to blurt out before walking straight past the ladies' room and out onto the sidewalk. The DC night was hot and muggy and her simple wrap dress clung to her damp skin. *What was I thinking?* Skye wondered as she looked around for a taxi. Did taxis even exist anymore? Or did everyone only use Ubers? These were things you didn't know when you lived in Paradise, right along with the difference between Somalia and Somaliland.

After trying unsuccessfully to update both her password and her credit card information on her Uber app, Skye decided to walk the twenty-five or so blocks back to the hotel. Why not? Her sandals were flat, it wasn't raining, and she'd done nothing all day but sit in lectures and eat her way through breakout sessions. Besides, this might very well be the last time in her life that she returned to a hotel room after a conference of any kind. The next morning she would put herself and her ideas for the girls' residence at the mercy of future benefactors, and she would do everything in her power to get the funding those girls deserved. Hopefully, she would find someone who related to her vision, who could see it like she could, as a small-scale equalizer in the midst of mass inequity in education. There were her ever-growing debts to be paid off, which was beginning to panic her, and families emailing her every day, wondering about the status of their daughters' promised school. But then, following that breakfast—and regardless of its outcome—she would return to Paradise, to her loving family, and she would resume driving carpool and fundraising for Aurora's school and volunteering to be a class mom. That was hardly so terrible, she berated herself as she trekked. It was a privilege, to live that life, one uncomplicated by illness or discrimination or crushing financial hardship.

And yet no amount of love for her daughter, her husband, or their shared life was enough to soften the blow of the realization—which had struck her tonight, at that hellish dinner—that she'd sacrificed herself and her own dreams. Skye pulled out her phone to call Gabe and saw that it was already silently ringing from a number with no caller ID. Without thinking, she swiped to answer the call.

"Hello?" said a familiar woman's voice, but one Skye couldn't quite place. "Is this Skye Alter?"

Suddenly she recognized the voice: it was their adoption case officer, Susan, who worked with an agency in Texas that provided birth mothers with housing and medical care during their pregnancies. She and Gabe had only met her once, but Skye still thought of Susan as one of the dearest people in her life, still sent her letters and pictures of Aurora and thoughtful little gifts at the holidays.

"Susan? Is that you? My god, it's good to hear your voice. Is everything okay?"

"Yes, everything's fine," Susan said in her comforting way that even now, all these years later, could settle Skye's anxiety in seconds. "I'm sorry to call so late. Truthfully, I was expecting to leave a voicemail. No one answers their phone these days!"

"I'm in DC for work, so now's a good time, actually."

"You're teaching again? Good for you! You were always so passionate about your work."

"Oh, no, not officially. I mean . . . never mind that. How are you?"

There was a brief pause before Susan said, "I was actually checking in with you. How's Aurora?"

Skye frowned but kept walking. "Aurora? She's fine. Great, actually. Very much enjoying her summer."

"So, I'm doing some maintenance on our database of adoptive families, some updating, and I was wondering if you and Gabe have reconsidered your position?"

"Our position?" She stopped walking.

"Sorry, I don't mean to be so formal. Just that when you adopted Aurora, you told the agency you were only interested in one child. We are going through, um, all of our families that have completed successful adoptions to see if they might consider adopting again. Nothing specific, if a need arose, something like that."

"Yes, absolutely," Skye said without hesitation.

"What was that?" Susan asked. "One of us is breaking up."

"Yes, of course we are interested," Skye said, feeling like she was careening around a racetrack on a car going a hundred miles an hour. "I mean, it would have to be the right circumstances, the right timing, but yes, I do think it's something we would consider."

"Well, that's wonderful news. Thank you. I'm going to update your profile to active, which is really a formality. Perhaps you'll also want to update it, include any family updates, moves, that sort of thing."

"Yes, that's right," Skye said, because she wasn't sure what else to say, and she couldn't quite parse if she'd done something wonderful or irreparably damaging. She'd just finished a dinner which had forced her to face the harsh truth that, at least compared to her ex-colleagues, her career had been completely derailed. Another baby hardly seemed like the right answer; in fact, it seemed like the worst possible move if she wanted to get her professional life back on track. But saying no to Susan—shutting down that possibility for good—was impossible.

Even once she'd closed the door behind her, located her phone, and pressed Gabe's smiling photo on her Favorites list, she was shocked by the sound of his voice.

"Gabe?"

"Hi, love. How was dinner?"

"Is that you?" She jumped up and began pacing the drab gray room. How had she not noticed that hideous quilted bedcover?

"You called *me*, honey. Is everything okay?"

Suddenly Skye felt a jolt of regret. She shouldn't have called him yet. What was she going to say? *I randomly got a call from the adoption agency asking if we'd consider another child, and because I've been crazy lately, I said yes? Without asking you how you felt. Or discussing it in any way. Not even to mention the rising debt I've accumulated, another rather major thing you know nothing about.*

"What? No, no, everything's fine. Sorry, I was just . . . distracted. It ended up being a really nice night."

"It did?" Gabe said, his joy and relief obvious. "I'm so glad to hear that. You were nervous about it."

"Yes," she said, trying to sound normal. "I mean, don't get me wrong, it was embarrassing—I told a woman with a PhD in economics who speaks enough languages to be considered a polyglot that I'm a Girl Scout troop leader in Paradise. But besides that, it was good to see people. To have an adult conversation that wasn't centered on kids or workouts."

"That's great, honey. You needed that. Any luck with the fund-raising?"

"Not yet," Skye said. "But tomorrow's benefactor breakfast is my best chance. Plus, it's been good to reconnect with a bunch of people—now it won't be strange if I follow up with them later."

"I'm so happy to hear that. Plus, you picked a good night to be away. Kiddo's got the pukes."

"No! Is she okay? Do you think it's the stomach bug or something she ate?"

"Stomach bug, for sure. Esther texted me that both of hers have it, too. She's finally sleeping, but I'm getting my towel pile ready."

"I'm so sorry I'm not there. And so ecstatic I'm not there. I think we went through every towel in the house last year."

"Excellent."

Skye finally smiled. "I'll take an earlier train home tomorrow to relieve you. Hang tight. Tell Aurora I love her, okay?"

"I'll tell her using a bullhorn from another room."

"Gabe? I love you, too."

"Love you, honey. Enjoy your solo hotel room and try not to feel too badly about me sleeping on our daughter's floor with only the sound of splashing vomit for company."

Skye flopped onto the bed and then bolted up again, unsure what to do with her nervous energy. "Good night," she said, hoping it sounded like she wasn't hiding anything potentially life altering. "Call me if you need me."

He made a kissing sound through the phone and disconnected the call.

Ohmigod, ohmigod, Skye chanted in her mind, walking into the bathroom to turn on the shower before immediately turning it off again. *How could I not have told him? What if he says no?* She dialed Peyton. It rang twice before she received one of those automated text responses saying that her sister wasn't available.

Dammit. She stubbed her toe on the folding luggage rack and then whipped around and kicked it on purpose. It smashed into the wall and her rolling duffel bag dumped its contents all over the floor. Her phone rang from back in the bathroom. She couldn't wait to tell Peyton everything, but when she plucked her phone from the sink, something made her press Decline.

22

Porsched In

A re you kidding me?" Peyton asked as she pulled into Skye's driveway. Her sister was sitting in a wicker chair on the porch, a tennis racket propped up near her legs.

"What?" Skye asked, all innocence.

"I told you to wear all white. Elena was very insistent."

"I'm not comfortable with all-white rules," her sister said as she grabbed her racket and walked to the passenger side.

"It's not a racist thing! It's more like a country club thing," Peyton said.

"Same difference."

Peyton suppressed a smile. Skye wore hot-pink running shorts and a black tank that read "The Future Is Female / Science Is Real / Black Lives Matter / No Human Is Illegal / Love Is Love" in rainbow colors down the front. Her hair was yanked into a messy bun and she had on not a stitch of makeup, and naturally, she looked amazing. Peyton had spent nearly two hours getting ready, including but not limited to a professional ponytail from a nearby salon, an eyebrow wax, and a spray tan. With so much flesh exposed in her skimpy white tennis dress, she'd agonized over every inch of it, making sure her legs were hairless and her décolletage dewy and her cheeks rosy and her under-eyes concealed. Skye had definitely forgotten all about their plans that night until exactly ten minutes before, when Peyton had called to tell her she was on her way, and still she looked a thousand times better.

"That shirt's a little aggressive, don't you think?" Peyton asked as she backed onto the street.

Skye yanked on the bottom, stretching it over her perfect breasts, examining it. She shrugged. "I had to do *something* to counteract the conservatism tonight. They may not be wearing their MAGA hats tonight, but don't kid yourself—they want to."

"Who, exactly, are 'they'?"

"The same people who belong to super fancy country clubs with all-white dress codes!"

Peyton laughed. "Aside from your statement shirt, can you keep the politics to a minimum tonight? I don't know these people at all, and it was really nice of Nisha to arrange it."

"Nice of Nisha? I'm not sure that's how I would describe it."

Peyton reached across the seat and poked Skye in her thigh. "It's going to be a fun night, you'll see. And remember, it's for a good cause."

"Yeah, your career," Skye said.

"Yes, that. Thanks. But also, underprivileged children. Your specialty."

Skye gave Peyton a look.

"What? I went to a City Harvest fundraiser one year. It was ridiculously over the top—at Cipriani, celebrities galore. The grand finale prize—a private dinner cooked by Eric Ripert in your own kitchen, with John Legend singing and Chrissy Teigen serving—was so popular that they sold it twice. For over a million dollars each time."

"Your point?"

"You may not agree with the means, but that whole insane spectacle raised over four million dollars to help feed hungry New Yorkers. I think that's worth it, don't you?"

Skye raised her eyebrows.

"And yes, I have got to get back in that anchor seat—not only for me, but for my family—and the quickest way to making that happen is to follow Nisha's explicit instructions. If she says I should attend a night at a country club, well . . . I'm grateful it's not equine therapy at this point. Or sensitivity training. Or rehab."

"Rehab? Is there something you're not telling me?"

"Everyone goes to rehab when they screw up in the court of public opinion. Doesn't matter for what—drunk driving, sexual harassment, racial insensitivity—rehab is always the answer."

"You sound really authentic right now. It's lovely," Skye said. "But in all fairness, shouldn't Isaac be the one considering rehab, not you?"

Peyton glanced at her sister. She couldn't remember a single time in the last forty years when she'd withheld important information this long from Skye. It was more than uncomfortable—it was unnatural.

Her phone rang from its magnetic holder on the air-conditioning vent. "Is it Kenneth? I have three calls in to him, and I haven't heard back yet."

"It's Mom," Skye said. "Isn't she in Iceland?"

"Somewhere cold. St. Petersburg?" Peyton said, jabbing the answer button while making a left turn. "Hey, Mom!"

"Hello, dear. Why is the connection so awful? Can you hear me?"

"I hear you perfectly, Mom."

"Listen, I only have a second, but I was talking to Nancy Blumenstein, and she said that her daughter—who's married to an ER doctor who went to Yale, by the way—told her that she saw on the Facebook a picture of Skye. And she was all dressed up at some super fancy party!"

"Who? The daughter? Or the ER doctor? Or Nancy Blumenstein?" Peyton asked, grinning at Skye, who had covered her mouth to keep from laughing.

"Your sister! Do you know what party she was at? Because I certainly don't. Not that you girls ever tell me anything, but I do like to have some idea of what goes on in your lives. You should have heard the way Nancy said, 'Oh, you didn't know?'"

With this, Skye snorted.

"Why don't you ask her yourself?" Peyton said. "She's sitting right—"

Skye punched her hard in the forearm.

"I'm sure she's sitting in her own living room right now, hoping that you'll call."

"I will do that, dear. So . . . any word yet?"

"Word?" Peyton parroted, although she knew exactly what her mother was asking.

"On what's going to happen with Isaac! Linda Shapiro in my book club said that judges aren't being very lenient with this college admissions scandal. Apparently, they want to set examples."

"Well, Linda Shapiro sounds pretty smart."

"She should know—her son is a partner at a prestigious law firm, and he tells Linda everything. Plus, he and his wife bring their children to visit every three weeks when she's in Boca for the winter—how lovely is that?"

Peyton said, "Mom, can I call you tomorrow? A friend invited me to play in a tennis round-robin, and I'm pulling into the parking lot."

"Of course, dear. Have a good time. Send my love to Max and Isaac, if they allow phone calls under house arrest."

"He's not under—" But her mother had disconnected the call. She executed a three-point turn to back the car into a tight spot.

"We're Porsched in!" Skye said, looking at the cars on both sides and across the lot. "Why are we here again?"

"Shhhhhhhh! Just be a decent wingman, okay? And can we keep the crunchy crap to a minimum?"

"The 'crunchy crap'?"

"You know, the lectures on plastic straws and making your own almond milk and coral-safe sunscreen?"

"Roger that. No politics, no global warming, no environmental responsibility. Anything else I should leave out, Ivanka?"

Peyton glared at Skye, trying not to laugh, when a man in a monogrammed polo shirt and a belt embroidered with miniature golf balls asked, "May I help you?"

Peyton offered him an enormous smile. "Yes, thank you, we're guests of Ms. Elena Popov," she announced, as though they were being hosted by the queen of England and not the wife of an infamous, Madoff-level con man.

"Of course, right this way." He led them through the posh, high-ceilinged lobby and out a back door. "The courts are straight down that way, just follow the path."

"Is it a coincidence that tonight is being hosted by the high-profile wife of a white-collar criminal?" Skye whispered. "Are you sure this is the right choice?"

"Elena does a lot of wonderful things for the community," Peyton said. "In 2016 she founded a not-for-profit that provides one hundred percent of needed supplemental nutrition over the weekends for local food-insecure schoolchildren, and it's grown to over sixty counties. She has personally funded college scholarships for first-generation immigrant children, advocated in front of the House of Representatives for autistic children, and has established a corporate matching program for all kinds of charitable donations. Her husband might be a scumbag, but I assure you she is not."

"Well, I stand corrected," Skye said. "I actually didn't know any of that. In honor of Elena's good works, I will try to behave myself tonight."

"You're a peach," Peyton said.

The sisters hadn't taken more than a dozen steps before a woman's voice rang out. "Oh, look, everyone, Peyton Marcus is here!"

"Ugh, I see at least three sets of parents from Aurora's school," Skye said quietly through her own gritted teeth and painted-on smile.

Peyton linked her arm through Skye's so she could politely drag her to the first court, where a group had gathered. She could feel people begin to recognize her, and she offered each one her well-honed public winks that said, "Yes, it's me, the famous person you know from television, but tonight I'm a regular civilian, so please don't embarrass yourself."

The two dozen men and women parted and, like a graceful gazelle who'd just emerged from a herd of anteaters, Elena appeared. Extremely well-groomed and surgically enhanced anteaters, but still: no four-hundred-dollar-per-ounce snail-enriched face cream or glittering Gucci tennis shoes could give these women even a shred of Elena's poise or presence. And no award-winning plastics guy, regardless of his talent with scalpel or silicone, could give them her body. At nearly six feet tall and barely breaking a hundred ten pounds, Elena looked stunning in the delicate, spaghetti-strapped tennis dress that merely skimmed her nonexistent hips. Platinum hair floated down her back, and her skin shimmered from designer cheekbone highlighter or vigorous sex with her tennis coach, or both. Even from the sea of white—white skin, white clothes, white strings—Elena radiated lightness.

"I'm so glad you could make it," Elena said, grasping Peyton's hands and kissing her on both cheeks, as if a crisis manager hadn't arranged the evening because it was mutually beneficial to both women.

"Thank you so much for having me!" Peyton said. She could feel Skye's gaze burning into her back. "I hope you don't mind that I brought my sister? Elena Popov, this is Skye Alter."

"Skye, it's a pleasure to meet you," Elena purred, extending a hand with perfect, white-lacquered fingernails. She leaned closer and lowered her voice. "And I absolutely love your shirt."

Skye looked pleased. "Thanks for letting me tag along. This is a beautiful—"

They were interrupted by one of the four tennis pros, each of whom was male and disconcertingly gorgeous. "Welcome, ladies and gentlemen, to the Paradise Racquet Club's charity round-robin," said the one who seemed to be in charge. He was six foot four or five, with the lean, powerful look of a purebred greyhound. "My name is Alfonso. With me tonight are Guillermo, Luca, and Christophe. We'll divide you into groups and everyone will rotate between courts. But first! Reinforcements!" Alfonso waved toward the path where a single-file line of well-scrubbed and polo-clad servers marched toward the courts, holding trays brimming with drinks.

Everyone cheered. There were gin and tonics, vodka sodas, frozen rosés, and the club special, a very fine tequila on the rocks mixed with agave and lime juice. Naturally, if none of these appealed, they would be delighted to mix up your drink of choice.

Peyton plucked a frosé from the tray and handed one to Skye. They clinked their monogrammed Corkcicle cups together and Peyton said, "There are worse ways to spend an evening."

Peyton wasn't sure if it was the alcohol, the piped-in eighties music, or the four spectacularly hot tennis coaches who flirted indiscriminately with every man and woman in attendance, but over the next ninety minutes, for the first time in weeks, she managed to bury the feeling that her life was falling apart. They played out some points and then switched partners, moving up and down the line of courts according to whether they won or lost. It felt good to move and to hit a few balls, and by the time the group began filtering toward the restaurant's deck, which overlooked the expansive eighteenth hole, Peyton felt almost relaxed. But as she walked past a table full of chatting tennis players, that changed.

"Do you think they're getting divorced?" one pretty brunette in a tank and skirt asked a pretty blonde in nearly the exact same outfit. "I mean, why else would she be here alone?"

"I don't know, maybe he's on house arrest? Like with an ankle monitor, or whatever?"

"It's just crazy to me that she's out and about—partying, practically—in light of . . . the situation."

Someone must have kicked them each under the table, because both women whipped around at the exact same time. The brunette's face registered shock; the blonde smiled at Peyton and smoothly said, "I hope you don't mind us saying so, but we're all really big fans of yours."

Peyton stared her right in the eye. "You're too kind."

The entire table clearly sensed the awkwardness, because they all began nodding heads enthusiastically. "Seriously, we just love watching you in the morning," a third woman called across the table.

Peyton felt a squeeze on her shoulder and knew without looking that it was Skye. A warning.

"That is so nice to hear," Peyton said with a fake smile. "And I do appreciate your concern regarding my . . . situation. It's comforting being around people who understand." She paused for a moment to allow it to sink in and then cheerily waved goodbye to the group.

"And you were worried I was going to talk about *almond milk*?" Skye murmured.

"Elena!" Peyton called out, beaming and waving as they approached her table.

Even though everyone else wore their tennis clothes to dinner, Elena had showered and donned a floral chemise dress with barely-there straps and no bra. In her platform espadrilles, she easily exceeded six feet, yet she glided around the table to double-kiss Peyton with the grace of a figure skater. "I'm so glad you both could join us. Come, let me introduce you to everyone."

Elena indicated for Peyton to sit to her right and for Skye to sit to Peyton's right. The moment they sat, a college-aged waiter with floppy blond hair filled their glasses with prosecco.

"Peyton, Skye, this is Eric, my lawyer," Elena said, wrapping both her arms around the neck of the man sitting on her left. He feigned being upset, and she kissed him on the lips, lingering so long that Peyton could almost feel his stubble on her own face. "Okay, okay, so we are special friends, too!"

Peyton could see Skye giving her a look, but she ignored it.

"Next to Eric is Mathilde"—Mathilde, who looked barely out of her twenties, offered a wan smile—"and over there we have Paulina and her husband, Barry. Paulina and Barry are newlyweds!"

"Aw, congratulations," Peyton and Skye said at the exact same time, in the exact same manner, which made everyone laugh. There was a brief moment of silence, but Peyton immediately stepped in.

She knew she was skilled enough to carry a conversation with a potted plant if the situation arose, and she never shied away.

"So, how do you all know one another? Please, give us the full,
unedited version. Where are you from, how did you meet, who do
you hate?"

Elena smiled. "Well, of course you know already about me. The
press has made certain of that!"

The entire table laughed.

"But enough about that, tonight is about you!" Elena said, wrapping both her hands around Peyton's right bicep. "The package you
donated is amazing."

"It's truly my pleasure," Peyton said, although since Nisha had
arranged everything, Peyton wasn't entirely clear on the details.

She was interrupted by the auctioneer, a woman in a pantsuit
with a severe bun and reading glasses, who stepped up to a podium
and spoke into the microphone. "Forgive me for interrupting your
dinner," she said, her deep, full-bodied voice a surprise. "But we simply can't wait to get started."

A team of waitstaff fanned out across the balcony and distributed
hand paddles to each person while the auctioneer explained the rules
and highlighted some of the available prizes, and then, before they'd
even had their appetizers, the auction began. People bid frantically on
clothes from local boutiques, massages and facials from local spas, gym
memberships and gift baskets. At Peyton's table alone, the guests snapped
up "free" sessions for weight training, interior decorating, acupuncture,
and nutrition counseling. The table to their right won dog training, life
coaching, and closet purging, and the table to their left snagged couples
therapy, self-defense, home organizing, and chef-delivered meals. All
around them, white-clad tennis players vied ferociously for box seats for
the Giants, the US Open, the Yankees.

The preppy waiter produced a tray of mini plates. He set down
blistered shishito peppers, an assortment of Mediterranean dips and
pita squares, and a mushroom flatbread. "Our starters tonight," he
announced.

Elena plucked a pepper and delicately bit the flesh. "Delicious," she declared, while the men stared, but there was no time for chat because the auction, having exhausted the supply of smaller prizes, had progressed to the vacation opportunities. In fewer than ten minutes the auctioneer extracted top dollar for free weeks in a Mount Snow ski house, a Deer Valley condo, a Hilton Head beachfront manse, and four nights on a yacht that was currently docked in the BVI. Peyton almost bid on a fishing charter in the Florida Keys for Isaac, but stopped herself at the last moment: she couldn't afford to throw money around like that with her job so uncertain.

The auctioneer announced a brief break for dinner, after which they would get to the evening's final prize, something she called "the News Junkie Experience." Elena winked at Peyton.

The booze did its job, the conversation meandered comfortably through noncontroversial topics, and soon little crystal bowls of white chocolate mousse appeared. The waiter took coffee orders, but before her mint tea had even arrived, Skye abruptly stood up and said, "Please excuse me. I'm so sorry, but I must leave now."

Peyton jumped up after her sister. "Are you okay? I can't leave yet; they haven't auctioned off my package."

"I'm fine," Skye said quietly, in a tone Peyton knew meant exactly the opposite. "You stay. I'll get an Uber and I'll talk to you later."

Peyton watched as Skye strolled across the balcony and down the stairs. She turned to the table and offered up her most accessible smile. "Please excuse me for a moment."

She ran after her sister, whom she found, shivering, in the club's gravel parking lot.

"What was that all about?"

Skye looked at her. "I can't take another second of it. The whole thing was just so . . . vile."

"Oh my god, you are always *so dramatic*!"

"I need a shower after that."

"It's an auction for charity, Skye. I think you're overreacting."

"Not a single person there tonight cares in the least about

underprivileged children. Or charitable giving. Or doing the right thing. This whole night is a disgusting sham."

Reflexively, Peyton started to protest, but she stopped. "It's the tiniest bit gross."

Skye glanced up. "The tiniest bit?"

"Okay, it's full-blown hideous. There, I said it. However, I am unclear how this is all that different from what you've been doing, trying to raise money for your residence? I mean, just to put it all out there, Henry—back when he agreed to finance the project—didn't give a rat's ass about underprivileged girls from the inner city. He was forking over the cash because some consultant told him that's what companies need to do in 2021 for the sake of appearances. I'm not saying that's right, or admirable, but does the end justify the means? In both cases, I think the answer is yes."

Skye sighed. "I hate you sometimes."

"You hate me most when I'm right."

"Can we get out of here now, please?"

"I have to congratulate the winning bidder of my package. Pick a date when they're going to come by the studio for a tour, sit at the anchor desk, have lunch afterward. They're expecting it to be a big-ticket item!"

"I hope your winning bidder has some availability in the fall, because it doesn't seem like you're doing much studio touring or anchor-desk-sitting this summer. Just saying." Skye gave a sly half smile.

Peyton blinked. Who else would ever speak to her like this? The same person who wouldn't hesitate to tell her when she looked fat, or old, or tired, or bloated. Who regularly told her that an idea, outfit, or life plan was one thousand percent, unequivocally bat-shit crazy. Only a sister could be thoroughly unimpressed with your public accomplishments and accolades but would screech in joy and support when you finally learned how to parallel park or make it through a cavity filling without fainting.

Peyton barked out a laugh. "Maybe we should offer a leave-of-absence discount."

"Maybe pair it with a soon-to-be-permanently-unemployed insurance certificate?" Skye paused, looked at Peyton. "Too much?"

"Yes."

"Sorry."

"I left my tennis bag in there," Peyton said pleadingly, motioning toward the clubhouse.

"Get in the fucking car," Skye said, grabbing Peyton's miniature YSL crossbody bag and digging out her keys and handing them over. "We're leaving."

Peyton took the keys and climbed behind the wheel. She pecked out a quick text to Elena: *So sorry! My sis isn't feeling well. Send me the contact info for the winning bidder and I'll get in touch tomorrow.* She hit send and then said, "Nisha is going to kill me when she hears we left early." She eased out of the parking spot, taking extra care not to hit all the Porsches, and began heading back to Skye's house.

Skye fixed her eyes on Peyton. "You need a friend right now, not a crisis advisor."

"She's both," Peyton said.

"Hardly. Sending you into that snake pit. What, exactly, did that do to rehabilitate your reputation? I'm sorry, P. Your reputation is not the primary problem here. It's your daughter. Your marriage. And me."

Peyton pulled into Skye's driveway, put the car in park. "I don't know what else to do. Tell me, because I'm willing to do it! I screwed up, and now I need to do everything in my power to try to make it right again."

"You mean *Isaac* screwed up so much."

Peyton was certain her sister could hear her heart pounding through her chest. It was never going to be the right time to tell Skye that her anger at Isaac was misplaced, but if she didn't, her sister might always hate her husband. Still, she couldn't force out the words.

"We can't let this ruin all our lives!" Peyton said. "Mistakes were made. I'm not denying it. But we have to do the hard work now to move forward."

"Move forward?" Skye asked, her eyes flashing. "Eight girls hoping for a different chance, a year at one of our schools—Peyton, it was the dream I worked on for two years. Not to mention the fact that I'm tens of thousands of dollars in debt, and Gabe has no idea!"

Peyton turned to Skye, who was wrapping and rewrapping a lock of hair around her forefinger. "I didn't know that."

"Yeah, well, now you do. When Henry agreed to the funding, I started buying things. All the things. Mixing bowls, throw pillows, towels, school supplies—you name it, I bought it. Is it all necessary? Yes. But does that matter, now that there's no residence? Nope. I have a basement full of enough supplies to furnish an entire house, a massive outstanding credit card bill, and eight families whose lives have been turned upside down, all thanks to me."

"I can write you a check! Seriously, for as much as I can."

"I don't want a handout from you."

"It is not a handout! And I wish it could be more but I don't have it. It's insane how much money I make each year and we've managed to save almost nothing. Between the apartment, Max's school, vacations, and general asshole-level spending on whatever I felt like . . . there's almost nothing left. In the greatest of ironies, the only real nest egg we've built and protected has been Max's college fund. We started the day she was born and squirreled it away. Now she may not even go to college!"

Skye sighed. "She's going to college, P. It's not going to be Princeton, or possibly anywhere like it, but she'll go somewhere that's perfect for her."

The mudroom door to Skye's house opened, and Gabe stepped out. "You guys want to come in? Or are you just going to hang in the driveway?" he called.

"I'll be right there," Skye called back, flashing him a smile. Then she turned to Peyton. "Have you ever stopped to think of the most ridiculous thing in all of this?"

Peyton's head was starting to throb. "What, that Mom is the happiest one of all three of us?"

"No. Look how differently our lives turned out compared to what was prescribed for us in high school. I was the straight-A student who went to the great college, and I've become a glorified housewife. You were the teenage fuckup who ended up at some branch campus, and you became one of the most famous news anchors in the country."

"Okaaaay . . ."

"But neither of us are where we want to be! I mean, no one hates the word 'balance' more than I do, but we sure haven't found it, have we? I frittered away an incredible education combined with genuine passion and, forgive me for saying it, but I think real talent, to helicopter parent my six-year-old. You got the dream job, but along the way you sacrificed unquantifiable amounts of time with your family and missed out on large swaths of your daughter's childhood."

Peyton turned to look at her sister. "Thank you for that. I'm about ready to go find a very high bridge."

"Yeah, well, take a number and get in line. My point is this: We both seem to be at a crossroads here. For shit reasons, no doubt. But maybe it's time we both take honest stock of our situations and try to make some positive changes?"

"Why do I feel like I'm listening to a Brené Brown TED talk right now?"

Skye laughed. "I have been liking her lately. Anyway, I have to run. But think about it."

"Think about how I selfishly chose my own career over being a better mother to my daughter and missing, as you so eloquently put it, 'large swaths' of her childhood? I will add it to the list of things I berate myself about nightly."

Skye climbed out of the car. "You're a great mom, and we both know it. Besides, I'm hardly preaching from a place of moral high ground here: you don't think I realize that I've poured my heart and soul and ungodly amounts of money into a charity that, yes, I believe in and know will help others, but that I'm also depending on to save my sanity and correct my shitty career choices so far? Because I do."

"Well, on that note, I'm headed home to drink a bottle of vodka and listen to Leonard Cohen before shopping for guns online. Thanks for the pick-me-up."

"Welcome!" Skye said cheerily before slamming the door. "If you do off yourself, please remember that I've always wanted that white leather jacket of yours. . . ."

Peyton gave her the middle finger, but she was grinning as she shifted into reverse.

23

Heavy Pour

Mmm," Max said, climbing out of the passenger seat of her mother's car. She took a deep breath and decided that yes, the air was qualitatively cleaner and fresher in Vermont.

"That's the one," Peyton said, pointing down the hill. "On the end." They each lugged their duffel bags down the steep staircase that connected the parking lot to a row of townhouses. "I can't imagine doing this in two feet of snow," Peyton said.

"I can't imagine doing anything in two feet of snow," Max replied.

Her mother laughed. "I'm not sure I realized how much I've turned you into a city kid. Surely I've told you about the kind of winters we had in Pennsylvania? How we had to walk three-quarters of a mile just to get the bus, and it was always—"

"Yep, you definitely have."

"Here we go." Her mom unlocked the door and swung it open with a flourish. "Country life!"

Max was oddly relieved to see that her mom had returned, at least partially, to her old level of enthusiasm. The moping and obsessive watching of ANN had been starting to become concerning.

They stepped into the ski condo, which although it looked like all the others from the outside—ugly aluminum siding, attached wooden ski closets, swing-out windows from the eighties—was, on the inside, a modern, minimalist dream of all glass and steel.

"Not what I was expecting," Max said, checking out the floating staircase and the nearly two-story-high stainless fireplace. "But I love it!"

"Me neither and me too," her mom breathed. "When Sean said we were welcome to stay here, I was picturing lumpy couches and Crock-Pots. I should have known better."

They were supposed to be at Canyon Ranch for their annual mother-daughter spa weekend, something she and her mom had been doing—with varying degrees of success—since middle school, but Max had seen some emails her mom had left up on her iPad. The first was to Nisha, asking for her thoughts on a letter she'd written to the president of Princeton, pleading Max's case and reassuring him that Max had no involvement in or knowledge of the scandal whatsoever. The second email had been to Max's dad, explaining that Peyton was going to cancel the spa trip this year, considering how expensive a weekend it was. Her father had replied understanding the decision but encouraging her to find a cheaper option, something to keep the tradition going, especially then. The final email her mom had written was to Sean asking if his offer still stood to use his place up in Vermont for a weekend. And here they were.

"It was really nice of Sean to let us use his place," Max said, hoping her mom didn't think she missed Canyon Ranch. She didn't. All the rich ladies wandering around in their workout clothes, discussing the health benefits of matcha tea and stuffing their faces with "clean" food and spending lots of hours and even more dollars in the boutique buying yoga mats and fluffy socks and cashmere robes and other things they didn't need because it was something to do. No thanks.

They unpacked the groceries they'd bought on the way and chose adjoining bedrooms on the lower level. "What's first?" her mom asked eagerly. "Hiking? Biking? Leaf peeping? Forest bathing? Tell me."

Max laughed. "Why don't we go get lunch at that place we passed in town? I'm actually starving."

"Done! Lunch. Sounds perfect."

Max glanced at her mother warily, but she wasn't being sarcastic or mocking, just genuinely excited. She was obviously trying.

They drove back down the mountain to town and found the bar and grill Sean had recommended. The twenty-something hostess looked like she might faint when Max and Peyton walked in.

"Oh my god, you're Peyton Marcus," the girl breathed without a hint of self-consciousness.

Max could feel her own cheeks redden, she was so embarrassed for this girl, but her mom deftly handled the situation.

"It's lovely to meet you," she said, offering her hand to the girl. "My daughter and I would love to have lunch. Any chance you have a good table for us? Maybe something with a nice view?"

The girl's skin was now a mottled shade of red, and she was nodding. "Of course, how wonderful, yes, right this way. Please, follow me."

She led them through a drab dining room and out a back door, where a nearly empty porch looked out over an expansive mountain lake. "This section isn't really open right now, but if you'd like . . ."

"You're such a dear," Peyton said, flashing the girl one of her most winning smiles. "We would love."

"Hey, Mom, you still got it," Max whispered as they sat. She was happy to see her mother give her a wink. Depressed Peyton was far worse than Public Peyton.

The moment they opened their menus, they were greeted by an equally enthusiastic waiter, a man in his sixties with white hair in a ponytail.

"Ladies! What can I get you for lunch today?" he practically sang.

When he left, Max exhaled. "Why is everyone so happy here?"

Peyton shrugged. "Maybe it's a country thing? I've heard rumors there are people who are content to live in the moment, focus on the good, real glass-half-full types. I just don't happen to know any of them."

Max laughed. "Brynn was like that. It was so annoying. In third grade Mrs. Covington nicknamed her Bright Side Brynn, and it just stuck."

"You miss her, don't you?"

Normally, a question like that would irritate Max, but whether it was relief that her mother no longer seemed suicidal, or the fact that she was looking forward to a weekend away, Max didn't feel her usual involuntary wave of rage.

"A lot. I guess I never realized . . . we didn't really need other friends because we had each other." Max paused. "Had."

A different waiter came to take their order, and he was blessedly less enthusiastic. After they ordered, Peyton peered at Max.

"Would you want to go to Hong Kong to visit Brynn?"

Max's eyes widened. "Yes! Definitely."

"Well . . . Dad and I still haven't gotten you a graduation present. In all the . . . with everything that happened, I'm afraid that slipped through the cracks."

"Are you serious?" Max said, wondering what had happened to her mother. Did she want something? What was her agenda?

"Completely." Peyton sipped her iced tea. "Why shouldn't you go visit your best friend in her new home?"

Max exhaled. "I would love that. So would she. We were trying to figure if she could come here since she's taking a gap year, but I was going to be away at school. . . ."

Her mother opened her mouth and quickly closed it.

Max waited.

Again her mother parted her lips, started to speak, and, shaking her head, stopped.

"Are you having a stroke?" Max asked, obviously kidding, but her mother didn't laugh.

"About Princeton . . ."

"Mom, can we not? Just for, like, this weekend? It's been really nice getting away from all of it, and I appreciate you planning this"— she waved her hands toward the rolling green lawns outside the window—"I really do. So much. But I need a break from the college stuff."

"Okay, okay. I'll stop." Her mother cleared her throat. "Am I allowed to say how glad I am that we're doing this? Plus, it's really nice not to be working now so we can stay an extra day."

Max peered at her. "How are you feeling about work? I know you weren't expecting to be, um . . . out the whole summer."

Her mom's eyes widened. "No, I certainly wasn't. They're doing what they feel they need to." She leaned forward and lowered her voice. "But it will be fine. Because it has to be."

Was her mother tearing up? Max felt a stab of panic. She was trying her best to express interest in her life—something she certainly didn't do enough of—but now she'd gone and made her cry.

"I didn't mean it to . . ." Max said. "I'm sorry."

"No, no, it's not you. It's just . . . everything. Here you are, being so understanding, when I'm the one who's ruined your life."

"I do have a future, don't I?"

"Of course you do, sweetie. The brightest one. I . . . I just . . ." She dabbed fiercely at her eyes with her napkin.

"I was really looking forward to going away," Max said quietly, almost in a whisper.

Her mom nodded.

"It's just . . . high school sucked. Like, in every possible way. And I know I was hatefully obnoxious about Princeton when you and Dad were so excited about it. . . . I'm sorry about that. I don't think I even realized what a special place it was. Is. Could have been. But, well . . . ever since I got in, I've been researching it, and I had actually gotten excited to go. Did you know they have a whole, dedicated outdoor education program, where they take you on the most amazing trips, all over the region?"

Peyton shook her head. "I didn't know that."

"And their Program in Visual Arts looks incredible. They get the most amazing visiting filmmakers and guest artists. . . ." She looked down at the table. "It's super ironic, I guess, that when I was offered a spot, I thought there was a better fit for me somewhere else, and now that the opportunity has been taken away, I can't think of a more perfect school."

"Oh, honey. I'm so . . ." Her mom's eyes widened, as though she'd been struck.

"No, no, I didn't mean it like that," Max rushed to say. "It's fine. It will be fine. I don't really know what's next for me, and that's not where I thought my life would be right now."

"Max . . ."

Max held up her hand. What had she been thinking? Here was her mother, already upset enough about everything, and now Max was piling on. "Let's change the subject," Max said. "Skye told me you won Homecoming Queen! How could you never have told me that before?"

"She told you what?" Her mother looked at her, confused.

"That you won Homecoming Queen in high school! That you were the first junior in the history of the school to win it. I had no idea."

An empty laugh. "What's to tell? That I won some award for being popular? A lot of good it did me. I'm thankful every single day that you're so much smarter than I was. My god, though, I worked my ass off for that job. Overnight shifts, weekends, backwater towns you can barely find on a map. I was so lonely for those years, living in random places, working odd hours, moving around all the time. . . . My friends were in New York or L.A., dating, partying, traveling. And it seemed like I was locked in this hopeless grind of local police blotter stories. I kept asking myself if it was worth it. . . ."

"Well?" Max asked.

"Well, what?"

"Has it been worth it? You've made it—times a thousand. No one can argue that. Was it worth it?"

"I'm going to get back to that desk if it kills me," her mom said, but something about her expression made Max wait. Her mom bit her lower lip, the way she sometimes did when she was concentrating, and furrowed her brow. "Although, in hindsight, I worry that I missed too much time with you."

"No. You were always there when I needed you. Or Dad was. And you two are pretty much the same person." Max meant it—when she looked back, she always remembered seeing at least one parent around, probably more than she'd wanted to.

"You mean that?"

"I'll never forget the time you came and spoke to my eighth-grade class for Take Your Working Mom to School Day. You were incredible! People still talk about it."

Her mom smiled, but it looked sad. "You're sweet to say that. I hope so. I don't know what it is—your father's arrest, of course, but maybe my big looming birthday, too—I keep thinking about where we all stand now. What's going to happen. And if I'm doing anything right . . ."

"Don't get all somber on me again!" Max said, trying for jokiness. "I mean, we just got you out of the sweatpants!"

"Sorry, sorry," Peyton said, waving her hand. "I promised you we wouldn't have to talk about it this weekend, and here I go again."

"I asked, Mom. It's okay."

"What do you think about trying that chakra class Sean told us about, at his yoga studio?" her mom asked, delicately forking her quinoa.

"Where everyone sits around on yoga blocks and the instructor bangs all the gongs?"

"Yes!" Peyton laughed. "Apparently it's very aligning."

"What does that even mean?" Max asked.

"I have absolutely no idea."

"Chakras and gongs it is."

Guess what?? Getting plane tix for grad present to . . . drumroll . . . HK! Max pecked the letters on her phone and, as she always did, wondered what time it was in Hong Kong.

All of Max's electronics rang instantaneously. Propping her laptop on her chest, Max clicked accept on the FaceTime call and Brynn appeared on her screen, looking like she'd just woken up.

"What time is it there?" Max asked, squinting for a closer look. Brynn's short, choppy hair was a total mess, and whatever shirt she was wearing was stretched at the neck so much that it hung off her shoulder.

Brynn rubbed her eyes. "Are you serious? About coming to visit?"

"Yes!"

"My fucking god, this is the best news I've heard in a very long time."

Max grinned. It was crazy how much she loved Brynn. How much she missed having a friend like that. Brynn pushed herself up, her laptop shaking as she climbed out of bed. "I'm just going to get water—keep talking, I'll be right back."

"Did you decide between Australia and Southeast Asia?" Max yelled at the screen. "I'm so freaking jealous of you right now."

"So come!" Brynn said, bounding back into view and climbing under the covers. "You said it yourself, you have nothing better to do."

"Yeah, I'm looking into a few things."

"Like?"

"Like applying now to start in January. There are actually a bunch of schools that do that. I don't know. I need to get a job as soon as possible, something more substantial than scooping ice cream. Save some money. Figure out a plan."

The door to their adjoining bathroom opened and her mom appeared wearing a bathrobe and rubber slippers. "I'm so relaxed I could scream," she said, padding into Max's room.

"Hi, Mrs. Marcus!" Brynn called from Max's screen.

"Is that Brynn?" Peyton sat down next to Max and leaned in. "Hi, sweetheart! Stop calling me Mrs. Marcus, it makes me feel old."

Brynn laughed. "You're the coolest old person I know. Next time you take Max away for the weekend, can you bring me, too?"

"Of course. I'll let you two talk; I'm going to shower. Brynn, say hi to your parents for me, okay?"

Her mom cinched the robe belt tighter around her waist and headed to the bathroom, closing the door behind her.

"I actually have to go," Brynn said, rolling her eyes. "I promised my father I'd go grocery shopping with him."

"Have fun with that," Max said. "Talk later?"

When Brynn's face had disappeared, Max started transferring the video clips she'd shot throughout the day. She'd captured a "Welcome to Vermont" sign from their car ride, a few seconds of the maniacally happy restaurant staff that would be hysterical on a loop, a totally random clip from when she sneaked into the empty yoga studio and banged a gigantic gong, and some selfie takes—shot with a tripod—of her stretched out on one of the condo's couches with a cup of tea and a paperback. She had a pang of concern. Was it too much? Her fingers flew over the keyboard, cutting, pasting, brightening.

Her mom emerged from the bathroom. "What time do you want to go for dinner?" Peyton asked, toweling off her hair.

Max stared at her screen. "A half hour? I'm almost done with this."

"What are you working on?"

Normally, Max would've muttered, "My channel," or "Today's vlog," in a tone that made clear to her mother to lay off the inquiries, but after her FaceTime with Brynn and a general sense of well-being that she hadn't felt in ages, Max looked up from her laptop. "Here, look. I'll show you."

She half expected her mother to make up an excuse, but to Max's surprise, Peyton immediately joined her on the bed.

"Oh, I love that!" Peyton said, pointing to a clip from the car ride. The highway stretched ahead of them, but then, in a clearing off to the side, Max had captured a huge group of curious deer. There were probably two dozen of them, the mamas eating and the babies scampering.

"Cute, right?"

Max scrolled through the rest of the day's material and was shocked that her mother not only asked eighty-five thousand questions—that was her job, as both her mother and a journalist—but that she actually seemed interested in the answers. How many times had Max tried to explain to her the purpose of a vlog? Or why strangers wanted to watch them? Or what made one more compelling, artistically speaking, than another? But tonight, as Max showed her mom the list of eight thousand people who subscribed to her channel, who commented and DM'd her and asked questions and signed up for notifications for new posts—well, it seemed to get her attention.

"And how many of these people would you say you know?"

"Know, like, in real life?" Max shrugged. "I don't know exactly, probably a couple dozen? Some girls from Milford, a few people now from Paradise, Brynn and a couple of her friends. But mostly, they're strangers."

"Incredible," her mom said. "I really admire how you mix it up. Every day is something different, but whether you're observing things in nature or being a fly on the wall of a pointed social interaction, or creating an ode to the city you so obviously love, you give it such a unique perspective. Not many people can do that, you know."

Max felt a warmth spread in her chest. Her father said things like that all the time, but she couldn't remember the last time her mother had complimented anything other than workouts or food choices. "Thanks."

"So . . . I spoke to Daddy today. He sends his love."

Max could feel her mother looking at her. "Oh, yeah?"

"The judge is recommending a three-week sentence."

"In *jail*?"

"In a minimum-security federal penitentiary, yes."

"Dad's going to *jail*? I mean, we all knew this was the probable outcome, but my god, to hear it's actually happening. This is all so fucked."

"Sweetheart, he misses you so much. He asks about you every single day. I know it's hard to understand at your age, but parenting sometimes makes you lose your mind—even the really smart, even-keel parents completely lose it sometimes. Deep down, you know who your dad really is. What he's really about comes down to one word: you. And if there's one thing I've learned along the way, and I'm still learning even now, it is that you have to be there for the ones you love, even when they royally mess up. *Especially* when they royally mess up. You can't shut him out like this forever."

"I don't plan to shut him out forever. But I'm not ready to forgive him yet."

"I know it might be hard to see right now, but you have everything ahead of you—everything. One day this whole awful situation is going to be a tiny blip in your rearview mirror, and you're going to be a world-renowned cinematographer—or a contented stay-at-home mom, or a skilled tradesperson, or a surgeon—who knows? All I'm trying to say is that Daddy and I both love you so much, and this too shall pass."

Max glanced up. "Did you really just say that?"

Her mom's face broke into a smile. "I'm sorry. Nisha's been saying it to me lately, and it makes me want to end her life."

"Yeah, I'd want to kill her, too," Max said. She shut her laptop and turned to her mom. "But it's not just me who's completely screwed over. Is there any way that we can help Aunt Skye? With her charity? It's so unfair that this thing that she dedicated two years of her life to might now not happen because of us."

"Honey—" Her mother's voice caught. "It's . . . it's not . . . Everything is more complicated than it seems."

"Complicated? It seems pretty simple to me."

Peyton stood up and strode over to the closet, where she yanked out a small tote bag.

"You're *leaving*?" Max asked.

"No! Look what I brought!" Her mom carried the tote over to Max's bed and began to remove things one by one.

"Oh my god—are those what I think they are?" Max picked up a four-pack of chocolate-frosted cupcakes.

"They sure are. And I brought these, too." Movie-theater-size bags of Sour Patch Kids, Raisinets, and Swedish Fish hit the bed.

"Are you *sober*?" Max asked, unable to believe what she was seeing.

"Not for long, I hope," her mother answered, and produced a bottle of Veuve Clicquot. She held it aloft like a trophy.

"But I'm only seventeen!"

Her mother sighed. "I suppose most mothers would be happy their teenagers want to follow the alcohol laws." She bounded off the bed once again and retrieved from the bathroom two water glasses and a washcloth. The cork popped off into the washcloth with only one twist, and they both cheered.

Max accepted a glass, examining the fizzy contents. "Heavy pour," she said. "You've done this before."

"Hah! There's no reason on earth I can't enjoy a little champagne with my beautiful daughter."

"Except: underage," Max said, grinning.

"What are they going to do?" Peyton said, clinking her glass with Max's. "Arrest us?"

24

Lighten It Up

Peyton poured herself another cup of coffee and dialed Kenneth.

"Mr. Grinfeld's office," his assistant said brightly, even though she most certainly knew it was Peyton calling.

"Hi, Liz. Happy Monday! Is he available?"

"And who may I ask is calling?"

Peyton inhaled. "Just me, Peyton. Calling like I have every Monday morning for the last nine years!" She tried to keep her tone light.

"Of course, Peyton. Putting you through now."

She waited at least two minutes, which was a minute and fifty-five seconds longer than normal.

"Peyton?" Kenneth boomed. "What can I do for you?"

"I'm calling for an update. You said you'd call by end of day Friday, but I never heard from you. Has there been any word from ANN?"

"Nothing yet. I have a call with Joseph scheduled for this afternoon, but I wouldn't get my hopes up."

Peyton realized that her fingernails were digging into her palms. "Oh? And why is that?"

"Nothing definite. Just a feeling. I'll call you later today when I know more. Peyton? I hate to run, but I have to take this call."

He hung up without saying goodbye.

She glanced at the microwave clock, which read 9:33 A.M. Sean would be done with the post-show meeting, but when she called, his phone went straight to voicemail.

"Hi, it's me. Just wanted to check in, hear how everything's going with you. Call me when you get a chance? Okay, bye!"

It was the second time she'd left a message; after the first, he'd texted her an apology, saying everything was "so crazy" and he'd get back to her as soon as he could.

Peyton was just about to call Nisha when Max appeared in the kitchen, wearing joggers, a tattered tank top, and high-top sneakers. As usual, her hair was piled on her head.

"Hi, honey," she said, bracing herself for a cranky, early-morning teenage response. The weekend away with Max had been wonderful—even better than she'd allowed herself to hope—but Peyton had been up most of the night, haunted by Max's confession that she felt lost and confused about her future. It had been such a rare admission from Max, who was normally so tough, and Peyton couldn't stop thinking about it.

She stood up and wrapped her arms around her daughter. "Can I make you some breakfast?"

"No thanks," Max said, more cheerily than she had in ages. "I'm going to meet some friends at the diner."

"Some friends?"

"Mom."

"What? Inquiring minds want to know if this group happens to include Oliver?"

Max pretended to be busy with filling her stainless coffee mug, but Peyton could see the blush creep up the back of her neck.

"I think it's great that you two are . . . friends. That one time I came to visit you at work, he couldn't have been nicer."

"Mmm. So, you good with me taking the car?"

"Sure thing, honey. Just keep in touch, okay?"

"Yep," Max said, hightailing it out of the kitchen. Peyton heard the door slam a minute later. She was thrilled that Max had a group now, and possibly even a boyfriend. She wasn't quite sure she'd realized how lonely her daughter had been these last weeks—or really since Brynn left. Now, with her whole future uncertain . . . Peyton hated thinking about it.

Her phone rang.

"Hi," she said to Nisha. "I was just going to call you!"

"Listen, I can't really talk right now, I just wanted to see how you were doing with updating your social media? After your leaving the tennis fundraiser early, I really feel like you need to appeal directly to the public."

"Um, yes, definitely. I spoke to the woman who oversees my social accounts, and she said the best way was to choose a dozen or so photos, write the captions, and send them to her. Then she'll post a few every week."

"Fine," Nisha said. "Remember, we're going for really personal here. Humanizing. Happy family events, okay? And do not be afraid to include Isaac—you aren't hiding from anything."

"Roger that," Peyton said, joking, but still a little taken aback by Nisha's abrupt manner. "Hey—I know this is super last minute, but any chance you want to meet tonight for a drink, or dinner even? I'm happy to come to you."

"Would love to but I can't tonight," Nisha said.

Peyton waited for her to elaborate, but Nisha said nothing.

"Got it. Well, another time, then?"

"Mmm. Copy me on the email you send to her? So I can see the pictures?"

"Yes, of course. Say hi to Ajit for me. And the boys. We miss you guys!" She hadn't meant for it to sound pathetic or accusatory or sad, but it managed to come out as all three.

"Will do. Talk soon," Nisha said, and hung up.

No one would ever accuse Nisha of being warm and fuzzy, but when had she become so cold? So distant? They hadn't seen each other since the brunch at Nisha's apartment the morning after Isaac's arrest, and that had hardly been social. Even when they were both crazed at work and juggling a thousand different things, they always made time to meet for a quick coffee or cocktail. Making a mental note to follow up with her friend, Peyton sent a text to her TV Moms group.

Hi! Last minute but anyone want to meet for a drink tonight?

She waited five minutes, and when no one responded, she added: *Also, mi casa es su casa! Bring the fam and come visit this weekend. Pool, porch, chickens, cocktails . . . the suburbs await.*

Again, another five minutes passed and then ten, and there was no response.

Trying not to attach any meaning to her friends' radio silence, Peyton flipped open her laptop and began to scroll through her nearly eighty thousand pictures in Photos, looking for the just-right humanizing pictures that Nisha had requested. The first one she chose was of Max, age one, wearing a tutu in a pumpkin patch, her pigtails and chubby cheeks perfectly squeezable as she gummed an apple. Peyton smiled to herself, remembering the afternoon she and Isaac had driven to the farm on Long Island. She wrote, "My baby girl's first Halloween!" As a counterpoint, Peyton scrolled forward sixteen years, the faces and places blurring by, before she found the exact photo she was looking for: Max at her high school graduation, a peace sign pasted on her mortarboard and a giant smile on her face, ready to embrace her whole future. Peyton felt a tightening in her throat as she added the photo to the album and wrote, "So proud of the woman she's become!"

She scrolled some more and chose a photo of Isaac and her, the weekend she proposed to him. Pale from seasickness and hair wild from the salty air, she helped him hold up a giant striped bass. Both of them were grinning. She remembered how they'd gone back to their little room at the Montauk Inn and made love and talked about all their plans for the future. She typed, "My man, the love of my life." Without thinking, she added a couple more of her favorites, the pictures that stood out in her mind to this day, among the tens of thousands casually snapped over all their years together: one of Isaac cupping a newborn Max in the palms of his hands; Isaac holding up a toddler Max on miniature skis in Vermont one winter; a picture from an ANN holiday party where Isaac, looking gorgeous in his tuxedo, stood in the center of a group of her colleagues, making them all laugh. She smiled now, remembering how proud of him she'd been that night, how grateful that he was hers.

A few months earlier Skye had sent Peyton a zip drive with a bunch of old family photos she'd scanned from albums she found in Marcia's storage closet. It took a few minutes, but Peyton located the drive and chose her favorite: her and Skye, both in middle school with bad bangs and braces, at a family bar mitzvah. She captioned it "My better half." Unable to resist adding another, she found one of the three of them in their driveway in Pennsylvania. Skye was plopped down on the cement reading a Beverly Cleary book, while Marcia helped Peyton ride her new two-wheel bike. Their father had just left with his hygienist, and while Peyton couldn't remember who had taken the picture, she could still recall the feeling that her life had been irrevocably changed.

Refilling her coffee, Peyton ran across a picture that made her instantly smile: it was all her TV Moms before they were moms, at Buddakan on opening night. Cocktails littered the table in front of them; they wore skimpy dresses and enormous white smiles, their arms slung over one another's shoulders. She captioned it "My kick-ass friends from our early TV days." Good god, that seemed like another lifetime. Had they ever been that happy and free? That *young*? But wait, she could remember another picture, from only six months ago. It took some searching, but Peyton soon located exactly what she was looking for. They'd all somehow managed to escape their jobs and husbands and kids and responsibilities and steal three days together at a resort in Mexico. In the photo they were floating in the pool with floppy sun hats and brightly colored margaritas, laughing. Always laughing. She captioned it "My girls."

The photo reminded her to check her texts, but not one of her friends had responded about meeting up for drinks or coming to visit her in Paradise. She slumped back in the uncomfortable wicker dining chair and stared at her screen. There, practically calling out to her, was the photo that would complete her social media collection. It was from last year's Thanksgiving, which Peyton and Isaac had hosted. All of them—Skye's family, Gabe's mother, Marcia, Max, and even Brynn, who'd stopped over to say hello—sat in the living room, stuffed after an epic spread, and watched Aurora do a choreographed dance to a Justin Bieber song. Peyton had snapped the picture while standing on a couch to make sure she captured the whole scene, and every single person was laughing and clapping.

The tears came on so swiftly, so fiercely, that Peyton could barely stand up. She had to get away from the computer, her phone, all those thousands of photos that showed in bold, living color what she had jeopardized. She staggered into her bedroom and flung herself on Isaac's side of the bed, which was ridiculous because he hadn't spent so much as a single night at the cottage in Paradise. How could she have done it? Why? What was she *thinking*? She'd asked herself this so many times over the last weeks and months, and while it made her feel slightly better to say she did it for Max, Peyton couldn't lie to herself any longer. She'd risked it all—her marriage, her relationship with her Skye, her friends, her career, and, worst of all, her daughter's future—in some foolish attempt at being perfect. At keeping up appearances. To make sure that no one ever saw the real Peyton, the one who constantly felt like an imposter, and who, despite all the achievements, was convinced she deserved none of them.

25

Cake-Scented Vortex of Hell

Skye stalked all three floors of the newly renovated library, her heart pounding as she scoped out the quietest available cubicle. Libraries were another place that made her feel old. When she was a kid, growing up in Pennsylvania, her local town library was militant about three rules: no eating, no talking, and return your books on time. But here, at the Paradise Community Library that looked more like MoMA, none of those rules applied. Except for one small, quiet reading room, people spoke in normal tones. Cellphones rang. Laptops dinged and chirped. People pecked away on keyboards and munched on kale chips and slurped down liter after liter of Smartwater and Vitaminwater and Hint water. Toddlers tore through the stacks and babies wailed and mothers threatened. Teenagers who'd told their parents they were doing homework huddled in corners. TikTokking. And the books! If you checked out ten and didn't read a single one before your three weeks ran out? No problem! Just log on and extend it. It was like the entire place was unrecognizable, a virtual hub of socializing and chatting and eating and drinking and nonreading and barely any writing and zero studying. But still, it was a thousand times better than trying to work at a Starbucks or—shudder—her own house, so Skye kept coming back.

Her phone rang with a blocked number. Reflexively, she sent the call to voicemail, waited thirty seconds, and then read the garbled transcript. It was from yet another debt collector, wanting to know when she was going to make her next payment. She deleted it and took a few breaths. Just yesterday, right after Gabe had left for work, she'd packed Aurora and about six hundred dollars' worth of towels and bed linens into the car and headed to Bed Bath & Beyond. The sales associate was hesitant to accept items so far past the return window, but the manager made an exception when Skye started crying. From there she'd made returns to Target, West Elm, and Walmart, but she had barely made a dent in either her basement or her credit card debt.

After she finally settled down at a desk that was a touch too close to the graphic novel section for her liking (those kids tended to be the loudest), she logged onto the Wi-Fi and, as she'd promised herself, knocked out a few emails that had been haunting her. Feeling productive, she read and reread the draft of the email she'd written the week before but still hadn't worked up the nerve to send out. It described her plans for the residence and a bit about the first class of girls in what she hoped was an interesting and evocative way. Only at the very end did she ask for leads on people who might be interested— personally or professionally—in helping to underwrite the project. Should she be more direct? Less? Ask sooner? Share more? Skye agonized before slamming her laptop closed in frustration. How was she back here again, scrounging around for money and begging people to donate? Her anger toward Isaac was unhealthy, she knew this, but she couldn't help it. It was one thing if you made the choice to ruin your own life, but that the fallout also affected Max and eight completely deserving children made it much harder to swallow.

A disgruntled-looking teenage boy sauntered over and raked through the graphic novels. He made strange lip-smacking noises, and he glared at Skye when he caught her staring. She grabbed her laptop and headed to the library's café for some coffee. Was she emotionally damaged for assuming he was going to pull out a gun and start to shoot the place up?

From the café she texted Gabe and asked him: *Am I crazy to think some kid dressed in all black and making angry noises in the library is a school shooter?*

Yes.

Why? Don't you ever think about it? She knew he did.

Of course. Too often. Our country is broken.

Then why don't you think my library guy is a killer?

Because he's at the library!

Skye considered this. It was a fair point. She sipped her coffee and checked the time: the conference room would be all hers in fifteen minutes. Yes, she'd frittered away precious minutes looking for a quiet place to work, but soon she'd be able to move into a private room for ninety straight minutes—more than enough time to edit and send the email to everyone she knew, so long as she stayed focused—and she would still make it on time to meet Max and Aurora at the mall.

She copied and pasted her exact text to Peyton. *Am I crazy to think some kid dressed in all black and making angry noises in the library is a school shooter?*

You'd be crazy not to, Peyton wrote back instantly. *Don't think, just leave! Trust your instincts!*

Skye smiled.

Collecting her coffee and bag, she headed to Conference Room 2, and after adjusting the temperature and the lighting and unpacking her laptop, she settled into her seat. She took a deep breath. Here it was. Her ninety minutes of focus. The hour and a half she'd been waiting for all day. She was ready. She was going to *crush* it. The room was cool and quiet, Skye was fed and caffeinated, and her daughter was safe and happy. She'd been lucky that Isaac had a contact who'd been willing to fund this, but now it was time for her to make it happen. She wasn't a quitter, at least not yet. She took a few deep breaths, channeled some positive words of encouragement, and opened her laptop. An email from J.Crew popped up announcing their annual fifty percent off sale, and instinctively, Skye clicked on it.

A new-for-fall hot-pink sherpa kid's coat led her to check a few other sites to make sure no one did a cuter version at a better price, which led to a list of new fall trends on BuzzFeed and then straight to a slideshow of the summer's bestselling five-star products on Amazon. Before she could even register what was happening, Skye had ordered a specialty moisturizing mouthwash despite not having a particularly dry mouth, a set of magnetic measuring cups for all the baking she never did, and an extremely cute sunglasses organizer even though she only owned two pairs. There was a knock on her conference room door.

"Hi! Sorry! I think I signed up for this time slot?" said a bubbly blond teenager in a Paradise soccer T-shirt and shin guards. Her blond braid reached her lower back. Her pert nose was spattered with freckles. Even her teeth were bright white.

"Of course," Skye said with a warm smile, despite her panic. How had she just squandered away her precious ninety minutes surfing clothing sites and buying a bunch of stupid stuff she didn't need? Why was it so damn hard to focus these days?

She packed up and headed to the parking lot. Her phone rang as she was backing up, another blocked number that she screened. It rang again. And again. Was it another debt collector? She felt dampness spring to her underarms. They had been *stalking* her lately. It made her feel like a criminal, rather than someone who would have had the funds to pay for her perfectly legitimate charges before this shit show of a misunderstanding. Why were they so relentless, so completely single-minded? When the ringing started again, Skye stabbed the button on her car's screen and screamed into the speakerphone. "Stop calling me already! I've told you everything you need to know. The stalker-calling is not helping anyone. I'm going to have to report you to—"

"Skye? Is that you?" a woman's voice rang out over the car's speaker.

Skye's eyes widened. "Hello? Who is this?"

"Skye? It's Susan, from Forever Families?"

"Oh my god, Susan! Of course, how are you?"

"Is now a bad time? It sounds like you might be in the middle of something."

Skye forced a laugh. "Sorry about that! I thought you were some-one else. Now's a great time," she lied, nearly rear-ending the car in front of her. "I'm just going to . . . There!" She pulled off the road and turned on her hazards. "I'm all yours."

"I typically like to have these conversations in person. . . ."

"Are you calling to say that our file has been reactivated?" Skye's voice was high-pitched, how it got when she was lying. How had she not told Gabe yet that she'd decided—without so much as talking to him—to add their names back into the adoptive parents' database? It was insanity.

"Well, yes, to an extent. I must say, that was a bit of an investiga-tive call on my part, to gauge your current situation, your position, your willingness . . . all of that."

Skye frowned. "Our position?"

"I'm not being clear here, am I? I have to say, we have a bit of an unusual situation here, one that I haven't personally encountered before." Susan cleared her throat.

"Is something wrong?" Skye's mind flew to Aurora, even though she knew she was safe with Max, and both girls were on the way to meet her at the mall.

"No, no at all. I know this might come as a bit of a shock, but Aurora's birth mother is pregnant again . . . and she wants you and Gabe to adopt the baby."

A horn sounded from somewhere behind her. On the radio, John Mayer was singing his insipid lyrics about daughters becoming lovers and mothers. Cars flew by, drivers turning to glare at the person who'd double-parked and inadvertently blocked a part of the road. The air inside was suddenly humid, almost stifling.

"Skye?"

She felt her heart hammering. Was she having some kind of a cardiac event? Anxiety? Her breathing was shallow, and the air felt depleted of oxygen. Quickly she rolled down her window.

"Say nothing, of course! Obviously, you'll want to talk to Gabe and take some time to think about it. I have one detail more, however, that may . . . affect your decision."

"Don't tell me the gender! I don't want to know the gender!" Skye shouted, and then slapped her hand to her forehead. How could those be the first words she'd managed?

"It's not about the gender, although we do know and would be happy to share that information at whatever time felt right. I was going to say that the birth mother—Shayna—is already almost seven months along."

Skye did the math. "She's due in October!"

Susan murmured, "It's quite soon. I do know she was hoping to keep the baby, but recent circumstances have made that impossible."

A group of laughing teenagers crossed in front of the car.

"Skye? Is there anything else I can answer for you?"

"What? Oh, um, I don't think so. I'll call Gabe, of course, and we'll talk it over and get back to you. Is there a deadline? I know that's not the right word, I'm sorry, but when should we let you know? I mean, obviously Shayna wants a decision sooner than later, but I'm not even home right now. . . ."

Susan's voice was soothing. "I know this must be quite a shock, to get a call like this out of the blue. You two should take whatever time you need and get back to me when you're ready, okay? And don't hesitate to call if there's anything I can do to help or provide you with any additional information."

"Right. Got it. I mean, thank you."

The call disconnected but Skye's heart rate didn't decrease. She put the car in drive and somehow arrived at the mall, even though she didn't remember driving there, or parking, or walking inside. It was only the sound of her daughter's voice that shook Skye out of her fugue state.

"Mommy!" Aurora's voice rang out, and Skye felt a pair of arms wrap tightly around her waist.

"Chickpea!" Skye said, bending down to scoop Aurora into a hug. She pulled her to her chest and spun. Aurora's legs swung through the air and she squealed.

"Did you have so much fun with Max?" Skye asked, leaning in to kiss her niece on the cheek. She was shocked to hear how normal her own voice sounded. Like she hadn't just received a life-changing call.

"We really did," Max said. Aurora nodded in agreement.

"Someone is in dire need of clothes that fit for school, and let's just say that shopping is not her favorite activity." Skye tapped Aurora on the head.

"Well, it's not mine either," Max said. "That is the domain of Auntie Peyton, am I right?"

Aurora nodded. "Auntie Peyton loves to buy new clothes."

"She sure does," Max said, and Skye laughed.

"Mommy! Look at that! Do you see that! I want that! Can I have that?" Aurora screeched in a desperate voice Skye had never before heard. Before Skye or Max could say a word, Aurora bolted into Justice and fixed her gaze on a floor-to-ceiling display of sequined, monogrammed makeup bags.

"This was such an amateur mistake," Skye muttered, following her daughter into the store.

Max laughed. "Don't worry, the phase doesn't last long. Don't you remember how much I used to love this place? And look at me now." Max motioned to her super-high-waisted belted mom jeans, ribbed tank, and Doc Martens, all in black.

"Yes, but she's only six!" Skye said, watching Aurora run her little hand across every reachable item. "That means we could have *years* of it."

Skye took a deep breath and nearly choked from the piped-in scent of birthday cake. Or was it jelly beans? Frosting? Whatever it was, it clung to her throat and the back of her tongue like a bad mouthwash. Aurora had never begged for Skye to buy her anything, at least not until she'd first walked into a Justice, that sparkling, glittering vortex of hell. Now the store activated some primal, involuntary switch in her little girl's brain. Aurora was in a frenzy, running from display to display, examining and stroking and sniffing every piece of merchandise she could fit in her tiny hands.

"Honey, we are not shopping here now," Skye said as calmly as she could while watching her six-year-old gaze at a pair of sequined jeggings with rips in both knees.

"But, Mommy! I love these!" Aurora bolted again, this time to a rack of "gift ideas." There were rainbow initial pillows and bath bombs in every imaginable flavor. Everything was in a shade of light blue, pink, or purple. Ninety percent of it featured a unicorn, and if it lacked a unicorn it had a llama. There were fuzzy blankets and BFF necklaces and heart-shaped sunglasses. Backpacks with giraffes wearing headphones. Nightshirts with "Girlz Rule!" in glitter. Bed desks and diaries with locks, diaries with picture frames, diaries with unicorns—so many diaries. There was an entire wall of furry slippers and—god help them all—a makeup display geared toward the six- to ten-year-old crowd, where every lip gloss had a taste and every eye shadow had a sparkle. Gigantic hair bows. Temporary tattoos. A whole slew of things no child needed: dangly pierced earrings, sports bras, boy-short panties.

"Mommy, please," Aurora said urgently, pointing to a rack of pajamas. "Pretty please may I get something? I love so much things. Pretty please with a cherry on top?" Her tone was sweet and polite, but also nearly hysterical. Skye had never seen her daughter like this—not at a toy store, not anywhere.

She started to say no and scoot them all away from the store's heroin-like addictiveness, but Max gently placed a hand on Skye's shoulder. "It's an easy yes," she said quietly. "There aren't many of those."

Skye looked into her niece's beautiful brown eyes, so wise beyond their young years. "You think I should get it for her?"

Max nodded. "They're fleece pajamas. Who cares? Be a hero and say yes. Think of it as an investment in the future: giving in on the small stuff makes it less likely she'll need to come in ten years and show you her new nipple piercing. She won't be asking permission for that one."

Skye shuddered at the thought of anything piercing anyone's nipples. "You didn't!"

"I didn't! I thought about it. But this?" She pointed to her nose ring. "That was strictly to piss off Mom."

Skye looked back to Aurora. "Which ones do you like the most?"

Aurora squealed again. "These. With the unicorns. I *love* them."

Skye examined the fleecy one-piece pajamas: they were purple with pink paws on the feet and hands and a sparkly silver unicorn horn poking up from the hood. It had no message swathed across the butt and no revealing bits whatsoever. *Could be worse,* she thought, as she nodded her acquiescence.

Aurora whooped. "Thank you, Mommy, thank you so much! I am going to wear them every single night, forever and ever."

Skye and Max laughed as Aurora took off again to check out another display.

"See? Easy yes," Max said.

"How did you get so wise?" Skye asked, nudging Max's arm.

"You think I'm smart?" Max asked, widening her eyes. "Mom told you that the judge decided?"

Skye nodded. "Three weeks?"

"Yep. Three weeks in the clink. Plus a fine and community service. He got off pretty easy, right?"

Skye reached out and touched her shoulder. "I don't think he would agree that he got off easy. Jail is still jail."

Max peered at Skye, curious. "Why are *you* defending him? I've heard you talk to Mom, and you've sounded like you hate him."

Something about the way Max's mouth pinched and turned down, all the hurt and confusion stamped on her face, made Skye's throat constrict. Her hands flew to her eyes, but the tears felt completely beyond her control.

"I'm sorry," she said quickly, as Max's expression turned to concern. "I've just been very . . . emotional lately."

"No, I'm sorry!" Max breathed. "I shouldn't have said anything about your charity. My mom explained the whole thing, and I know it's a really hard situation. . . . I make everyone cry lately."

"Please, honey, don't. *You're* the one who's been affected here,"

Skye said, wiping at the tears that wouldn't seem to slow. There was that feeling again, like she couldn't quite breathe. How was she going to tell Gabe? What if he didn't want the baby? What did it mean for the residence? How was she going to pay off her debt?

Max stroked her back, clearly unsure what to say.

"I don't know why I'm like this. . . . It must be perimenopause. Anytime a woman over forty cries, it's perimenopause."

"Mommy? Why are you crying?" Aurora asked, appearing out of nowhere. She clutched an overstuffed pillow in the shape of a poop emoji.

"What, sweetheart? I'm not crying, love. I was just . . . talking to Max."

Aurora held the poop pillow over her head. "Can we get this, Mommy? Please?"

Skye tried to answer, but her voice came out choked.

"Aurora, honey, no one wants a giant pile of poop on their bed," Max said reasonably. "But you know what? I've been searching everywhere for a purple lip gloss. Not pink. And it must have sparkles. Will you see if you can find me one?"

The little girl dropped the pillow at her feet and took off toward the makeup display, delighted with her assignment.

"Thank you," Skye whispered.

"It's okay to cry, you know," Max said.

"This is not a tragedy, I recognize that," Skye said, watching as Aurora carefully removed every lip gloss in the display case and examined it. "But it somehow feels like the residence is doomed, that it won't ever happen now. I'll never find another investor, and I'll spend the next eight years like the last: not working, micromanaging my kid's life, surrounded by über-wealthy people with the wrong priorities. Not to mention massively in debt." The words came easily, but in her mind, it was only *baby, baby, baby,* over and over again.

Suddenly Max's arms were around her, hugging her close. "I'm sorry, Aunt Skye. I know it's not—I really do—but it feels like this is somehow all my fault. Like my dad wouldn't have done this if it weren't for me."

Skye waved her hand. "Look at me, talking to you like you're thirty and not seventeen. It's because you act like you're thirty! But seriously, honey, I'm fine. I may not look like it now, but I will be. *We* will be."

"Max! I found it! Purple lip gloss with pink sparkles, just like you wanted," Aurora announced, thrusting the tube in front of her cousin's face. "I picked the prettiest one."

Max accepted the lip gloss like it was a delicate, rare bird. "Wow," she breathed, gazing at it with joy. "This is exactly what I wanted. Thank you!"

"Will you open it now? Please? I want to taste it!"

Max and Skye both laughed.

"Come on," Skye said, taking the lip gloss from Max and adding it to the pile that already included the unicorn one-piece. "This one's on me."

26

Torture on a Tatami

The car was cool and comfortable, the air-conditioning on full blast, but Peyton's hands were sweaty on the steering wheel. As she stared at the empty tracks in front of her, she wondered if it was physiologically possible to feel nervous about seeing your own husband. First-date jitters for someone you'd shared a bed with for nearly two decades? Her foot hammered the floor.

By the time the train lumbered into the station and the first wave of passengers stepped onto the platform, Peyton was holding her breath. She watched as people poured off the train, every shape and size of commuter, with only their exhaustion and misery in common. They climbed into Ubers and taxis and shuttle buses and SUVs with school stickers on the bumpers and every imaginable brand of luxury sedan. Within sixty seconds the platform was almost empty, everyone dispersed to enjoy a short evening at home. Three hours, maybe, where they would assist with homework, and help clear the dinner table, and hear every last excruciating detail about the most recent drama with the Board of Ed, and read bedtime stories, and threaten consequences if children emerged one more time from their rooms, and wish they wanted to have sex with their spouse when all they actually wanted was to grab a pint of ice cream or a beer and zone out to whatever insipid thing they were watching on Netflix before it was time to pass out so they could do it all over again the very next day. And the day after that. She closed her eyes for a moment. Was she becoming one of them?

Finally, Peyton spotted Isaac at the very end of the track. He was wearing jeans and her favorite shirt, a bright blue polo that made his eyes pop, and carrying a bouquet of sunflowers. She gave a friendly honk and waved when their eyes met. A quick glance in the mirror confirmed that her freshly blown hair still looked good and her eye makeup hadn't melted. It mattered. She wanted him to want her again.

"Hey," Isaac said, pulling open the passenger door and climbing in.

"Hi, honey!" Peyton's voice was higher than she'd intended. She leaned over to kiss him, but he turned slightly so she would get his cheek. Undeterred, she said, "You look great. Rested. And those flowers are gorgeous."

He glanced at the bouquet in his lap but made no move to hand them to her. "You think Aurora will like them? I didn't have time to stop at a toy store."

"Aurora?" Her voice caught in her throat. "I'm sure she'll love them! I signed both our names on the robot toy I bought her, too."

The sushi restaurant that Aurora had chosen for her seventh birthday because it featured an indoor koi pond with fish and an entire wall of chirping parakeets was only a mile away, so there wasn't much chance for discussion before Peyton pulled into the parking lot.

"Right this way," the host said, grandly motioning for them to follow. "The rest of your party is already here."

They followed him past the pond and the birds to the very back of the restaurant, where he opened a curtain to reveal a small, private room. There, sitting on the floor with their legs dangling into the cutout space around the sunken table, was their entire immediate family.

"Please remove your shoes," the host said with another exaggerated flourish before he abruptly departed.

There was a moment of awkward silence. Then Marcia said,

"Welcome to the only place in America where you have to pay to sit on the floor and eat your food with cold feet. Come in, don't be shy!"

"Grandma!" Aurora said. "This is their culture!"

"Says the seven-year-old," Gabe said, and everyone laughed, the ice not quite broken but beginning to melt. He climbed to his feet and gave Isaac a half hug with a shoulder thump. "Good to see you, man. It's been a long time."

"You too, Gabe." Isaac handed the sunflowers to Aurora. "Happy birthday, sweet girl! I can't believe you're ten today."

"I'm not ten, I'm seven!" Aurora shouted, appalled.

"Seven? Not a chance. At the very least you must be nine." Isaac laughed good-naturedly, and Peyton could feel herself beginning to relax. She watched as Isaac looked around the table, smiling at each person, until he got to Max. "Hi, sweetheart," he said softly.

"Hi, Dad," Max said. The words were as flat as her expression.

Max was flanked by Skye and Aurora, so Isaac eased himself down next to Aurora and gave her a few moments of attention, asking her serious questions about her day. Then, leaning over her, he whispered to Max, "It's really good to see you."

Although she was certain no else could detect a thing, Peyton could see the slightest wobble of Max's lower lip. This was the first time Isaac and Max had seen each other in weeks.

Peyton lowered herself into the well area beside Isaac. She made sure her thigh pressed against his, but he didn't seem to notice. The waitress appeared. They ordered cocktails and some starters to share—edamame, vegetable spring rolls—and Aurora very sweetly requested a Shirley Temple. Then there was silence.

"Mom, how was Tahiti?" Peyton jumped in, addressing Marcia, who was watching the table with an amused expression. She was wearing a shapeless skirt, topped with a sleeveless shirt and a scarf, a combination that irritated Peyton for no good reason.

"People always confuse Tahiti with the whole of French Polynesia," Marcia began.

"Did you bring me a present?" Aurora interrupted and everyone laughed.

Marcia smiled. "Of course," she said, yanking her gigantic tote from the floor to her lap. Plastic crinkled as Marcia extracted various bags and pouches within the tote, placing each on the table in front of her, along with a banana, a tin of Altoids, a sandwich-sized Ziploc full of over-the-counter medications for every imaginable ailment, a brush teeming with strands of hair, a fistful of loose receipts, and an empty M&M's packet.

"Here!" Marcia exclaimed, pulling out a hot-pink organza bag with a cinch tie. "This is for you, sweetheart."

"Thank you!" Aurora breathed, as she removed a neon woven bracelet with a tiny black bead in the middle.

"You see that, there?" Marcia pointed to the bead. "That's a Tahitian pearl! A real one. They're known for their black pearls."

"Cooooool," the little girl breathed.

Marcia went back to the organza bag and pulled out more trinkets. There were Tahitian tea bags, packets of Tahitian vanilla, and woven jewelry with questionable "pearls," which she passed around the table and, in the case of Peyton, who was sitting the farthest away, tossed.

"Thanks, Mom," Skye and Peyton said simultaneously, as they each took a necklace and some tea bags.

"I got some extras of everything," Marcia said. "For my dates."

"Your dates? What kind of dates?" Isaac didn't say it meanly, but Marcia glared at him.

"My dates as in my *beaus*. Or really, soon-to-be beaus," she said, as though this clarified things.

"What's a beau?" Aurora asked, admiring the neon bracelet that Max had tied on her wrist.

"Men that Grandma can travel with and kiss and love," Marcia said matter-of-factly.

"Aurora, sweetheart, do you want to make some wishes in the koi pond?" Gabe asked. He removed a dollar from his wallet and handed it to her. "Go ask someone who works here to give you change for this, okay? Then you can throw the coins into the water and your wishes will come true!"

Aurora grabbed the dollar and jumped up, beelining for the curtained door.

Skye turned to Marcia. "Have you lost your mind?"

Marcia shrugged. "Don't be such a prude, dear. It's natural. And lovely."

Peyton laughed. "That wasn't your perspective when you found out I was sleeping with Brian my senior year."

"Well, that's because *Brian* looked like a derelict drug addict. I'm meeting the most fabulous men. Gentlemen, all of them."

"How are you meeting so many men?" Isaac asked.

Marcia peered at him, her eyebrows arched. "I have an app! Really quite easy to use. The quality of people on it . . . I've been very impressed." She held up her phone for everyone to see, and Max snatched it.

"Oh my god, Grandma, this is Tinder for old people! I'm so impressed!"

Marcia shot Peyton an I-told-you-so look.

The waitress appeared with their appetizers.

"Would you like to order the rest now?" the young girl asked timidly.

"Should we keep it easy and share a mixed assortment of sushi?" Peyton asked, looking around at everyone. "Heavy on the tuna, salmon, and yellowtail, a little lighter on the more exotic stuff?"

There were nods all around, except for Marcia. "I don't eat raw fish!" she said loudly to the waitress, just in case the girl had a hearing problem. "I'd like an order of chicken teriyaki, please, with sauce on the side, and an order of steamed broccoli, no butter."

The waitress wrote frantically on her pad.

"Also, a Diet Coke with no ice, that I'll drink right now, and after that I'll take a hot tea—caffeine-free, please, anything but chamomile, which I loathe—with my entrée. The chicken is all white meat, yes?"

Peyton looked over at Skye, who was shaking her head and trying to suppress a smile.

"Do you know if the teriyaki sauce is bottled or made in-house?" Marcia asked.

The waitress stared at her; Marcia explained, "I find that bottled sauce has so much added sugar. I'm not diabetic, not strictly speaking, but one can't be too careful."

"You are allergic?" the waitress asked. "To teriyaki?"

"No, dear, that's not at all what—"

Peyton turned around to the waitress, who was standing behind her, and placed a hand on the girl's forearm. "She's not allergic. Don't worry. I think that's everything, thank you so much."

The girl gave Peyton a grateful look and bolted.

"She's traumatized," Max said. "Grandma broke her spirit."

"Nonsense!" Marcia said.

"Skye?" Isaac's voice was tentative, nervous.

Looking surprised that he'd addressed her directly, Skye met his gaze and moved her head ever so slightly as if to say Go on.

Isaac coughed. "Were you able to find another investor after . . . Henry pulled his support?"

Instantly it felt like someone had come in and pressed the mute button on the entire restaurant: the music, the people laughing at the adjacent bar, all of it. Peyton once again became acutely aware of the dampness under her arms.

"Another investor?" Skye's laugh was hollow. "Um, no, I didn't. Not for lack of trying, but I suppose there aren't many people walking around looking to invest over a million dollars in a residential school for underprivileged Harlem girls."

Skye's words were benign enough, but her tone was dripping with uncharacteristic sarcasm. Even Max's eyes widened across the table.

"I'm so sorry to hear that," Isaac said.

"A little late for sorry," Skye shot back, glancing down at her plate.

Peyton inhaled, trying to suppress a wave of nausea. It was making her physically ill, listening to Skye blame Isaac. It was enough already—she'd allowed them to live this lie for long enough. Peyton jumped to her feet.

But like a flash, Isaac was standing too, next to her, tugging firmly on her wrist. "I need to speak with you," he hissed into her ear, while he pulled her toward the exit. "Please excuse us."

"I can't let them talk to you like that any longer," Peyton whispered as soon as the heavy curtain closed behind them. "This has gone on too long."

Isaac was still gripping her wrist. "I appreciate that. But you and I agreed, and I haven't changed my mind."

"But they're our family. Your relationship with Max! What if Skye never forgives you?"

Isaac's shoulders slumped, but he merely nodded. "We'll explain everything one day. We'll make Max understand—even if I don't entirely understand myself. But not now. I'm more . . . equipped to deal with this now. We've discussed this."

"But, Isaac, it's sickening how—"

He stared hard at her. "I mean it."

Peyton looked into his eyes, noticed how they'd recently softened more around the corners. She placed her hand flat on his chest. "Okay," she said.

Aurora appeared with an excited description of her hundred pennies, and she chattered as Isaac and Peyton escorted her back to the private dining room. The conversation had shifted to politics, and Peyton was happy to see Max engaged in the heated debate. Moments later the heaping trays of sushi arrived. During the meal Max, Gabe, and Marcia did the heavy conversational lifting, with a few comic additions from Aurora, but Peyton noticed that she, Isaac, and Skye were nearly mute.

"Speaking of which," Marcia suddenly said, although no one was speaking about anything, "I think we should acknowledge that this is someone's quote-unquote 'last meal' and wish him the best in his next endeavor. Isaac, may your stay be—"

"Mother!" Peyton interrupted at the exact same time Max said, "Grandma!"

Marcia raised her eyebrows. "What? We're not all capable of acknowledging reality? It feels very strange indeed to merely ignore the elephant in—"

"That's enough!" Peyton snapped, glaring at her mother.

"Oh, leave her alone, Peyton," Skye said sharply.

Peyton swiveled to Skye, shocked at her tone. Not since they were children could she remember a time when Skye had sided with her mother.

Gabe raised an arm. "Now, let's all just take some deep breaths and—"

Peyton cut him off. "And what?"

Isaac's voice next to her was a warning. "Peyton."

For a brief second the glare on Isaac's face silenced Peyton: he stared at her with a rare intensity. But almost immediately her mind rocketed through the possibilities. *What if Skye and I become estranged forever when she realizes it was me and not Isaac? Can my relationship with Max withstand this revelation? How can I continue to let my husband take the fall for this? Our marriage is already tanking; how much more can it take?*

Marcia and Max were watching the action like they were at a tennis match. Gabe was staring at his plate.

"He didn't do it!" Peyton whispered. The moment she uttered the words, she felt equal parts relief and horror.

"What do you mean, 'he didn't do it'?" Skye asked.

"He didn't do it." Peyton's voice was much quieter now. She sounded in control, but she felt like she was spiraling.

Max shook her head. "Mom, I love you, but you're sounding—"

"He didn't do it."

"Peyton," Isaac said, but he sounded more resigned than angry.

Peyton felt the lump in her throat harden as she looked at Max. "Your dad didn't bribe anyone. He didn't break the law. He didn't even know about it. It was all me. I did it."

•

"Come in," Marcia urged. "I'll make hot chocolate with Baileys."

"I can't, Mom. I've got to get home and talk to Max."

Marcia snorted. "There's not a chance in hell your daughter is going to speak to you tonight. Leave her be. She'll be more willing tomorrow, or the day after that." When Peyton didn't respond, Marcia reached over and gently lifted her chin. "Come."

Nodding, she switched off the car. They walked together to Marcia's two-bedroom on the ground floor; neither spoke as she unlocked the door and turned on the lights.

"Go, sit. I'll make the drinks."

It was a relief having someone tell her what to do, and Peyton listened. She sank into the couch, the same one from her childhood home, because why on earth would someone buy a new couch if it wasn't broken? The place was immaculate, almost impersonal if it weren't for the lone framed family photo on the bookshelf and the small pile of albums on the coffee table. Peyton grabbed the top album and began to flip through the pages. It was from a family trip they'd taken to the Bahamas when Max was five.

"My god, how could that have been almost twelve years ago?" she asked, accepting a steaming mug from her mother.

"Such a fun trip, that one. I think that was before your sister and Gabe were married? Or actually, I should say, before they were married *to each other*."

Peyton exchanged the album for another one. This one was from the year she'd graduated Penn State and gone to work at a small news channel in Tennessee.

"Remember you helping me move into that apartment? My god, it was so grim," Peyton said, pointing to a page of grainy photos.

"Vile," her mother agreed. "But you were so excited anyway. Your first job. Your first real apartment."

Peyton flipped through the pages. There were photos of her dressed in her Ann Taylor skirt suit for her first day; her entire team out to dinner together at a Mexican restaurant; Thanksgiving dinner back in White Plains, the very first year they'd celebrated without Skye because she had been in Uganda.

"I was so young. So optimistic," Peyton said.

"You still are," her mother said automatically, although neither was technically true.

"Back then I couldn't even imagine a life like I have now. How is that even possible? When did it all change?" She sipped the cocoa, and the Baileys felt like liquid warmth in her mouth.

"You grew up," Marcia said matter-of-factly. "It happens."

"Yes, but when did *I* change so much? Back in college and those early years, it was all about the story. I was a reporter. A journalist. The stories might not have had a national reach, but they were important to the people in these places. Now what do I do? I'm a talking head." Peyton waved her hand, practically punching the air. "No, I'm not even that. Talking heads have their own opinions! I'm a teleprompter reader! I can read, that's what I can do. Essentially, I'm a third grader."

"A very well-paid third grader."

"A very well-paid third grader who has still not managed to save almost anything, and who might never work again."

"Peyton, I'm not going to sit here and pity you; you know that's not my style. Shit happens. Men leave. Jobs go away. People mess up. In your case, it seems like you've nailed all four. But so what? No one's dead, thank god, spit three times." Her mother spat three times. "And you're a fighter, just like I am. It might take a little while, but everything's going to be fine."

"Isaac didn't leave," Peyton said.

Marcia raised her eyes.

"We agreed to separate for the sake of appearances! Besides, it's Max I'm most worried about. You saw how she was with Isaac when she thought this was his fault, and she actually adores him. What chance do I stand?"

"Sweetheart, I know it can be easy to miss when it's your own child—I think I might have missed it with you—but eventually you need to stand back and admire the person they've become. It's almost never the person you wanted, or expected, them to be, but once you can see them as separate from you, it's pretty incredible how much you can respect them for the path they've chosen."

Peyton peered at her mother. "There is so much to unpack there, but all I'm really hearing is that I'm not what you wanted me to be, but Skye is?"

"Yes," her mother said, nodding solemnly. "That's right."

They both burst out laughing.

"She checked all the boxes, your sister did. Perfect grades, first-seat violin, well-mannered boyfriends, academic scholarships. Check, check, check. She was as easy a child to raise as they come. You were the exact opposite: parties, sneaking out, drinking. Those loser boys. Refusing to study. Every word out of your mouth hostile. At least, that's how it all felt to me then. But now? I see this incredibly accomplished woman who fought like hell for everything she wanted. Who found a truly happy partnership and built the kind of career most people can't even dream of—and, of course, had a whip-smart daughter of her own who, in a beautiful demonstration that all is right in the world, is giving her mother a run for her money."

"You can say that again."

"But that's the point! Max is doing exactly what she should be doing—for her. Just as you did. She's a mini you, Peyton, in all the best ways. And as for Skye—"

"Your favorite."

"Yes, my favorite. All those perfect grades and violin recitals don't mean a damn thing if you don't listen to your own, inner heartbeat. I love Skye more than life itself, but until *she* realizes that she's living in the wrong place and doing the wrong thing—for her—she's always going to be tortured."

Peyton closed the album. They sat for a moment, sipping. "How did I fuck everything up?" she whispered.

"You were selfish. You thought of yourself and not of Max."

She nodded, knowing that was right. "I really do think some part of me was trying to save her from what I went through. To keep her from making a stupid decision when she was seventeen that she'd regret the rest of her life."

"I'm sure that's true. But you'd be lying if you said that was the only reason."

"When did you get so smart about this stuff?"

Marcia smiled, and got up to get the bottle of Baileys. "Peyton Marcus, if you and that sister of yours would stop mocking me long enough to listen, just once, one of you might actually learn something." She returned and topped them both off.

The tears that came this time were both heavy and light, a strange mix of sorrow and relief.

"Go," her mother said gently. "Take your boo-hooing home and make things right with Max. And your sister. And your husband. And your viewers. My god, woman, you've got a lot of repenting to do."

Peyton burst out laughing through her tears. She gave her mother a hug. "You're a crazy old bat, but I love you."

"You're a conniving criminal, but I love you, too."

Peyton held her mother tight, unable to remember the last time they'd been like this, and she didn't ever want to let go.

27

Ivy League Outcast

L et your breath come and go naturally. Don't try to control it, just feel the breath moving in and out of your body. Try not to judge your breathing. Perhaps you're noticing things other than your breath. Noises in your surroundings, or feelings in your body. See if you can return to—"

"Max, honey?"

". . . your breathing. If you become aware of thinking, bring yourself back to your next inhalation and—"

"Mackenzie? Can you hear me, sweetheart?" Her mother's voice echoed from the bottom of the stairs, and even with the newest AirPods turned to their highest noise-cancellation capabilities, Max couldn't block it out.

Exasperated, she yanked the pods out and exercised every ounce of self-control not to throw them across the room. Eight minutes. Eight fucking minutes of peace and quiet was all she needed to complete the first lesson of her new meditation app, but was that possible? Of course not.

Just as she'd swung her legs onto the floor, her mother appeared in her doorway.

"I was doing a meditation exercise. I was two minutes from being done."

"Sorry, honey, I didn't realize. I was trying to tell you that I'm running to CVS, if you want anything."

"CVS?"

"The pharmacy."

Max went to stick a pod back in her ear, but her mother sat down on the edge of her bed. It was all Max could do not to place both feet on Peyton's hip and nudge her off. *Leave, leave, leave,* she silently willed.

"Max. Honey, can you look at me?"

Max raised her gaze to meet her mother's, briefly.

"I know this is hard. I know everything, especially between us, feels impossible right now. But . . ." Peyton's voice broke. "Please try to understand. I made a mistake. A huge, awful, inexcusable mistake. And I'm so sorry."

Max could hear her mom's voice break, but she kept staring at the darkened screen of her phone.

"I'll regret what I did to you every single day for the rest of my life. Maybe one day, when you're a mom yourself, you'll understand a little bit more how or why I could have done something so stupid, but something that stemmed from . . . a place of really intense love for my child. For you."

Almost instantly, the feeling of pressure in Max's throat expanded. She'd be damned if she was going to cry.

"I get it, Mom, I do. I'm not a complete idiot, and I don't think you need to have a kid to understand that in some admittedly super fucked-up way, you were doing it because you wanted what was best for me. Even if that means you didn't trust me enough to do what was best for myself."

"Max, that's not—"

The tears started to flow down her cheeks, but Max's voice was strong and confident. "I've barely spoken to Dad for the entire summer! How could you let me think that he did this?"

"Max—"

"Not to mention all those girls, and it makes me . . ." Her voice trailed off.

"I know," Peyton said quietly. "I'm going to figure out a way to help. I don't know how yet, but I'm not going to stop trying until I find her other investors."

Max wiped under her eyes. "I'm trying hard not to be a bitch right now, I swear, but can you please leave me alone?"

Her mother opened her mouth to say something but changed her mind. She nodded and closed the door.

Taking a deep breath, Max returned to her meditation app, but an email notification caught her attention before she could resume. She swiped it open and started reading.

Dear Max,

I'd like to take this opportunity to introduce myself. I am the Dean of Undergraduate Students, and I look forward to welcoming you to our beautiful Princeton campus for Orientation Week. I'm including a link to the entire week's schedule; I encourage you to peruse the many options and begin to plan your time.

Max's eyes widened. How had this woman gotten her name? This was the first Princeton email she'd received since they'd rescinded her admission. It was clearly a mistake, and she knew she should delete it, but Max couldn't stop reading.

Prepare to bond with your residential college in our small-group experiential trips, before rejoining the large community back on campus. Our world-class professors will be holding breakout sessions in their specialties, and our dining halls will be showcasing their various cuisines. All of our athletic facilities are available to you, as are a sizable sampling of our laboratories, art studios, and libraries. Residential college advisors will be on hand to help facilitate your move-in, and every evening, there will be a mixer with music and refreshments on the lawn of Nassau Hall. Nature lovers will want to consider joining our Frosh Trip with a hike to the Delaware Water Gap or some rock climbing in The Gunks.

Please do not hesitate to get in touch if there is anything I or my team can do to make your transition to Princeton as smooth as possible. My office doors are always open, and I hope to meet each of you during the first few weeks of school.

All my best,
Deanna Cook

Her mind flashed to the previous spring, when Max and her parents had attended a campus tour. The prospective students and their parents had hailed from everywhere: Montreal, Tampa, Dubai, Santa Fe, Asheville, and Hawaii. Their tour guide, a senior English major who specialized in nineteenth-century literature and walking backward, obviously loved her time at Princeton. That night, Max's parents left for their off-campus hotel and Max nervously accompanied her freshman buddy, a girl named Molly whose sulky demeanor and sarcasm immediately charmed Max, to a night out. The two parties they swung by weren't her scene, but they weren't as horrible as she'd envisioned. But when they ended up at some junior's apartment, right in the middle of a heated game of Cards Against Humanity, something inside of Max switched: she could see herself belonging there. Maybe it wasn't her first choice in terms of visual arts, or the campus only an hour from the city, but the people were cool and smart. Diverse. Interesting and *interested*.

Sitting on her bed, in a bedroom that wasn't her own in a town she didn't really live in, Max had an obvious but nonetheless crushing epiphany: some of those people from the campus tour, and all the ones she'd met at the New York City lunch event for accepted students, would be starting their freshman year in two weeks. Enrolling in challenging courses and meeting new people; going to parties and on hikes. She didn't even *like* hiking, but she suddenly wanted to give it another chance. Instead, Max would head back to the city, back to her parents' apartment, and she would wait. Wait for her father to start a jail sentence for a crime he didn't commit. Wait to see if her mother ever worked again. Wait to see what on earth Max could possibly do with her own life now that, thanks to the internet, she'd been branded a liar and cheater for all eternity.

Fuck this! Max slammed shut her laptop, grabbed her phone, and pulled on a pair of Converse sneakers that were still wet from last night's excursion out back to see the Ladies. She made it to the kitchen before she remembered that her mother had taken their only car.

Oliver picked up on the first ring. "Are you *calling* me?" he said, instead of "Hello."

"It's an emergency. Can you come pick me up? I need to get out of this house."

He laughed, and Max couldn't help but smile. "So, by 'emergency' you mean 'I need a break from my mother'?"

"Something like that. Anyway, I can see you don't have to be at work until two today."

"What's in it for me?"

"You really need an incentive to get out of your own house? Come on, Stroker. Get moving."

She could almost hear him shaking his head. "See you in ten."

Rummaging through the pantry toward the very back, she extracted a family-size box of Lucky Charms and poured a gigantic bowl. How had her mother not found these yet? Max had bought the Charms plus oversized boxes of Cinnamon Toast Crunch and Cocoa Krispies and smuggled them into the house in a goddamn duffel bag like it was cocaine. She packed her backpack as she ate: handheld video camera, laptop, external hard drive, and a supplemental microphone since the one on her computer was garbage. She threw in two bottles of water and a couple of her mother's disgusting diet granola bars and was standing in the driveway by the time Oliver arrived.

"Here," she said, handing him the cranberry one as she climbed into the front seat. "I also have lemon if you'd rather."

"Wow, you shouldn't have." Oliver waited until Max had buckled, then began to reverse.

"You can thank my mother. Apparently, they're, like, practically negative calories. Burns more to chew them. Or something."

"Mmmm. You're selling it really well." He tossed the unwrapped bar over his shoulder; it landed with a thud on the backseat and slid to the floor. "So, you going to tell me where we're going?"

"Let's drive around. I'd like to get some footage of the town for tonight's vlog."

He turned to glance at her; Max noticed his acne had cleared considerably. "I've been watching, you know. I mean, not every night. But I've definitely seen a few."

Max's eyes widened. "You have? What, did you sign in under an assumed name or something? I haven't seen your email address."

"Something like that." Oliver brushed the hair out of his eyes and made a sudden right turn onto a private street. "Have you been down here? Sickest houses ever."

Oliver rolled slowly down a tree-lined lane, which was flanked on both sides by stately mansions. Not knowing exactly why, Max began to film them: an imposing stone castle with spires; a chic modern farmhouse with black steel windowpanes; a dramatic glass house set far back from the road; a gated colonial with a circular driveway; and finally, at the very end of the cul-de-sac, a sprawling estate with a main house, a guesthouse, a separate six-car garage, and a stable, where Max could just make out a stable hand leading a magnificent horse.

"This is unreal," she murmured as she filmed, still uncertain how she would use the footage. "I mean, it's not like people don't have money in the city. But you never see it like this, all splayed out over acres and acres."

Oliver executed a three-point turn. "I imagine the people who live in houses like this are tortured by conflicting needs: they want complete privacy, but they definitely also want everyone to see how much money they have."

"This is what it's all about," Max murmured, nearly forgetting that she was still filming. "This is why they're all doing it."

"Doing what?" Oliver asked, but Max didn't answer.

They drove down another private street, past more beautiful homes, and then headed into The Village, with all its designer shops and high-end restaurants. Teenagers climbed out of hundred-thousand-dollar cars; their mothers adjusted their Hermès handbags on their barre-crafted shoulders and waved to one another with diamond-laded hands. Children toddled after them, clutching the newest iPad, little ears covered in enormous Beats headphones, begging for more time on Roblox. And the fathers, few that there were, murmured agreement to things they wouldn't remember even five minutes later because they were checking the latest market fluctuations on their phones.

Max hung out the passenger-side window, capturing all of it like she was seeing it for the very first time. "This is why parents are liter-ally buying their kids' admissions to Ivy League schools. So they can have all this. What a dream, right?"

Oliver pulled into a tiny parking lot behind a local hardware store that sold exclusively Yeti brand everything and turned the car off. Without thinking—and for the first time ever—Max handed him her camera and motioned for him to record her.

"My name is Mackenzie Marcus, and for anyone who may not know, I'm the one whose father has been convicted of trying to buy my way into Princeton." Max could see Oliver's eyes widen, but he held the camera steady and she continued. "I didn't ask for anyone to interfere on my behalf. *My* dream was to go to the American Film Institute for their video-editing program. And I'm at fault for not insisting that I was going to pursue my dream, no matter how impor-tant my parents thought it was to go to an Ivy League school."

Max took a deep breath. Her throat was dry and her hands clammy, but a calmness settled over her. This was good. This was right. These were things she'd been thinking for months now—years, actually—and she finally had the clarity to say them aloud.

Oliver gave her an encouraging nod, and she continued speaking directly to the camera. "So, I'm here to tell you that I'm going to spend the next year busting my ass applying to art schools with great video programs, even if my parents think schools like that won't prepare me for the 'real world.' What's really unfair, of course, is that either way, I'll be fine. Because I was lucky enough to be born into a well-off family. I can't deny that privilege; I can only try to use it to help other people. So I'll also spend this upcoming year doing everything I possibly can to help my Aunt Skye get her charitable program back on track. All the children she was going to help deserve it. Does anyone care about them? Well, I'm here today to say 'Yes. I care.' And I want to help. It may not be much, but all the money I earn scooping ice cream or babysitting is going directly toward ensuring this girls' residence actually happens."

Max made a slashing motion across her neck; Oliver laughed and switched off the camera. "That was great," he said. "Bit of an abrupt ending, but great."

"I'll clean it up in post," Max said, taking a sip from the steel water bottle she'd brought with her. "Thanks for doing that."

Oliver turned, looking straight out the windshield. He had a strange look on his face.

"What? Did I say something?"

He shook his head.

"Why are you being weird?"

Turning back to look at Max, he gave her a funny smile. "Lunch at the Trivet before my shift starts?"

Max shrugged, hoping she appeared more casual than she actually felt. "Sure, why not?"

He put the car in gear, and Max tried to suppress a funny, awkward-feeling smile of her own. "A burger with a side of *E. coli* sounds perfect right now," she said, and his laugh gave her a warm feeling.

Later that night, after completing her own six-hour shift at the Ice Cream Shoppe, Max was too exhausted to edit her earlier footage. She surfed and clicked through YouTube and TikTok, unmotivated to do much more than stare passively at her screen, until a text from Skye came through.

You up? her aunt asked.

Y. It's 11. That's like 7 pm to a teenager

Hahaha true. Just checking in. How are you doing?

Max considered this. How *was* she doing? The whole incident at the sushi restaurant and its ensuing fallout had been surreal. It was comforting to know that her dad hadn't done this awful thing—and so great to have him at the Westchester house, even if he was sleeping in a guest room—but now there was her mother to contend with.

Doing ok. Extremely ready for some distance from your sister.

I hear that. But go easy on her, ok?

Nope. Strong NO.

She f'ed up, no doubt about it, but she's not a bad person

In your opinion

Max! Come on.

Subject change: how's Aurora?

Skye replied with a happy face emoji, followed by a crazy face one.

Max laughed. Feeling energized, she switched over to uploading her footage. As she scrolled through the footage of Paradise town, she felt a little trepidation over showing her face and giving her name for the first time, but it vanished when she thought of Skye's residence. Fingers flying across the keyboard, Max quickly superimposed the charity's name and link on the video and attached a big, splashy graphic of the house's architectural rendering that Gabe had, months before, emailed the entire family. In a text box underneath, Max wrote an impassioned description of how the residence would serve the inner-city girls and provide them with access to the very best public education the United States had to offer. It wasn't hard—Max believed in Skye's mission with her entire being. She wrote and edited, clipped and perfected, and by the time she finally pressed Publish, she felt drained but satisfied, and she fell almost immediately into a deep, exhausted sleep.

28

Mommy Needs a Ritalin

It flickered once before the book light went dark. Sighing, Skye unclipped the light from page 326 of her novel and slid it onto her night table. She propped her phone between her chest and chin and positioned her book so its flashlight shone on the page and not in Gabe's direction. If only she could concentrate. Her mind flipped back and forth between the baby (the baby!) and the scene from the sushi restaurant, three days earlier, when Peyton had stood up in front of everyone like she was accepting an Oscar for Best Actress and admitted to ruining all their lives. The digital clock on Skye's night table read 2:27 A.M. Normally, she'd call her sister and Peyton would no doubt be awake, organizing her underwear drawer or shopping online for suitcases or raiding the supply of Thin Mints she kept hidden in her pantry. But not tonight. It was insane that her own sister didn't know Aurora's birth mom was pregnant, yet here they were.

Without much hope of a response, Skye texted Esther. *You awake?*

She waited for only a moment before the three dots appeared. They were followed by *I am now.*

Sorry, did I wake you?

*Yes, but I'd be getting up soon for bathroom visit #2. What's up?
All ok?*

Skye smiled and adjusted the shoulder of her nightgown, which kept twisting around her neck. Gabe found the gown exceedingly sexy, which, considering it was made of a thick cotton and covered every inch of flesh from her collarbone to her ankles, probably did not say a great deal about his bedroom hopes and dreams.

Sorry. But now that you're up . . .

????

Skye looked hard at those question marks. Why did it feel like a betrayal to tell her about Peyton? How insane was it that she felt a moral loyalty toward Peyton, some bizarre need to protect her? But it had been like this since the dinner: no matter how desperately she wanted to tell Esther, or the checkout guy at Stop & Shop, or the lady who did alterations at her dry cleaners, Skye hadn't uttered a word. And since Skye couldn't imagine ever telling another human being about the baby before her husband or her own sister, she hadn't told Esther about that yet, either.

Sorry, it's nothing. Just can't sleep.

Come on over! One kid came in at 11, the next one usually shows up around 3.

Skye thought of Aurora, happily asleep in her own bedroom right next door, a great sleeper since the first day they'd brought her home. She climbed out of bed while pecking the letters into her phone: *I'll come in the a.m. with coffee. Go back to sleep!*

She padded down the hallway and into Aurora's room, where a bedside night lamp projected a million tiny stars onto the ceiling. A white-noise machine hummed quietly from a carpeted corner. Aurora looked like an angel child, peacefully sleeping on her back with her hands folded gently across her chest. She barely stirred as Skye climbed under the covers.

"Mommy?" Aurora whispered, her eyes still closed.

Skye snuggled closer under the covers and pressed her warm body against her daughter. What would it feel like to snuggle a baby?

Memories of Aurora as a swaddled newborn, wearing little hand mitts and impossibly soft cotton beanies, flooded her with emotion. She could still conjure up that baby smell, so unlike anything else in the world. And the feeling of unrestrained joy the first time she smiled. And rolled over. And sat up. And army-crawled backwards. The weight of a baby in her arms and against her chest, a feeling so exquisite that it almost hurt.

"It's me, sweet girl."

They lay like that without talking for nearly thirty minutes. Aurora's breathing had long steadied when Skye carefully extricated herself.

"Honey?"

"Ohmigod!" Skye exclaimed, and her heart rate surged.

"It's just me," Gabe said, appearing next to her, the general outline of his body now visible in the bit of nightlight coming through Aurora's half-open door. "Come here, I didn't mean to scare you."

Skye gratefully walked into his open arms. During the day, when they both wore shoes, they were nearly the same height. It would work the same without the shoes, she'd often think—height was immutable, after all—but it didn't. Something about the plushness of the carpet or maybe her own willingness to relax her posture, to let herself sink into her husband, made it feel like Gabe towered over her. It was the warmest, most protective feeling in the world. She breathed him in.

"Is Aurora okay?" Gabe asked, hugging her tightly.

"She's fine. I couldn't resist a quick snuggle."

Skye couldn't see his face, but she could feel that he was smiling. "Leave the child alone, woman! All we ever talk about is how amazing a sleeper she is. Do you want to undo that?"

"I miss . . . I miss the time when she was a baby."

He lifted her chin to his face, ever so slightly, and she could see that he was smiling. "I do too, sometimes."

Skye's heart beat a little faster. "Maybe we should think about another?"

Gabe took her hand. "Come on, honey. It's the middle of the night."

"No, for real. I'm curious. What would you say?"

"I'd start with 'Come back to bed.'"

It wasn't the right time, she knew that. Instead, Skye followed him back to their bedroom, the one room in the house that, according to all the experts, was supposed to be their private, personal sanctuary. Was that even possible? Did such people exist, parents who kept their own bed neatly made and their night tables free of board books and pacifiers, their dressers devoid of bottle heaters or kindergarten drawings or a heaping stack of Pokémon cards? Skye and Gabe's bed currently contained two of Aurora's stuffed animals that Skye must have missed before she'd gone to sleep; there was a mini hot-pink piano with a coordinating bench under the wall-mounted television; on the little side table that adjoined Skye's reading chaise was a stainless steel bento box with the remnants of Aurora's cheese, apple, and peanut butter cracker bedtime snack.

No one would call it a sanctuary, but still, despite the cluttered surfaces and a small heap of dirty laundry that never seemed to disappear, Skye loved their private area. How many evenings had she and Gabe flossed their teeth next to each other, gargled, brushed? How many mornings had she sneaked into his shower, nudging him out of the hot water stream while he feigned outrage? How many nights had they lain in bed together, having just had sex, or about to have sex, or debating whether or not they were too tired to have sex, and laughed?

Back under the covers, Skye rested her head on Gabe's bare chest. He stroked her hair. "Are you thinking about Peyton?"

"Yes," Skye said, her body tense.

"She made a mistake. A huge one. But she's still your sister."

"Of course she's still my sister!" Skye said, instantly regretting her tone. She took a deep breath. "But that's the problem. This is pure, unadulterated, *classic* Peyton. How could I not have seen it earlier? Why am I even surprised that someone who's been obsessed with appearances her entire life would pay to ensure her daughter got into a prestigious school? I mean, Max didn't even *want* to go to Princeton! And the biggest irony of all of it is that she probably could've gotten in on her own."

Gabe was quiet for a moment. "I'm not going to defend Peyton. But I don't think she fully understood that making a so-called charitable donation in exchange for extra consideration was illegal. Immoral? Obviously. But there's no way she knowingly broke the law."

"But—"

"Let me finish. Beyond the legal definition, I also don't think she did this for strictly selfish reasons. I think we should all give her the benefit of the doubt and assume she thought she was helping Max. In a misguided and ethically questionable way, yes. But I believe she thought that Princeton would be an incredible college experience for anyone—that it would be in *Max's* best interest. From everything you've told me, Peyton would've killed to go to a school like Amherst, which we both sometimes took for granted. Yes, her moral compass was way off in the way she approached it, but she was only trying to make that happen for Max."

Skye pushed herself up on her elbows. "I don't understand how she could be so selfish. And shortsighted. Was any of this difficult to predict?"

"But we've all made mistakes, and we've all needed forgiveness."

"Not at this level."

"Maybe not. But if I recall, your sister was basically the only person who was supportive of our relationship from the very beginning. Everyone else rushed to judgment. I'm a cheater. You're a home wrecker. Our relationship could never last, considering I was married to someone else. When your mother and my parents and pretty much all of our friends said we were being rash and stupid and selfish, Peyton was the only one who even *tried* to understand. Who got that my marriage was a mistake. Who could see that what *we* had was the real thing. Who had confidence that we were both decent, honest people with the best intentions, despite the lousy way it all went down. And you know what? I've never claimed to feel super close to your sister, or to understand all of her life choices, but I will never forget that. She showed up for us then. And even though it's hard and there's a lot of hurt, we—you—both of us—need to show up for her now."

"Easy for you to say," Skye murmured, feeling like a horrible person.

"No, it's not easy for me to say. You're upset over what she did to Max, and I could literally kill her for what it ended up doing to you. I've watched you work like hell for two years now to build the girls' residence from scratch. Learning everything there is to know about the real estate market. Permits. Zoning. Finding an equitable way to identify potential students. Coordinating with the school district. Interviewing and vetting potential housemothers. Raising the money, planning the construction, putting out all the fires along the way. I've never been prouder of anyone in my life, and then your sister makes one very bad call and your whole project implodes. You think I'm not *angry*? But when you take the emotion out of it, you and I both know that she never, ever could have predicted that the fallout from this would have affected you this way."

"Well, that's a big part of the problem, isn't it? She didn't think about anyone but herself. And maybe, maybe, in a super twisted way, Max—if I really dig deep and give her the benefit of the doubt, then I suppose I can see that a little—but the rest of us? My charity? Her own husband's reputation? All necessary casualties in Peyton's master plan."

"You make her sound like a sociopath."

"Hey, if the shoe fits."

"She's your sister, Skye. The only one you'll ever have. Be mad at her. Hate her momentarily. But please remember that she's suffering, too."

Skye rested her head back down on Gabe's chest, ran her fingers lightly over his hair. She sighed loudly, for effect. "Why did I marry such a decent human being?"

He kissed the top of her head and gently pulled himself out from beneath her. "Really just a tired human being," he said, his voice heavy with exhaustion. "Now, we both need to get some sleep." Almost immediately he began to snore.

Feeling a shiver of cold, Skye pulled her Amherst hoodie closer around her and smiled at the memory of the day Peyton visited her on campus and insisted they buy matching sweatshirts. Yes, it was true that, like everyone, Peyton at times could be bitchy and thoughtless and self-obsessed. But more often than not, she went out of her way to help the people she loved. Just like she had that weekend at Amherst, and all the other times Skye had called her sobbing over a guy or a job or, once, a pregnancy scare. Peyton always knew how to make it better. She wasn't perfect—god knew Skye could list a hundred times when she'd wanted to murder her sister. But when things got real and the ugly crying began, Peyton showed up. Every single time.

Skye reached toward her darkened phone and stared at it for a minute before typing:

I hate you right now but I love you always

And then, even though it was 4:02 A.M., the three dots popped up instantly. Skye smiled even before the reply appeared.

Just remember, my boobs are better than yours

Skye laughed and turned her phone upside down on her night table. She slid in next to Gabe, curled herself around his body, and fell into a deep, satisfying sleep.

"It's here!" Esther said, snatching her phone off the outdoor table like it contained a secret code to happiness. "Who do you have?"

Skye snatched her phone. "Dolin. You?"

"Dolin too! Oh my god, I'm so happy!"

Skye called to Aurora, who was shrieking as she ran under a sprinkler. "Aurora, guess what? Vaughn is going to be in your second-grade class this year!"

"I am?" Vaughn asked. He wore European-style swim trunks and his toenails were painted blue. The water from the sprinkler had drenched his tortoiseshell glasses, but he didn't seem to notice.

"Yes! Plus, you both have Mrs. Dolin, and she's the best second-grade teacher."

The two children looked at each other, shrugged, and ran back into the water.

Esther brushed her hair back behind one ear, revealing a tasteful but gorgeous diamond stud. "I'm looking at the class list, but I don't recognize most of these kids' names."

Skye scrolled through the attachment. "Well, there's Ezra, who belongs to Ronnie. She once invited me to a class she attends at nine in the morning—on Tuesdays—for flower arranging. No, no, I'm wrong. Not flowers. *Succulents*."

Esther stared at her, holding her Moscow mule in midair. "Succulents?"

"Mmm. Yep. Let's see here. There's Arlo, who apparently is a genius. Like a real one, not just according to his mother's assessment."

"What makes a six-year-old a genius?" Esther asked, taking a sip.

"I have no idea. Genetics, probably. The mom is a pediatric neurologist. She has four kids under nine and is some kind of competitive tennis player. Her husband's also lovely. Plus, they go on the most fabulous family vacations and post loads of pictures and everyone always looks so happy and fulfilled. It's really . . . something."

Esther laughed. "Are you going to make me beg? Because I will."

Skye laughed. "I really, truly don't know! For a while I figured maybe a drug problem—I mean, how else are you going to do all that without copious amounts of Adderall—but now I'm not so sure. She might just be really competent."

"I hate her."

"Clearly." Skye looked across the fenced backyard toward the grill, where Gabe was dutifully tending to the burgers and dogs. "Honey? What's your timing? Should we get all the kids dried off?"

In response, Gabe held up a spatula and waved it.

"I guess that's a yes?" Esther said. "Thanks for having us over. Holidays are always super weird as a single parent."

"Labor Day is not a holiday. Aurora asked us this morning what it celebrated, and neither Gabe nor I could tell her." She walked toward the spigot and turned off the water. "Kids, it's time for lunch."

Aurora and both of Esther's children groaned and booed. "Come on," Skye said, hating how much she sounded like her mother. "If anyone wants ice cream tonight, you'll go get changed out of your bathing suits."

Esther was still staring at her phone. "Who's Magnolia? My god, dramatic enough name?"

"Hah! Her mother's name is Donatella. I don't know her well, but Aurora had a playdate with Magnolia a few months ago, and Donatella called me the night before to 'run through' the schedule. Snacks, outdoor activities, that sort of thing."

"I don't believe you," Esther said, laying out paper plates with American flags at the children's picnic table.

"Not only that, but about thirty seconds after we hung up, I got an email from her summarizing what we'd just discussed."

Esther shaded her eyes with her hand and looked at Skye. "Where do we live?"

"Guess this is not a good time to tell you about Charlie's mom. She's in love with her au pair."

"So? I'm in love with my au pair, too." Esther squinted.

"Yes, but you don't want to have *sex* with your au pair."

Esther poured water from a pitcher into paper cups. "My life is so *boring*! I get up, feed my kids, go to work, come home, feed my kids, and do it all over again. Where do these people find the *time*? I mean, between the shopping and the workouts and the sex with the nannies—I just don't understand. But . . ." She looked at Skye.

"What?"

"I probably shouldn't say anything. I'll jinx it."

"You met someone! Who?"

"Not my au pair!"

Skye laughed. She shook a bagful of baby carrots onto a paper plate. "Who is he?"

"He's a co-worker. But a new one! He just relocated from the L.A. office. He followed his ex-wife to New York, because she wanted to be near her family and he wanted to be near their children, so . . . I like that already."

"Me too. What's his name?"

"Gavin."

"That's it? No last name?"

Esther shook her head. "Not yet. I'll see where this goes before giving you full Google capabilities. But . . . I like him."

"Aw, honey, you have no idea how happy this makes me."

"It's really kind of amazing dating at forty, once you already have the kids and the salary and don't actually *need* the man. It's very free- ing to focus on whether or not you actually like each other. Anyway. It's still early."

Skye noticed the smallest red spots appear on her friend's cheeks, and she felt a surge of happiness. Esther never complained—not about work, or about raising two kids alone—and she always said she never had the time or the inclination to date.

"So, when do I meet him? Maybe you can bring him to dinner? Or if you'd rather go out, we can do that, too. I promise I won't—" Skye stopped, noticing that Esther was looking across the yard at Gabe, who was barreling toward them.

"Honey?" Skye called out, trying not to sound irritated that he wasn't carrying any food. "Everything okay?"

He had a strange look on his face. "Can I speak with you for a minute?"

"Ruh-roh," she heard Esther mutter under her breath.

"Actually," Gabe said, turning to Esther, "can we leave Aurora with you? Just for an hour."

"Gabe, honey, what are you talking about? We invited Esther and the kids here—"

"Go," Esther said, waving her hand, as though this wasn't the weirdest suggestion ever. "Be gone."

"No, of course we're not leaving our own house! Whatever it is, it can wait until after we've all had dinner—" Skye gave Gabe her best pointed look but was silenced by his stare.

"One hour. Skye? Get in the car, please."

Skye looked at Esther, who had managed to maintain an impassive expression despite the awkwardness of the situation. "Go! We're fine here. We've got hot dogs and burgers and television if we need it. Seriously, *go*."

"Okay, I'm, uh, I'm just going to get changed," Skye said, glancing down at her bathing suit.

Gabe motioned toward her cover-up. "Come on, we're just going for a drive."

"A drive?"

He didn't answer. She shot a thank-you look to Esther, told Aurora they'd be right home, and followed Gabe to the driveway.

"Have you lost your mind?" she asked.

He got into the driver's seat and started the car.

"I don't even have shoes on!" Skye climbed into the passenger seat, searching his face the entire time. "Are you dying?"

Gabe put the car in drive. "No."

"Is it your parents? My mom? *Cancer?*" She whispered the last word.

"No."

His refusal to elaborate was unnerving. Then it hit her, so hard it nearly took her breath away.

"You're having an affair. You're leaving me." As soon as she said the words, she knew it was true. Not that things had been bad lately, but there had been more tension since Isaac's arrest. Sex happened less often. They bickered more. There wasn't as much spontaneous laughter and fun.

"Skye?" He glanced at her, and for a moment she stopped breathing. "I mean this very nicely, but shut the fuck up."

"So, you're not having an affair? I need to hear you say it."

"I'm not having an affair."

"But I have this strange gut feeling," she murmured. He'd found out about the credit card bills. That must be it.

"Your gut is full of shit." He pulled into the parking lot of a little French café.

"They're closed for Labor Day. Everywhere is."

"We're not here for the coffee."

"Gabe, honey, what is it?" she asked, leaning forward, wondering if her life might be about to change forever.

He reached across the car and took her hands. "Why didn't you tell me?" he asked, his voice cracking.

"Tell you what?" Skye asked, her stomach tight with tension. "Aren't we here because you have to tell *me* something?"

"I'm so . . ." He cleared his throat. And then said nothing.

"What? Gabe, I'm going to die if you don't tell me."

"I want the baby," he said. His voice was so quiet that Skye wasn't sure what he said.

"The what? You want the *baby*?" It took saying the words herself before she finally understood. "Oh my god, you do? You want the baby? Are you sure?" She didn't know when she started crying, but the tears were there, pouring down her cheeks.

"I do. Of course I do! It's Aurora's biological sibling! How in the world could I not want that for her? But . . . but . . ." His face registered a swift pain, like a sudden stomach cramp.

"But what?" she asked, feeling like she was on an emotional roller coaster. Terrified, then ecstatic, and terrified again.

"I don't understand why you didn't tell me. Why I had to find out from Susan and not from you."

Skye's hand flew to her mouth. "Susan told you?"

"She emailed us both, a few minutes ago."

Skye wiped her nose with a crumpled tissue from the cup holder. "I made a mistake."

"No doubt," Gabe said, not unkindly. "But why?"

"I didn't think you'd want to adopt another child—you've always said one was the perfect number, and whenever we've talked about adopting another, or trying ourselves, or whatever, you always shut it down. So definitively. Always 'Aurora is perfect and let's not press our luck. Our family is complete.' And then this happened . . . and I wanted it so badly, and I knew you didn't—or I thought you didn't."

"But I do want the baby," he said softly.

A fresh wave of tears came. "What changed?" Skye asked.

Gabe considered this. "I've never wanted two kids in general, and I do think Aurora is all we quote 'need.' But this baby isn't any baby—he or she is Aurora's brother or sister! I don't think any of us planned on this—especially her biological mother—but I can't fathom a world in which we don't give our Aurora's sibling a home . . . with her."

"Yes!" Skye said, her voice breaking.

Gabe squeezed her hands. He looked her straight in the eyes. "We're having a baby."

Skye felt like she could barely breathe. "We're having a baby."

"Here, call Susan right now," he said, handing Skye his phone. "The email with her phone number is already up."

"Oh my god. Now? I can't believe this is happening." Skye clicked on the number and watched it dial. It rang four times before going to voicemail. Skye switched the phone to speaker.

"Hello. You've reached Susan at Forever Families. I'm sorry I missed your call. If this is an emergency, please hang up and dial 911. Otherwise, please leave me a message with your phone number, and I will call you back at my earliest convenience. Thanks, and have a great day!"

The machine beeped to begin recording. Skye opened her mouth but couldn't say a single word. Gabe looked at her encouragingly, and she tried again, but she couldn't find the words.

He slid the phone from her hands and held the microphone to his mouth. "Susan? This is Gabe Lee. I know this is a strange thing to leave on voicemail, and of course there's lots more to discuss, but

Skye and I are one thousand percent in. Can you call me back as soon as you get this? Thanks." He hit End and grinned at Skye. "Congratulations, Mama."

She smiled back at him. The tears still flowed, but her voice had returned. "I love you."

29

At Least the Ladies Are Loyal

ood morning, girls," Peyton said. At least the chickens were
happy to see her. "Can I get anyone some breakfast?"

The loudest one, a redhead with significant girth, crowed
back. When Peyton glanced in her direction, she flapped her wings
and crowed again.

"I hear you, Firetruck. I'm moving as fast as I can." Firetruck was
the only hen Peyton had named, since she was the only one with
enough personality to deserve one.

Peyton walked slowly back to the house, her legs tired and heavy,
her boots wet with the early morning dew. She hadn't slept more than
a couple consecutive hours in the week since The Dinner. It didn't
help that she refused to take so much as a Tylenol PM because she
wanted to be clearheaded and available should Max or Isaac—who'd
been sleeping in the guest room—feel a sudden, middle-of-the-night
urge to talk. So far, they'd only spoken to each other, and not to her,
but she was determined to stay vigilant.

The fridge drawers in the pantry were stocked with neatly labeled
snap-lock containers. Glass, of course, to ensure the fowl didn't ingest
even trace bits of BPA. Yesterday, when the chicken chef had dropped
off a full week's supply of home-cooked food, Max observed that the

woman bore an uncanny resemblance to Carole Baskin from *Tiger King*. Peyton laughed aloud, not only because Max's assessment was dead-on, but because she desperately hoped the joke was an olive branch from her daughter. It wasn't. When Peyton asked Max if she thought Carole had murdered her husband and fed his body to the cats, Max raised her eyebrows and walked out of the room.

Surprised to find she was humming as she worked, Peyton pulled the top two containers from the fridge, grabbed a wooden spoon, and headed back to the coop. The clucking increased, led as usual by Firetruck, and Peyton worked as quickly as she could.

"Here, sweet girls," she said, spooning out the vegetarian risotto into the coop's food dishes. It looked and smelled delicious enough to serve to her own family, were it not six in the morning, and the hens went wild. "Just wait! Wait until you've had these." Peyton plunged her hand into the second container and sprinkled a mixture of sun-flower seeds, pumpkin seeds, and shelled hemp on top of the risotto. "Luckiest fucking fowl on God's green earth," she murmured.

When the food dishes were full, Peyton adjusted their AC and wiped down the French doors. It took six one-liter bottles of water to top off their water dishes, but their clucked appreciation made it worthwhile. She would miss them when the farmer took them back next week. It was inconceivable summer was already over, that in a few short days they'd head back into the city. Isaac was due to start his twenty-two-day sentence, and the prospect loomed above them all like a death cloud. Every time her mind landed on the thought of Isaac in jail, her rib cage felt like it was cinching her lungs. How was she going to cope with the actuality of jail when she couldn't bear so much as a passing thought?

The screen door banged. Peyton turned around and was shocked to see Max walking toward her in a nightshirt, an inscrutable expression on her face.

"Sweetheart, are you okay?" Peyton searched Max's eyes.

But Max only held out her open hand, palm forward: *Stop*.

Peyton froze.

Max folded her arms over her chest, clearly feeling the morning chill, and it was all Peyton could do not to hand over her own sweatshirt. But something told her she shouldn't move or speak or breathe.

"Please listen. Without interrupting," Max said as Peyton furiously nodded. It felt almost surreal to have Max looking at her, acknowledging her, wanting to tell her something—in the most wonderful way—and Peyton wasn't going to screw it up.

"I'm angry," Max said quietly. And then, more loudly, "Not just angry. Infuriated."

Peyton nodded again, but Max raised one eyebrow in a warning, and she immediately stopped. She would stand there silently and immobile, forever if she had to, if that's what Max needed.

"I really could kill you right now. For what you did—for what you took from me. I'm hurt, too."

Instinctively, Peyton opened her mouth to apologize, but she remembered and quickly shut it.

"Hurt that you had so little faith in me. When I think of how stupid or incompetent you must think I am . . ." Max's voice caught in her throat, and, as though their two bodies were connected by a physical tether, Peyton's throat also tightened. "Not even to mention how stupid or incompetent you were! A journalist! How could you not know better?"

Peyton opened her mouth, but Max held up her hand.

"But." She let this word linger, a life preserver in an ocean of misery. Max took a deep breath. "But I have thought about it a lot, and talked with Dad about it, and written in my journal about it, and talked to Brynn. And while I'm not ready yet to forgive—and I will certainly never, *ever* forget—I do understand that somehow, somewhere, in some totally messed-up alternate reality, you were operating from a place of love. And besides, I'm so freaking tired of being angry. I've been angry for weeks, and it feels like years. I want it to stop."

Peyton exhaled so forcibly that she felt light-headed. When had this person standing before her—probably the human being she knew best in the world—grown so wise? So mature? When had she shed her girlhood and assumed the role of a full-grown, thinking and feeling woman?

Stepping toward Max, Peyton could almost feel her daughter's warmth, the softness of her nightshirt, that distinctive Max scent that no shampoo or moisturizer could ever mask, the smell Peyton would recognize anywhere.

Max stepped back. "I'm not finished. I want you to know that I'm open to the idea of working on our relationship, so long as you are willing to work on *all* the parts of it."

"Of course," Peyton said, nodding.

"Do you even know what I mean?"

Peyton looked down at her mud-splattered boots. "Not really."

"See?" Max hugged herself even tighter. "This is part of the problem."

"Tell me!" Peyton urged. Then, lowering her voice, she said, "I want nothing more than to be close to you. Please, tell me how. Be patient with me. I will try my hardest to do whatever you ask."

Max appeared to consider this. "You need to butt out of my life for the foreseeable future."

It felt like a kick in the stomach, but Peyton worked to keep her expression neutral.

"I mean, like, be there as a supportive mom and not as a control-ling, over-involved one," Max said. "Try to understand that I'm not you. I don't care about clothes and makeup. I want to go to college to learn more about the subjects I love, not because a bunch of other people will be so impressed by the school's reputation or whatever it is about Ivy League schools that makes you all go so fucking crazy."

"I hear you," she said. "I think I finally get that one loud and clear."

"I want to go to film school," Max said. "And I want you to be there for me, cheering me on, telling me I can do it, and not the mom who makes it very clear through every word and action that you think art schools are for losers or misfits or other kinds of weirdos who can't get into 'real schools.'"

"I don't think that!" Peyton said.

"You actually *said* all those things last year when I was applying to colleges!"

"Yes, but . . ." Peyton thought back to the previous summer, when she and Max and Isaac had sat around their kitchen table, debating the merits and pitfalls of at least a dozen schools. She wasn't proud of it—and she didn't specifically remember saying it—but she had to admit that Max was probably right. "I'm sorry," she whispered.

For the first time since she'd walked outside, Max's face softened.

Peyton felt the knot in her throat tighten even more. "I'm sorry," she said again. "For everything. For all of it. I've failed at the one job I have as a mom besides keeping you safe and fed—making you feel loved for the person you are."

Max shook her head, and it was obvious she agreed.

"I hear you. Probably for the first time in way too long. I hear what you're saying, and I'm going to change," Peyton said, looking into Max's eyes.

Max offered the smallest smile and Peyton felt an involuntary rush of tears. "You better," Max said. "Because you've been a complete fucking psycho, and I want my mom back."

"Don't you think 'complete fucking psycho' is a bit harsh?" Peyton asked, with a tearful laugh.

Isaac's voice rang out, surprising them both. "No, I'd say that's pretty accurate." He was standing on the porch in a pair of shorts and a sweatshirt, a cup of coffee in hand.

Peyton's and Isaac's eyes met. She could tell, in the way that comes from being married to someone for many years, that something in him had softened.

She gave him a look. *Thank you.*

"Okay," Peyton said, wiping underneath her eyes, trying not to think about the fact that her hands were covered in chicken germs. "Well, this complete fucking psycho has a proposal. What do you both say about going to the diner for breakfast? I haven't had a pancake in decades."

Max's eyes darted to her father, who nodded. "Chocolate chip pancakes," Isaac countered.

"With a side of extra-crispy bacon," Max added.

"Make that two sides, and you have a deal," Peyton said.

Isaac looked first at Max and then at Peyton. He reached a hand to each of them. "Let's all go together."

Was it the early September heat or just nerves? Peyton wondered, as she jogged toward Skye's house, still smiling from the breakfast with Max and Isaac. For the first time in as long as she could remember, the three of them had laughed. There was still a long way to go, she understood, but she finally felt like she could breathe again.

Aurora answered the door with a huge grin. "Aunt Peyton!"

"Hi, sweetheart. I love, love, love your hair. Look at how gorgeous you are!" Peyton said, following her niece inside. Aurora's usual braids were gone, and her hair was a wild, glorious afro.

"Can Max go swimming with me today? Please?" Aurora begged, yanking on Peyton's arm. "Pretty pretty please?"

Peyton followed Aurora into the kitchen, where Gabe sipped coffee.

"Hey," he said. "How's your day going?"

"Please can we swim? Pretty please?" Aurora hopped up and down.

"You'll have to ask Max, sweetheart. I think she's working later tonight, but I'm not sure. How about I ask her when I go home?" Peyton asked.

Aurora nodded. Gabe closed the copy of *Rosie Revere, Engineer* and pushed it aside. "Aurora, why don't you get changed into your suit? We can do the sprinklers together while we wait to hear from Max."

Without another word, Aurora bounded out of the kitchen.

"How's it going here?" Peyton asked, glancing around the kitchen, which looked, unusually, like a disaster area.

"Just great," Gabe said. "Skye has taken to her bed with what she's calling a cold, so I'm trying to pick up the slack. We've done a lot of reading. Some Magna-Tiles. And we started on her 'All About Me' poster."

"I cut out a unicorn and a heart and a star from a magazine!" Aurora called from the stairs.

"Homework in second grade?" Peyton said.

There was quiet for a moment and then Gabe said, "If you want to see her, you're welcome to go up."

Peyton cleared her throat. She hadn't smoked regularly since getting married, but she was suddenly desperate for a cigarette. "Thanks. Do you think she'll want to see me?"

Gabe looked at Peyton. "Honestly? I don't know. But you're her sister. I don't think she really has a choice."

"Right," Peyton said. Her hands shook as she made her way up the stairs. She knocked on the door and waited, but there was no answer. Cracking it open, Peyton peeked her head inside. Skye stared her at her from under the covers, her hair a mess and her skin blotchy with red streaks.

"What happened to your face?" Peyton asked.

Skye touched her cheek with her fingertips. "Aurora did a 'face mask' on me. She didn't tell me that she made it herself in our kitchen, using whatever ingredients she could reach."

"Yikes. Any idea what she used?"

Skye shook her head. "No, but it's better this morning. Last night it looked like I was in a car accident."

Peyton barked out a laugh. "It still looks that way."

Skye smiled. "Thanks."

"What do you have?"

Skye coughed deeply. It sounded dry and chesty. "The plague. A cold. Depression. All of the above." And then: "You can come in."

Peyton closed the door behind her and perched on the very end of Skye's bed.

There was an awkward silence, made even worse by the fact that neither could remember feeling awkward around the other.

"Did Gabe tell you?" Skye asked.

"Tell me what?"

"Aurora's birth mother is pregnant again."

It only took Peyton a second to understand. "What! For real? You're having a *baby*?"

Skye smiled wanly. "We're having a baby. Due at the end of October."

Without thinking, Peyton threw herself on her sister, wrapping her arms around Skye's bundled body. "A baby! You're having a baby! Oh my god, I cannot even handle this! When did you find out? Does Aurora know? What's the gender? The end of October is, like, tomorrow. This is so incredible!"

Skye wriggled out from under her and propped herself up; she clearly couldn't hide her delight. "I already bought a Moses basket," she said, holding up her phone so Peyton could see the photo.

Gabe brought up two coffees, and Peyton nearly knocked him over with her congratulatory hug. She and Skye surfed websites of baby boutiques, placed bets on gender, and brainstormed cute ideas for telling Aurora and, after her, their mother. It was so tempting to leave it at that, to let the happy news drown out the rest of it, but Peyton knew she couldn't put off the inevitable.

"I'm sorry," Peyton said, her voice suddenly hoarse. "I know this"—she waved her hand at the rumpled bed and the messy room with strewn clothes and dirty dishes on every surface—"is all my fault. I can't even imagine how much you hate me right now."

Skye's eyes narrowed. "I don't hate you," she said, pulling the covers up higher, to her chin. "I want to murder you, but that doesn't mean I *hate* you."

"The residence. You had everything in place. All those girls. I'm sick about it. And I'm so, so sorry." Again the tears came without warning, but this time her crying was hysterical, uncontrollable. Peyton had tried so hard not to terrify Max with her own overwhelming emotion, but the nearness of her sister, her *person* for as long as she could remember, triggered all-out sobbing.

Immediately Skye was out from under the covers and wrapping herself around Peyton. Her body was warm and her scent—sweet but not cloying, like a touch of maple syrup—was familiar. Peyton clung to her sister, burying her face in Skye's neck, soaking her pajama top with her tears. "How will you ever forgive me?"

Skye put both hands on Peyton's shoulders and gently pushed her away. She tipped Peyton's chin up the way she would to get Aurora's attention. "Listen to me," she said quietly. "I forgive you. I'm not going to give up. Somehow, I'm going to raise the money I need. It's time for me to tell Gabe about the debt I accumulated, because I know it's wrong to keep that from him."

"You have no idea how—"

Skye interrupted her. "Let me finish."

Peyton nodded as she wiped under her eyes with the sleeve of her sweatshirt.

"I can even sort of understand why you did it. But my god, Peyton—this is her *life*. Her *future*."

The tears felt like they would never stop. Peyton nearly choked as she said, "I hate myself so much. Not just for doing it—that's bad enough—but for thinking that my brilliant, beautiful daughter *needed* me to do it. She didn't. It was my dream, not hers."

Skye placed her hand on Peyton's arm.

"If I'm being completely honest with myself, somewhere, somehow, I knew it then, too. I just absolutely refused to accept it. What's wrong with me?"

Skye shrugged. "I say blame Mom."

Peyton cracked a smile. "When in doubt."

"Have you told Max all of this?"

"Yes." Peyton reached across to Skye's night table and plucked a tissue from the box. "She's agreed to work on our relationship. There's a lot I'm getting to know about my kid these days, most of it pretty amazing. I just—" Peyton's throat seized up once more. "I don't know why I didn't see it before."

Scooting closer, Skye wrapped her arms around Peyton. "Because you were an idiot. Sometimes an asshole. In other words, human."

"I'm sorry," Peyton whispered.

"I would like to be apologized to more, but I desperately have to pee," Skye said, and hopped off the bed. Peyton rolled her eyes when she saw that her sister, who by all accounts hadn't left her bed in forty-eight hours, looked positively chic in crisp white cotton pajamas.

"I've got to get home," Peyton said. "Will you promise to call if you need anything? I'm obviously not going to make you chicken soup, but I can definitely figure out where to purchase the very best."

Skye coughed again and offered a little wave. "Will do. Say hi to Max and Isaac for me."

"I will. And, Skye?" Peyton smiled. "I love you."

"I love you, too. Now get out of here, please? I need to enjoy this time without my husband and child."

Peyton pulled the door closed behind her and waved goodbye to Gabe and Aurora, who were having a catch in the backyard. Isaac was reading the paper on the front porch when she returned, and she felt a wave of relief when he indicated she should join him.

"Thanks for pushing Max to talk to me," Peyton said, propping her feet up on the wicker table.

"She was ready. It was all her," Isaac said.

"I know you had something to do with it, and I really—"

She was interrupted by Max, who burst through the front door clutching her laptop. Her eyes were wide; she looked shocked.

Peyton leapt up, ready to tackle whatever it was: illness, house fire, act of war. "What's wrong?" she practically shouted. "What happened?"

Isaac also turned to Max, a look of sheer panic on his face.

Max said, "I went viral."

Peyton saw Isaac's nose crinkle in confusion. "You did what?"

"My vlog went viral."

Isaac cleared his throat. "And that's a good thing, right?"

"Was this something you *wanted* to go viral? I think that's what Daddy's asking."

"Yes, of course!" Max turned the screen around and hit play. The three of them watched in silence as Max's professional-looking video diary unfolded with its Paradise mansions and teenagers in Range Rovers, all overlaid with her searing commentary. Even as they watched, the number of viewers continued to climb.

"Is that really four hundred *thousand* people?" Peyton asked. She was concerned that Max had attached her real name and face to it—wasn't there a security risk in doing that?—but she quickly reminded herself that Max knew what she was doing. Her daughter was an artist, a filmmaker, and she had a different way of processing what happened to her. And that was okay. It was more than okay—it was healthy and right.

Peyton reached out, stroked Max's gorgeous, unruly hair, and said, "I think you've done an amazing job editing this; clearly it resonates with hundreds of thousands of people. You must be so proud. I know I am."

Max's lower jaw dropped open. She broke into a huge smile. And for the first time in as long as she could remember, Peyton felt the anxious knots in her throat, her chest, her stomach, her lower back, her temple, loosen all at once.

30

Always Kiss the Keepers

I t felt weird being back in her own bedroom in her own apartment in the city in which she was born and raised. Nothing had changed, physically speaking, during her summer in Paradise, but for a reason Max couldn't quite put her finger on, her New York bedroom felt different. A little foreign. Like it didn't fit her anymore.

She heard her parents jabbering down the hall, making breakfast, the espresso machine hissing in the background, a normal Saturday morning. That part was really nice, all being under the same roof again. Nothing was perfect—far from it, considering her father was forty-eight hours from beginning his jail sentence for a crime her mother committed—but things seemed more settled. Her mother was trying. Her parents were meeting Nisha later in the morning, but then they were going to buy last-minute tickets for whatever Broadway show popped up on StubHub. Just the two of them, like they used to, and Max was surprised at how happy it made her. Sunday she and her dad were going to spend the entire day together, his last before he had to turn himself in Monday morning. So far, they'd agreed on brunch, followed by tennis, and probably a little fishing at the Boat Basin. Like her mom, her dad seemed to be in bizarrely good spirits, all things considered.

Tiptoeing to her bathroom so her parents wouldn't know she was awake—no matter how well behaved they'd been, there was still zero reason to speak to them before nine in the morning—Max peed, brushed her teeth, and climbed back under the covers. A quick check of her YouTube channel left her breathless: up to 2.5 million views and still climbing. She settled in to read the comments, but her eyes froze at the very first one, a GoFundMe link, posted by someone calling him- or herself WeCare.

The sliding graph at the top of the page showed a goal set at $1,000,000, a number that Max couldn't even process, but it was the second number that made her dizzy—$422,550 raised so far toward the goal. As she watched, the figure jumped to $422,600, followed almost immediately by $422,675.

"Wow," she murmured, scanning the donations down the right side of the screen: $50, $250, $36, $800, $5. They went on forever, donated by individuals and couples and families and companies and a whole bunch of "Anonymous." One unnamed person had donated $3,600 with no comment. It was incredible. Indescribable. Surely this amount of money could get the project back off the ground! And it was growing every second. But a thought struck, and it panicked her: Who was WeCare, and how did Max know this person was legit? Like every crowdsourced fundraising site, GoFundMe was plagued with fraudulent claims. The entire thing could be some scam set up by a tech-savvy teenager in India. Panicked, Max texted Brynn.

Did you set up the GoFundMe? she typed.

Three dots and then: *Huh?*

Dammit. That would have been her first guess.

She climbed out of bed, yanked on a sweatshirt, and headed to the kitchen.

"Good morning, sweetie," her dad said, glancing up from the *Times*. "You're up early."

"Do either of you know who set up an online fundraising page and linked it to my latest vlog?" she asked, knowing she may as well have been asking her parents if they wanted to discuss the pros and cons of various coding software.

"I'm sorry, what?" Her mom furrowed her brow.

"Linking what to what?" her father asked, frowning.

"Nothing. Never mind." Her mind was racing, and none of the possibilities were good. Maybe it was Gabe? She knew he subscribed to her channel, and he often left encouraging comments. He also wasn't a complete tech moron, like most middle-aged people. But no, he'd have told Max ahead of time.

"Do you want some coffee?" her mom asked.

Her phone rang from the kangaroo pocket of her sweatshirt. Oliver's name popped up on her screen, and instantly she knew.

"It was you, wasn't it?" she asked as she answered, without so much as a hello. "Please say it was you."

Max could see her parents looking at her strangely. She didn't even realize she was holding her breath until Oliver said, "Yeah."

"Oh my god, you're amazing," she exhaled.

"Who are you talking to?" her mother asked.

Max walked back to her room and kicked the door shut behind her. "What made you think of that? Have you seen how much it's raised already?"

"Yeah, I get a notification every time someone donates. I had to turn them off, they were so constant."

A growl emanated from under the bed and Max remembered to pull her feet up to safety. "Oliver, seriously, this is going to be life-changing. For Skye, yes, but mostly to those girls."

There was a moment of quiet.

"Are you still there?" Max asked.

"I'm here." He coughed. "Look, I did what anybody would've done. I had no idea it was going to take off like that. I think it's really cool that you're trying to help your aunt and those girls."

"I don't know what to say."

"Don't say anything. I think the vlog you made is pretty incredible. I think . . . you're pretty incredible."

She was grinning like a maniac and relieved he couldn't see her. Impulsively, Max said, "What are you doing today? Want to go fishing?"

"*Fishing?* Is that code for something?"

"No," she laughed. "Like, actual catch-fish-with-a-rod. I've got the gear. I'll come to you. What do you say?"

"I mean . . . sure?"

"Great. I'll text you my train. Pick me up at the station?"

"I can't tell if you're kidding or not."

"Be at the damn station." Max ended the call and pulled on jean shorts, a cute tank top, her hiking boots, and a hoodie.

Her mother looked at Max like she'd just announced her plan to enlist in the army, but her father smiled. "You remember the code to the lock?" he asked. "Have fun."

Grabbing an empty backpack, Max rode the elevator to the building's basement and walked through the aisles of storage lockers until she located her family's unit. Once inside, she carefully packed the backpack with her father's well-organized mobile tackle box, a miniature cutting board, two camp chairs that folded to the size of one-liter water bottles, and a handful of tools, including pliers, a hook remover, and a knife. Using carabiners, she clipped two folding rods onto the outside of the bag and slung the whole contraption over her shoulder.

Oliver was waiting at the train station, as promised, when her 10:37 A.M. from Grand Central pulled in. He took her backpack and raised his eyebrows, clearly impressed. "You weren't kidding."

"I checked," she said, climbing into the front seat. "We'll be at high tide in about two hours, so it's not perfect but it's pretty good."

"Unreal," he said as he merged onto the highway. "What kind of city girl goes fishing?"

"A country girl at heart," she said. "Right lane, please. And take the next exit."

After directing Oliver to Bass Pro Shops for a couple boxes of frozen squid, they headed to a rocky outcropping on the Sound, a place Max had read was good for shore fishing. They clambered out onto the rocks, and Max began to assemble their gear. Oliver stared at her, mouth agape, when she pulled a slightly thawed whole squid from the cardboard box and used the bait knife to deftly decapitate it. She sliced the remaining squid into triangle-shaped ribbons and, not having any sort of towel or tissues, wiped her slimy hands on her jean shorts.

"No fucking way," Oliver said, his admiration obvious.

"It's just bait," she said with a shrug, trying to keep from smiling.

"Does it make me a pussy if I don't want to touch it?" Oliver asked, and frowned at the sludgy pile in front of them.

"Yes," Max said, laughing. "A big one."

Over the next few hours, Max taught Oliver everything her dad had taught her: how to choose the right sinker weight, change out the rod setups, and free up jammed reels. She demonstrated the best ways to rig the bait, and exactly where to grasp a fish while removing a hook so you wouldn't cut your hands on their spiny parts. They discussed different strategies for removing swallowed hooks; how to ensure a fish met the legal minimum size requirements; the best way to kill it quickly and humanely. They caught more porgy than anyone could eat in a week, and soon Oliver had negotiated a deal in Spanish with one of the men nearby to trade some of the keeper porgy for a couple of cans of Bud Light and some Fritos. Max switched out their rods to snapper setups, and they both stretched out on a flat rock, sipped their warmish beers, and idly watched their bobbers floating on the surface. When he leaned over and kissed her gently on the lips—once, very simply—it felt like the most natural thing in the world.

Later that afternoon, after Oliver had headed to his shift at the Ice Cream Shoppe and Max had trained back to the city, she walked from Grand Central to her building with a bulging backpack of fish fillets and an enormous smile. When was the last time she'd had that much fun? When had seven hours felt like thirty minutes? That day, as they had stared out over the water, Oliver quietly admitted he wasn't close to either parent, and Max had been struck with a realization: not since Brynn had a single person in her life needed her, confided in her, or treated her like a friend.

"Impressive!" her father said as she unpacked her carefully wrapped fillets. "Porgy is delicious, especially the way your mother cooks it."

Peyton came over to inspect the fish. "I was just wondering what we were going to make for dinner. Nice work, Max. It's like *Little House on the Prairie* on the Upper East Side. I'm into it."

As her mother started pulling flour and chili powder and soy sauce from the cupboards, Max scrolled through the pictures she'd taken that day. There was one of Oliver's horrified face while she sliced the bait; another he took showing her reeling in a fat thirteen-incher; and her favorite, a selfie of both of them, holding their beers and squinting in the sun. She decided to post one that Oliver had snapped of Max proudly holding up what looked like a massive, person-sized fish, using only her thumb and two fingers. Her dad had taught her which fish she could hold by the mouth and which had razor-like teeth that necessitated the use of a tool; he'd also demonstrated how to thrust the fish out in front of your body, which would make it look quadruple the size in pictures.

"My haul," she captioned it. Then, without thinking about it too much, she tagged Oliver's name right on the fish's face. She grinned, remembering Oliver's shock when Max had planted a kiss directly on the fish's lips.

"Did you just kiss the *fish*?" he'd shrieked. The only people in hearing distance, two older men with lines in the water, had smiled.

"Of course," Max had said. "My father taught me that you always kiss the keepers." Then she'd leaned over and planted one on Oliver.

Her mother's voice pulled her back to the present. "What are you laughing about?" she asked.

Max could feel her cheeks redden. "What? Nothing."

A notification pinged: she'd been tagged on Instagram. Quickly opening the app, certain it was Oliver posting his own photo, it took her a moment to see that she'd been tagged by the American Film Institute.

The American Film Institute had tagged her? Max frowned. Yes, she'd mentioned them in her vlog, said that it was her real first-choice school, but that didn't explain why they'd tag *her* in something they'd posted. Quickly tapping on the thumbnail, she inhaled when she saw the full-sized photo. It featured one of those old-fashioned letter boards with plastic white letters, and it read WILL YOU JOIN US, MACKENZIE MARCUS? in all caps.

"What the . . ."

We would like to invite Mackenzie Marcus to the class of 2025! Her grit, moxie, and desire to serve others aligns perfectly with AFI's values. Max, we hope you'll join us. P.S. New Jersey is just fine, but wait until you see Los Angeles in the winter!

"Oh my god, oh my god, oh my god," Max murmured, her voice getting louder with each repetition.

Her mother dropped a spoon, which hit the counter before clattering to the floor. "What's wrong? What happened?" She sounded panicked and resigned at the same time.

"No way!"

"Max? Honey, what is it? You're really worrying us," her father said.

Max limply held her phone out. "Here. See for yourself."

Her father took the phone and Max watched as his eyes moved back and forth across the screen. "Amazing," he said.

"Isaac!" Her mother was shouting now. "What is it?"

"Max has been offered . . . They posted this sign . . . Here, see for yourself." He handed Peyton the phone.

"Mackenzie! This is incredible. *You* are incredible! I didn't even know you'd applied. . . ."

"I didn't apply!" Max shouted. "They must have seen my vlog. I mean, obviously they know about the whole . . . admissions thing.

And I guess this is their way of saying that they know it's not my fault."

She clicked over to her email, and sure enough, there was an email from someone named Peter Handel. "It's all here," Max said as she read it. "An email from the dean of admissions. Their entire admissions board is so impressed not only with my talent but also with my determination and my willingness to advocate for others. They say that I'm exactly the kind of candidate that they're always looking for, and that I'm welcome to start immediately or to defer for a year, whichever I want."

"Come here," her mother said, pulling Max into a hug. Her father wrapped his arms around both of them.

"Incredible," he said, his voice breaking.

"I tried my absolute best to fuck up your life, and look—you not only turned it completely around, you did it on your own terms. I . . . I am so proud of you."

Max pulled back and examined her mother's face, searching for signs of sarcasm, of inauthenticity or martyrdom, but there were none. Only a smile that radiated with genuine joy.

"Thanks, Mom. I'm going to call Oliver, okay?" Max didn't miss the look her parents exchanged, but she didn't mind.

Oliver picked up on the first ring. "Two actual phone calls in one day," he answered, and the sound of his voice, its warmth and intimacy, made her smile like an insane person. "Please tell me you're not calling to suggest night fishing?"

"You know, I wasn't, but that's not a bad idea. What time are you off tonight?"

Oliver had kept his job at the Ice Cream Shoppe despite pressure from his parents to quit. Once school started again, they'd railed on and on that senior year academics were important, that his first-semester grades still counted toward college admissions. Despite being the ones who'd insisted he get an hourly wage job in the first place because that kind of work looked good on applications, they hadn't intended this to be a long-term commitment. His job now was to be a student, to work on his applications, and *not* to scoop ice cream. But Oliver had refused to quit.

Through the phone, Max heard the shop bell ring, and Oliver said, "I'm sorry, we don't have anything sugar-free. It's only real ice cream."

"Unreal," Max laughed.

"Stormed out without saying a word," Oliver said.

"Put me on speaker and go to Insta for a second." There was rustling. "Okay, now search for American Film Institute."

"Looking," he said, before his tone quickly changed. "Max, this is you!"

"Yeah, I know. Crazy, right?"

He was quiet for a moment, and she knew he was reading the caption. "Wow! What are you going to do? Are you going to go? Like, right this second? Jump on a plane and get out of here? Go."

It stung for a second, this easy encouragement to leave, but he was a genuinely good person, and genuinely good people wanted what was best for those they cared about. "I mean, I don't know?" she said. "I certainly have all the stuff ready, the shower caddy and the extra-long twin sheets. Part of me is dying to fly directly to California and not look back. But . . . my dad is starting his sentence the day after tomorrow, and I can't imagine being that far away now, or leaving my mom all alone."

It felt strange that Oliver didn't know the real truth—that it was really her mother who'd paid off the guy.

"I hear that," he murmured.

"Besides, now that we've raised all this money for Skye's residence, I'm thinking I might stick around and help my aunt get everything going again. She's going to have a ton to do, plus a new baby. I could be a huge help."

He was quiet.

"You still there?" she asked.

"So, hypothetically speaking, were you to defer and spend this year helping out your aunt, it might make sense for you to move back to Paradise? And, like, stay with her?"

Max could picture his pale skin reddening with embarrassment, and she was filled with the urge to reach through the phone and kiss him. She'd never admit it—not yet, at least—but she'd been thinking the exact same thing.

"Who knows?" she asked, unable to erase the grin off her face. "Anything is possible."

31

Get in Line

Peyton dug around in her closet until she found the black pants, the ones that looked like proper slacks but felt like sweatpants, and yanked them on. She paired them with a white V-neck T-shirt, a loose linen blazer, and a pair of insanely comfortable slipper flats that she'd purchased on a whim after Instagram told her they were Meghan Markle's favorite. Wrapping her hair in a loose, chic knot, she applied only the barest of makeup—tinted moisturizer, a swipe of mascara, a neutral lip gloss—and appraised her appearance in her bathroom mirror. Clean, put together, and professional, without even a hint of glamour: exactly the goal. From her jewelry box she plucked a necklace that had been a Mother's Day gift from Isaac and Max. It was a very delicate rose-gold chain with a dainty, off-center letter *M*. It wasn't fancy or particularly expensive, but it was her favorite, and she smiled remembering the brunch when they'd given it to her. Lastly, she splayed her hand and took a moment to admire her most prized possession. The engagement ring was far from huge by New York standards. They'd been so young when she proposed to Isaac, and the center diamond he'd presented her with a couple weeks later was lovely but modest. He'd offered countless times over the years, on birthdays and anniversaries, to upgrade with a larger stone or a fabulous new setting, but Peyton always refused. The ring was not visually impressive, but she loved it. Maybe one day Max would have a daughter or a granddaughter, and the small but lovely ring would get passed down the generations, accompanied by the story of how much its original owners loved each other. Peyton smiled as she pulled it from her finger and gingerly placed it in her velvet-lined jewelry box. Her hand felt naked without it—she touched that ring multiple times throughout every day—but she forced herself to leave it.

Next she flipped open her laptop and opened a folder labeled "Paperwork." She'd been working on it over the last few weeks, adding relevant emails and bank statements. It only took a few minutes to open each file and print them all, place them in a plastic sleeve, and tuck the whole thing in her purse.

When she finally emerged from their bedroom, Peyton felt a welcome sense of calm.

"You look nice," Isaac said, glancing up from the couch, where he was reading a giant hardcover memoir by Michelle Obama.

"Thanks," Peyton said, sitting down next to him.

"Why'd you get dressed to go pick up the food? And why are you going to pick up the food in the first place? Send Max. Or better yet, ask if they'll send one of the kitchen guys to deliver it. They've done that before, haven't they?"

Peyton scooted down and rested her head on his shoulder. He felt so warm and strong. "Yes, but I have a couple errands to run. I don't mind swinging by and picking it up."

"Errands on a Sunday night? Are you having an affair?"

Peyton laughed. "An affair? Add it to the list." She reached her hand to his chin, turned his face slightly toward hers, and kissed his lips, a long, soft kiss.

"Mmm, what was that for?" he asked, looking pleased.

"No reason."

"You're definitely having an affair."

Peyton kissed him once more and stood up. "Max in her room?"

"Yes. Although I think she said something about seeing Oliver tonight."

"Tonight?" She frowned. "It's your last night at home, and I'm literally on my way to pick up dinner."

"I'm assuming she meant afterward. Late. Like when almost-eighteen-year-olds begin their nights." He must have noticed Peyton looking distressed, because he added, "Let her have fun, P. God knows she deserves it, and you said yourself he seems like a nice boy."

"He does. But tonight, of all nights . . ."

"Honey, if everything had gone as planned, she'd be living in her freshman dorm right this very moment, doing whatever she wants. So I think we cut her a little slack. Let her see her boyfriend. The truth is, it's not even our call anymore."

"Did she say he's her boyfriend? Did she call him that?"

Isaac picked up his book again. He shook his head as he reopened it, but he was smiling. "You're an insane person. Go. Be gone. I love you."

"I love you, too."

She knocked on Max's door. When there was no answer, she pressed her ear to the door and heard the water running. Normally, she wouldn't barge in on Max in the shower, but there was nothing normal about that night.

"Max? Sweetie? Can you hear me?" she called through the cracked bathroom door.

"I'm in the shower!"

"I know, honey, sorry. I'm running out to pick up dinner, and I wanted to make sure you were going to be home? Daddy said something about you seeing Oliver tonight?"

The glass shower door slid open and Max stuck her head out. "You know I wouldn't miss Daddy's last meal," she said, water dripping onto the floor. "I'm going to see Oliver afterward. He's coming to the city. We're going out."

"Out?"

"Yes. Out." Max flashed her a smile, a rare authentic one. "And since I overheard you and Daddy talking about me like I'm nine years old, and I understand that inquiring minds want to know, Oliver and I *are* seeing each other."

"Seeing each other?"

"It's like there's a parrot in my bathroom."

"Sorry," Peyton said, smiling. "Does that mean you're boyfriend-girlfriend?"

"*Moooooooom!* You're embarrassing yourself."

"In case you haven't realized this yet, I was put on this earth to ask you probing and uncomfortable questions about every aspect of your life. And just so you know, I'll never stop. Not when you're eighteen, not when you're thirty, not when you have kids of your own. FYI."

"Noted."

"I'm running out to get the food, I'll be back in a bit," Peyton said.

"Can you close the door behind you?" Max called.

"Sweetheart? I love you. More than life itself."

"You too!"

There was a lightness in Max's voice that wasn't usually there, and it made Peyton's heart surge. She sounded *happy*. She had a boyfriend and plans for her future and she had done it on her own terms.

Her phone rang in the elevator. Why would Kenneth be calling her on a Sunday night? Probably to prep her on how to react—or really not react—when Isaac presented himself upstate the next day to begin his sentence. She figured there would be paparazzi to contend with, but she hadn't considered what that would look like. They'd decided she would drive Isaac and accompany him inside for however long she was permitted to stay, and Max would remain at home, but that was as far as they'd gotten.

"Hello? Kenneth? Can you hear me? Kenneth?" The call showed as connected, but all she heard was silence. They tried each other a few more times, crossing calls, until Peyton stepped out of her building and the call finally connected.

"Can you hear me now?" he asked, sounding peeved.

"Yes, sorry," Peyton said. It was swelteringly hot for a mid-September night, and almost immediately she felt her blouse start to stick to her body. This was not the time to start sweating, she thought. Not tonight.

"I'm calling with some good news," Ken said. "*Very* good news."

"Really? I barely even understand what those words mean anymore."

"I just got off the phone with Joseph." He paused.

"Okay . . ."

"And it was a very productive conversation."

Peyton exhaled. Her doorman turned to look at her with concern. She gave him a little wave and turned to hail a cab. "Are you going to make me beg?"

"Not surprisingly, the ratings tanked with Vivi in your seat. They want you back, effective immediately."

It was exquisite. And certainly predictable. How many summer mornings had she wasted watching that imbecile child flirt with Jim and fake her way through delivering the news? How many excruciating so-called interviews had she watched Vivi conduct, always wanting to reach through the screen and strangle her delicately beautiful neck? How many times had she and Sean texted during the broadcasts, wondering what had happened to their previously well-rehearsed and beautifully choreographed morning show? It had eaten at her—kept her awake at night and anxious by day—and yet here they were, not eight weeks later, and ANN was finally admitting what Peyton had known from the beginning: she was the one viewers wanted.

"Well, not effective immediately, per se, but forty-eight to seventy-two hours after Isaac's sentence commences, to let the story run itself though the news cycle. Is he still due upstate tomorrow?"

Peyton hesitated for just a moment.

"Yes. I'm driving him up there tomorrow."

"Well, you're looking at Wednesday. Latest, Thursday."

A yellow cab pulled up to the curb and Peyton slid into the backseat. "Just straight down Park for the moment, please," she told the driver.

"Peyton?"

"I'm here," she said, checking her phone for the address. "Kenneth, I appreciate this call, I do. You told me all along that ANN would be back, and it's very gratifying. My answer is no."

"You cut out for a minute. What did you say? Your answer to *what* is no?"

"To ANN's offer to return. I need time."

There was a beat of silence, and then Kenneth's voice began a slow increase in volume. "What are you talking about, 'need time'? That's not how this works, Peyton! They put *you* on a leave of absence and it's up to *them* to decide when you come back."

"I understand that. But I don't accept their terms," she said calmly.

"It's not your call!" Kenneth was all-out yelling. While he often sounded exasperated, it was unlike him to raise his voice. "You have a contract. A very detailed and expensive contract!"

"I'm aware of that. And I'm going to depend on you to figure out some loophole to get me more time, because I'm telling you: I am not going back to ANN this week."

"Peyton."

"Kenneth."

"There's no loophole and you know it. They're going to take you to court if you refuse to come back."

With this, Peyton snorted. She didn't mean to, but in light of everything else that was going on, the conversation was ridiculous.

"Tell them to take a number and get in line."

"What? I can't hear you. Peyton?"

"Sorry, Kenneth, I have to run. Thanks again for everything. We'll talk soon."

She disconnected the call. That wasn't so bad, not for one of the conversations she'd been dreading the most.

"Ma'am? Address?" the driver asked.

"Right, sorry." She opened her Notes app, where she had saved the information earlier that day. "Eighty-second and Amsterdam, on the southeast corner, please."

The ride was quick; there was no traffic on a Sunday night, and even though there were a thousand things she could be doing—probably *should* be doing—Peyton merely sat back and watched the scenery go whizzing by. The couples out for evening strolls, the children scootering up and down the sidewalks, the dogs of every size and type pulling at their leashes, all of them enjoying the warm weather and the relative serenity before another week of work and school resumed.

When the taxi slowed to a stop, Peyton added a hundred-percent tip and swiped her phone across the Apple Pay sensor.

"Hey, thanks," the driver said, noticeably surprised.

"Thank you," she replied, before climbing out and shutting the door. She gave him a little wave as he drove off.

Taking a deep breath, Peyton glanced at the sign above the foreboding double metal doors. She dialed Isaac, who answered on the first ring.

"I hope you're calling to ask if we also need red wine?" he said, without saying hello. "Because the answer is yes."

"Honey? You know how you've been wanting to do that fishing trip? The one where you go walking into the water and camp out and everything?"

Isaac laughed. "It's called fly-fishing. And the camping part can actually be very luxurious, I've been telling you that for years."

"Well, I've been thinking about it, and I want to go."

"You what?"

"I want to go! You've been saying forever that it's your number one bucket-list trip, and I think we should do it."

"Peyton? Are you feeling okay? Where are you right now?"

"I'm totally fine, I promise. And as soon as I'm permitted, I want the very first place we go to be on your fishing trip. Just the two of us. For as long as you'd like."

"Did you say as soon as *you're* permitted?"

"Isaac? Please listen carefully. I don't want you to worry, okay? I am fine—more than fine, actually. I'm great, because I'm doing something that is long overdue."

"Peyton, I don't—"

"Shhhhh. Just listen. I'd like you to call Nisha, and then I want you to walk into Max's room and tell her how much I love her. Isaac? I love you more than anyone in the world, and I'll be back to you as soon as I can."

It took superhuman effort to press End Call, especially since she could hear him starting to yell. Her phone rang again immediately, but she silenced it and returned it to her purse. Her legs felt heavy, but she inhaled deeply and took a small step forward. Then another and another, until she was climbing the staircase in front of the Twentieth Precinct. Two uniformed officers walked outside as she stood, frozen, staring at the door.

"Ma'am? Do you need directions?" the young female one asked.

"Hmm? Oh, no, thank you," Peyton said. They held the door open for her, and she thanked them as she entered. Directly inside was a metal detector; to her right there was a desk with a bored-looking officer doing paperwork.

"Can I help you?" he asked, sounding disinterested.

"Yes. My name is Peyton Marcus, and I would like to speak to a detective," she said as confidently as she could manage.

"A detective? What's it concerning?"

Peyton coughed and then cleared her throat. She took a deep breath, held it for just a moment, and said, "I am here to confess to a crime."

Acknowledgments

While I began writing this book what feels like forever ago, a large part of the heavy lifting took place during the unexpected and unprecedented time of a global pandemic. As any author can attest, there's no such thing as an "easy" book, and I've struggled mightily, and for many different reasons, with nearly every novel I've written. But never like this. Losing Susan Kamil in 2019, the brilliant editor who championed me, believed in me, and cheered me on when I doubted everything, was devastating. When COVID-19 struck and the world first reeled, then shut down, tapping into any small shred of creativity—especially for a book that's supposed to be a beach read—felt impossible. People everywhere were scared, sick, and dying. Like so many others, my young children were suddenly home and looking to us for their schooling and socializing. We were isolated from friends and family; our usual extensive support system evaporated in an instant. But through it all, these three people never gave up on me, even when I may have wanted them to:

Sloan Harris, thank you. Your honesty and forthrightness in good times and bad means everything to me. Thank you for always being my champion and friend. Our thirteen years working together have been the best of my career, and I especially love how our families have come to know each other and spend time together. I wouldn't want to do any of this without you.

To Kara Cesare, my editor, who stepped in so seamlessly when the very worst happened, thank you. You were no doubt mourning your own loss but never hesitated to extend your hand and heart to a new author. Whether it's the shared hometown roots or simply your instinctive, incredible warmth, I feel like I've known you forever. Thank you for taking a book—and an author—you merely inherited and making us both your own. I am forever grateful.

And to Lynne Drew, my UK editor, the one who has been there from day one, thank you. Whether we're sitting at my dining table working on a manuscript together or sharing cocktails at book events in London or—currently—bemoaning our joint homeschool situations, I am so grateful to have you in my life. Thank you for the often overlooked work that you've done to make each and every one of my books the best it can be. I adore you.

Thank you to the people at Random House who have made me feel welcome from the beginning: Gina Centrello, Andy Ward, Robin Desser, and Avideh Bashirrad. And to the incredible team who helped turn a rough manuscript into a polished novel and then introduced it to the world with passion and professionalism: Debbie Aroff, Maria Braeckel, Susan Corcoran, Madison Dettlinger, Belina Huey, Michelle Jasmine, Leigh Marchant, Steve Messina, Colleen Nuccio, Paolo Pepe, Melissa Sanford, Jesse Shuman, and Susan Turner.

Thank you to everyone at my home across the pond, Harper-Collins UK, for so brilliantly publishing my books: Charlie Redmayne, Charlotte Brabbin, Roger Cazalet, Isabel Coburn, Kate Elton, Alice Gomer, Holly Macdonald, Hannah O'Brien, Rachel Quin, Michael White, Jaime Witcomb, and Kimberley Young.

A million thanks to Felicity Blunt for spot-on manuscript reads and all-around terrific advice. Julie Flanagan, you're a behind-the-scenes wizard and a welcome editorial voice—thank you for all you do. To Heather Karpas and Kristyn Keene: you can run but you cannot hide. I'll find you both always.

To my friends who are more like family: Helen Coster, Vicky

Feltman, Julie Hootkin, Audrey Kent, Mandy Lewitton, Leigh Marchant, and Arian Rothman, thank you for title inspiration, outdoor socially distanced dinners in a variety of cold and unpleasant places, and sanity-saving Zoom calls during quarantine where we discussed everything from the state of our country to the best foot peels on Amazon. I love you guys and all your people, too.

To all my actual family, who keep me sane and drive me crazy—like all the best families. Mom and Bernie, Dad and Judy, Jackie and Mel: thanks for being such supportive and loving parents and grandparents. Dana and Seth, Dave and Allison: who's luckier than us? Raising our kids together has been the joy of a lifetime. And to the rest of the Weisberger, Zuskin, Cohen, and Kelberg clan, I feel so fortunate to have you all in my life.

To R & S, my loves. You're finally starting to understand what it is your mommy does, and it's been such a pleasure sharing it with both of you. You two are the lights of my life.

And lastly, mostly, to Mike. There is nothing better than sharing this great adventure with you. You make all of it possible, every minute of it. I love you.

About the Author

LAUREN WEISBERGER is the #1 *New York Times* bestselling author of *When Life Gives You Lululemons, The Singles Game, Revenge Wears Prada, Last Night at Chateau Marmont, Chasing Harry Winston, Everyone Worth Knowing,* and *The Devil Wears Prada*—all of which were bestsellers. *The Devil Wears Prada* was published in forty languages and made into a major motion picture starring Meryl Streep and Anne Hathaway. Kevin McCollum, in partnership with Elton John, is adapting *The Devil Wears Prada* for the stage. Her books have sold more than thirteen million copies worldwide. A graduate of Cornell University, she lives in Connecticut with her husband and two children.

laurenweisberger.com
Facebook.com/lauren.weisberger
Instagram: @laurenweisberger

About the Type

This book was set in Caledonia, a typeface designed in 1939 by W. A. Dwiggins (1880–1956) for the Mergenthaler Linotype Company. Its name is the ancient Roman term for Scotland, because the face was intended to have a Scottish-Roman flavor. Caledonia is considered to be a well-proportioned, businesslike face with little contrast between its thick and thin lines.